BOOKS BY JILL BARNETT

THE
Days of
Summer

JILL BARNETT

POCKET STAR BOOKS
New York   London   Toronto   Sydney

A Pocket Star Book published by
POCKET BOOKS, a division of Simon & Schuster, Inc.
1230 Avenue of the Americas, New York, NY 10020

Copyright © 2006 by Jill Barnett Stadler

Originally published in hardcover in 2006 by Atria Books

ISBN-13: 978-0-671-03536-5
ISBN-10:   0-671-03536-3

This Pocket Star Books paperback edition May 2007

10 9 8 7 6 5 4 3 2 1

POCKET STAR BOOKS and colophon are registered trademarks of Simon & Schuster, Inc.

Cover illustration by Robert Hunt; Handlettering by Dave Gatti

Manufactured in the United States of America

For information about special discounts for bulk purchases, please contact Simon & Schuster Special Sales at 1-800-456-6798 or business@simonandschuster.com.

This writing life I've stumbled through has brought me
an abundance of riches, the most valuable a
friendship of twenty years.

To Kristin and Benjamin Hannah, who have stood by
my side and protected my back through all the wins and losses.
Only the angels could have sent you.

Life can only be understood
backwards;
but it must be lived forwards.

Søren Kierkegaard

PART ONE

1957

A hurtful act is the transference to others of the degradation which we bear in ourselves.

Simone Weil

CHAPTER

1

Southern California

Warm and motionless nights were natural in LA, a place where so much of life was staged and the weather seldom competed for attention. There, events and people stood in the limelight. On most nights, somewhere in the city, searchlights panned the sky; tonight, in front of the La Cienega Art Gallery. All the art show regulars were there in force, names from the society pages, old money and new, along with enough existentialist poets and bohemians to fill every coffeehouse from Hollywood to Hermosa Beach.

Well-known art critics chatted about perspective and meaning, debated social message. They adored the artist, a vibrant, exotic woman whose huge canvases had violent splashes of color charging across them, and wrote about her work in effusive terms as bold as the work itself, likening her to the abstract expressionists Pollock and de Kooning. Rachel Espinosa was the daring of the LA art scene, and Rudy Banning's wife.

Rudy came to the show late, after drinking all afternoon. His father was right: he was a sucker—something that was easier to swallow if he chased it with a bottle of scotch. The searchlights were off when he parked his car outside the gallery. Once inside, he leaned against the front door to steady himself.

A milky haze of cigarette smoke hovered over the colorless sea of black berets, gray fedoras, and French twists. In one corner, a small band played an odd arrangement of calypso and jazz—Harry Belafonte meets Dave Brubeck. The booze flowed, cigarettes were stacked every few feet on tall silver stanchions, and the catering was Catalan—unusual—and done to propagate the lie that his wife, Rachel Maria-Teresa Antonia Espinosa, was pure Spanish aristocracy. This was her night, and her stamp was on the whole production.

She stood near the back half of the room, under canned light and in front of one of her largest and latest pieces, *Ginsberg Howls*. The crowd milled around her but most managed to stay a few feet away, as if they were afraid to get too close to such an icon. A newspaper reporter for the *Los Angeles Times* interviewed her, while a staff photographer with rolled-up shirtsleeves circled around her, snapping photos with sharp, blinding flashes.

Rachel turned on for the camera, striking a carefully choreographed pose Rudy had seen before: arm in the air, a martini glass with three cocktail onions in her hand. Tonight she wore bright orange. She knew her place in this room.

Rudy helped himself to a drink from a cocktail tray carried by a passing waiter, then downed the whiskey before he was ten feet away from her. She didn't see him at first, but turned with instinctive suddenness and looked right at him. What passed between them was merely a ghost of what had been—the days when one look across a room could evaporate everything around them. His wife's expression softened, until he set his empty drink on a passing tray and grabbed another full one, then raised the glass mockingly and drank it as she watched him, her look so carefully controlled.

"Darling!" Rachel said quickly, then turned to the reporter. "Excuse me." She rushed forward hands outstretched. "Rudy!" When he didn't take her hands, she slid her arm through his and moved toward a corner. "You're late."

"Really?" Rudy looked around. "What time was this charade supposed to start?"

"You're drunk. You reek of scotch." She pulled him away from the crowd.

"Are you trying to shove me off into a corner? I'm six foot four. A little hard to hide." Rudy stopped bullishly and turned so she was facing the room. "You crave attention so much. Look. People are staring."

"Stop it!" Her voice was quiet and angry.

"I know, Rachel."

"Of course you know. No one force-fed you half a bottle of scotch." Her deep breath had a tired sound. "Dammit, Rudy. Do you have to ruin everything?"

"You bitch!"

Her fingers tightened around his arm. Murmurs came from those nearby, and people eased closer.

"I know," he said with emphasis. The music faded and the room quickly grew quiet. Rudy had the laughable thought that if it wasn't a show before, it certainly was one now.

"What are you talking about?"

Apparently lying and persona were all that was left of the woman he'd married. Strange how confronting her felt nothing like he'd imagined. "You want me to shout it? Here? For everyone?" He waved his hand around. "For that reporter, *darling*?" His breath was shallow, like he'd been running miles. His vision blurred around the edges, and the taste of booze lodged in his throat. "I will shout it to the world. Damn you. *Damn you, Rachel!*" He threw his drink at the painting behind her, and the glass shattered in a perfectly silent room. He stumbled out the front door into the empty night air. At the curb, he used the car's fin to steady himself, then got inside.

Rachel came running outside. "Rudy!"

He jammed his key in the ignition.

She pulled open the passenger door. "Stop! Wait!"

"Go to hell."

She crawled inside and tried to grab the keys. "Don't leave."

Rudy grabbed her wrist, pulled her across the seat until her face was inches from his. "Get out or I'll drag you with the car." He shoved her away and started the engine.

"No!" She closed her door and reached for the keys again.

His foot on the gas, the car raced down the street, straddling lanes as he struggled for control. Tires screeched behind them, but he didn't give a damn.

"Rudy, stop!" She sounded scared, so he turned the next corner faster. The car fishtailed and he floored it again. She hugged the door and seemed to shrink down into someone who actually looked human, instead of a goddess who painted intricate canvases and saw the world with a mind and eye unlike anyone else's. Ahead the stoplight turned red. He slammed on the brakes so hard she had to brace her hands on the dashboard.

"You're driving like a madman. Pull over and we can talk."

"There it is again, Rachel, that calm voice. Your reasonable tone, so arrogant, as if you are far above the rest of us mere mortals because you don't feel anything."

"I feel. You should know. I feel too much. I know you're upset. We'll talk. Please."

"Upset doesn't even come close to what I am. And it's too fucking late to talk." The light turned green and he floored it.

"Rudy, stop! Please. Think of the boys," she said frantically.

"I am thinking of the boys. What about you? Can you ever think about anyone but you?" He took the next corner so quickly they faced oncoming traffic, honking horns, the sound of skidding tires. A truck swerved to avoid them. It took both of his hands to pull the careening car into his own lane. At the yellow signal, he lifted his foot off the gas to go for the brake, paused, then stomped on the accelerator. He could make it.

"Don't!" Rachel shouted. "It's turning red!"

"Yeah, it is." He took his eyes off the road. "Scared, Rachel? Maybe now you'll feel something." Her whimpering sound made him feel strong. His father was wrong. He wasn't a weak fool. Not anymore. The speedometer needle shimmied toward seventy. The gas pedal was on the floor. He could feel the power of the engine vibrate through the steering wheel right into his hands.

"Oh, God!" Rachel grabbed his arm. "Look out!"

A white station wagon pulled into the intersection.

He stood on the brakes so hard he felt the seat back snap. The skid pulled at the steering wheel, and he could hear tires scream and smell the rubber burn. Blue lettering painted on the side of the station wagon grew huge before his eyes:

ROCK AND ROLL WITH JIMMY PEYTON
AND THE FIREFLIES

The other driver looked at him in stunned horror, his passengers frantic. One of them had his hands pressed against the side window. A thought hit Rudy with a passive calmness: they were going to die. Rachel grabbed him, screaming. With a horrific bang, her scream faded into a moan. The dashboard came at him, the speedometer needle still shimmying, and everything exploded.

CHAPTER

2

Seattle, Washington

Three hours ago, a complete stranger stood in the doorway of a downtown apartment and told Kathryn Peyton her husband was dead. The stranger, a local police detective, wanted to notify her before some reporter did, but the news flashed on the radio within minutes after she closed the front door.

"Twenty-six-year-old singing star and entertainer Jimmy Peyton, whose fourth record went number one last week, died tragically tonight in a deadly car accident in LA."

Hearing the report on the radio made her husband's death more real—how could this be happening?—and when Kathryn called Jimmy's mother, she was told Julia Peyton was devastated and unavailable. So Kathryn dialed her sister in California and talked until nothing was left to say and staying on the phone was empty and painfully awkward.

A few reporters called to question her. She hung up and unplugged the phone. Later came the knocks on the door, which didn't sound as loud from her bedroom, and by midnight they'd left her alone. In her bedroom with the curtains drawn, it was easy to ignore the doorbell, to turn off the phone, to lie on their bed holding Jimmy's pillow against her, holding on so tightly every muscle in her body hurt.

The smell of his aftershave lingered on the pillowcase; it was on the sheets, and faintly recognizable on the oversized blue oxford shirt she wore. Sheer panic hit her when she realized she would have to wash the pillowcases and sheets; she would have to get rid of his shirt, all of his clothes, or turn into one of those strange old women who hoard the belongings of the one they'd lost and who kept rooms exactly as they had been—cobwebbed shrines to those taken at the very moment they were happiest. Now, alone in the dark, Kathryn cried until sleep was her only relief.

The ringing of the bedside alarm startled her awake, then made her sick to her stomach, because every night when Jimmy was on the road, he would walk offstage and call her. *I love you, babe. We brought down the house.*

But in this surreal world where Jimmy no longer existed, the alarm kept ringing while she fumbled in the dark for the off switch, then just threw the damned clock against the wall to shut it up. A weak, incessant buzzing still came from a dark corner of the room, and she wanted to put the pillow over her head until it stopped, or maybe until her breathing stopped.

Eventually, she got up and turned off the alarm. A deep crease on the wall marked where she'd thrown the clock. The paint was only three weeks old and blue like the sheets, like the quilted bedspread and the chairs, blue because Jimmy's latest hit song was "Blue."

Kathryn dropped the clock on the bed and walked on hollow legs into the bathroom, where she turned on the faucet and drank noisily from a cupped hand. She wiped her mouth with Jimmy's shirtsleeve, then opened the medicine cabinet.

His shelf was eye level. A clear bottle of golden Vitalis she had bought last week. A red container of Old Spice without the metal cap. She took a deep breath of it and utter despair turned her inside out. The bottle slipped from her fingers into the wastebasket. Seeing it as trash was more horrific than seeing it on the shelf. Didn't that then mean it was all true? When all was in order on the shelf, life still held a modicum of normalcy.

She carefully put it back exactly where it belonged, next to a small black rectangular case that held Gillette double-edged razor blades, which she looked at for a very long, contemplative time, then she reached for a prescription bottle with "James Peyton" typed neatly in epitaphic black-and-white. *Seconal. Take one tablet to sleep. Count: 60.*

Take one tablet to sleep. Take sixty tablets to die. She turned on the faucet and bent down, a handful of red pills inches from her mouth.

"Is that candy, Mama?"

"Laurel!" Kathryn shot upright, the pills in a fist behind her back, and looked down at the curious face of her four-year-old daughter. "What are you doing up?"

"I want some candy."

"It's not candy," she said sharply.

"I saw Red Hots, Mama."

"No. It's medicine. See?" Kathryn opened her hand,

then put the pills back inside the bottle. "It's just medicine to help me sleep."

"I want some medicine."

Kathryn knelt down. "Come here." Laurel would have found her. *Laurel* would have found her. Shaking and numb, she rested her chin on her daughter's head, surrounded by the scent of baby shampoo and Ivory soap, a familiar, clean smell. It took a long time for Kathryn to let go.

"I can't sleep."

Jimmy's face in miniature stared up at her. Every day she would look at that face and see the man she loved, and Kathryn didn't know if that would be a gift or a curse. "Let me wash your face. You can see tear tracks." She used a warm wash rag to clean Laurel's red face. "There. All done." Kathryn straightened and automatically shut the mirrored medicine cabinet. In her reflection she caught a flicker of a pale, shadowed life and had to brace her hands on the cold sink. It was achingly painful to realize she was here and Jimmy wasn't.

Eventually she would clear out the medicine chest; she would put things in the trash without panicking, wash the sheets, and do something with his clothes. They weren't him, she told herself; they were only his things.

"Does the medicine taste like candy?" Laurel pointed to the prescription bottle.

"No." Kathryn made a face. "It's awful." She dumped the pills into the toilet and flushed it. "We don't need medicine."

It was amazing how skeptical a four-year-old could look.

"It's late," Kathryn told her. "You can sleep in our—in my bed."

Laurel jumped up, all excited and so easily distracted. "Because Daddy's gone?"

"Yes. Because Daddy's gone."

The last time Laurel Peyton waved good-bye to her father was from the backseat of a long black Cadillac that belonged to the Magnolia Funeral Home. Waving good-bye was normal when your father was on the road all the time, but the camera flashbulbs and reporters alongside the car were anything but normal.

The three women inside the car—Kathryn, her sister, Evie, and Julia, Jimmy's mother—tried to shield Laurel from the faces at the car windows, until the press, dressed in their amphigoric darks, were left behind and stood crowlike at the edge of the grave site while the Cadillac continued down the hill.

Behind them Kathryn saw only a monochrome Seattle sky, and scattered all over the lush green lawn were absurdly bright clumps of fresh flowers, bits of life scattered over a place that was only about death. The tires crunched on the gravel drive and sounded as if something were breaking, while rain pattered impatiently on the roof of the car and the electronic turn signal ticked like a heartbeat.

Jimmy's mother tapped the driver on the shoulder. "Young man. Young man! Can't you hear that? Turn off that turn signal!" Julia Laurelhurst Peyton looked as if she were carved from granite. Only Jimmy could ever seem to crack through her veneer.

Laurel began to sing one of Jim's hit songs in a

slightly off-key young voice. Feeling sickened, Kathryn glanced at Julia, who was looking out the car window, her face away from everyone else in the car.

Evie took her hand. "She doesn't understand, Kay."

"She will soon enough," Julia said without turning, her voice serrated and burned from too many cigarettes. She opened her purse and pulled out her cigarette case. "You must make her understand, Kathryn. It's your job as her mother."

Her job as a mother was not to swallow a handful of Seconal. Her job as a mother was to go on hour by hour and day by day. Her job as a mother was to do what was best for Laurel, at the expense of anything else, because Jimmy wasn't there.

Julia tapped a cigarette against the back of her hand, then slid it between her red lips and lit it. Smoke drifted around them. "My son was a star." She looked at Kathryn, at Evie. "You saw the reporters there." Julia took short drags off her cigarette. "Tomorrow, they'll play his songs on the radio."

Kathryn wondered if she would constantly search the radio for his songs. She began to silently cry.

"Don't, Kathryn." Julia held up her hand. "Don't."

Evie handed her a tissue. "She can cry if she wants to."

Julia crushed her cigarette in the ashtray. "Laurel? Come see Grandmama." She patted the seat next to her, but Laurel climbed in her lap instead. Julia began to hum the same song, holding her granddaughter tightly, and soon tears streamed down her slack and chalkish powdered cheeks.

Six long hours later, it was Kathryn who hung on tightly to Laurel as she ran through the waiting reporters at the front doors of their apartment building.

"Kay, I'm sorry," Evie said. "We should have hired some security." She blocked the closing elevator doors as a couple of persistent newsmen shouted questions at them.

Thankfully no one was on the tenth floor while Kathryn waited for Evie to unlock the apartment door. "Look, Evie. Laurel's sound asleep. I want to be a child, oblivious to that chaos downstairs. I want to wake up and have it be a bad dream."

Evie quietly closed the door behind them. "Go on. Put her to bed."

A few minutes later Kathryn walked into the living room.

Evie stood in the corner over a bar cart with an ice bucket and crystal bottles of decanted liquor. "I'm getting us drinks. Strong drinks. God knows I need one." She studied Kathryn for a second. "What am I saying? I should probably just give you a straw and the whole bottle."

Kathryn unpinned her hat and tossed it on the coffee table. "Today was bad."

"Your mother-in-law didn't make it any easier. Look at me, Kay." Evie patted her cheeks. "Am I pale? Do you think I have any blood left since leaving Julia's, or did she suck it all out of me?"

"You're awful."

"No, she's awful. I'm truthful."

Kathryn unbuttoned her suit jacket, sank into the sofa, and let her head fall back on the pillows. Above her was the hole in the acoustical ceiling left over from a swag lamp. One of those things they'd meant to fix. The iron poker near the wood box was bent from when the movers ran over it. The mirror over the fireplace hung a little crooked. Everything was the same, yet nothing would ever be the same again.

"You're a sweetheart for putting up with that woman. She's so critical." Evie dropped ice cubes into a couple of highball glasses. "What do you want to drink?"

"Anything."

"I don't know where you get your patience. Pop used to check his watch every two seconds if anyone kept him waiting, and Mother was just like I am: intolerant of anyone who disagrees with us. You are the saint of the family, Kay."

"No, I'm no saint. I just loved her son."

Evie paused, ice tongs in her hand. "It broke my heart when Laurel started to sing."

"My first urge was to put my hand over her mouth."

"I can't think of anyone better to sing a Jimmy Peyton song than his daughter. The only reason you didn't know what to do was because Julia makes everything so uncomfortable."

"It's not Julia. I don't understand the world anymore. It seems so wrong, Evie, so unfair. I want to shout and shake my fist at God and tell him he made a huge mistake. Jimmy had so much left to give the world. He was going to make it big. I knew it. You saw it."

"Everyone saw it, Kay."

"We had such big dreams. The sheer waste of his life makes me want to scream."

"You can holler the walls down if you want. It is unfair. Do whatever you have to do to get through this horrible thing."

It was a horrible thing. Everything was changing and out of her control. Her skin hurt; it felt too small for her body, like the changes to her were happening in a matter of days. She glanced at the crooked mirror above the fireplace to see the ravages of sudden widowhood right there on her face.

Evie clattered through the bottles on the cart. "Where are those silver things that go on the bottle necks to tell you which liquor is which?"

"Laurel thought they were necklaces. She put them on her storybook dolls." Kathryn dropped her hands away from her strained face. "It drove Jimmy nuts, but he didn't have the heart to take them away from her."

Evie held up two of the bottles. "I wonder which one is the scotch."

"The brown one."

"Funny." Her sister sniffed one of the bottles. "Bourbon."

"I'll take bourbon and Coke."

Evie dumped bourbon into the glass and splashed a small bit of Coke over it.

"One night Laurel made me tell her what each necklace said. She named her dolls Bourbon, Scotch, Rum, Gin, and Vodka. Jimmy and I laughed about it." Strange how his laughter was still fresh in Kathryn's mind, and for just the briefest of moments, she didn't feel locked in some dark, parallel dimension made for those left behind.

Here." Evie handed her a drink and sat down, folding her legs under her. They didn't speak.

Her years with Jimmy filed through Kathryn's mind like frames in a documentary. His laughter, his fears, his tears of excitement when he first saw their daughter in her arms, squalling and hungry. She could hear him singing the songs he had written to her, and for her. She heard the first thing he ever said to her—and the last: *Just one more night on the road, babe. I'll be home tomorrow.*

Her sister set her glass down. "Lord, that tastes good. Maybe a few drinks will wash away the bitterness of Julia's tongue."

"Do you think what she said was true?"

"I doubt it," Evie answered. "But which tidbit of your mother-in-law's viperlike wisdom are we talking about?"

"That society treats women without men as non-entities."

"Oh." Evie laughed bitterly. "The idea that widows should be strong because it makes people uncomfortable to see someone's grief."

"Well, she is a widow. She should know."

"She's a black widow. They eat their mates. She deals with her grief by denying yours. She also said single, independent women have their life preferences questioned." Evie raised her chin and mimicked Julia's husky voice: "'You are a divorcée, Evie dear, and marrying a divorced woman is like going to the track and betting all your money on a lame horse. Divorcées are only fair game for men who want to get them into the bedroom but would never consider marrying them.'"

"You shouldn't let her get to you."

"You've had more practice dealing with her than I have, Kay."

"I might be getting a lot more practice." Kathryn

rested her glass on her knee and stared into it. "Julia wants me to give up this place and move in with her."

Evie turned sideways on the couch, facing her. "You cannot live in the same house with that judgmental woman who will suck every bit of life from you. Half the time I want to muzzle her. Even now, when I should feel terribly sorry for her, she can say something that makes me just want to pop her."

"Underneath, Julia is as fragile as I feel. You saw her in the car. She needs Laurel, and with Mom and Pop gone, Laurel needs to know her only grandparent."

"The woman is an emotional vacuum."

"She's never that way with Laurel. It's sad, really, the way she was talking today about her son the star, as if all she had left of him would be those few minutes when some radio station played one of his songs. I have Laurel. Maybe Jimmy's mother should, too."

"You're Jimmy's wife. She should treat you better."

"He used to say it wasn't me. She couldn't let go of him. I look at Laurel and I'm so scared about what kind of parent I'll be. What if I cling to her? How do I do this alone? How do I know what's right and wrong, and how do I protect her?"

"The same way you did when Jimmy was alive. You can't completely protect her from everything."

"Laurel doesn't have Jimmy anymore, but if we move in with Julia, at least she would have his mother. This apartment isn't the same. All the colors look so faded. Nothing is sharp or clear. It feels empty. I don't know if I can stay."

"You can stay with me, Kay. It's wonderful on Catalina. The island is small and safe. The house is small, too, but we all can fit. There's room in back to build a small studio for your kiln and wheel."

"You said you were going to plant a garden there."

"Who needs a garden? My faculty meetings are always in the mornings. I could watch Laurel in the afternoons and evenings while you work. Please. Think about it."

"I love you for offering, but it would be a disaster. Besides the fact that you just bought the place, you have one bathroom. You know we'd be on top of each other."

Evie took her hand. "I wish you would."

"I know you do." Kathryn looked around. "Maybe I'm being silly and I should stay here."

"Oh, hell, Kay, I don't know. I can't tell you what to do. I worry about you both living with that woman."

The doorbell rang.

"Ignore it. They'll go away." Kathryn took a drink. The bell kept ringing and ringing.

Evie shifted. "I can't stand it. I'll get it."

"No. No." Kathryn stood. "I'll do it." When she opened the front door, a flashbulb went off and everything was suddenly white.

"*Star* magazine, here. We'd like an interview, now that you're Jimmy Peyton's widow."

"Leave her alone!" Evie was suddenly standing behind her, a hand on Kathryn's shoulder. "Go away!" Evie reached around her and slammed the door, swearing.

Kathryn buried her face in her hands. "I don't know if I can do this."

"Mama?" Laurel was standing in the dark recesses of the hallway, a stuffed duck Jimmy had given her tucked under one arm.

Kathryn rushed to pick her up. "Are you okay, angel?"

Laurel nodded, hugging the duck, but she kept staring curiously at the front door.

"That kind of thing wouldn't happen at Julia's." Kathryn looked pointedly at her sister. "She has the front gates and hired help."

Evie nodded.

First and foremost, Kathryn knew she had to protect her daughter. Today people had said the stupidest things: *It'll get better with time. God needed Jimmy more. You're young, dear, you'll marry again.* She could only imagine how Laurel might interpret any one of those comments. And how long would it be before the newspaper people finally left them alone?

"Mama?" Laurel framed Kathryn's cheeks with her small hands and brought her face very close, the way she did whenever she wanted someone's sole attention. "Those people at the door want to view you because you're Daddy's window."

The words took a moment to register. Kathryn turned to Evie. "I'm a window."

Her sister looked as if she were trying not to laugh.

"I'm a window," Kathryn repeated—it was all so ludicrous—then laughter poured out of her, uncontrolled, like water running over. She couldn't stop. It was just laughter, she told herself, a silly emotion, really, and panic edged it—a sound that was closer to shattering glass—and she knew then her laughter was anything but natural.

CHAPTER

3

Orange County, California

On that long stretch of land between LA and San Diego, towns grew quickly and sprawled all over one another. Amusement parks with gravity rooms and wild toad rides replaced boysenberry fields and orange groves where people could pick all the fruit they wanted for a fifty-cent piece. Tracts of shake-shingled homes with attached garages sold out before the houses were even built, and traffic signals sprang up on street corners suddenly too busy for stop signs.

Public transportation? It was an afterthought. Cars were necessary in Southern California, and oil was big business. Hammer-shaped oil pumps lined the coast highway all along Huntington Beach, where tar spotted long stretches of sand and stuck like gum to broken seashells, litter, and the murky green kelp that washed ashore. The locals called it Tin Can Beach—it looked like a dump, so everyone just used it as one.

If tar was the automobile driver's grim trade-off for

pumping oil up from the ground, so were the skeletal black oil towers on Signal Hill and the churning refineries off Sepulveda Boulevard, with their tall, cigar-shaped towers that spit white smoke and all those acrid smells into the sweet California air. A popular joke regularly ran through the LA nightclubs that Southern Californians paid the prices for their automobiles in dollars and scents.

But the truth was, people spent money on cars for mobility and freedom, so they could be in control of where they went and when. They bought homes because they liked to think they owned a piece of a place where the sun shined most of the time and movie stars lived large and died tragically.

The coastal resort town of Newport Beach was all prime property. The ocean was clean, the sand fine as sugar, and there was no litter anywhere. Pristine white yachts pulled into private docks along the isles, where sprawling California-style homes carried addresses as distinctive as those in Beverly Hills. Whenever the Santa Ana winds blew in, the scent from the eucalyptus trees above Highway 1 cleared the sinuses better than Bano-Rub, a petroleum-jelly-and-camphor mixture that helped launch Banning Oil into the petroleum by-products industry and gave Victor Gaylord Banning enough money to buy up a chunk of Newport's exclusive Lido Isle with hardly a dent in his bank accounts.

It was a Thursday afternoon, maybe three o'clock, and Victor was home in the middle of the day, facing a wall of windows—all that stood between him and the civilized edges of the wide blue Pacific. He stared at his reflection in the glass, seeing only the physiognomy of the one person he vowed he would never become. His father had been weak, unable to succeed in anything except failure.

Victor grew up in a house of discontent, with only his sister, Aletta, as champion against a mother whose elusive approval he could never capture, because she saw in Victor only his father standing there in miniature, a constant reminder of her bad choices. It was Aletta who paid the biggest price for their father's failures. She died a useless death when there was no money to save her, and Victor was abandoned by the one person he depended upon.

For his mother, Aletta's death was complete devastation. She couldn't bear to look at the only child left, so she would lock him in the closet for hours. Eventually she saw suicide as the only release from her agony. She didn't want to live in a world with only her weak husband and his look-alike son, who, try as he might, would never be a substitute for the girl child she truly loved. To Victor's complete dismay, he cried for days after his mother killed herself, unable to control his emotions. The Banning legacy was jagged and sharp and part of him, no matter how he tried to prove otherwise.

Today, his cheeks and eyes were proof that sleep escaped him. He hadn't shaved since yesterday, when he went to identify the bodies of his son and daughter-in-law, filed in long stainless steel cabinets at the LA morgue. Until a few days ago, he hadn't seen or spoken to his son, Rudy, in almost ten years. His only source about anything in Rudy's life had been Rachel. What Victor was feeling at that very moment—had he allowed it inside—would have brought him to his knees. Grief was crippling. Allowed in, it made the strong weak.

At the sound of his Town Car pulling in, he moved to a narrow window where he could see the driveway through the waxy leaves of a fat camellia bush. Next to his Lincoln the boys stood side by side, wearing similar striped T-shirts and stiff new jeans cuffed up. Although four years apart, they looked like Bannings: blond hair, square jaws, and wide mouths, all inherited from his own grandfather. Their skin was pale, their expressions thinly serious, and they had their mother's thick, dark eyebrows. Cale, the younger, took hold of Jud's hand. They looked like bookends that didn't quite match.

Victor saw only their vulnerability, as they clung to each other like scared little girls. They would never be able to stand on their own. Rachel had ruined them. He'd seen enough and walked away, wondering exactly what he would have to do to turn them from pussy little boys into the men they needed to be to make it in his world.

Soon he heard the hushed voices of the help, and the hurried steps in the entry hall of children he had never spoken to. His driver came into the room, his chauffeur's cap in his hands. "Your grandsons are here." Harlan wasn't a huge man, but he was stronger than an ox and looked a little like one. He was an ex–middleweight boxer with a flat, broken nose and porcelain front teeth Victor had paid for. "Do you want me to take the boys upstairs?"

"No. I'll be out in a minute. They didn't give you any trouble?"

Harlan shook his head. "They sat in the backseat

whispering about riding in the limousine. Thought it was pretty special."

"Is the MG back from the paint shop?" Victor asked.

"Yes sir."

"Check the paint job on the running boards and the hood."

"I checked it this morning."

"Good." His son had loved the MG, but that had been back in the days before Rudy threw the car keys at him and walked away from everything Banning. "Let the boys wait in the entry for now," Victor said evenly. "I'll be out soon."

Harlan left, and Victor poured a scotch, wanting to be somewhere else—a sweeter time—the few in his life he could count on one hand. Under his feet, the wood floor creaked, and he looked down at the hairpin edges of a trapdoor to the fallout shelter, something his architect insisted he needed. But it was a useless hole in the floor that did nothing to protect him from the real fallout of his life: his son had died hating him. A scotch didn't help. Mistakes wouldn't dissolve in alcohol—although Rudy had certainly tried. So Victor remained there, his feet on the cracks of the trapdoor, a useless drink in his hand, facing the largest ocean in the world and the worst of his sins.

Cale Banning stood with his older brother in the hallway of a strange house, in a strange neighborhood, waiting to meet a stranger—the grandfather he'd never known he had until a few hours ago. Their suitcases and toys were piled up in the hallway, stacked in a hurry and looking as confused as he felt. He tugged on his brother

Jud's shirt. "How come I don't remember this grandpa? Why wasn't he ever around? Didn't he like us?"

"Who knows?"

Cale stared at their things and thought they looked like they didn't belong there.

Jud sat down on the stairs, his elbows on his long skinny legs, his hands hanging between his knees. "I remember his car," he told Cale. "I saw it drive away from the house a few times."

"Did you ever see him?"

"No."

Cale searched the hollow room for something familiar. High on the wall above the staircase was a window of colored glass, like in church. "Look up there."

"I saw it," Jud said distractedly. "It's one of Mom's paintings."

Cale studied the painting hung near the stained-glass window; it was huge. Once, when he'd asked his mother why she painted so big, she told him large canvases had bigger things to say, and he wouldn't understand until he was older, so he should ask her again when he was Jud's age. He looked at Jud. "Do you know why Mom painted big pictures?"

"No."

"It's supposed to say something." Cale studied the colors of red and blue, green and yellow slashed across the painting above him. Her studio had never been off-limits. She usually smelled of something called linseed oil and her clothes were covered in paint splotches that made about as much sense to him as the paintings did. But inside her studio, the two of them would drink bottles of Coca-Cola, eat egg salad sandwiches and

Twinkies, and she would talk to him while she painted with huge long strokes of color that involved her whole body and seemed to make sense only to her. As she stood back and away from her work, she told him there were messages in art about life and the way people thought and felt, that sometimes the messages were hidden, secrets only some had the eye to see, but the soul of the artist was always there if anyone chose to look close enough.

"Jud? What does a soul look like?"

His brother looked at him. "You're weird."

Cale sat down and rested his chin in his hands. "I miss her."

Jud didn't say anything, but slid his arm around him, so Cale leaned against his shoulder, because if his parents were really dead, then Jud was all he had left.

When he glanced up, a man stood off to the side. His father's father was tall and looked a little like his dad. But his hair was a mix of blond and brown and gray. He was looking at him with an unreadable expression. Cale straightened. "Why did you bring us here?"

Jud stood up so fast it was like he had a fire in his pants.

But their grandfather remained silent.

Why didn't they know him? Why didn't he say anything? Why did their mom and dad have to die and leave them with no one but him? Cale wanted to hit something, maybe this grim-faced man who stood away from him. "How come I don't know you? Are you really my grandpa?" Cale took a step.

Jud grabbed his arm and hauled him back. "Stay here."

"You're Cale," his grandfather said finally.

Cale stood in the taller shadow of his brother. "Yes."

"And you're Jud." His grandfather shook his older brother's hand as if he were a grown man, but didn't offer to shake Cale's. "Come with me," he said to Jud, then went out the front door with Jud following.

Cale was his grandson, too, so he ran after them, dogging his brother, who was beside their grandfather. Cale ran past both of them and turned, half-running backward in front of his grandfather. "Where are we going?"

"To the garage."

"Why?"

"I want to show your brother something."

He wanted to show Jud but not him. "What?" Cale asked.

His grandfather kept walking.

"What do you want to show him?" Cale stayed ahead of him because he was afraid if he stopped now his grandfather would walk right over him. "You don't like me," Cale said.

His grandfather looked at him. "Does it matter if I like you?"

"Yes," Cale said.

"Why?"

"Because you're my grandfather. It's your job to like me."

He laughed then. "Good answer, Cale."

For just a second, Cale thought his grandfather might like him after all.

"What makes you think I don't like you?"

"You won't talk to me."

"Does that bother you?"

"Yes."

"Why?"

"Because I haven't done anything wrong."

"So you think that you have to do something wrong for someone to not like you?"

Cale knew sometimes people had no reason at all not to like you. "I don't know," he answered truthfully.

"Think about it, and when you have an answer you can knock on this door and tell me." His grandfather turned to Jud, holding the door open. "Come inside, son."

Jud disappeared inside.

When Cale tried to sneak a peek, his grandfather blocked the doorway. "What if I told you that I like Jud because he's the oldest?"

Cale stood stick-straight, arms at his sides, like soldiers in tall red hats who guarded queens and refused to show people what they were feeling.

"Answer me," his grandfather said. "What would you say to that?"

"I would say that you're a stupid old man."

His grandfather's expression didn't change. "Perhaps I am," he said finally, and closed the door in Cale's face.

Cale lay in bed, listening for silence in the hallway. A tree outside the window moved in the wind as he lay there, his heart beating in his ears, his breath sounding loud and hollow beneath the covers. His brother was all the way down the hall in the house of a man who said they were supposed to call him Victor. Not Grandfather or Grandpa. Victor.

When only silence came from the hallway, Cale bolted from the bed and went straight to the closet. He

carried an armload of clothes back to the bed, pulled up
the covers, then socked them a few times so the lump
looked like him sleeping.

His grandfather's bedroom was at the end of a long,
dark hallway on the second floor. The double doors
were slightly open and a shaft of bright light cut across
the wood floor. Cale followed the sound of Victor's
voice coming from inside. His grandfather was yelling
on the phone.

"What the hell do you mean you can't get the paintings? What auction house? Where?"

Cale stopped two feet from the door.

"Tell them they aren't authorized to sell. Those paintings belong to the family. Screw the contract! You're my
attorney. Stop that sale. Hell, if you have to, buy them all. I
don't care how much it costs. I want every last painting."
His grandfather slammed down the phone, swearing.

Cale waited until he saw Victor walk into his bathroom, then moved quickly toward Jud's room and
slipped inside.

Jud sat up on his elbows. "What do you want?"

"Can I sleep here?"

"Have you been crying?"

"No. I wasn't crying," Cale lied.

Jud lifted the blankets. "Come on."

Cale ran over, jumped in the air, and rolled into the
middle of the bed.

"Move over, you hog," Jud said, shoving him.

"I'm not a hog." Cale stared up at a black ceiling,
worried that tomorrow would be as bad as today and
yesterday. He pulled the covers up.

A second later the light came on, bright and blinding,

and Victor stood in the doorway. "What are you doing in here?"

Cale felt instantly sick.

"Never mind," he said in the same angry voice he'd used on the phone. He crossed the room and pulled off the covers.

Jud looked too scared to say a word.

"In this house, we sleep in our own rooms." Victor pulled Cale up, put his hands on his shoulders, and marched him to his own room, where he flipped on the light and paused before he pointed at the lump on the bed. "You know what that tells me?"

I'm in trouble. But all Cale said was, "No," in a sulky voice.

Victor threw back the blankets. "It tells me that you knew damned well you were supposed to stay in your own bed."

Cale didn't admit anything.

"You are eight and I'm a lot older. There isn't a trick you can pull I won't see through." He threw the clothes into a corner. "Now get into bed."

Cale crawled in and lay board-stiff, his eyes on the ceiling.

"Do you want the light on?"

"No," Cale said disgustedly and jerked the covers up over his head as the light went off. He could see through the white sheet.

His grandfather filled the doorway, backlit from the hall light. "Banning men don't need anyone, Cale. We stand on our own." He closed the door and the room went black.

* * *

Jud awoke to a sound like someone beating trash cans with a baseball bat. By the time he reached the window, the neighbor's dogs were barking. It was after midnight, and misty fog hovered in the air. Cale lay sprawled in front of the wooden garage doors, two metal trash cans lids next to him, one of them spinning like a top, the barrels rolling down the concrete driveway toward the street. His little brother had tried to look in the high glass panes of the garage doors. Jud opened the window and called in a loud whisper, "Are you nuts? Get back inside. Hurry up!"

Cale sat up, rubbing the back of his head. "I want to see the red car."

"Moron! It's the middle of the night."

"I know, but he won't let me see it. He won't let me talk to you or sleep with you. Besides, he's asleep."

"I was asleep, but someone woke me up making more noise than a train wreck." Their grandfather stepped out of the shadows and walked toward Cale. There was a threat in the way he moved.

Jud leaned out the window. "Don't you hurt him!"

His grandfather looked up, frowning. "I'm not going to hurt him."

"How do we know that?" Jud yelled. "We don't even know you!" He raced down the stairs. By then the chauffeur was outside his room over the garage, dressed in pajamas and carrying a shotgun, and Cale glared up at Victor with a stubborn look on his face . . . one that was exactly like their grandfather's.

"Don't hit him," Jud said.

"I'm not going to hit him," his grandfather said in an exasperated tone. He looked down at Cale. "Do you think I'm going to hit you?"

"I don't care if you do."

"This is all your fault," Jud said. "You should have shown him the car, too."

The chauffeur came down another step. "Mr. Banning?"

"I've got it, Harlan." His grandfather sounded tired. "Go back to bed."

The chauffeur turned back up the stairs.

"Harlan, wait! You—" Victor pointed a finger in Cale's belligerent face. "Apologize for waking him up."

For a moment Jud thought Cale was going to say no. The silence seemed to stretch out forever, then Cale faced the chauffeur and didn't look the least bit apologetic when he said, "I'm sorry I woke you up."

"It's all right, son." Harlan went back upstairs, leaving the three of them standing silently.

"So, Jud. You think I should show Cale the car?"

"Yes."

"Okay." Victor took a key from the pocket of his robe, unlocked the door, and held it open. "Go inside, both of you, and look all you want."

In a flash of brown Hopalong Cassidy pajamas, Cale slipped under Victor's arm and Jud followed. The MG was low and lean, its chrome sparkling. The tan top was folded down and the glass in the headlamps picked up the reflection of too-bright overhead lights. You didn't see that kind of car anymore, except in old movies. It was square, with running boards, tan leather seats, and a red paint job that made it look like a miniature fire engine.

"Wow!" Cale walked around the MG, then put his hands on his knees and made a face in the side mirror, then more faces in the polished chrome grille. He was just a little kid with his pajamas buttoned wrong and leaves from the driveway sticking to his back and spiky hair, which looked as if it were angry.

Their grandfather leaned on the fender. "I bought this car for your father."

Jud didn't know the MG had been his dad's. He could only picture his dad behind the wheel of that old two-tone Ford. But something wild had lived inside his father, like the red car.

"Jud." His grandfather opened the car door. "Get in."

He slid into the soft leather seat and placed his feet on the pedals. His little brother crawled into the passenger side, chattering, cranking the window up and down and punching the door locks, while Jud just held the steering wheel in both hands and stared out the low chrome-edged windshield, trying to feel something familiar: a sense of his dad, whatever was left behind—if anything was ever left behind after someone died. A strange kind of hunger came over him, sharp and intense: this car belonged to him. He wanted this car more than anything he'd ever wanted in his life.

Beside him, Cale was up on his knees, bouncing and gripping the seat back. "Someday I'm gonna have this car. I'm gonna be just like my dad and drive it every-where."

Jud shot a quick look at his brother, then up at the old man, who was watching him with an unreadable expression. Jud turned back around. *No, little brother. No. This car's going to be mine.*

CHAPTER

4

Kathryn paid the driver and got out of an orange cab that smelled like dirty ashtrays. Laurel ran up the front steps of Julia Peyton's home, an English Tudor gabled house with leaded glass windows, stone chimneys, and lush gardens flanking a downward sweep of sheared lawn.

"You're late, Kathryn." Julia stood at the front door dressed in heels and pearls. "I expected you before lunch."

"The movers took longer than I'd thought." Kathryn snapped her purse closed, annoyed at herself for automatically making excuses.

"Grandmama! Grandmama!" Laurel jumped up and down. "We're coming to live with you!"

"Yes, you are. Come give me a hug." Julia opened her arms and Laurel ran into them.

Kathryn turned to look back down the hill at the tail end of the cab as it disappeared around the iron gates. In the distance, a metallic sheet of water spread out to the cloudless blue horizon, broken only by a green hump of land called Bainbridge Island and the snow-dusted Olympic Mountains. *Puget Sound. This is the place where eagles drift by.* A line from one of Jimmy's songs. Too many lines came to her now, not just as song lyrics—but the words gave a timelessness to his thoughts and proof he had once lived.

With a loud hiss of air brakes, a green-and-yellow Mayflower moving van turned up into the driveway. It was done, she thought.

"Come along now, Kathryn. There's so much to do." Julia disappeared inside with Laurel still chattering excitedly.

Unmoving, Kathryn clung to her handbag with both hands and stared up at the imposing house where her husband grew up, and where now her daughter would do the same. In the useless days since Jimmy's death, nothing had changed the feeling that she was trapped between him and their child. Trapped. She felt it now. She had no home anymore. She had no husband. Laurel was here. Julia was here. Some part of her must still be here? That's what she told herself.

Kathryn put one foot in front of the other and said, "I can do this."

Within two weeks, the tension between the women in Jimmy Peyton's life could be cut with a knife, and Kathryn, who didn't handle conflict well to begin with, was quickly losing her will to fight Julia.

The first incident happened when Kathryn unpacked Jimmy's framed records. Just looking at them tore her apart, so she put them in a box and sent them up to the attic, only to come home a day later to find them displayed in the front entry hall, where everyone could see them the moment they stepped through the door. Crying, she hid them under her bed. At dinner that evening—meals that nightly consisted of Jimmy's favorites—Julia confronted her.

"You took down Jimmy's records."

"Yes."

Her mother-in-law angrily chain-smoked through dinner, until the silence was thick as cigarette smoke and sitting there became unbearable. Kathryn stood. "It's time for your bath, Laurel."

"Let the child have dessert." Julia dropped her linen napkin on her plate and slid a bowl of ice cream in front of her granddaughter.

Kathryn sat down again and stared at the heavy gold draperies on the windows. Underneath them were pale sheers covering the glass panes. She felt as invisible as those sheers.

"Johnny Ace's family gave his records to a museum," Julia said.

"The records should go to Laurel someday."

"Laurel will know they're important if they're hanging in the entry." Julia's voice was clipped. "I took down a Picasso and the Matisse."

Later that night, Kathryn rehung the records, then walked to her bedroom, closed the door, and lay there staring at nothing and feeling everything. From then on, she came in the house through a side door or the kitchen.

Between the time she had agreed to let their downtown apartment go and their actual move, Julia had redone Jimmy's bedroom for Laurel, but the adjoining playroom remained untouched from Jimmy's childhood. A few nights later, Kathryn walked in on Julia with Laurel in her lap while they looked at old slides through a viewfinder.

"Come sit with us, Kathryn. I don't believe you've ever seen these photos."

"Come, Mama. Come here. Daddy had a red tricycle just like mine."

Already Laurel sounded like Julia. *Come here. Come with me. Come there. Come. Come. Come.*

So Kathryn looked at photo after photo, each one drawing a little more of the life from her. She didn't tell Evie when they talked on the phone that night, because she didn't want any more stress. These days she folded so easily under pressure. But she slipped the rental section of the Sunday morning paper under her arm and in the quiet of her bedroom began to circle the ads.

On the sly the next week, she looked at a small house in Magnolia with a backyard and a view of the sound, and she came home later than she'd planned and rushed right to the kitchen to make Laurel lunch. On her way to find her daughter, Julia stopped her. Kathryn tried to escape. "I'm taking Laurel a peanut butter and jelly sandwich."

"It's one o'clock. She's already eaten. I gave her a ham salad sandwich."

"Laurel doesn't like ham."

"Of course she does. It was Jimmy's favorite." Julia took the plate from Kathryn and set it on a nearby table. "Come. I have something to show you." She led her out through the back of the house, past the new swing set

and jungle gym, to a break of cedars that bordered the
back lawn. Julia stopped. "Look, Kathryn."

Between those trees was a small building, a miniature
of the big house. Julia handed her a key. "Go inside."

What Kathryn had assumed was a playhouse for Laurel was a large open room with shelves along the walls
and a deep work sink and tiled counter under a wide
front window.

Julia leaned against the counter, her hands resting on
the rim. "You can see Laurel's play area from here. And
from that long window. I thought we could put your
wheel there. The kiln is around the corner so this room
won't get too hot. And that refrigerator is for the clay."

"I don't know what to say." And Kathryn didn't. "This
is wonderful."

"Good." Julia cupped a hand around a match, held it
to the cigarette hanging from her lips, then tossed back
her head and exhaled smoke. "I know coming here
wasn't easy for you. I wanted you to know I'm glad
you're here." For a raw instant, Julia stared at her with
the expression of an animal caught high in a tree, staring
down at the hunter and his gun. "Enjoy it." Julia turned
and left.

The studio of Kathryn's dreams couldn't have been
any better. Light and warmth came through the window;
the tiles were gleaming, the room pristine, new still, no
earthy smell of damp or baking clay. The walls were
white, stark, and clean, without a trace of life. As she
stood there, her past was wiped out, her future haunt-
ingly empty.

But something else haunted her. She looked back to
where Julia had just stood and realized she understood

her mother-in-law's terrified look. Only that morning Kathryn had seen it in the mirror.

Over the next few days, Kathryn stopped reading the rental ads and Julia stopped telling her what to do and how to feel. Kathryn was dressing after a shower when she heard Laurel singing. It sounded like she was jumping on the bed next door.

Kathryn ran into the hallway. "Laurel! Tell me you are not jumping on your grandmother's bed." She entered Julia's suite for the first time.

Laurel was bouncing jubilantly on her grandmother's silk-dressed bed and chanting, "I love coffee, I love tea . . ."

"Stop it!"

Laurel looked at her midbounce.

"She's fine, Kathryn." Julia came out of her bathroom rubbing cold cream on her face. "I told her she could jump on it." Her robe matched the room, which was a clean soft white. Even the furniture, including a dressing table in one corner and a hi-fi in the other, were painted white, and the suite was luxuriously decorated from the carpet and the bed linens to the silk draperies on two long mullioned windows that looked out over the water. Between those long windows was a five-by-eight-foot canvas of bold colors, contemporary like most of Julia's art. Kathryn felt the blood drain to her feet.

"It's impressive, isn't it?" Julia used a tissue to wipe the cream off. "There's another over the bed."

Kathryn faced the bed where Laurel was still jumping.

"The artist is Espinosa. I bought them a while back.

Their value must be rising, although Lord knows I paid enough for them to begin with. The gallery called a week ago. The artist died recently and her family has been trying to track down all her pieces. The canvases fit so perfectly in here I don't think I want to sell them. I decorated the whole room around them."

Kathryn found her voice. "Do you know who that artist is?"

"Rachel Espinosa. A Spanish artist."

"She was married to Rudy Banning."

"Banning?" Julia sat down. "Banning?" There was a hollowness to her voice and her skin was gray. She looked up at Kathryn. "He killed Jimmy. Rudy Banning killed my son."

"Rachel Espinosa Banning died in the same accident. She had an art show that night. Didn't you see the newspapers?"

Julia shook her head. "I couldn't read them. I didn't want to read them. I was afraid to read them."

"She and her husband left the show arguing. He lost control of the car."

"My God." Julia stood. "My God . . ." She walked into the bathroom and shut the door.

Kathryn was left to stare at the paintings, first one and then the other, until they all blurred together and she couldn't see them anymore.

Later that night, Kathryn awoke from the throes of a nightmare and sat up, startled at the sound of Jimmy's music playing so loudly from the next room.

Laurel came to her bed. "Mama. The music's too loud. Make it stop."

Kathryn tucked her in. "Stay here. I'll ask Grandmama to turn it off." What the hell was Julia thinking? She rapped on the door. "Julia?" Inside, she froze. Her mother-in-law stood on the bed, a long kitchen knife in her hand, the painting slashed from one corner to the other. "Julia!"

Calmly, she sliced down the other side and faced Kathryn, then stepped down to the carpet. "I don't want them in this room. In this house." Julia started toward the other painting.

"Wait! Don't."

"I need to destroy it. They destroyed my life. They killed my son."

"You said the family wants the paintings."

"They do." Julia looked so small and lost and confused, not like someone capable of setting your teeth on edge. She merely looked half there.

"Then don't destroy them. To never sell them back is the best revenge." Wicked words, she knew, but that made saying them all the better. "Never sell them."

Julia looked from the knife in her hand to the other painting on the wall. She took deep breaths and wiped at her tears with the sleeve of her silk robe, then handed Kathryn the knife. Kathryn put her arm around her. "It's okay."

"Nothing will ever be okay again." Julia started crying and leaned against her, no longer hard as stone but frail and brittle as shale.

"Come with me," Kathryn said. "You can sleep in one of the guest rooms tonight. I'll have the paintings removed tomorrow."

"I'll never sell them. You're right, Kathryn. We will never sell them."

PART TWO

1970

We often make people pay dearly for what
we think we give them.

Marie Josephine de Suin de Beausac

CHAPTER

5

Newport Beach, California

The soil was rich in this Golden State, dark as the oil pumped up from its depths. Bareroot roses planted in the ground bloomed in a matter of weeks, and every spring the lantana tripled in breadth, filling the narrow property lines between homes where every square foot was valued in tens of thousands. Roots from the pepper trees unearthed backyard fences, and eucalyptus grew high into the blue skies, like fabled beanstalks, shooting up so swiftly the bark cracked away and fell dusty to the ground. If you knelt down and dug your hands into the dirt, you could smell its fecundity, and when you stood up you might look—or even be—a little taller.

Billboards sold everyone on growth, and the coastal hills swelled with tracks of housing because people hungered for a false sense of peace from the Pacific views. Newport was not the small resort enclave it had once been, with new restaurants now perched on the waterfront, housed in everything from canneries and beam-and-glass buildings to a grounded riverboat. Luxury homes stood on most lots, which had been subdivided into smaller shapes that couldn't be measured in anything as archaic as an acre. At the entrances to entire neighborhoods, white crossbars blocked the roads and were raised and lowered by a uniformed security guard in a hut, a kind of cinematic image that brought to mind border crossings and cold wars. But the guard wasn't there to keep people out; he was there to keep prestige in.

The Banning boys grew into young men here, tall and athletic, golden like everything in California. Thirteen years had changed who they were, now brothers separated by a demand to be something they weren't. They wanted to win. They had everything, except their grandfather's approval.

As soon as the opportunity arose, Victor Banning had bought the homes on either side of him, torn them down and renovated the Lido house until it spanned five lots, encompassing the whole point. The place had three docks, boasted a full basketball court and seven garages.

Today, Banning Oil Company was BanCo, involved in everything from petroleum by-products, fuel, and manufacturing to the development of reclaimed oil land. Annually listed as a Fortune 500 company, it was the kind of proving ground hungry young executives clamored to join.

Hunger wasn't what had sent Jud Banning to work for his grandfather the previous May, when he'd graduated from Stanford Business School in the top five percent with a master's in corporate finance along with degrees in business and marketing. Expectation sent him there, Victor's idea of natural order.

Every summer since the start of high school both Jud and his brother had worked for the company in some capacity—mostly peon. But a career working for his grandfather wasn't the golden opportunity Jud's grad school buddies imagined. For as much as the house and business had changed, Victor hadn't. He was still difficult and demanding. Nepotism didn't feel like favoritism when Victor Banning was the one doling it out.

It was early spring now, a time of year when the morning marine layer seldom hung over the coast, so the sun glinted off the water and reflected from the glass of waterfront homes across the isle; it soaked through a wall of windows on the water side of the Banning home. The dining room grew warm, sunlight spreading like melted butter over the room and over Jud Banning, who was sound asleep at the dining table.

He sat up, suddenly awake. And just as on the last three mornings, the housekeeper stood over him holding a carafe of coffee. He glanced around the room, a thread of panic in his voice. "What time is it?"

"Early." Time was either early or late in Maria's eyes. Days, weeks, and months were noted only if they held religious significance—Ash Wednesday, Lent, the Assumption of Mary. You could ask her when the steaks would be done and she'd tell you how to butcher the cow. She had come to work from Mexico as cook, housekeeper, and nanny two days after Jud and Cale arrived, and thirteen years later she was still the only woman in an all-male household. She set the coffee and a mug down with a meaningful thud. "You fall asleep here every night, Jud. Papers everywhere."

"I know. I know."

"Mr. Victor is coming home today. You want him to see you like this?"

"He won't. The board meeting is today."

"Beds are for sleeping. Desks are for working. Tables are for eating."

"I've never eaten a table," he said, deadpan. She merely looked at him, so he changed the subject. "I won't be here next week. I'm going to the island with Cale tomorrow."

"That boy." She shook her head and headed for the kitchen. "He never comes home."

"He's busy with school."

"He's busy with the girls," Maria said and disappeared around the corner.

Jud could hear the sound of Barbara Walters's voice on the *Today* show coming from the kitchen TV, a sign he wasn't late. Under the charts and graphs, notes, and P&Ls piled on the table he found his watch; it read seven fifteen. He slipped it on and ran both hands through his shaggy hair. He didn't cut it, just to annoy Victor. Unlike Cale, Jud kept his revolts on a more subtle scale.

Around him were weeks' worth of paperwork, but stacked on a nearby chair were glossy black presentation folders with his proposal ready for board approval. Today was the first Friday of the month, and the board meeting would begin as always at precisely 10 A.M. From the moment he'd been able to negotiate with another supplier, he knew this was a winner of a deal. It would cut the proposed cost for new oil tankers by over two million dollars, a figure he expected would bowl them over.

So an hour later, he came down the stairs whistling as he tied the knot in his new tie, then shrugged into his suit coat and stopped by a mirror for a quick look. Tugging down on his cuffs, he said, "Old man, have I got a deal for you."

A few minutes later Maria met him at the door. "Take Mr. Victor's newspapers with you." She dumped them on the box of folders he carried and opened the front door for him. "It's Good Friday. You go to church."

"Sure thing." He hadn't been in a church since his college roommate got married.

The static, machine-gun racket of an air compressor came from the garages, where there was room for seven cars, plus a full maintenance bay and workshop. Harlan had his head under the hood of Victor's silver Bentley. Three sports cars were parked in the small bays on the left side. A '59 Porsche 1600D roadster, a '63 Corvette convertible, and a Jaguar XKE. All of them belonged to Cale. All of them were bright red. But his brother never drove any single one of them with the regularity of a favorite. No matter how many expensive red sports cars Cale bought, none would ever be a replacement for their dad's MG.

The MG was parked in the fourth bay, gleaming like California sunshine because Harlan was a man who truly loved cars. Every Banning automobile ran to its capacity as a finely tuned machine, engine smooth, body always washed, and the chrome and tires polished.

Jud opened the driver's door, dropped the folders on the floor, and threw his briefcase on the passenger seat. He opened the trunk and tossed the newspapers inside—

the *Los Angeles Times,* the *Examiner,* the *New York Times,* the *Wall Street Journal,* the *Register,* the *Daily Pilot,* and the *San Diego Tribune.* He didn't understand his grandfather. If you'd read one paper, hell, you'd read 'em all.

Harlan lifted his head out from underneath the Bentley hood and grabbed a rag from the back pocket of his gray work coveralls. He spotted Jud, frowned, and glanced at an old Banning Oil Company clock on the back wall, then switched off the noisy compressor. "You're leaving early. Your grandfather's plane isn't coming in until nine thirty."

"I need to be there early."

But Harlan's expression said what every Banning employee knew. No one did any board business before Victor arrived. Harlan stuffed the rag in his pocket and went back to work.

Jud let the engine warm up and backed out, waited for the electronic gates, tapping the steering wheel impatiently before he honked the horn twice and sped away.

The Santa Ana headquarters for BanCo occupied the top seven floors of the Grove Building, a glass, metal, and concrete structure that took its vanilla name from the old orange groves that had been plowed under to clear the building site. From Fifth and Main, towering glass buildings bled from one mirrored image into another, looking nothing like farmland. Sound carried up from the nearby freeways, the constant hum of cars along Interstate 5, and the air had an energized buzz, a swarming sound of human activity that hung above busy streets at lunchtime and after five.

On the fifteenth floor, no traffic noise came into the

boardroom as Victor Banning sat in front of his unopened proposal folder and listened to Jud talk.

"I know Banning has never dealt with Marvetti Industries," Jud said. "But I've met with them and found their tankers to be top of the line."

Victor heard the word "Marvetti" and stood up. "This meeting is over." A pointed pause of absolute silence existed for a nanosecond, then the board members dropped their folders and fled the room like rats from a sinking ship.

Jud stared at him, red-faced. "What the hell was that all about?"

"We'll talk in my office." Victor headed for his private office.

Silently, Jud followed him inside and shut the doors. "Okay. What's going on?"

Victor took his time. He sat down at his desk, a large, impressive piece of rectangular furniture that put space between him and everyone else. "You tell me."

"Tell you what? You cut the meeting off in the middle of my presentation."

"To stop you before you made a complete fool of yourself."

Immediately Jud's hackles went up, his body language stiff and all too readable. Sometimes Victor forgot how young he was. By the time Victor was twenty-five, he'd learned to be ruthless, how to protect his ass and his business. He had a wife and child at home and he worked eighteen-hour days with single-minded purpose.

"I wasn't going to make a fool of myself. Do you think I don't know how to make a presentation?" Jud drove a hand through his goddamned long hair. "Shit . . ."

"You're standing knee-deep in shit right now with this Marvetti deal."

"Marvetti's company has the rigs ready for purchase. We don't have to wait for Fisk to reinforce their tankers. We don't have to order the tractors separately. With Marvetti, it's all one deal and the tanker reinforcements have already been done. All at a cost that's a third less."

Victor just looked at him. He hadn't done the right research.

"This deal—my deal—will save the company two million dollars." Jud held up two fingers. "*Two million dollars.*"

"I can't believe my own flesh and blood could be so fucking stupid. Just what did they teach you in six years of college?"

"Enough to figure out how to cut a deal with one of the biggest suppliers in the world."

Victor laughed at him.

"We've never dealt with Marvetti before." Jud tapped his chest. "I got us in. Me."

"You actually think I can't make a deal with anyone I want?"

His grandson had no quick comeback. The kid wasn't stupid, just green. Jud's voice was quiet when he said, "I checked the company records. There's no record of any deal with Marvetti."

"Why do you think that is?"

"Because we didn't have an in."

"Who told you that?"

"Joe Syverson said there was a rumor that Marvetti hated you."

"I wouldn't do business with him when I was small

potatoes, and I sure as hell won't do it now. You should have asked me, not Syverson."

"The last time I asked you a question, you said you weren't going to wet-nurse me through my job. You told me to learn to think for myself."

"'Think' is the definitive word, Jud."

"Go to hell."

"For Christ's sake, stop glaring at me and calm down. Tell me how this deal of yours came about."

"I ran into Richard Denton at the club a few months back." Jud began to pace in front of Victor's desk. "He asked me to have drinks with his foursome. Marvetti's sales manager was one of the group."

"So they came after you."

"No." Jud spun around and faced him. "That's not what happened. I had to work my butt off for this deal. I did everything but kiss his ass."

The kid never saw it coming, Victor thought. "Was Fitzpatrick there?"

"Yes."

Victor looked up at Jud. "So you think men like Denton and Fitzpatrick are going to welcome you into their inner business circle just like"—Victor snapped his fingers—"that? Why would they do that? Because you went to Stanford? Because they like your looks? Because you drive a hot little MG, wear cashmere sweaters, and can shoot three under par on the back nine? Or do you think it just might be because you're my grandson?" Victor leaned forward, his palms flat on the desktop. "You're a snot-nosed kid just out of college."

Jud's head snapped back as if Victor had punched him.

"You're twenty-five years old and you have a helluva lot to learn." Victor took a long deep breath and sat back in his chair. "First rule of business: Examine the offer. Don't look first at what kind of deal they're giving you. Look at what's in it for them."

"I know what's in it for them. A multimillion-dollar deal with BanCo. That's what I can give them," Jud said, wounded pride in his voice.

Victor understood pride in all its forms. "You're exactly right."

Jud looked confused. He ran on ego instead of instinct, something he had yet to develop.

"If a smart businessman wants something and can't get it, he looks to his opponent's weakest spot." Victor paused, then said, "In my case, you're it."

Jud spoke through a tight jaw. "Just what do you want from me?"

"I want you to do your job. When you start a deal, you make damn sure you know everything there is to know about who you're dealing with. Especially their motives. You find out their shoe size, their kids' names, their goddamn blood type. Know how much they paid the IRS last year. Know every fucking thing there is to know before you ever negotiate anything."

"What's wrong with Marvetti? Why won't you deal with them?"

"I'm not going to do your job. You need to use your head, dammit. I want you to understand that—"

"You want me to be perfect!"

"No. I don't believe in miracles." Victor would have bet Jud wanted to hit him right then. He took a deep breath. "What I want is for you to learn to work the same way I do. I want you to think like I do."

"Why in the hell would I want to be like you?"

Victor stood up. "You cocky young fool. You have no idea of the mistakes ahead of you."

"Yes I do. I'm looking at my biggest mistake, old man. I thought I could be part of this company. You're the one who's mistaken if you think I ever want to be anything like you!"

"Then you're stupid, and I've never thought that of you, Jud. You wanted to learn this business. Then watch me and goddamn learn it!"

"I didn't ask to be raked over the coals every time I turn around! I can't do anything right around you!" Jud leaned on the desk.

They were almost nose to nose. Victor straightened, then spoke in a calmer tone. "Your only problem is that you're young. And you don't like to admit you're wrong."

"With you I'm always wrong."

"You're not always wrong. You just think you know everything."

"Then I guess I am just like you."

In the utter silence that followed, Victor asked himself how many mistakes it would take to crack through this kid's hard head. He thought Jud was like Rudy in that and he looked at the angry young man standing before him and felt as if he'd been thrown back in time. Rudy would have run the company into the ground, but Jud was whip-smart, took chances, and he was the stronger of the boys. Unlike Cale—who was screwing his way through Loyola—a woman would never get between Jud and the business. Jud didn't think with his fly.

"You think I'm tough on you? Well, I am." Victor sat again, leaning back in his chair and never taking his eyes off Jud. "I built this business by being tough and I'll be damned if I'm going to lose it because you're too hard-headed to listen and learn."

"So what am I supposed to tell Marvetti? My grandfather said no deal. I can hear the buzz now. 'Jud Banning is a real pussy. A puppet. He does exactly what his grandfather tells him.' Great . . . just great."

"You want me to give you all the answers and I'm not going to. I didn't have anyone to tell me what to do. Solve this yourself. Show the world the kind of a man you are."

"So in this hard-edged, tough business world of yours, you become a man by welshing on a deal? How in the hell will anyone ever take me seriously?"

Victor leaned back in his chair, crossed his arms, and merely looked at him. He refused to lead Jud through life by the nose.

"Damn you, Victor. This is my deal. I have to lose my respect and integrity because you don't like Marvetti?"

"You lost your integrity when you let his flunkies lure you into a business deal with him. Find out for yourself why. Then you come and tell me how good your deal is."

Anger, humiliation, and something almost elemental were in Jud's taut features. "I want the chance to make my own mark on this company, to do things my way."

"Your way is wrong." Victor didn't move. Jud was pigheaded but Victor knew he wouldn't cross that final line—the one that would send his butt out of the company. The silence between them was tense, and silence between people said more than words ever could. "Go on." Victor waved a hand and looked away. "Get out of here." He picked up a folder on his desk, but when Jud was almost out the door he called his name. "Don't come back until you're ready to do things the right way."

Jud jerked open the door. "You mean your way."

"Yes. I mean my way."

Loyola University Marymount College, Del Rey Hills, California

There were no doctors in the Banning family. Cale wasn't trying to follow in some relative's hallowed footsteps. He defied Victor's rule of natural order, but not for the sake of defiance. When Cale was young and someone asked him what he wanted to be when he grew up, his answer was always the same. While his friends vacillated between a cowboy one week and a fireman the next, he saved the life of everything from earthworms to a neighbor's half-drowned cat. Whenever a seagull flew into the almost invisible glass windows of the Lido house, Cale would put the senseless gull in a box with a beach towel warm from the dryer, and an hour later the bird would have flown away.

Those nights he would sleep without moving. He would crawl out of his bed the next morning, the sheets still tucked in, and later Maria would swear he'd slept on the floor or in Jud's room. The truth was, he never tried to sleep in Jud's room after that first month. Their boyhood closeness was just that, part of boyhood. Jud was his brother, but like those unsuspecting seagulls, Cale had slammed headfirst into a glass wall Victor built between them enough times to not fly there anymore.

By the time Cale started high school, he sought his comfort from the opposite sex. At college those first few years, partying was preferable to catching some Z's, and he had a new freedom living away from home. Everyone slept in dorms, which was where he headed that afternoon as he left the student post office with an envelope from the University of Washington.

A cool afternoon breeze swept in from the Pacific, pushing the smog farther inland and away from the campus perched on a bluff above the western fringes of the LA basin. Students sat on benches and lounged across lawns surrounded with the clean smell of mown grass and beds of rosebushes with flowers the size of an open hand. As on most days, older priests and nuns played boccie at one end of the green, a spot called the Sunken Garden, and some students tossed around a Frisbee at the other end. A banner painted with a bulldog behind bars and the cry *Pound the Zags!* hung between two huge magnolia trees in the middle of the mall, because tonight—the last night before spring break—was the night when Loyola challenged Gonzaga for the number one position in their division.

Cale's mind wasn't on the big game when he left Saint Robert's Hall and headed straight for the senior apartments, a three-story stucco-and-wood building that could have easily melted into any block of apartments in any part of LA. Four seniors shared each two-bedroom unit, but the place was empty when he tossed his books on an orange Formica table, grabbed a cold Coors, and headed for his room, which smelled like old socks, wet towels, and pizza. He sat down on the bed, staring down at the white envelope for a long time before he opened it and unfolded the letter.

March 24, 1970

Dear Mr. Banning:
We regret to inform you that you do not meet
our requirements for admission into the University
of Washington School of Medicine.

Blah . . . blah . . . blah . . . He crushed the letter into a ball and rested his head on his fists. Every letter was the same. The rejections from the first-tier schools had come rapid-fire fast—Harvard, Stanford, Johns Hopkins. The rest came week after week, like some unending boxing match he was destined to lose.

The door flew open with a bang and his roommate and teammate shuffled in, singing off-key Creedence Clearwater. "Down on the corner, out in the street, Willie and the tall boys are playin', on the home court tonight."

William Dorsey was the grandson of a big band leader whose musical talent was not passed on to subsequent generations, but whose showmanship was. Will loved a cheering crowd, whether it was on the basketball court or in the dorm back in their freshman year when he was the only guy who could chug a six-pack of

Colt 45 malt liquor in under three minutes and not throw up. He was a basketball star. Six foot six, a loose walker, all rubber arms and legs, and on the court he was magic in motion. His jump shot was tops; he could score more points in two minutes than any other player in the division; and it was no surprise when he was unanimously voted captain of the Lions. Scouts had been around him at almost every game.

Will kicked the door closed and stopped to blow a ritual kiss at a color eight-by-ten photo of Jeannine Byer, a knockout blonde, a Mount Saint Mary's nursing student. He gave Cale a quick glance, then stopped. "Who died?"

"Me." Cale held up the crumpled letter.

"Another one? Which school?"

"U Dub."

"Ah, hell, man. You didn't wanna go there anyway. It rains all the time." Will dropped his books on the floor, picked up a metal wastebasket, and balanced it on his head. "Here." He pointed to the basket. "That letter belongs in here. Those sorry bastards. One throw. Come on, man. Go for it!"

Cale pitched the letter into the air; it arced across the room and dropped inside the basket with a soft ping.

Will lifted Cale's Coors can to his mouth like a mike. He blew into it, making a hollow sound. Mimicking Howard Cosell, he said, "We have an-*nuther* goal scored by Cale Banning tonight. He is well on his way to breaking *all* . . . ex-*zisting* records for med school rejection! But there's hope! This erudite fuckup of Loyola has *not* exhausted *all* his options. Canada? Mexico? The third world countries? Or if all else fails, *Mis*-ter Cale Banning can apply to Uncle-Sam-Wants-U, where he will swiftly be transferred to the renowned University of *Da Nang*!"

"Funny." Cale threw a wet towel at him. "University of Da Nang, my ass."

"Hell, if I were sending men into the jungle, I wouldn't want dropouts leading the way." Will swept a couple of eight-track tapes off the bed, fell back flat on the mattress, and crossed his big feet. He was wearing squeaky huarache sandals he'd bought for a buck on a weekend trip down to Tijuana over Thanksgiving break. "When I was dreaming of the draft, I was thinking NBA, not U.S. Army." He folded his hands behind his head and lay staring up at the ceiling before he raised his head off the pillow and looked at Cale. "Your MCATs aren't doing it?"

"Med schools are packed. No one wants to go to Da Nang."

"Too many body counts on the news. Was that the last of your applications?"

"No. I haven't heard from San Diego, Texas, and USC."

"What are you going to do if they all say *nada*?"

Head down, Cale rested his elbows on his knees and rubbed his eyes. "I don't know."

"I can't believe you gave away your GPA for a forty-inch bust. Did you go to any classes last year?"

"Some."

There was a long pause before Will asked, "Was she worth it?"

Cale laughed bitterly. "No."

"Have you talked to your grandfather yet?"

"Oh, yeah. Sure. I'm looking forward to that conversation."

Will picked up a basketball and began to toss it from hand to hand. "Victor Banning. The great and powerful Oz. I only met him once. Kept wishing I had a crucifix to hold in front of my face."

"One of his better qualities."

"He has to be able to help you. With his connections?" Will quit tossing the basketball and faced Cale. "What would happen if you had a heart-to-heart talk with him?"

"He doesn't have a heart."

"Talk to him."

"I've spent years trying to talk to my grandfather. No one talks to Victor. He talks to them. Every time I go home, I hear about how I'm throwing my future away. It's one of the many reasons I don't go home." Cale looked down, then shook his head. "God, Will. How could I screw up so bad?"

The only sound in the room was the basketball bouncing off the ceiling, then nothing but a long silent pause. Will held the basketball at chest level, looking at him. "Bad-*ly*," he said, and threw the ball at Cale.

Instinctively, Cale caught it, then laughed. "Kiss my ass, you literate jock."

Will grabbed the ringing phone. "Timothy Leary's House of Hash. You smoke 'em, we coke 'em." His gaze shifted to Cale. "Yeah, he's here . . . somewhere. Let me see if I can find him. Oh, I think I see his foot. There! Yes! In the corner! He's buried under . . . Wait! Wait, I need a skip-loader here." He paused for drama, then shook his head. "Uh-oh. Too bad. Looks like he's a goner. Make a note for his epitaph, will you? 'Here lies Cale Banning, who, on April 3, 1970, suffocated to death under the largest pile of med school rejections in the history of the modern world.'" Will held out the phone and whispered, "It's Jud. Lucky Mr. Four-F."

"Hey, there, big brother."

"Hey, you." Jud's bass voice sounded exactly like their dad's. Cale always had to take that one extra second to remember who was on the other end.

"Will Dorsey is a nutcase," Jud said.

"Yeah." Cale looked at Will. "I know. You ought to try living with him. It's like being trapped inside a Ferlinghetti poem."

Will flipped him off and jogged into the bathroom. A couple of seconds later, Cale heard the shower running, then the tinny notes of a transistor radio playing a Jimi Hendrix song. "What's going on?" Cale asked Jud.

"I'm on a pay phone at the steamer dock, waiting to board the boat. I'm going to the island a day early."

Damn . . . He'd forgotten this was the weekend they'd planned to meet at the Catalina place. "I can't leave yet, Jud. There's a play-off game tonight."

"I know. I just wanted to let you know I'm going over early. I've got to get out of here today."

"What's wrong?"

"What isn't wrong." Jud sounded disgusted.

"Victor."

"Yeah, well, don't get me started. I'll tell you about it tomorrow."

They hung up. He hadn't seen Jud in months. Cale used school as an excuse to avoid going home; it had become a comfortable habit. He used sports, studying, anything to weasel out of going to Newport. Nothing waited for him at home but Victor's expectations. He grabbed his game gear from under the bed, slung the athletic bag over a shoulder, and hammered on the bathroom door, then opened it. Steam hit him in the face. "How long are you going to be in here?"

"Till I'm clean."

Cale turned down the radio.

"What's going on with Mr. Perfect?" Will asked.

"Jud's not perfect."

"He's a helluva lot closer than anyone I know."

Cale glanced in the mirror at his foggy reflection. Smeared and far from perfect. Maybe his grandfather wasn't the only person he was avoiding. Jud had been accepted to his first choice—Stanford—for both undergraduate and graduate studies. He wouldn't have any idea what a rejection letter looked like. Cale's most insurmountable problems were a piece of cake for Jud, who skated through life on silver skates, never slipping, never falling. Never failing. Jud first took off for college when Cale was still in high school, and he knew he would never forget that summer, because Victor gave Jud their dad's MG.

By August it was just Victor and him, which meant they lived in a house of silence until a long weekend or school vacation when Jud came home. Life was pretty much a set formula. Jud set the bar; Cale usually failed to meet it. From the very day they drove up to their grandfather's home in that long black limo, his life had been very different from his older brother's, and he had the feeling that was exactly the way Victor wanted it.

Cale zipped his shaving kit closed. "I'm going to

meet my brother tomorrow at the Catalina place. Since it looks like you're gonna stay in that shower till graduation, I'm heading over to the gym. I'll shower there." He closed the door, but stopped in the middle of the room. The torn envelope sat on his bed. Talk to Victor, Will had said. Cale could just hear his grandfather now. *You young fool. You let a girl snatch away your dreams. Your only job was to go to college and study, not skip classes and screw some sweet young thing.* Victor had an uncanny ability to zero in on an open, bleeding wound and stick a knife squarely into it.

Cale threw the envelope in the trash. No way he would go to Newport now. Will had been right on when he'd called Victor the great and powerful Oz. He was. But for Cale, no place was home.

CHAPTER

6

During the years she lived with Julia, Kathryn Peyton had lost herself. Her mother-in-law hadn't been old when Jimmy died, only fifty-five to Kathryn's twenty-three, but she was frail, her bones the first thing anyone noticed about her and much of what gave her the hard look that went along with her controlling nature. With Laurel in the house, Julia's mind stayed sharp, but her body hadn't. Those bones shrank into nothingness over twelve years, and even Julia, with her sheer determination to control everything, couldn't stop her own death.

Those same twelve years had shrunk Kathryn into a nonentity. She was Laurel's mother, Julia's daughter-in-law, a reclusive artist known only through the pieces sold. No Kathryn. Her life had been dissected into two precise pieces—before Jimmy died and after Jimmy died. Everything before was only a dream, everything afterward alien territory.

It wasn't until recently that she had faced her own existence with clearer eyes, and saw what it had been— one distraction after another. Laurel needed her. Julia needed her. Her work—a place to hide from what she was really feeling. Then one day she was living in her dead mother-in-law's home with no one to tell her what to do or how to live. She didn't fit anymore and felt swallowed by the emptiness of her own existence. Until Evie called with a plan. She was getting married and moving to Chicago, so Kathryn should buy the house on Catalina Island. The timing was perfect. Nothing was keeping her in Seattle. "After all, Kay," Evie said, "you're almost thirty-six years old."

So Kathryn bought the house and moved to Santa Catalina, a small Channel Island off the coast of Southern California, where everything was different. From the island village of Avalon, the moon looked as if it rose right out of the sea, and the palm trees stood so tall, like hands waving hello in the sea breezes. It was lazy here; things began only with an arrival from the mainland—a regatta, a steamship, or a seaplane. This was the land of glass-bottomed boats, of coves named after jewels, of starfish and abalone shells, a place where people preferred to drive golf carts instead of cars.

Esther Williams had leapt off an island cliff on horseback once, creating a small but dramatic piece of cinematic and island history. The movie studios had shipped a herd of buffalo over to film a Western, and left them to become part of the place, like the wild boars and herds of goats and other seemingly mythic animals. So, given all the elements, Catalina became the magic isle, a place that rose out of the fog, an emerald in a sea of sapphires, a place where the fish could really fly.

Here the rain didn't come down in sheets of water so thick they blocked out life going on around you. Island sunshine made things appear clearer. You could see all the sharp edges and soft curves of life. Here, when you looked into a mirror, you saw what you had become, not what you had been.

Hiding in excuses wasn't so easy in the clear air and sunshine, or inside a small house filled with rooms as colorful as her sister's personality. So perhaps it wasn't all that surprising when Kathryn shared a pitcher of margaritas and a platter of nachos earlier that evening with a man named Stephen Randall, whom she'd met at a Chamber of Commerce meeting the week before. She had sat down alone in the bar of the local Mexican restaurant and felt reckless for even showing up. She knew how to hide; she didn't know how to date.

Just drinks, he told her when he'd come into her shop one afternoon. But tonight he came into the bar with his arms full of yellow daffodils, so drinks moved on to appetizers, and he left hours later with her home telephone number. Funny that she didn't regret giving it to him, even now, as she set an overflowing vase on a glass table in her bedroom. His flowers were the same sunshine-warm shade as the walls. Happy colors, Evie called the paint she'd used inside the house. Daffodils were happy, like snapdragons, and pansies, and lost women who moved to small islands in the blue Pacific.

Wilmington Pier, Los Angeles Harbor

Laurel Peyton stood on the corner as the local bus pulled away from the wharf and headed back toward downtown LA. A slight breeze lifted her hat, so she pressed it down, picked up a large, rusty brown suede purse, and rushed toward the boat as she did almost every Friday, when she routinely made the two-hour boat trip home.

The SS *Catalina* was a three-hundred-foot white steamer, a ship really, but everyone called it a boat. As always, the *Catalina* was docked in the last slip, where nothing but an expanse of blue-gray water stood between her huge hull and the Channel Island she serviced. On most days, you could see the island from almost anywhere along the Southern California coast. Against the western horizon, Santa Catalina Island looked like an enormous sleeping camel, sometimes shrouded in marine mist and sometimes sitting there so clearly you could almost make out the saw-toothed outline of the trees along its ridges.

Laurel joined the long line waiting to board. The late afternoon sun was hot and shone at eye level. The sun was more intense in California, especially at the very end of land and on days like today, when no cool wind blew in off the ocean. People shifted in line and muttered impatiently, removing jackets and sweaters. Kids whined or ran about. Their mothers ignored them, fanning themselves with island pamphlets and folded-up guide maps.

Although she hadn't lived in California a year yet, Laurel could spot the tourists with the innate eye of a native. Men in dark shirts wore straw hats with black hatbands and socks with their sandals. Women in floral print dresses carried white patent-leather purses and wore nylons. California women were true to the golden land and wore only their tanned skin, polished with a bit of baby oil.

Laurel glanced left at the sound of a deep male voice coming from a bank of pay phones. The young man leaned casually against the wall, his back to her. He was tall, with light brown hair and the lanky build of a movie idol. He wore khaki shorts and a polo shirt the color of fresh lemons, his skin looking darkly tanned against that light clothing. On his feet were sandals—no socks.

The line shifted with an almost unanimous sigh of relief as two crew members came down the gangplank and unlocked its chain. He glanced over his shoulder and she forgot to breathe. Paul Newman and Ryan O'Neal rolled into one. He was too old for her, really—in his mid-twenties—but when he walked past her, he winked.

She counted slowly to ten before she turned around, and had lost him while pretending to be so casual. The boarding line was backed up to beyond the turnstiles, four or five people wide. The Gray Line tourist buses in the parking lots still unloaded passengers, but he was tall enough to stand out in any crowd, so she systematically scanned the dock from right to left.

"Excuse me, missy." A man tapped her on the shoulder. "You're holding up the line."

A gaping distance stood between her and the gangplank. "I'm sorry." She rushed forward, her face red, struggling to sling her bag up her arm.

A familiar crewman greeted her at the gangplank. "Going home again?"

"Sure am. Looks like you have a full boat."

"Spring break starts today. The next couple of week-ends will be pretty wild. College kids. High school kids. Heard last year was almost as wild on the island as Palm Springs. This might be the last calm crossing for a while."

Her frozen smile hid the truth: she had no idea what spring break on Catalina Island was like. She and her mother had lived there only since summer, after they had moved away from everyone and everything they'd ever known. Halfway up the gangplank she looked back over the crowd, searching, but the line was now just heads and hats and people milling together like spilled marbles. Once on board, she searched for that handsome face and yellow shirt, but soon gave up and went to find a seat.

An hour and a half later the seat felt hard as a rock. The sun glowed low on a vibrant pink horizon, a golden ball magically balancing itself on top of the blue sea. Passengers shifted to the bow, where the colors of the sunset looked like fire, which meant no lines in the snack bar. Inside, she stared at the black menu board with its crooked white letters. She glanced back and Paul O'Neal himself stood three people back. He smiled. She smiled back.

"What can I get for you?" The worker behind the snack counter waited impatiently, a plastic smile on his face.

She glanced quickly at the board and blurted out the first thing: "A white wine." There was complete silence for an instant, the kind where you wish the floor would swallow you up.

"Can I see your ID, please?"

She dug through her bag pretending she had an ID. "It's here somewhere. I'm certain of it." She moved her face so close she could smell the old sticks of Juicy Fruit gum in the bottom. "Give me a second." Her cheeks felt hot. She shoved her wallet into a dark corner at the bottom and looked up. "I'm sorry. My wallet isn't here."

"I can't serve you any liquor without an ID." Why did his voice sound like he was hollering on the ship's loudspeaker? "Can I get you something else?"

She glanced at the board, then at her bag. "No wallet," she lied, then walked away without looking back. She straight-armed one of the swinging doors, and the air hit her flushed face.

At the back of the boat, the seats were sheltered from the wind and spray. She sat down on a bench where she could lean her head back against the side of the ship and hide. Seagulls drafted alongside the boat and the mainland was a distant outline of dusky hillsides, where pinpoints of light began to sporadically wink back at her. It was still light out when the ship's overhead lamp flickered on. The light was bright and white, so she opened her bag and pulled out her book, then reread the last page she'd read on the bus.

Someone came around the corner and stopped—a yellow shirt. She pulled the book so close she couldn't read a word. The change jingled in his pocket as he sat down next to her.

How do I pretend I'm not the moron who was just carded?

He set down a plastic glass between them and sipped a beer.

Was she supposed to reach for it? If it wasn't for

her . . . well, she would just die . . . again. She shifted and looked down at the lonely glass.

"Are you going to let the ice melt in that wine?"

She lowered the book. "What?"

He handed her the plastic glass. "This is for you."

"Oh. Thank you." My God, but he was good-looking, and watching her with eyes the color of blue ice. "It's good. Thanks."

"That's heavy reading you've got there. Is it for an economics class?"

"No."

He laughed. "What kind of girl reads *Wealth of Nations* for fun?"

She closed the book and looked at the front jacket, then at him. "It's a shame really. I had nothing else to read. I left all my Barbie comic books at home."

"With your wallet?" he shot back.

"Yes." She had to laugh, too. "With my wallet."

"Okay," he said. "I deserved that Barbie comment. I didn't say that right at all, did I?"

"No, you didn't."

"And here I was trying to impress you."

"You were? Why? Do I need impressing?"

He watched her for a long few seconds. "Maybe I was wrong again."

"Maybe buying me a drink was impression enough. That was very sweet of you."

"You looked thirsty."

"Did I?" She laughed softly. "I thought I looked embarrassed."

"That, too." He sipped his beer and glanced out at the water.

She stared down at the drink in her hands and felt every awkward second of silence. "So what do you like to read?"

"After what I just said, I'm surprised you aren't asking me if I can read."

"Actually, I was thinking your reading material might be the kind that has staples in the centerfold."

He burst out laughing. "I deserved that."

"You probably did."

"You've got a great sense of humor."

"You sound surprised."

"I don't think I'm going to answer that. I'll just get into more trouble." He stood up. "I'd like another beer before they close. Do you want another drink?"

"No, thanks."

She was smiling, probably a goofy smile that told the entire world what she was thinking. He was coming back. She sipped her drink at the railing, watching the island and the glimmering lights of Avalon, home after her mother moved them there when Laurel graduated high school. Moving was tough when she'd lived in a place where her friends had been her friends since they'd all played in a sandbox together. In a new town, Laurel was suddenly the outsider. All those lights before her and not a friend among them.

"We're almost there." He walked toward her, a dripping beer bottle in his hand.

"That didn't take long."

"No line."

She felt different when he looked at her—like he was doing now—as if she weren't a friendless, lonely thing. She longed to say something clever and memorable.

"Okay." He braced his arms on the railing next to her, his beer in his hands. "Time to come clean. You didn't leave your wallet at home."

"No."

"So, I'm guilty of contributing to the delinquency of a minor." There was a softness around his eyes and mouth, no judgment or censure.

"You could say that."

"How minor?"

Laurel contemplated lying. In the right clothes, she looked at least twenty, but wanting to be older didn't make you older. She faced him. "I'm seventeen."

He choked on his beer. "Seventeen? You're kidding."

"No. I'll be eighteen soon."

He watched her, probably half hoping she would suddenly age five years, then swore under his breath. His gaze dropped to the drink in her hand. Without a word he took it and tossed it in the water.

She drew back from the rail and crossed her arms in front of her, equally silent, her body brittle, her knees locked.

He looked surprised at what he'd done, but not apologetic.

"You paid for the drink," she said. "You can do what you want with it."

He lifted his hand toward her cheek, almost approachable again, almost apologetic, and standing close enough for her to smell his aftershave. "You're in high school?"

"No, I'm in college."

"At seventeen?" Clearly he thought she was lying.

"I skipped the third grade. I graduated high school

just after I turned seventeen." She could almost read the word "jailbait" in his expression.

The loudspeaker crackled on. "Attention, please, we are now arriving at the Avalon dock, Catalina Island. Make certain you have all your personal belongings. All passengers will disembark on the starboard side of the ship. For safety, please securely hold the hands of all young children as you leave." The loudspeaker cut off.

She gave him a direct look. "Do you want to hold my hand securely as we disembark?"

He didn't laugh.

"I guess my age killed your sense of humor."

For just a moment she thought he wanted to say something kind to her, but a group of young kids scattered away from the nearby railing and jumped up and down, shouting, "We're here! We're here!"

"We're here," she said over their noisy little bouncing heads. The kids ran around them in rambunctious circles. She broke eye contact, and when she looked up again he was shaking his head.

"I'm sorry." He walked away and never once looked back.

She stood there, empty, embarrassed, ashamed, and upset. Maybe because of him. Maybe because of her. Listlessly, she picked up her thick book with its conservative literary jacket and dark, unaffected type. The things you could hide . . . She slipped off the paper jacket. Hot pink lettering glared back at her from the real cover—*The Adventurers*, by Harold Robbins. She dropped the other jacket into a nearby trash can, tucked the book under an arm, and made her way toward the gangplank.

Behind the hills the sunset glowed pink, and a noisy

hum came from the crowds. Pole lights lit the dock and shone down on the boarding ramp. Only a few hundred feet down the dock was Crescent Street and the heart of town. Local boys sold newspapers and, for fifty cents, offered to cart suitcases in red wagons to side-street hotels and cozy island inns. The crowd split around girls in white shorts and sandals who handed out flyers with discount coupons for abalone burgers, lobsters, and pitchers of draft beer at two for one.

But nowhere in that crowd below her did Laurel see a tall, handsome man in a lemon yellow shirt. He had disappeared as if he had never existed. And for her, he didn't exist. Not really, because she didn't even know his name.

Victor checked the clock on his desk, stood—his foot on a floor button that buzzed his secretary—and effectively brought the magazine interview to an end. The interviewer's questions had just gone in a direction he disliked. "I have another appointment."

"But I have more questions, Mr. Banning . . . Victor. It's only five thirty. You know this is our cover story."

Victor laughed at him. "I wouldn't be talking to you if this weren't your cover story."

The door to his office swung open and his secretary recited, "The car's waiting, Mr. Banning. You're running late."

The journalist still sat there, a tape recorder on the arm of the chair and a shiny Italian pen in hand. He wore a clipped beard and his dark curly hair in a ponytail, which fell halfway down the back of a five-hundred-dollar suit.

Victor came from behind his desk. "I see I've reduced you to silence, which is best. We don't speak the same language, son." He left the young man juggling his pad and recorder, stammering for him to wait, and headed down the hall toward his private elevator.

The article would label him a corporate villain. At his center he was a hardscrabble oilman born in a boom-or-bust era, and the polar opposite of a journalist out to cauterize enterprise and whose radical point of view smacked of being all too trendy. An ill-fitting sobriety emanated from men like him, a languidness in the face of the real and vital things that changed the world around them.

That reporter's Berkeleyesque scorn was detectable even when cloaked by a professional voice. With high degrees from expensive schools, his kind persuaded courts to stop the building of freeways, put hundreds of people out of work, boondoggled, and stopped progress to save a damned frog. Victor could have respected them if they were actually doing it for the frog, but men like him were faux avant-garde—the ultimate luxury for those who already had everything.

Victor and men of his ilk made things better for everyone: gas stations with car washes and streets fitted with drains so they wouldn't flood; tax dollars that fed the public schools and highways, and opportunity for golden equity in land and homes with values that rose monthly.

Later, at home, he took an overly long shower—an attempt to wash off the grit of an interview that implied what he had accomplished in his life was all wrong. His annoyance was difficult to shake off. The seeds of it stayed with him even as he traveled north along the 405, Harlan at the wheel of his Bentley.

In the distance, covered in a green veil of haze, were the rolling hills connecting San Pedro to Palos Verdes. Victor could remember those hills when they were just purple wildflowers, waist-high mustard, and a crumbling Spanish hacienda with its scattering of guest ranches, land deeded before California was ever a state. Now streets with expensive homes cut along those hillsides, looking as pronounced as veins on the arm of a growing economy.

It was change. It was good. So he told himself he didn't mind articles written about men like him—a generation hungry for success and power, winners who carried with them accomplishment and the pride of building something out of nothing, instead of making a brouhaha out of nothing in order to sell magazines.

Lately he'd been the topic of too many articles, and the human interest ones made him clam up faster than today. Perhaps he was annoyed now because he'd had a touchy interview for *Look* six weeks ago. Newspapers and magazines sent women reporters for human interest stories, armed with his family history and seeking an angle that was lonely, silly, and romantic—something his life was anything but.

Victor had been married twice and in love only once. He'd worked most of his life, hardest when he had a wife and young son. Anna died with no warning, and he couldn't remember crying for her, a woman forbidden to him whom he'd married after a long chase.

His son was a stranger, barely three when he buried Anna. Victor remembered thinking he had nothing in

common with Rudy other than bone and blood and the
same last name. His son cried every time Victor came
home—took one look at him and ran away, disappearing
for hours in some nook of the monstrous Pasadena
house that belonged to his wife's family.

The day Victor found his son cowering in Anna's
closet symbolized their dismal relationship: the father
who had been locked in a closet and his son who sought
refuge in one. It was a long time before Rudy could sit in
the same room with him, longer still before he accepted
that Victor was the man who fathered him.

Victor had spent his childhood fighting for acceptance.
Not even for his son would he fight for acceptance again.
Soon he recognized in his own son's expression his
father's look of failure. He and Rudy were doomed from
the start. The Banning curse had skipped a generation, and
nothing Rudy ever did changed Victor's opinion that he
was a weak young man, destined for nothing. The only
thing his son ever had the strength to do was walk away
from Victor and stay away.

The second wife also walked away from Victor, and
he never regretted that. She was a convenience—she'd
done the chasing. The women and marriages, even the
affairs were long gone, and he was left now with his only
progeny, Cale and Jud.

The radio phone between the car's seats rang, his
attorney calling with news. "Jameson's kid agreed to sell
the painting."

Victor didn't move. "How much?"

"Half a million."

"Cut the deal," Victor told him in a voice more even
than he actually felt. To finally win was almost a physical

thing, live and sweeping through him like some kind of drug. "Any word on the other pieces?"

"That Seattle gallery claims they've lost track of the client."

"Then we need to find the client."

"No one will release the name, Victor. It's been thirteen goddamn years and I can't even buy that name out of those people."

"Raise the offer another quarter of a million," he added. "And the commission another ten percent. That ought to prod somebody to locate who bought those paintings."

After making arrangements for delivery, he hung up and rested his head against the back of the seat while Harlan turned the car into the Loyola parking lot. In an instant so real he would never be able to explain it, Victor caught a whiff of Arpège and sat forward sharply. On the seat across from him were the images of his son and daughter-in-law, an echo of another time and clearer than any memory should be; they held hands. Rachel was pregnant and Rudy didn't look like a failure.

"The game's already started." Harlan opened the back door.

The images across from Victor evaporated in the overhead glare of parking lot lights, but what they represented stayed with him and made him pensive and touchy. Once inside the gym, they took seats in the middle of the crowded bleachers. By 9 P.M., Loyola was losing, so Victor sent Harlan to get the car and stood hidden in the shadows of the bleachers.

He watched Cale trot down the basketball court, weaving in and out of the other players with long-legged agility and a sure-footedness that helped him score three points. With that single basket, the energy in the gymnasium changed. The crowd noise grew louder; they were on their feet. The university band began to play with the crowd clapping and singing, "Down on the corner . . . Out in the street."

Rudy had played basketball, too, but was never good enough and spent his games mostly on the bench. Victor could have missed every game and it wouldn't have mattered.

But this game changed in under five minutes. Dorsey cut quickly, stole the ball, dashed past his opponent, his grin as big as the sections on the basketball. Then he became all business and shot the ball in the opposite direction, right to Cale, who let the ball fly. It arced through the air, then hit the rim with a deep thud, bounced, and went straight up in the air.

Nothing moved in that gymnasium but the ball. It came down on the rim, swirled around and around. On the edge of defeat or victory, players jumped up, arms reaching for the ball. The ball fell into the net and the white numbers on the scoreboard flipped: *89–87 Loyola.*

Pom-poms flew into the air and the university cheerleaders tumbled across the wooden floor. The crowd cheered and stomped their feet so loudly you could barely hear the time buzzer. Players and coaches swarmed all over one another, and a teammate ripped Cale's jersey in two and ran around him, holding the torn piece with his number, twenty-three, high in the air. They shouted, "Banning! Banning! Banning!"

Victor didn't know he was smiling. He felt something he couldn't ever remember feeling for Rudy.

Maybe a hundred feet stood between Cale and him. They hadn't spoken since Christmas. He placed one foot in front of the other, closing the distance.

"Cale!" An attractive young blond girl raced down from the bleachers and across the court, her ponytail flying, her long tanned legs running straight toward the knot of Loyola players. She wore a Mount Saint Mary's sweater and flip skirt, and flung her arms around Cale, who caught her and spun her around, laughing as she kissed his cheeks.

Victor stopped, unable to move forward. Another girl he can throw his future away on. Cale hadn't learned a thing from last year, from any years. Victor turned away in disgust and walked out of the gym without looking back. He wasn't there when Cale set his roommate's girlfriend down and tugged affectionately on her ponytail. And when Cale slung a towel around his sweaty neck and looked around the gym for the one person in his life to whom winning was everything, Victor was already on his way home.

CHAPTER

1

The Island Theater was housed inside the old casino and always busy on the weekends, so Laurel studied the coming attractions on posters lit with small strings of Hollywood lights. A group of girls her age joined the back of the line, chattering. Shannon worked part-time at her mother's shop, so Laurel stepped out of line and moved toward them, then waited for a pause in their conversation. She tapped Shannon on the shoulder. "Hi."

"Laurel. Hi. I haven't seen you in weeks."

"I'm home for spring break."

Shannon introduced her, then said, "The town's going to be really crazy. Spring break always is. The beach gets packed. The bars. Guys and girls all over the place. Parties in the hotels. It's pretty wild. You haven't been here for Easter yet, have you?"

Laurel shook her head. "I'm not here much anyway, because of school. Just some weekends and holidays."

"Laurel already graduated." Shannon explained to the

other girls. "She goes to cooking school in LA. What's that place called again?"

"Pacific Culinary Institute." The school was one of only three in the country that offered Cordon Bleu courses and certificates. The classes were small, tuition steep, and they accepted only one out of every few hundred applicants. The administrators and internationally famous instructors there would have cringed at the phrase "cooking school." One of them could easily have waved a boning knife under poor Shannon's nose and said, "Culinary institute. Cooking school is for the people who work at Denny's."

"You want to be a cook?" one of the girls asked, as if Laurel were nuts.

"I want to be a professional chef."

"Like the Galloping Gourmet?" One of them giggled.

Shannon gave the girl a pointed look, but Laurel laughed. "Graham Kerr is a good chef."

"Why would you want to be a chef? You'll have to work in a hot kitchen, just to cook food for other people? Why not just be a housewife?"

"Ouch!" someone said. "That wasn't nice, Karen."

"Well, I mean, isn't that like being some kind of glorified slave?"

Shannon punched Karen in the arm. "I wouldn't talk. You said you wanted to be a nurse. I'd rather cut vegetables and take out the garbage than change sheets, give sponge baths, and clean bedpans."

"You don't meet cute doctors in a restaurant kitchen." Clearly Karen had a plan.

At the box office, Laurel paid her admission and

stepped aside, waiting for them. They bought their tickets, then the girls looked at her and at Shannon.

"Well, we're going inside now," one of them said.

"Do you mind if I tag along?" Laurel spoke to Shannon. A couple of the girls exchanged strained looks. Karen stared pointedly at Shannon. It was one of those long moments of telling silence and Laurel felt awful, but she kept a plastic smile on her face.

"Sure," Shannon said without much enthusiasm. "Come on."

The lobby was crowded and the concession counter hummed with activity, surrounded with the crackle of popcorn popping, the hollow rattle of ice in an empty cup, and the whirring of the drink dispenser. It smelled like popcorn and hot dogs and Laurel was hungry almost instantly. A pack of local boys joined them and swept the girls toward the counter. Laurel ordered Coke, popcorn, and Butterfingers, and when she turned around, the two groups had all paired off. Five boys. Five girls. And her. While the others were talking, she edged her way to Shannon and whispered, "I'm sorry."

"It's okay. You didn't know we were meeting them."

"I'll just ease away. I don't mind sitting alone," she lied.

"No," Shannon grabbed her arm and turned to her boyfriend. "Jake? This is Laurel Peyton. I work for her mom."

He seemed genuinely nice and before she could sneak away, he introduced Laurel to the other boys. She made some lame excuse and turned to leave, but they stopped her.

"You can't sit alone."

The girls weren't happy. She wasn't alone, but a few minutes later, when the heavy red curtains parted and the lights dimmed, she decided even sitting alone would have been better than sitting in the middle of a long row of seats with snuggling couples on either side of her.

M*A*S*H flashed on the screen, and by the time Sally Kellerman was Hot Lips, the couple on her right was making out. Laurel set her Coke down and bumped into Karen's knee. "Sorry."

A boy's hand closed over her thigh. Karen's boyfriend had the wrong girl's leg. She removed his hand, but they shifted positions and now were leaning on her arm. On her other side, Shannon was locked in a long, deep kiss with her boyfriend. Hunched in the center of her seat, surrounded by lovers, Laurel shoveled handfuls of popcorn into her mouth, ignoring the soft whispers and moans next to her.

The film suddenly fluttered over the screen, then snapped off. The audience groaned and everyone sat in the dark. The lights came on and the manager came out to a round of boos. "Sorry. Sorry. The film's broken, so there will be free passes for everyone at the box office. But don't leave your seats. We will be showing *Love Story*."

The audience clapped and whistled as the lights dimmed and Ryan O'Neal stood on the huge screen. Both Laurel and her mother had watched every single episode of *Peyton Place*, her mom always joking that they had to be loyal to the name.

Laurel settled into her seat with the jumbo Coke, the tub of popcorn, and the huge yellow box of Butterfingers to hold on to instead of a boyfriend's arm. Instead of being in a romance, she would watch one, forced by lousy luck to dream of happily-ever-afters.

The camera panned in on O'Neal, sitting alone in the bleachers as he said, "What can you say about a twenty-five-year-old girl who died."

It seemed a cliché, a man sitting at a bar drowning his troubles. But bars supplied the perfect environment to beat yourself up for making stupid mistakes, so Jud was living the cliché in a small beachside bar in Avalon that night. The bartender whipped through drink orders and Three Dog Night blasted from the requisite jukebox in a smoky corner. Deep in the recesses of the place, couples played pool and drank.

In under an hour, the place had swelled with people until the noise level measured many decibels. Jud sipped the foam off a beer, trying to shut out the saccharine song that was sending "joy to the fishes in the deep blue sea" and the obnoxious noise from a nearby table, where a group of college guys from UCSD were slamming back shooters and singing their college fight song in a key that didn't exist. They acted as if the world was theirs. That kind of partying had lost its appeal before his third year of college. He felt suddenly old. Today he'd hounded after a young girl who was jailbait, and he'd managed to convince his grandfather he was a first-class fuckup. This morning he'd thought the world was his. Now he felt like the world had him by the balls.

Right after he'd left the company offices with his crushed pride and his tail between his legs, he'd wondered bitterly if what happened this morning was another way for his grandfather to manipulate him. Victor was happiest when he stirred up trouble. But now, when he wasn't angry anymore, Jud knew Victor didn't play games with his business deals.

Earlier, Jud had called his connections and scheduled a lunch for the next week, but he felt skittish about it. As much as he'd hated to hear the truth from his grand-father's mouth, those men would not have welcomed him into their business ventures. He had been so full of himself, so glad to be accepted, he couldn't see their motive anymore than he could see that that girl today was under twenty. Seventeen? Could have been real trouble there.

He stared into the bottom of his beer glass, still chewing over the mysteries of Victor versus Marvetti until he decided none of it was going to solve itself tonight. He scanned the place. Bars never seemed to change much, still smoky, still smelly, still one of the few places on earth where you could be in a crowd and feel completely alone. The empty summer house on the cove held more appeal for him than a smoke-filled bar, where too many college kids on spring break needed to let loose. He downed his beer, paid, and went outside, where he could breathe again.

It was dark and cool in the shadow of the door, and the air tasted salty with the water just a hundred feet away. Neon light from the beer signs in the front win-dow fell onto the bricked street like brightly colored snakes. Along the beach, palm trees cast shadows that looked like giant forearms with splayed hands, and beyond, the water was cavern black out into the harbor, until the running lights flickered in a staggered chain from where the weekend boat traffic moored. The smell of the tide made it seem like summer, and it was warm for April, maybe sixty-five degrees.

There were no cars about, only the occasional electric hum of a golf cart or the clicking spokes of a bicycle. On a bench next to the sand, a couple made out. Jud lit a cigarette, took a drag, then remembered he was going to quit. He took another hit then crushed it out with his foot.

At the north point, where the street ended with the old casino, people spilled out from the movie theater. Ahead of the crowd, a girl walked faster than most, wearing a car coat, her hands shoved deep in the pockets. She had great legs. A group of kids sped past in two golf carts, shouting and waving as they passed by her. She waved and watched them disappear, then she shoved her hands back in her coat pockets and walked on, staring down at the ground as she passed under a streetlamp.

In the warm light, her brown hair brushed her shoulders; her face was distinct and familiar, because she looked so much like Jacqueline Bisset. It was Jailbait, and this was his chance to apologize, but he hesitated. The bar door swung open and almost clipped him, forcing him back and into the shadows. Jukebox music blared into the night and the UCSD guys stumbled out like a family of apes, laughing loudly and shoving one another around.

They began to giggle and took him back to those times when he acted like an asshole for fun. In a haze of mind-numbing tequila they turned and immediately zeroed in on Jailbait. She kept walking, sidestepping away from them and nearer the sand. To her credit she looked straight ahead as they surrounded her. "Excuse me," she said too brightly and squeezed between two of them.

"Hey, there, sweet thing." The group tightened their circle around her.

"Please. You're drunk." She tried to push through them.

"Come here." One who looked like a linebacker roughly pulled her against him. His friends whistled and cheered.

"Stop it!" She pushed at his chest as the huge jerk tried to kiss her.

Jud stepped away from the building. "Let her go."

"Please stop. Please . . . Don't!" She sounded terrified.

Jud gripped the guy's shoulder. "You. *Now*. Leave the girl alone."

"Oh, yeah. Sure thing, asshole."

Jud grabbed his arm and jerked it away from her. She stumbled backward, out of the guy's reach, and fell down.

Jud spun around . . . right into the guy's fist.

"Get him." His friends chanted. "Get him!" They formed a circle around Jud, who ducked a punch and looked for Jailbait. He threw wild punches and twisted out of their grip twice, then one of them pinned his arms back. "I got him! I got him!" It took two of them to keep him pinned while they punched him. Jud could taste the blood in his mouth. His eye hurt. He blinked, trying to see her, but the edges of his vision blurred. The linebacker walked straight toward him, laughing, fists up, and beat the hell out of him.

CHAPTER

8

Laurel sank down next to her dreamboat as he lay unconscious on the pavement. One eye was already swelling. He had a cut on his cheek, and both his nose and mouth were bleeding. "Please wake up. Please." The streets were empty, but she could hear the distant footsteps of the bullies, who ran away down a side street after she'd screamed for them to stop, then screamed over and over.

"Help! Someone help! Please . . ." She lifted his head off the hard brick into her lap. "Please wake up. Can't you hear me?" Where was everyone? The doors to the bar were closed. They probably didn't even know there had been a fight. It was eerie, such silence in the aftermath of something so terribly violent.

He groaned, then winced and slowly opened his eyes.

"Oh, God, I'm so sorry. Can you move? How badly are you hurt? What can I do?" Her words all came out in a rush.

He grunted something she couldn't understand,

swore, then rolled out of her lap onto his hands and knees. Silent, his breathing labored, he shook his head and tried to get up.

"Here. Let me help you."

"No!" He jerked his arm away from her and stumbled to his feet, weaving slightly. "No."

"Please. You're hurt because you tried to help me."

His face was beaten and flushed and he looked like he might fall down. "I'm fine." He spit blood, then swiped at his mouth and stared down at the blood on his hand with a disgusted look.

"You need a doctor."

"What?" He looked up again, scowling at her from the one eye that wasn't swelling.

"I'll call a doctor."

He turned away like someone embarrassed. There were leaves and dirt on his back, so she brushed off his shoulder. "Jesus," he scowled at her. "Just go home. You shouldn't be out walking around town this late. You're asking for trouble."

"I was walking home."

He pressed his hand to the cut on his mouth and stepped away from her. "Then go home."

"This wasn't my fault. You can't blame me."

"Go—home."

She didn't move.

"Go home where you belong," he yelled at her. "Go home, little girl, and leave me the hell alone!"

His harsh expression turned blurry from her tears, and she ran—her face hot and flaming—around the corner and down the street into the small plaza by her mother's studio and pottery shop. Laurel stood there, directionless. In front of her was the dark shop with its Closed sign hanging in the door. That sign seemed to say everything. One word that defined her life: closed. She sat down on the edge of a tiled fountain, where water spilled into a shallow pool.

Again he'd made her feel young and foolish, like some thirteen-year-old with a silly crush making a pest of herself. He called her a little girl to put her down for being seventeen—as if she could change the year she was born. And no one wanted to be twenty-one more than she did, instead of stuck in some kind of hinterland between a teenager and an adult. She didn't belong anywhere: on this island, with those girls, in Seattle; even her age was undefined. There was a time when she could have talked about what she felt with high school friends. Now, whenever she spoke with them, scattered as they all were in colleges all over the country, there were more long silences than meaningful words. None of them knew what to say to one another anymore.

Things would have been easier, maybe, if her father were alive. Somehow she knew he could have given her the answers she needed during the moments when living became so hard and ugly. Without a dad, she felt as if she were hobbling through life on one leg, when most other people had two.

Her grandmother Julia claimed her dad had been a star and made Laurel promise to never forget. It was important to her grandmother, the star thing. At first Laurel had been too young to understand the difference between a music star and a star in the sky. To children, stars were stars. Confused, she'd asked her aunt, Evie, what stars were, one night when they were standing together outside and the night sky was filled with them. Her aunt had told her that the stars were magical things, other worlds so far away that sometimes it was impossible to believe they really existed. Laurel had been probably seven at the time, an age when she had blind faith in magical things and grew up trying to believe in fathers who were never there.

He was an image in a faded photograph, a name on a record that hung on the wall of her room. He was a star—something impossible for her to believe ever existed. And now, as she sat there feeling inconsequential, she looked up in the sky and searched those stars, wanting them to magically spell out the answers to all her most important questions, like why did people have to die? Why did life move so slowly? What was real love like? Why was she so lonely? She felt as if she were in a different dimension than everyone else and destined to watch life from outside.

Sitting on the edge of the fountain, she could see copper and silver coins sparkling back at her, the water and lights making them seem bigger than they actually were. There must have been close to a thousand forgotten wishes in the bottom of the fountain. When you didn't believe in magical things like wishes, you never set yourself up for disappointment. You understood that all too often things looked bigger than they really were.

Laurel pulled a couple of pennies out of her pocket. Two cents. There was a joke in that somewhere. She turned her back to the fountain and closed her eyes, then tossed the pennies over her shoulder and made a wish for someone to love her.

* * *

Kathryn could hear the night frogs in the side garden through an open window in the living room, so she sat down in there with a book. It was almost eleven when Laurel came in the front door and hung up her coat. "Hi, Mom." Exhaustion was in her voice, her shoulders sloped in defeat.

"How was the movie?"

Laurel shrugged.

"You look so pretty," Kathryn said brightly. "I bet you turned some heads tonight."

Her daughter looked at her as if she'd slapped her, then ran out of the room sobbing and slammed her bedroom door closed.

"What did I say wrong now?" Kathryn said to the empty room. Everything had been so much easier when Laurel only worried about a Halloween costume or a book report or if she performed some complicated ballet position correctly. In those days, Kathryn had all the right answers.

She tapped lightly on Laurel's door. "It's me."

"Just leave me alone, Mom. Please."

A blank white door stood between them, a wall of Kathryn's wrong words and wrong choices. She heard Laurel's muffled cries and reached for the doorknob, but a voice in her head said, *Don't barge in*. She understood self-pity and despair, feeling helpless, confused, and frustrated—apparently the normal state for a mother with a teenage daughter. She sagged down into an overstuffed chair and stared at the empty hallway as if she could divine answers from there, a thread and needle for the worn and unraveling seams of their relationship.

The awful truth was that the move here had made

Laurel miserable. Laurel was miserable, but Kathryn wasn't. She liked living in Evie's house. It was well over sixty years old, with a small floor plan, tall ceilings, crown molding, and hardwood floors. Lazy beach furniture filled the rooms—Victorian wicker, an antique French daybed, rattan—so different from Julia's formal white furniture. There had been little color in Kathryn's life except her own blue bedroom.

Evie had painted every room a different color. The place was all spring and sunshine, yellows and pinks. It felt like a woman's house. Here she wanted to drink tea from a flowered mug instead of a three-hundred-year-old tea service, her mother-in-law serving her without ever asking whether she wanted the lemon and sugar.

Moving to Catalina had freed Kathryn's spirit. But her freedom came at a price, one Laurel had paid.

Kathryn waited for the sound of crying to stop. This time she didn't knock. Inside, a muted hanging lamp and sandalwood candles lit the room. In the corner, flat on the floor, sat Laurel's bed, covered with an ethnic print throw and mirror-trimmed pillows from India. Evie was right. George Harrison, Ravi Shankar, and the Hare Krishna who stuck carnations in your face at the airport would feel right at home in this bedroom.

But the candles flickered softly against the walls, where Jimmy's guitar hung beside his records, some photos, awards, and framed copies of his handwritten music. Beneath this shrine to her father, Laurel lay curled in a lump on her bed, facing the wall and leaving no doubt that Jimmy's daughter still belonged to the day he died.

Kathryn sank down beside her. "You want to tell me what's wrong?"

"No." Laurel gave a sharp, caustic laugh.

She's too young to be so bitter. It's by my example. Her mouth was dry when she asked, "Do you want me to leave?"

"No." It was a while before Laurel spoke. "I want someone to think I'm special and beautiful and wonderful."

"I think you're special and beautiful and wonderful."

Her daughter wasn't rude enough to say, *Big deal*, but the words hung there in her silence.

"I don't know what I can do to make you happy."

Laurel reached out and touched her hand. "Look, Mom. It's not your fault. Sometimes, like tonight, you just say the wrong thing."

"What did I say?"

"It's a long and miserable story."

"I'm not going anywhere. I have hours and hours." She settled back against a couple of those gaudy pillows. It took a moment before Laurel started talking, and once she did, everything spilled out of her in a rush of emotion—the boy on the boat, the kids necking in the theater, the fistfight—all told with that double-edged intensity of youth.

Laurel looked at her. "I feel like I'm completely invisible."

Kathryn had watched her grow up and felt so proud, and so scared. One day, not that long ago, she turned around and no longer had a child for a daughter. The years had turned into a white blur while her daughter became a beautiful young woman. She wanted to tell her she was far from invisible, but Laurel wouldn't believe her. Kathryn pointed to a black-and-white photograph of

Jimmy onstage with his guitar. To anyone who looked at the shot, it appeared as if he were looking at the audience. "See this photograph of your father?"

Laurel nodded.

"It was taken one night when he was playing in Hollywood, at this club on the Sunset Strip. I can't remember the name. You were maybe three at the time. This was right after his third record went number one. He was about to start the final song and looked down at us. We were in the front row. He took off his guitar and came down to us, then stepped back on stage with you in his arms, set you down, picked up his guitar, and said, 'You wanna help me sing, little girl?'

"When you said, 'Sure, Daddy,' the place went crazy. They calmed down when he began to play and you stood there in front of hundreds of people, completely fearless. You couldn't have cared less who watched. You sang with him just like you always did at home. Didn't miss a single note."

Kathryn handed the photo to Laurel. "You had no idea, but everyone in that place, including your father, was looking at you and thinking how very wonderful you were."

Laurel sat cross-legged on the bed with the photo, then curled up with it as Kathryn stood. "Thanks, Mom," she said in a small voice, already half asleep.

But Kathryn didn't go to sleep that easily. She tossed and turned, haunted by images of fiery car crashes and slashed canvases, and woke with the sheets twisted around her legs, her pillow damp, and Jimmy's face in her mind. There were moments over the years when Laurel looked so much like him that Kathryn found herself imagining the worst: a mind-numbing fear that her daughter might follow her father's path to a fateful, early death. Kathryn had to fight her innate and desperate need to overprotect. She didn't want to be like Julia, who had taught her what it was like to live inside your child's life.

None of those fears ever materialized. Still, Kathryn hadn't had nightmares in years. She put on her robe and left the room, then made cup after cup of tea. When the eastern skies turned purple and gold and the sparrows and robins began to sing, she still stood at her living room window, no better off really than she had been. Laurel was so very young, and she desperately didn't want to be. She still believed and trusted the world that lay before her. Her daughter had no haunting consequences to keep her from running headlong down the wrong road.

But Kathryn was overwhelmed by an uneasy terror as she watched the day break and sipped tea, which had a sudden, bitter taste. It needed lemon and sugar. She walked into the kitchen, doctored her tea, drank it, and went into her bedroom.

She still tossed and turned, staring at the yellow walls, and told herself she was being silly, overreacting. Of course, fate had better things to do than to follow the Peyton women around, just to create havoc in two small lives.

CHAPTER

9

It was two in the afternoon when Cale unlocked the door to the Catalina house. "Hey! I'm here! Jud?" He dropped his bag on the floor and headed for the kitchen, tossing the newspaper and some magazines on the dining table as he beelined for the refrigerator. Leaning on the open door, he guzzled half a carton of milk—one of four inside. Jud had done the shopping: eggs, bread, lunch meat, cheese, steaks, potatoes, salad stuff, and fruit, even a jug of orange juice. There were probably new boxes of cereal lined up neatly in the overhead cabinet. Cale counted off Cheerios, shredded wheat, and corn flakes, pancake mix, syrup, coffee, creamer, sugar. The kitchen had everything needed for three squares a day. His brother—the poster boy for good nutrition. Hell, he even ate perfectly.

Cale tossed the lid from a container of spaghetti toward the sink like a Frisbee, missed, and grabbed a fork. Shoveling cold spaghetti into his mouth, he headed for the sliding glass doors to the deck. The beach lay a hundred feet away, and beyond, the glassy water of a slumbering cove. At the edge of the deck, hanging off the end of a lounge chair, were two really big and bony bare feet.

Jud lay in the sun, his arm slung over his face. He was snoring. Cale kicked his brother's feet. "Wake up, you lazy bastard, and say hello to your little brother."

Jud groaned, then mumbled into his arm, "Little my ass. You're two inches taller than I am."

"And twice as good-looking, too."

"Normally I'd argue that point, but I don't think I can today." Jud pulled his arm away. His face was a black-and-blue mess.

"I hope the other guy looks worse than you do."

"Got away without a cut." Jud tried to sit up and winced. "Damn, that hurts. Everything hurts."

"You look like everything should hurt. What happened?"

Jud rested his elbows on his knees, his hands hanging loosely between them, and he looked at him—at least, it looked as if he were looking at him. He wasn't too sure. Jud's eyes were so swollen it was more of a squint, like being stared at by a bruised pig.

"I tried to play Galahad and save some sweet young thing from a bunch of drunks."

Cale straddled a lounge chair and sat down. "I hope you won some reward for sacrificing your face. Is your nose broken?"

"Only swollen and hurting like hell."

"Tell me she gave you her phone number for your trouble."

"Nope. Not even her name." Jud shook his head,

winced, and buried his head in his hands. "Remind me not to do that again."

"What? Try to get lucky? Get into a fight? Or shake your head?"

"Uh-huh."

"So, big brother, you ended up battered and bruised and without a date."

"I'm not sure I looked very impressive passed out facedown and bloodying up the sidewalk. Stop laughing, asshole."

"I'm not laughing."

"I can hear it in your voice."

"Okay. I'm laughing."

"Hell, I didn't get in a single solid punch."

"Looks like it."

"Go to hell."

"I don't want to go home. Victor's there." Cale lifted the spaghetti container in a salute and with his mouth full said, "Good stuff."

"I made it last night."

"Before or after you ran into Joe Frazier?"

"Before."

"Here. Catch." Cale tossed him his napkin. "Your nose is bleeding."

"Again?" Jud blotted his nose. "Damn." He started to get up.

"Stay there. I'll get you something." Cale came back with two steaks from the freezer. "Here, put these on your face."

Jud frowned at the steaks. "They're frozen."

"Yeah, but steak is good for the black eye and ice for swelling. Two remedies in one."

"The best I can get is frozen steak from the future Dr. Banning?"

"Shut up and put 'em on your face. After they thaw, we can barbecue them."

"And I heard premed was hard."

That cut deeply, but Cale said nothing. He had studied five nights straight to get a low B on his last test in anatomy. He held up a magazine, centerfold open. "Here's a cure. Look at this."

Jud pulled the steaks off his face and lifted his head up. "Nice."

"Nice? That's all you can say?" Cale studied the centerfold again. "More than nice. I'd to like to meet a girl like her."

"You did last year and your grades went in the toilet."

Cale's big mistake now hung in the air between them. His brother lay there with meat on his face, yet Cale felt as if he'd just taken a punch.

Jud crossed his feet. "How's school going?"

"Okay."

"You keeping your grades up?"

"Jesus . . . You sound like Victor. It's bad enough I have to get flak from the old man. I don't need it from you, too." When Jud didn't say anything, Cale added bitterly, "I don't need you judging me."

"I'm not judging you." Jud pulled the steaks off again. "What's going on?"

"Nothing."

"Something's wrong. You're way too touchy. Come clean."

Cale tossed the magazine on the deck. "Med school.

Almost all of them have turned me down. Not even my MCATs—which I aced—are helping my apps."

"I thought Dorsey was just horsing around on the phone yesterday."

"He was and wasn't."

"All of them turned you down?" Jud sounded as if a college turning someone down was as unrealistic as Martian landings or statues of the Virgin Mary that cried real tears.

Right then, Cale wanted to hit Jud himself. "I've still got three schools left. University of Texas, UCSD, and USC."

"I'm sorry, bud."

"Yeah, well, there's not much I can do about it now." Odd, how it was harder for him to swallow his big brother's pity than his judgments. He felt like the wrong half of a man talking to the right half. "I don't know what I'm going to do if I don't get into one of these last three."

"They can't all turn you down." Jud lay back down. "You'll get in."

His brother's world was so easy. Just that easy. The spaghetti turned over in Cale's stomach and felt as if he'd eaten a pound of it. He sagged back in the chair, looking out at the water because he felt like nothing when he looked at his brother.

There was no breeze and a light haze in the sky, almost like earthquake weather, but seagulls were flying all over the place. In the moments before an earthquake, all wildlife vanished. Utter and complete silence ruled, as if the world were holding its breath.

Cale listened to the seagulls whining overhead, and a

few feet away, the quiet lap of the water against the sand. In the distance was the mainland. A wildfire burned in Malibu. A cloud of purplish gray smoke hovered over the hills, and Santa Monica had disappeared from sight. He followed the outline of the coast, the minuscule silver glint of planes in the sky over LAX—and the white clusters of beach towns, their piers, marinas, and homes staggered in the coastal hillsides.

Jud snored louder, lying there deep in sleep—something Cale hadn't had much of lately. *You'll get in.* His brother said it with such assurance.

"Yeah, Jud," Cale said quietly. "Easy as taking your next breath." He felt like his stomach was going to explode. Too much spaghetti. His next breath was as shallow as his confidence. Jud didn't have a clue what his life was like. Cale closed his eyes and the thought hit him that maybe the lump in his stomach wasn't from the mouthfuls of spaghetti he'd swallowed whole. Maybe it was his pride.

Jud woke up late in the afternoon with melted meat on his face. He heard Cale shooting baskets out front. Once inside, he put the steaks on a plate in the fridge and strolled out the front door. "Hey. Let me show you how the game's played."

Cale stopped, holding the ball in one big hand. "Yeah, right. Who just took a nap, Pops?" He casually tossed a hook shot over his head high into the air. It dropped through the net without ever touching metal. Crowing, Cale grabbed the ball, then faced him, dribbling it and shuffling back and forth.

"You cocky ass." Jud laughed.

"We'll see who's the ass, big brother. I'll give you six points. Two for old age, and four for your beat-up face. Remind me to teach you how to duck. Or throw a punch."

"I don't need your points, hotshot. Give me the ball and I'll show you old."

Cale gave him a shit-eating grin and shoved the ball right at his face.

Jud moved fast, twisted around, and went right under his little brother's long arms to score. "Two to zip! Screw your points."

They played one-on-one for forty-five minutes straight, faces red, hair stringy, sweat-soaked T-shirts stuck to their skin, legs and arms gleaming in the late afternoon sunlight. At the hour mark, bent eye to eye, they were like two dogs facing off in an alley, both panting so hard neither could speak. Jud had the ball, his face burning up and his eyes stinging from salty sweat. He rasped out the word "water."

Cale gave him a slight nod. At the same instant they looked at the garden hose. Whoever got there first won the water, and the added luxury of a few extra breaths while he waited for the other one to finish. It was a footrace. Cale stuck out his leg. Jud jumped it, side-stepped quickly, spun, and dove for the hose. He drank for a full two minutes while Cale stood there, hands on his knees, panting.

Sun-warmed water ran through the nozzle and he took a long time to drink, then let the cold water spill over his sweating head until it stopped throbbing. He shook like a wet spaniel and tossed the hose to Cale.

Jud walked over and picked up the ball, dribbling. "You gonna cry uncle?"

"Me?" Cale looked up from the hose and swiped his mouth. "No way. I'm just getting warmed up."

"Good," Jud lied and threw the ball right into Cale's stomach.

For just an instant his little brother looked as if he was going to heave, then they went at it again for another savage half hour. Jud bounced the ball through his brother's legs and jammed his elbow hard into Cale's gut. "Ooh, college boy. You're getting soft."

"Go to hell, Jud." Cale's body slammed him. "Who's soft, now, doughboy?" They were all over the court, legs and arms, punching and socking, until Cale slapped him in the head with the flat of his hand, stole the ball, then stood there, four feet from Jud, the ball bouncing from palm to palm.

Jud waited for an opening to the metronomic hammer of the ball on the asphalt and their hard breaths, then moved like lightning, stole the ball, laughing though his ribs hurt like hell. He held out the ball. "Come and get it, asshole."

Cale shot forward. Jud stuck out his foot and his brother skidded across the asphalt. They beat the hell out of each other in the name of basketball. By the time the sun set behind the hills, Cale's knees were bleeding, and Jud thought he was going to die, legs like rubber, his head killing him, but he wasn't going to lose. He stared into the crumpled look of concentration on Cale's angry red face, waiting for the patience Cale didn't have, and never had. His little brother's movements were jerky, blind, his motions looking desperate.

In the end, they lay on their backs on the warm ground, panting, hurting, bleeding, staring up at the night sky, which was clear and sharp, with no light of day left behind the hills. Music broke in the distance— drums and electric guitars. A band was playing some-where downtown. When Jud finally spoke, he said only two words: "You lost."

Cale raised up and pitched the ball at him.

Jud deflected it with his arm and lay there as the ball rolled away, his arm across his eyes, so tired he didn't know if he could stand. He sat up with a grunt and rested his arms on his bent knees. "You wouldn't have lost if you played with some patience. You give yourself away."

"I know how to play basketball."

"I'm just telling you how to win."

Cale wouldn't look at him.

"I'll light the barbecue and cook those steaks." Jud figured that was a peace offering. It was just a basketball game.

"I'm not hungry." Cale limped to the door and paused in the doorway, looking back, his expression bit-ter and intense. "I'm not staying home tonight." He slammed the door shut.

Jud stood up slowly, wobbled slightly. Standing just about killed him. He limped across the driveway to the hose and let the water run over his head for long sec-onds. The water pressure cut suddenly from the bath-room shower. Inside, he could hear Cale in the shower down the hall and thought about apologizing but stum-bled toward the kitchen. He wouldn't apologize for giv-ing his brother a little advice, or for winning. His swollen face had a date with an ice pack. He wasn't going anywhere tonight. Hell, he said to himself, I'll eat both steaks.

Laurel wanted to believe that somewhere in the big wide world was a boy who would love her. Of course, he could easily be in France while she was stuck on the western fringes of another whole continent. Alone, she walked along the crowded island waterfront, music from the live band on the pier drifting away from her, the scent of abalone burgers and caramel corn sweetening the night air. She bought some saltwater taffy and sat down on a bench, under the glow from brightly colored paper lanterns strung overhead. All around her was laughter, chatter, music—life, even if it belonged to other people.

At home, her mother was sitting in her chair reading novels about characters with lives bigger than theirs, or watching TV where nothing but the news was real. Instead of hiding in Seattle, her mother hid here.

Laurel felt as if she had been picked up and planted somewhere far from home. Miserable, she stuffed a piece of taffy in her mouth and watched people in pairs and groups on the sand. When she glanced up at the beach, she spotted an old man walking slowly away from everyone like some kind of lost soul and she wondered what went through the minds and hearts of other lonely people.

Another loner stood away from the crowd, facing the water, hands in the back pockets of his jeans, hip cocked, broad shoulders, and narrow waist—a classic masculine triangle. His height and sandy hair were all too familiar. He'd looked the same yesterday when he was standing at the boat rail before she told him she was seventeen.

This was her chance to set everything right. She would ask how he was feeling—as if nothing he could say would faze her—and say, "I haven't seen someone drop that fast since Cassius Clay beat Sonny Liston." Here was her opportunity to be witty, sophisticated, and worldly to someone who thought she wasn't. He wore an aqua blue polo shirt and she followed it through the crowd, but his steps were longer than hers and soon she had to run to catch up. She reached out and grabbed his arm. "Hey, there."

He turned and looked down at her.

Oh, God . . . It's not him. For an awkward, horrified instant she stood there. "I'm sorry. I made a mistake. I thought you were someone else."

"Lucky guy," he said.

"No. Not really." She started to turn away.

"Wait, don't go." He held his hands out, palms up. "I can be anyone you want me to be. Or if it's my lucky night maybe you'll take me instead of someone else. I'm quite the catch by the way—my name's Cale Banning."

"Cale?" she repeated dumbly, his flirting so unexpected. She sounded like an idiot, which was probably the real reason she had no dates.

"Yeah." He shoved his hands in his jeans pockets. "Like the vegetable, only with a *C*."

She laughed. "You're not going to believe this."

"Why? Are you Cale, too?"

"No."

"Cabbage?"

"No."

"Eggplant?"

She shook her head.

"Rutabaga."

"I'm Laurel . . ."

". . . like the tree," they both said together.

"Laurel Peyton," she added.

"Well, Laurel-Like-the-Tree Peyton." He took her hand. "Is this my lucky night?"

She melted right there. In a long, awkward silence, he studied her with sharp focus and made her wonder what he saw when he looked at her. Did she look empty and lost and clinging to his words?

"Since you didn't say no, come on." He pulled her with him.

"Where are you taking me?"

"Over there." He nodded somewhere but she couldn't see because of the crowd.

"Wait. Please."

He stopped. "Don't ruin my night and say no now."

"I can't see over this crowd. Where is 'there'?"

"You don't trust me." He was teasing her.

"I don't know you. And I don't trust you."

"Smart girl." He grinned and suddenly trust was no longer an issue. "Close your eyes, Laurel-Like-the-Tree Peyton, and just take ten more steps with me. We're on the beach with a few hundred other people, so you're safe. Just ten steps. Give me your hands."

"I can't believe I'm doing this." She held out her hands and closed her eyes. His fingers were calloused, and with her hands in his she felt light inside, a balloon someone had to anchor to keep from floating away.

He pulled her gently along. "You're cheating, girl. Keep your eyes closed."

"I'm not cheating."

"Just making sure." He took her hand again. "Okay, here we go. One, two, three . . ." He pulled her faster. "Four, six, eight, ten."

"Wait!" She dug in her heels, laughing. "Now who's cheating?"

"I'm counting, not cheating. Close your eyes."

She crossed her arms. "You call two, four, six, eight counting? Where did you say you went to school?"

"I didn't."

"Oh, that explains it. You didn't go to school." With every comeback, she laughed a little more, their banter the spun gold of a seminal moment, words she thought she would still remember in fifty years.

"I'm a senior at Loyola."

"Is that how they teach you to count after almost four years at a university? You should ask for your tuition back."

"No, that's how basketball players count. We count in goals—twos and threes."

"Basketball. You're so tall. I should have guessed."

He laughed. "If you are tall, then you must be a basketball player? That's discriminatory."

"Oh. I see now. Loyola? You're headed for law school."

"No."

"Well, we both know you sure aren't a math major."

"Let me count for you again. Two kidneys. Two lungs. Two hundred and six bones. I'm premed. We're here. Now you can open your eyes."

His face was the first thing she saw. She felt something odd looking at him, the actual weight of air on her exposed skin, hypersensitive, hypersensual.

He put his hands on her shoulders, turned her, but kept his hands there. "This is where I was taking you."

She had to lean back to look up at him. "Me and my two hundred and six bones?"

"You and your two hundred and six bones."

Just inches apart, they stood near the edge of the pier, where couples danced to live music. She was acutely aware of his hands on her shoulders; it felt as if it were the most natural thing in the world for them to stand together that way. One minute she had been alone, and the next a stranger was quickly changing into something more. Odd, how in a mere heartbeat life could change. She closed her eyes and gently swayed to the music, then remembered this same wonderful feeling from the boat yesterday.

"I'm seventeen," she blurted out.

He didn't say anything.

"I thought you should know. I'll be eighteen soon." She turned toward him then, and his hands fell away. In the absence of his touch, she felt exposed.

His expression was unreadable. "But you're seventeen now."

She nodded, waiting for him to say "Nice knowing you, kid."

"Like the Beatles," he said. "'I'll never dance with another, wooo . . .'"

She burst out laughing, half in relief and half because he went on to tease her by singing another two verses in a goofy voice. He didn't stop until the band struck up again.

"Good song," they both said at the same time, one of those rare moments of clarity when you realize that something might be choreographed by fate.

"Laurel," he said—just Laurel—and threaded his warm fingers with hers, pulling her around for a dance and setting loose a thousand fireflies in her stomach. So close, their bodies brushed lightly, and he smelled like Ivory soap and aftershave. She rested her hand on his shirtfront, where the cotton was soft and warm, as though it covered a good heart.

He moved his hand slowly across her lower back. It was the kind of touch a girl didn't forget, a little possessive. "Dance with me." But he wasn't really asking because they were already moving. Behind him, there were so many stars in the sky they should have lit up the whole island, like fireworks, or volcanic ash, or as if all the fireflies inside her had just flown free.

Dancing slowly, he placed her hand on the back of his neck, and over his shoulder hung an enormous platinum moon. "Tonight I want to dance in the sand with you, Laurel-Like-the-Tree Peyton. With everybody here watching us."

"Why would they be watching us?"

"Because you're the prettiest girl on the island." His expression told her he really believed what he'd just said.

Funny thing. At that moment she believed it, too.

When Cale was with a girl, time simply disappeared. There were no med school rejection letters, no sound of Victor's voice or expectations he could never satisfy, no perfect brother's footsteps to follow in. He didn't have to win or lose basketball games or play the game Jud's way. It was like going back in time to a place where he could drink Coca-Cola, eat egg salad sandwiches and Twinkies, and talk with someone who told him he could be anything.

He and Laurel sat on a beach bench and talked, struck by a hunger to learn everything about each other in a single night. A few people lingered around the pier after the band quit, sitting in the sand or on the steps to the pier; they talked near buildings with bars facing the water, and tried to keep the night alive in the same way Cale wanted to, while Laurel dug through a macramé purse slumped at her feet. Her brown hair, the color of polished walnut, hung down and hid her expression from him.

He'd understood quickly that the key to her thoughts showed in the pattern of her features: a hint of humor when she teased him, the laugh lines as he teased her; a look of mutual understanding between them the second he told her his parents were long dead, and the hollowness beneath her facial bones as she talked about leaving Seattle. A strange, bleak emotion like enmity changed the pallor of her skin when she admitted she'd never really known her father.

She felt things as deeply as he did. So much of his life sliced clean through him in deep cuts that took long years to heal, if ever. But when she looked up from her purse, holding a crumpled cellophane bag filled with saltwater taffy, he felt something like joy. Her smile spun of whimsy said Eureka! and Cale wondered which one of them had found gold.

The longer he watched her, the more he wanted to kiss her, to hold her body against his, hips pressed together, to touch her in secret damp places and lose himself inside this wonderful, lovely creature. He started to touch her—just to tuck her hair behind her ear—but pulled back, afraid if he did he might burn up right there. His hands wouldn't stop. He knew from dancing with her. But there was a newness and fragility to meeting a girl like Laurel, a sense that he could say or do the wrong thing and she would walk away.

"Want some taffy?" she asked.

"Sure. The cheeseburger, fries, beer, and ice cream weren't enough."

"I didn't eat all that. You did. I had a hot dog."

"You had half a hot dog."

"Half was enough. They make hot dogs from lips, hooves, and snouts."

"And intestines," he added without missing a beat. Their talk had a special rhythm, like two musicians who instinctively pick up on the next note. They had perfect pitch.

She unwrapped a piece of taffy.

"They're all the same," he said. "Red striped."

"Cinnamon." She held it up under his nose. "There is no other flavor."

"Where's the banana, the chocolate, the licorice? There are at least a dozen other flavors."

"If I'm going to eat it, I only want the best."

A rare lapse of silence balanced awkwardly between them. He hadn't been completely honest with her about med school. Not a lie exactly. He walled up that inadequate part of himself with jokes and teasing and didn't tell her he was failing at the most important thing in his life. She wanted the best, and tonight he needed to be more in her eyes, so he talked about basketball until he ran out of words.

She looked at her watch. "I need to get home."

"I'll walk you," he said, giving her no choice. He had no idea what she was feeling, if he'd bored her senseless talking about sports like some jock. Before she could turn away, he took her hand and caught a small smile on her face as they walked under a streetlight. Okay, he thought. This is good.

Too soon she stopped at the corner of Descanso Street. "That's my house." She pointed to a gray island bungalow a few doors down, where a lamp glowed from a table in the front window. The shades were half drawn, a too-bright porch light shone above the door, and he could see the mosquitoes and moths circling blindly in the light.

As they approached, he took a chance. "We're both free all week. Let's go to the beach tomorrow."

"Sure."

"What's your phone number?"

She rattled it off and he immediately forgot it. "How do you remember all the bones of the body?" she asked.

"I cheat."

"Okay." She wrote her number on his palm, then on each of his fingers. "Cheater's notes." She laughed, reminding him what that sound had done to him all night—a first taste of sugar when you'd lived your life on salt.

When she looked up at him, he felt taller, smarter, not the person he really was, but as if she were looking at someone she could love. He saw it in her face, in the stars in her eyes. He could leap tall buildings in a single bound. Maybe, just maybe, this was the girl who could love him for what he wasn't.

He tilted her chin up and leaned down to kiss her.

"The porch light," she said, annoyed. "My mom still waits up for me."

"No big deal."

"It's embarrassing."

He reached up and unscrewed the lightbulb. "Sometimes being tall is a good thing." It took a minute for his eyes to adjust to the dark. Standing there like that, their breathing mingled, mouths so close, Cale could taste cinnamon taffy in the air, and they did almost burn up when he kissed her. Incendiary—a tree burning from a lightning strike, a match to dry leaves, a flood of desire so strong he had to break apart and step back, relieved for the darkness that hid his flushed skin but couldn't disguise a longing heart.

"I'll call you tomorrow," he told her and she went inside without a word. He left, but stood under the corner streetlamp, compelled to look back at the house. Its angles were like the others on the street—ordinary—and nothing like the kind of place where an angel lived. Her silhouette was in the window, bent over the lamp. She looked right at him, stilled for a heartbeat or two, and placed her palm on the glass. He raised his hand, then stayed that way even after she'd turned out the light and he couldn't see her anymore.

Whistling, he walked home to the tune of a Beatles song, hands in his pockets, the fanciful presence of spring in the air, when nights were deep purple, when cinnamon taffy tasted like new love, and a dim life could suddenly brighten to endless possibilities.

CHAPTER

11

Kathryn kept her car on the mainland, stored in a San Pedro garage—you needed a car in LA. So every day she walked the few blocks to her studio and shop along Avalon's narrow streets, which splayed out from the waterfront like words on a Scrabble board and climbed up the hillsides to Spanish tiled homes scattered among the old-growth ironwoods. The town was touched in quaintness, with red and pink geraniums in planters and window boxes. Restaurants hung hand-painted signs and seldom used chalkboards, because you could smell the daily special a block away. The island's uniqueness was born in the constant, drifting call of seagulls and the fact that more people walked on the pavement than tires rolled over it.

At 9:30 A.M. it was sixty-five degrees, and sunshine already warmed the walkways and asphalt. Kathryn stopped at a small side-street market to pick up tea and sugar for her studio. Neighborhood stores like this one were mostly nostalgic. Gone were the mainland days of fresh home delivery from the Helms Bakery wagon and Adohr Farms milk truck. Inside, no racks of Wonder Bread decorated with real balloons, no giant pickle jar on the counter, or open boxes of penny candy under it, just the pungent aroma of freshly ground coffee. But the market wasn't cold and sleek and filled with more choices and brands than anyone ever really needed—the problem with things nowadays. Too many choices. Too many decisions. Life had become a supermarket.

In the checkout line, everyone in front of her talked about children and Easter services, the recent raise in library fines, so Kathryn glanced at the magazine rack next to the counter. Beneath the huge block letters of *Look* magazine was a headline touting "Growth and Achievement: Americans Talk About Their Work." The name in stark white on black caught her first, as five full racks of Victor Banning stared back at her. The boxes of tea and sugar slipped from her hands. She reached for the magazine as someone set her groceries on the counter. Banning Oil was BanCo now, and run by the scion and father of the man who killed Jimmy.

"They have a place here, you know."

Kathryn turned to the woman behind her. "What?"

"The Bannings. They have a house at Hamilton Cove. Don't come here as often as they used to, but Victor Banning—the man on the cover there—has a hundred-footer called the *Catalan*. You can't miss it when it comes in."

"Is this your tea and sugar?" The girl behind the counter looked at her. "You want the magazine, too?"

"No. That's all." Kathryn put the magazine back, quickly paid, and left. When she set the paper bag on the work counter in her studio, the brown paper was crushed from her grip and she couldn't remember walking there or unlocking the doors.

Banning Oil. Two words that could make her heart beat irregularly and turn her vision red. Banning service stations were part of the mainland, their big round blue-and-white signs hanging on street corners like 76 and Flying A, just blurs in her peripheral vision as she drove a few times a year over thoroughfares cluttered with businesses on both sides of the streets.

Yet with a single phrase—"They have a place here, you know"—her wonderful new world shrunk in size and went way off kilter. Back in the small bathroom attached to her studio she washed her face, as if she could wash away her raw feeling, then looked up into the mirror and braced her hands on the sink. She had been here before.

I have to let go of this, she thought. I'm not Julia. She made herself tea, which she sweetened with sugar, then became frustrated and overly angry when the lemon she kept on the counter was green and rotten. Her anger sent her out for another, so it was a while before she sat at her wheel and escaped the rest of the day. There was safety in the solitude of creation. She could lose herself there, even though it was sunny outside, the kind of clear day that made hiding difficult.

A little after five, when she walked inside the house, the phone was ringing. Stephen Randall wanted a date on Saturday. Kathryn said yes and hung up before she changed her mind. She had a queer feeling, not good, not bad, just a little scared at what lay before her. Evie wasn't home when she called, and Laurel's room was empty, so Kathryn went through her closet, looking for something to wear Saturday. When Laurel came home from the beach, Kathryn was sitting on the bed, surrounded by an explosion of out-of-date dresses, dark wool suits with skirts below the knee, and cardigan sweaters, clothes bought with Julia's approval. She looked at her daughter standing in her doorway. "I have twenty-five pairs of shoes and no clothes."

"These aren't shoes, Mother." Laurel dangled a patent-leather squash-heeled pump with a gold buckle from her finger. "Pilgrims wore these."

"I guess I'll have to take the boat over and do some serious shopping. You can help me come into 1970. Let's go the day after tomorrow."

Laurel's face fell.

"What's wrong?"

"I have plans, Mom. All week. It's spring break." She couldn't miss the panic in Laurel's voice, as if she thought Kathryn were going to take something away.

"Okay," she said calmly. "I'll go alone."

Her daughter stood there in a lace cover-up over her striped bikini, straw beach bag in one hand, a sunburned nose and tanned legs glossy with cocoa butter. She was pink and glowing with sunshine and something that looked like a wild kind of happiness, nothing like the blue, lonely girl crying into her pillow the other night.

"Are you home for dinner?"

Laurel shook her head. "I'm going out. I need to hop in the shower." Then she was gone. Kathryn was left in the middle of a Goodwill pile, struck by life again turning on a dime. Where was the White Rabbit? Two nights ago she couldn't sleep with guilt over moving here in search of her own happiness. *Selfish woman. Bad mother.* Phrases that became mantras in her sleeplessness. This morning, her past reached right up and slapped her in the face. Now, her achingly lonely daughter was far too busy to go shopping with her, a trip she needed because she actually had a date. Kathryn Peyton on a date. Her new mantra? *Change was good. Change was exciting. Change sent you in a new direction.* At least that was what Evie kept telling her.

Laurel had always dreamed about love, the same kind of love her parents had: love opened the soul; love filled you, completed you; love made you a woman. Once discovered, love was joyous and wonderful and uncomplicated. So what was this wild thing burning inside of her, something she was afraid to name and turned her into molten lava? She would go out with the resolve to slow things, but her body moved toward Cale's, inviting him to touch her in places deep and private. They went to the beach, ate burgers and ice cream, and kissed under the stars, telling each other about their lives and dreams, but not their fears. That would have made things too serious.

Still, between them everything moved unbelievably fast. A few kisses became long bouts of necking, and if Cale touched her in some ways she opened to his fingers and mouth and just let him do those things she craved. She told herself it was okay. They could touch and just stop. At home, she crawled into bed still wrapped in the soft damp remnants of what they had been doing, and in the morning the muscles under her arms ached from clinging for long hours to his wide shoulders and chest. Her nipples grew hard whenever she looked at him and when he kissed her, even when she was only thinking about him. Whose body was she living inside?

Four days after she met Cale, four days they had mostly spent together, he picked her up in a golf cart with a green striped awning edged in rope fringe.

"It looks like a candy cart," she said, climbing in.

"It is." He tossed a cellophane bag of red-and-white striped taffy in her lap, whipped the cart into a U-turn, and sped off.

Once they were out of town and up in the hills, he drove the golf cart as if they were trying to escape through a minefield, all jerky turns and fast starts that made her laugh and grab on to him to stay in the seat. They reached an uphill stretch and the cart barely moved forward.

She touched his arm. "You need to whip the mice in the engine."

"Funny."

"Should I get out and push?"

"No, just lean back and relax before I have to do something to quiet your smart mouth."

"Promises, promises," she said and Cale slipped his arm around her and French-kissed her all the way uphill. At the crest in the rise, the sea breeze swept over the hills, sang through the treetops, and touched her face with the sting and taste of salt. Below, the blue harbor looked like a snow cone with a bite taken out of it and bleached sails cut across rippling water. They sat on a carpet of wildflowers as blue as the cloudless California sky and that spread around them in the seemingly unending fields of a perfume commercial. Truthfully, she had never liked the island—it stood for everything she'd left behind—but it was soft up here and different with Cale. She found it easy to be lazy in this kind of spring.

Cale had been watching her (he did that a lot), then he leaned back on a blanket and stared out at the vista below. "Do you like it here?" she asked.

"We came here almost every summer after my parents died. Victor, Jud, and I. It was different."

"Different from what?"

"My grandfather didn't pit us against each other as much. He was busy with a woman he eventually married."

"I didn't know you had a stepgrandmother."

"I don't. Not anymore. She wasn't the grandmotherly type, too starlet for that." And he laughed. "But for a while, she kept Victor busy and out from between us."

"My grandmother took me everywhere, showed me everything," Laurel told him. "She talked about my dad all the time. She wore this dark, bleak sadness as if it were always part of her; it settled in the back of her eyes. She was afraid everyone would forget about him. It was like the Second Coming when they played one of his songs on the radio, and hard on my mom. Jimmy this. Jimmy that. But I loved the stories. They were all I had of him."

"Victor never talked about my parents. The subject was changed immediately." Cale turned to her. "But I can remember them." He spoke of his mother there on that flowered hillside and made her sound bigger than life. He talked about his father in a way that made Laurel long for a single memory, just one, a memory that was hers rather than those of the people who knew her dad.

When the sun began to drop, they ate food from a basket, drank beer iced in a cooler, and let the late afternoon sun loll them into each other's arms. He seemed contented to lie there without saying much, just drawing his finger over her bare back exposed by the halter top. "It's good to know you aren't perfect," he said. "You have a wart here."

Laurel twisted to look over her shoulder. "Where?"

He bent closer. "Here." His mouth closed over hers and they lay on their sides with little between them but thin clothing, anticipation, and sexual energy. She placed his roaming hand on her hip and held it there, until he pulled away with a sexual groan. Wanting more, she linked her arms around his neck and they were all tongues and mouths and raging blood. After a few minutes he slid his hands down under her clothes and it felt so good she couldn't stop him.

"Oh, baby, you're so sweet, so soft."

"Cale," she whispered. She didn't recognize the hunger and sexuality in her own voice.

He guided her hand over him and slowly moved it up and down, then touched her again, and they finished together, wet and throbbing, flushed and still clinging to each other. He pulled back. "Pretty girl. You're the best thing that's ever happened to me."

"It's too fast." She felt confused, guilty. "I'm not like this."

"I know that."

"Do you?"

He looked hurt, questioning, and unsure.

"We barely know each other."

"You think I'm going to try to get in your pants and then dump you?"

"It's crossed my mind."

"Look. I want to see you every day and every night this week. I want to see you, Laurel. I don't have someone else tucked away in LA. I want you."

"This week," she repeated the words bitterly and watched for the lie in his eyes.

"I said that wrong." He looked as uncomfortable as she felt. "Not just for this week. We can see each other on weekends and weeknights. You're in Westwood. I'm not that far away. Twenty minutes."

"I don't have a car."

"I have three cars."

She laughed. "No one has three cars."

"I do," he said seriously. "Three cars and a pickup. You want to use one?"

"No." She studied him and paused at the truth she saw. *I'm quite the catch.* His first words to her. "Oh, God," she said. "Are you rich?"

"I'm not rich."

He was lying.

"My grandfather is."

Her mind began to put it all together. "Cale Banning? Like the gas stations? Like Banning Oil?"

He nodded.

"Your family owns all those pumps along Pacific Coast Highway."

"The company's mostly moved on to petroleum products. Plastics and some shipping. We're down to only two refineries. It's not only Banning Oil anymore. A few years back, Victor, my grandfather, merged everything into BanCo."

"See? Oh, God . . . That just proves I don't know you at all." She lowered her voice to a whisper. "I keep letting you touch me. What does that make me?"

"I hope it makes you my girl."

"I've never done this with anyone before."

"I don't care. Wait, that's not true. I care that you only do it with me." He took a large school ring off his finger and put it in her palm, then closed her hand around it. "Okay?"

Laurel looked down at the ring in her hand. This was how all of her girlish dreams had ended. To belong to a boy. The Gidget ending. But the ring felt heavy in a way she couldn't explain and never expected. And even as she said, "Okay," she wondered why dreams were so different from the real thing.

Kathryn stood back from the front window when a tall boy with his arm slung possessively around her daughter reached up to unscrew the porch lightbulb. Motherhood kept her rooted where she was. What she saw outside was difficult to watch, her daughter in the boy's arms, their bodies pressed together like lovers', their hands all over each other. She'd dreaded this. Laurel was so young and inexperienced, but growing up terribly needy in a time of free love and a doing-what-feels-good attitude.

It wasn't virtue that worried her. She wanted Laurel to love and be loved. She wanted her to have great sex and babies and a happy life. But at seventeen everything was all fire and no substance. Her Laurel wanted love madly and had lived her life without male attention, thriving only on the dreamlike stories Kathryn had recounted about Jimmy and her. Now, when Laurel was just beginning to skirt womanhood, so needy for a man, and lonely to boot? Kathryn saw only a portent of something so frighteningly dangerous she had to step away from the window.

She was leaning against the counter with a glass of milk when Laurel came in, flustered, and said absolutely nothing, just stood there with her face flushed and her lips swollen from hours of kissing, wearing that tousled look and emanating a wild sexual energy the young could never hide.

"Where were you tonight?"

"Just hanging out."

The lies were starting, and Kathryn wanted to flinch at Laurel's words. *No, Mommy, I don't have my hand in the cookie jar.* "You're dating someone." Despite her best intentions, it came out like an accusation.

Laurel stiffened. "Were you watching us?"

"I was in the living room when the front light went out." She stopped. She had nothing to explain. "I think I should meet this boy."

Laurel didn't say anything at first and Kathryn wished she could read her mind. "I'm your mother, Laurel. If for no other reason than out of respect."

"He's nice, Mom. He really is."

Kathryn nodded. "Okay. That's good."

Laurel seemed to hesitate, then relaxed with a long sigh. "I'll bring him by the shop tomorrow." She turned to leave.

"Good night."

The words "Good night, Mom" echoed back from the hallway and she heard Laurel's bedroom door close. Now what? Everything was starting. She needed to talk it out. She needed to know what to do. It was too late to call Evie. But after a hellish night, she did call her sister the first thing the next morning and said, "She's so young, Evie. Laurel wants love for all the wrong reasons. What do I do when she wants to fall in love so badly?"

"You let her, Kay. You just let her."

The sea around Catalina was a myriad of abalone-shell blues, from aquamarine shallows near the island beaches to a deep ink blue along the distant mainland coast. Still as the morning air, the water glistened with sunlight, blindingly bright, as if reflected from a freshly cleaned mirror. The only motion visible was a subtle ripple of current, until a classic, mahogany runabout shot out from around an outcropping and cut diamond-like across the glassy water, heading toward the Banning home on a sleepy, private cove.

Jud powered down the boat as he approached their pier. Usually he could take the boat out and find peace in the blue solitude of the ocean. It never failed to remind him of his place—one man alone on the largest ocean in the world, like an ant staring down a herd of elephants. There, in the smallness of who he was, he could work things through. He could see with less clutter, and the insurmountable wouldn't appear so impossible. The ant had options. He could crawl onto the elephant's back and it would take him someplace else.

But today he came back to the house with no answers except the feeling—the reality—that his confidence was badly shaken. It stayed with him like a relentless headache that no medication could relieve. His grandfather had taught him the inflexible reality of life: either you won or you lost. There was no middle ground. You headed down a path that would lead you to one or the other.

At the dock, Jud jumped off, wrapped the towline around a cleat, and secured the other line. The hot, weathered boards burned the soles of his bare feet. Sweat dripped into his eyes and matted the overlong hair under his cap, as if it were July instead of April. Tooling around in this boat he loved appealed to him. Not just its leather interior, teak decking, and rebuilt V-8, though he'd spent time and sweat and money restoring it.

He and Cale bought the boat as a joint project a few years back. But Cale had trouble finding time to work, always living in the next moment. Cale worried about life passing him by. He saw everything in wholes—the whole world was speeding away from him, the whole world was against him, the whole world lay before him—while Jud was a detail man. He could sit patiently and wait for the perfect timing. It took cautious, thoughtful steps to get where you wanted to go. You couldn't just leap ahead without tripping.

That was part of what frustrated him so much about the Marvetti deal. He'd thought he'd done it all right, all the pieces there for the perfect deal—the best way to impress Victor.

Jud knew what Victor was really saying to him on Friday: he was a loser. His failure took physical form, a tautness invading his body that he couldn't shake even in the peace of a lonely sea. He arched his back and stretched in the sun, then grabbed a beer from the cooler. When he straightened, Cale was walking toward him from the house.

This was new. His brother had been avoiding him, the easiest way to make him out as the bad guy. Don't confront someone if you're ticked off. Avoid them and make them feel guilty. Jud jumped back on board and began to wipe down the boat. When he glanced up, his brother stood next to the boat guzzling orange juice from a carton. Jud dropped a large sponge into a water bucket. "Has anyone called?"

"No. But I just got up." Cale paused, then asked, "Who'd call this early?"

"Early?" Jud looked up. Cale was serious. "How are you going to get through those long hours as an intern?"

"That's why I'm resting up. Logging in sleep for the next few years." His voice was flip and screw-you. "Who's calling here?"

"I'm expecting some calls from the board members." Jud picked up his beer. "I left this number."

Cale looked around him, squinting a little at the sun. "How long have you been up?"

"I woke up about four with the Z Channel blaring on the TV. Couldn't sleep, so I took her out around sunrise."

Cale finished off the orange juice and tossed the carton in a trash can. He shoved his hands in his jeans pockets. "You're drinking a beer. It's ten in the morning."

"Call it breakfast."

"Beer for breakfast from the king of the kitchen?" The words dripped with sarcasm.

Jud kept wiping down the deck. "It's hot. I felt like a beer."

His younger brother didn't say anything more, perhaps aware he'd crossed a line, or that he couldn't egg him into a fight. Jud wrung out the sponge, annoyed at the grudge Cale carried. Hell, he was steamed too.

"Your face looks better," Cale said. "The swelling's gone."

"Yeah. I can shave without flinching."

"I guess I haven't been around much."

"No."

Cale was looking out at the mainland instead of at him. "I met a girl Saturday night."

"I just figured you were still pissed off because I kicked your ass at your own game."

"Ha! I let you win."

Jud started to argue.

Cale cut him off. "And if I were pissed, I'd bully you into a rematch."

"Bully me?" Jud laughed at him. "Right."

"Well." Cale half grinned. "Tempt you. All it took before was to shoot a few baskets alone. That's all it ever takes with you. Face it, Jud. You're easy."

"I didn't see you standing outside with the ball the next morning clamoring for a rematch." Jud remembered that Cale had slept until almost noon that day, then showered and left without a word.

Cale lowered himself into the boat. "Give me a rag. I'll help."

"You don't have to."

"Yeah, I do."

"No." Jud said distinctly and sat back on his heels. "You don't."

"I want to use the boat later."

"Then here." Jud tossed him a rag.

"I thought I'd take Laurel out in it this afternoon. Great girl."

"And she looks like Barbie Benton."

"No, but she has brown hair. Great legs, small waist." Cale stopped listing assets. "She's a knockout, but that's not what I like about her."

"Yeah, sure." Jud laughed out loud.

"Okay, okay . . . It helps. But you'd like her. She's really easy to talk to."

"I like my conversations in words that are more than one syllable."

"You're an ass, Jud. You know that?"

"Then why are you laughing?"

"Because you're a funny ass."

"You never laughed when I made cracks about the last one."

"Corkie? Once you've been made a fool of, it's easier to laugh at yourself."

"Good, then don't forget that, now that you've met a new one."

"You're warning me off and you haven't even met her."

"I'm not warning you off. Just reminding you to keep your head on straight this time."

"You're my brother, not my father, Jud."

"You were the one who was whining about med school."

"You sound like Victor again."

"If I were Victor, I'd make you feel as if you were worth about two cents. I just don't want you to screw up again. Okay?"

"Look. I know I made a mistake. Am I going to have to hear about it until I die?"

"It's not just that last girl, Corkie. Although she was the worst of the bunch. There's a pattern here. If it weren't for basketball, you might not have gotten into Loyola. Remember your senior year of high school? Wasn't exactly stellar. What was that cheerleader's name?"

"Sierra."

"Good God, how could I forget that?"

Cale's expression thinned. "I don't see you in any great relationship."

"We're not talking about me. We're talking about you. Now you find it easy to admit your mistake. A year from now this Lauren might be an easy-to-admit-mistake, too."

"Laurel, not Lauren. And she's different."

Jud just looked at him.

"She's a cooking student."

"What? Like home ec?"

"She wants to be a professional chef."

"You want med school."

"I know. I know." Cale shoved his hands in his pockets. "Trust me to make a better choice this time."

The boat was clean, so Jud stood and emptied the bucket over the side.

"You should meet her. You'll see she's different."

For some reason Cale wanted his approval of this

girl. That was unusual, so Jud faced him. "Bring her to dinner. We'll barbecue something."

"Tonight?"

"Sure."

Cale seemed to think about that, then said, "We're taking the boat out and I want to buzz over to the Isthmus. I'll make sure we're back before six."

"Here." Jud put the boat keys in Cale's hand. "The tank's half full." He headed for the house.

"This girl's the right one this time, Jud."

Cale followed him closely, reminding him of when they were kids and Cale shadowed him everywhere. This sudden need for approval was a different side of his brother. Jud studied him for a minute, and all of his anger dissipated. He had a hard time himself wringing a single drop of approval from Victor. But here was Cale, who needed some kind of victory—needed his older brother not to be Victor, something Jud understood. "Maybe she is the right one, little brother. Maybe she is."

Cale walked alongside him. "Tonight. You'll see I'm right."

"Okay. I'll hold back my judgment." Jud knuckled him in the arm. "Hell, Cale, even a blind monkey can find a peanut once in a while."

Kathryn Peyton pumped the pedals on the pottery wheel and a few pounds of clay coned up through her hands. Her movements were practiced and the only part of her life that had any rhythm. Last night she tossed and turned as she had so often lately, caught in the angst about her decision to pack up and move here, about

Laurel's desperate need to be loved and her longing for some kind of male attention in her life, roles she couldn't fill. By 4 A.M., each piece she'd created that week flitted through her head. She was counting artwork instead of sheep.

The shelves along the studio walls held tall, elliptical vases and deeply curved bowls, abstract urns, and large platters waiting for glaze and firing. All the pieces had a single, jagged line dividing them in half, a common thread. At 5 A.M. she knew the title of the collection, *A Mother's Mind,* and decided to glaze each side with deep contrasting color, then name each of the pieces for a different emotion. *Fear. Confusion. Need. Protection. Hesitancy.* Every piece would be numbered seventeen, Laurel's age.

When Laurel had come to work that morning with Kathryn the first thing out of her mouth had been, "Look at your studio. All those pieces? You've been working too hard, Mom." Her daughter wouldn't remember the last time Kathryn had filled a room with pottery, all abstract, most of it too tormented in design for easy sale, especially in the fifties, when people wanted Bauer bowls or Franciscan Ware, pieces you used, the days when "art" could never be thrown on a wheel.

In the years since, the oddly formed pieces she'd used to purge her grief had became seminal to her career and often sold at auction for more than her newer work. That collection had been titled *Jimmy.*

Now, she concentrated on finishing the newest piece, a huge open bowl with a waved rim and an unusual looped cut that twisted in and out of itself in a confused line. Once done, she sliced the piece from the wheel and added it to the shelf.

"Mom?" Laurel's voice crackled from the intercom. "I have Cale with me."

"Come on back." Kathryn released the intercom and washed her hands at the sink, then Laurel came in, dragging a tall young man about twenty-one or twenty-two with her and laughing at something he'd said.

As Kathryn untied her apron, that deep sound of her child's joy sank into her bones and blood. It had been so long since she'd heard Laurel laugh like that. The cause of that laughter was good-looking, golden in that California way, tanned and fit and blue-eyed, tall enough to grab attention in a full room. He was the reason Laurel stayed out late, came in with swollen lips, and said good night with a dream-spun look about her that made Kathryn unable to sleep.

"Mom, this is Cale." Laurel watched her closely, nervously.

It didn't take a genius to see this was important to Laurel. It just took a mother. Kathryn tucked her hair behind her ear, smiled, and shook his hand, which was big but warm and gentle. "Cale."

"Mrs. Peyton."

"So you're the reason I hardly see my daughter anymore."

"Yes, ma'am. I came to collect for taking her off your hands. But I'm going to have to charge you double. She's a real pain." His joke was so unexpected and refreshing that Kathryn laughed embarrassingly loud.

"Cale." Laurel jammed her elbow into his ribs and said quietly, "Stop it."

He doubled over, pretending to be in pain, and looked up at her as he was bent, gripping his ribs. "See what I mean?"

"I should have warned you, Mom." Laurel crossed her arms. "He's an idiot. And he goes to Loyola."

"The Jesuits might have a problem with how you phrased that sentence, Laurel," he said.

Her daughter laughed. "He's not an idiot because he goes to Loyola. I said that wrong."

The boy teased Laurel charmingly. No wonder she seemed so happy. But the look that passed between them made Kathryn feel old and uneasy. She didn't know which was worse, Laurel moping around the house or falling for this boy who put his hands on her daughter's bottom and lifted her against him for good night kisses.

"Cale's going to medical school in the fall." Laurel took hold of his hand and threaded her fingers through his.

All Kathryn could see was them standing on the porch, his hands all over Laurel. The fear in Laurel's eyes that Kathryn couldn't accept him. The rush of eagerness in Laurel's voice. The possessiveness already tangible between the two. "Med school," she managed to say. "That's quite a challenge. Which school?"

"I'm not certain yet." He glanced at his watch, then looked at Laurel.

"We're going out in his boat, Mom."

"I wanted to take Laurel to the Isthmus, Mrs. Peyton, then dinner at our place."

Not yet. Kathryn wasn't going to let them roll over her. "Are you over from the mainland with your family?"

"Just with my brother. You know, spring break and all. We keep a boat here all year. I promise it's safe."

"Who's going to be on the boat?"

Laurel looked as if she were fighting back the need to say something.

"Just the two of us," Cale said frankly.

Her daughter panicked, as if it just occurred to her that Kathryn might refuse to let her go. "Mom?"

"The boat is a runabout," Cale cut in quickly. "It's seaworthy and the engine runs perfectly. I've been on boats since I was eight, Mrs. Peyton, and I know this area well. We've had a place here for years and I grew up on these waters. I promise I wouldn't take Laurel out unless it was safe. We'll be back before dark. My brother's planning on barbecuing."

Kathryn looked at her daughter and her young man. *Just let her, Kay. Just let her.* She cut the cord. "Okay, then, you two. Have a good time."

"Thanks, Mom." Laurel, hurried over, kissed her, missing her cheek because she was in such a hurry to get back to holding the boy's hand. "Bye!"

They disappeared through the door before Kathryn could take a breath. She stood there feeling mixed emotions and sat down for a minute. Laurel was happy, which was a good thing. He was funny, polite, and he had an easy way about him. She liked his sincerity and nothing about him rang false. Med school was a big commitment, demanding, with little time to sleep. He had drive and goals.

But Laurel could get hurt. He was a senior at Loyola, which meant he was over twenty-one to Laurel's seventeen, eighteen in a few weeks. Laurel was on her own during the week and Kathryn had thought of it as no different from her daughter being away at college. Once Laurel was out of high school and working toward a career, Kathryn tried to let go. But her daughter was so young, and wanted so badly not to be. Already she appeared to be attached to this boy. In what, days?

You married Jimmy weeks after meeting him. She could hear Evie's voice now, telling her what to think. Her sister was the voice of reason. *Let go, Kay.*

There was no answer, right or wrong, here. Kathryn checked her clothes for clay and dust, then left the studio and crossed the few stone flags that led into the back door of her shop.

Shannon was at the register and looked up. "Hi, Kathryn. Wow, I didn't know Laurel was dating Cale Banning."

"What did you say?"

"Cale Banning. His family is loaded. Really loaded. You've heard of Banning Oil, haven't you? That's his grandfather."

Kathryn felt all the blood drain from her as Shannon rattled on about the family. "Banning?" It hurt to say the name.

"Yep."

She moved toward the front door like a cipher. Outside, she ran from the courtyard into the street, looking both ways, before she raced to the corner of Crescent, the words of the woman in the market pounding in her head. *They have a place here, you know.*

The steamship had come into port earlier and the town and beach were crowded with mainlanders. She searched for Laurel's pink sweater, for his tall, dark blond head. She walked down the sidewalk, between people, looking inside every storefront window. She wove her way across to the beach side of the street and stood on a bench, searching left and right.

The steamship blocked part of the harbor from view. She looked out toward the water, then jumped down and ran along the sand, searching for a runabout, trying to see her daughter near any of the boats moored closer to shore. *A hundred-footer. You can't miss it. House at Hamilton Cove.*

Kathryn frantically searched the bay, running down the beach, up onto the walkway, and all the way to the casino end of the harbor. She covered the whole waterfront. But they just weren't there.

CHAPTER

13

A woman stood away from the house, up on a rise in the secluded road that led to town. But Jud shrugged it off—tourists often walked out this far. He went inside, carrying a six-pack of beer and the last of the groceries from the golf cart. The house had been forgotten, except for Jud and his brother, who'd used it to escape the chaos of the mainland. Visitors didn't come to the Banning house on Hamilton Cove, so when the doorbell rang it caught Jud by surprise, loud and sounding like microphone feedback.

The woman standing on the doorstep was a stranger. "I'm looking for my daughter. And Cale Banning." She was fair-skinned—rare in a land of tans—with huge brown eyes and auburn hair. Her features were perfectly even, the kind born of good bones and genetic symmetry. If the daughter looked anything like the mother, no wonder Cale was tangled in love again.

"I'm Jud Banning. Cale's brother."

"Are they here?"

"I don't think so. He told me he was taking the boat out, with a girl he met. I just came home but—" He stopped. The woman looked as if she were staring death in the face. Paleness came over her in gray waves he could actually see. "Are you okay?"

He caught her before she hit the ground. "Damn." He kicked the door closed behind him and laid her on the sofa, then brought her a glass of water. Helpless, he stood over her. Should he throw it on her, or feed it to her?

To his relief, she opened her eyes, disoriented, and sat up too fast and put her hand to her head.

"Whoa. Take it easy. Here. Drink this." He handed her the glass and sat down next to her in case she keeled over again. She sipped it, then looked around the room, searching but looking cornered. Before, from a distance, he couldn't see her fragility. Now, sitting next to her, she was like glass so thin if he touched her he thought she would shatter. "They aren't here. The boat's gone from the dock. But we can radio them through the coast guard."

"No." She stared out at the cove beyond. "No. I shouldn't have come here. It's not an emergency." She stood up. "Don't say anything to them when they come back. Please. Nothing is more embarrassing than me overreacting. I just wanted to tell her something and thought if I could catch them . . ." Her words drifted off as she walked away.

She didn't convince him, and he wondered if she could possibly convince herself. "Wait." Jud caught up with her at the front door. "Let me give you a ride back."

"No."

"I can't let you walk back. You just fainted." He tried to lighten the situation. "My father would turn over in his grave." Her face went gray and he thought he might have to catch her again. "No argument. I'm taking you home."

She nodded and he helped put her into the cart. Every few moments on the short drive to town, he would look at her, sitting next to him in complete silence. Her color was better, her hands folded in her lap, but she didn't say anything until he asked for her address. He pulled up to the house on Descanso and killed the engine. All the way there his mind had been busy searching for answers why this woman was so upset. "He won't hurt her."

She studied him, looking for something, but only she knew what.

"Cale won't hurt your daughter. If that's what you're worried about. He's a good kid."

"I shouldn't have come. I met your brother. I just needed—I don't know—I needed to tell Laurel something."

"My brother's the one who always gets his heart broken."

"Thank you for the ride." She stepped out. "Stay there. I'm not going to faint again. The heat." She tossed off the excuse as she walked away.

Jud stared at the closed front door and thought that was one worried mother. The golf cart hummed back through town. Who was this girl Cale was involved with? His brother's girls were always trouble. He supposed he'd get an idea tonight. Dinner would be his opportunity to watch her closely, to see what kind of daughter this emotional woman raised. Back home, he parked the golf cart in the driveway. His brother was so stupid when it came to women. Same old pattern, he thought, then he heard the phone ringing and ran for the house.

Tonight Laurel and Jud would meet, and Cale was feeling anxious. He didn't know which was more important: what Jud thought of Laurel or what Laurel thought of Jud, of him, of the Bannings. He didn't analyze why it was important. It just was. Maybe all of it was important.

At half past five, they walked in the front door. Laurel stood in the open room looking around while Cale slipped off his jacket and hung it on a chair. In all the years he had come into this house, he had never thought of what it looked like through another's eyes.

Outside the wide windows, the weathered dock and blue-gray water stood off in the distance. That was the best of it. Nondescript pieces of furniture here and there. Ceramic lamps with white shades that disappeared against the same-color walls. An ugly starburst clock hung between a few metal-framed blurry black-and-white photos of Catalina fifty years before. The house was bland, flat, and unimaginative, as if it were designed by the kind of person who ordered vanilla ice cream when there were thirty-one other flavors.

Nothing of them was there. Not a single photo of Jud, Victor, himself, or of any people for that matter, and he wondered if that in itself didn't say what was wrong with the Bannings. He was suddenly self-conscious, feeling as if he were empty and nothing, and she would see that and not want him anymore.

He'd been inside Laurel's house one afternoon, where there had been photos in frames on the walls and tables, pictures of her from when she was small, with her mom, her grandmother, her aunt, with friends. Her life caught in single snapshots. He had relaxed in a comfortable chair in the small living room, drinking a Coke while she'd changed clothes. The lamp on the table next to him had been clear glass and filled with hundreds of seashells. Later she told him that she and her mother collected those shells, which were cracked and chipped, the kind that washed up on the shore, instead of the highly polished perfect ones anyone could buy in gift shops near the California beaches.

Her mother's wild pottery had been everywhere, on shelves and against walls that were the same yellow as a new Corvette. The room had fresh flowers in crazy-formed pottery vases on every table, and the whole place smelled clean and sweet the way women did.

Inside his dull island house the only thing Cale could smell was gym socks and beer. Two empty Coors bottles were on the table, his old tennis shoes under it. Yet standing in the middle of the flat landscape of his life was a wonderful girl, wearing a pink fuzzy sweater and tight yellow pants, a brightly printed scarf and dark pink lipstick. The two visions were linked in his mind: his monochrome life and Laurel standing there in full Technicolor. He had the strongest urge to wrap his arms around her and hold her until that color became part of him, too.

"Where's your brother?"

He looked around. "I don't know. He's here some-where. Jud!" He headed for the kitchen, then out back. The deck was empty and so was the dock. The boat had its canvas cover snapped in place.

"Cale," Laurel called out. "I don't think he's here."

A yellow smiley-face magnet held a scribbled note to the fridge.

> *Called back home on company business.*
> *Apologies to Laurel about dinner.*
> *Enjoy the steaks.*
>
> *J*

"I guess you won't meet my brother tonight. I'm sorry."

"That's okay. I'm sure we'll have another chance to meet."

"Actually, that apology was for me. Jud was going to cook. If I have to barbecue those steaks we're in trou-ble."

"Since one of us is training to be a chef, I expect that's a nonsubtle hint." She opened cabinets and the refrigerator, pulling out jars and spices and more, then pointed at a high cabinet near the stove. "Can you get that bottle for me, please?"

"This one?"

"Thanks."

He leaned against the counter, watching her.

"You're in the way." She shooed him away from the range.

He moved behind her and slid his hands over her. "I need to do something useful."

She turned around right into his kiss. After a couple of minutes she pulled away and rested her forehead against his chest, her breathing rapid. "This scares me, Cale."

"Don't be afraid."

"Be easy with me."

"I won't push you." He wanted to make her happy, to make her love him. She gave meaning to an empty dark place inside of him, a place that could all too easily pull him down to where he had to face all the wrong choices he'd made. He rested his chin on her head and could smell Prell shampoo and something sweet and rare like wild island honey.

She didn't move immediately, but seemed to be sorting out things for herself. When she stepped away, she was smiling and happy, no worry in her expression. He exhaled a breath he hadn't known he'd been holding.

"Ever heard of steak Diane?"

"No."

"Well, get ready because you're going to get to know it intimately."

"Sounds good. I like watching you work."

"You've got it wrong." She slid her arms around him and tied a silly red apron around his waist. "You'll know it intimately by cooking it yourself."

"I burn toast, Laurel. I'll screw up those steaks."

"I'll stand nearby with the fire extinguisher."

"But you're the chef."

"Stop whining. I can cook. You're the one who needs lessons. So, here are our new roles: I'm going to teach. You're going to learn."

He laughed because she was laughing. Laurel was

fresh air in a stale and airless room, and as she stood behind him, tying a ruffled apron around his waist, Cale knew cooking wasn't the only thing she was going to teach him.

Kathryn lay on her bed with her arm over her eyes as she had on that singular night thirteen years ago. But in her hand was a yellowed newspaper clipping.

Heir to Banning Oil Dies in Accident That Kills Rock Guitarist Peyton

Rudolph Victor Banning and his wife, artist Rachel Espinosa Banning, were killed in an auto accident in Los Angeles Friday night. Witnesses said Banning's car, a 1956 Ford Fairlaine, ran a red light and hit a Chevrolet station wagon driven by the manager for rock guitarist and recording artist Jimmy Peyton. Both the manager and Peyton died at the scene. Also in the station wagon were three members of Peyton's band, the Fireflies— Bobby Healy, Howard Went, and John Massey, who were treated for burns and are in serious condition.

Witnesses reported that Banning's car sped through the intersection and hit the gas tank of the station wagon, which burst into flames. Heir of oil magnate Victor Banning, Rudy Banning and his wife are survived by their two young sons, ages eight and twelve. Peyton, a Seattle-based musician whose recordings have topped the music charts, leaves behind a wife, Kathryn Fleming Peyton, and a four-year-old daughter.

The children weren't named. In those days, journalists protected the innocent. She understood that Laurel, Cale, and Jud were the true victims of that senseless accident. If she wanted to tell Laurel who the Bannings were to the Peytons because her daughter needed to know the truth, well, that was very different from telling her daughter only because she wanted to keep her away from one of the Banning sons. Truthfully, she was scared about any boy Laurel fell for. Was a Banning worse?

Yes. The answer came so fast it was sheer instinctive reaction—all emotion, no thought. But only a fool could separate herself from that night and the deep pain it brought. What was fair to her daughter and Rudy Banning's sons?

Kathryn had trouble thinking in terms of fairness. She wanted to hide Laurel away from Cale Banning. So what if Jud Banning had been kind to her? She didn't want to like either of the Banning sons. What would she have said to her daughter if she had actually found them when she ran up and down the streets so panicked? Would she have jerked Laurel away, then looked at the two of them—both innocent, both victims—and said, "Cale's father killed your father"?

The answer to that question became clearer hours later when Laurel knocked on Kathryn's bedroom door. "Mom? Are you awake?"

Kathryn ran for the bathroom and shut the door. Her face was red and blotchy from crying. She could hear

Laurel come into her room and an odd sense of panic came over her when she remembered the box of newspaper clippings on her bed.

"Mom!"

"Just a minute!" Kathryn walked out with white cold cream on her face and a towel in her hand. "What's wrong?" Her voice sounded surprisingly calm.

"Nothing. I just wanted to say good night."

The room was dark, but light from the streetlamp limned the shoe box lying open next to her glasses and the scattering of newspaper clippings on the disheveled bed. Kathryn crossed the room and began to gather everything up before Laurel saw it. She could feel her daughter watching her. "Look at this mess. I was reading some old articles on glazes." She shoved everything into the box, then into the closet.

Laurel seemed to be searching for words, and when she spoke, they came out in rush. "You liked Cale, didn't you, Mom?"

His father was drunk and killed your father. Laurel needed Kathryn's approval, something she could never give. "I don't know him well enough to like him or not."

"That doesn't sound good."

"He's nice-looking and made you laugh, and—I don't know . . . he's fine." She faced her daughter. "What do you want me to say?"

"Now you're getting mad."

"I'm not mad. I just don't want to make any quick judgments. It's not fair to you, to me, or that young man."

"Can't you just be happy for me?"

"Happy because you just met him?"

"No."

"You met him when?"

"Saturday."

"This is Wednesday. You've known him four days?"

"Five. But we're already making plans to see each other when we go back to the mainland. Loyola isn't that far from the school or from my apartment."

Kathryn wanted to scream, Get away from him! But Laurel had lost that hollow look, one Kathryn knew all too well. Did it really matter who made her daughter happy? She was so damned conflicted. But instinct told her to chose her words carefully. "I'm not trying to criticize or ignore your feelings, but I don't want to see you get hurt."

"Why would you just assume he's going to hurt me?" Laurel looked upset. "Why are you so sure he's going to dump me?" Her words held all the insecurity of a girl who thought she wasn't good enough for someone to love.

"Oh, honey, that's not what I meant at all. Any boy would be lucky to have you. He's going to medical school in the fall. From everything I hear, medical students don't have much spare time."

"I hadn't thought about med school being something that could mess things up." She looked thoughtful and Kathryn had no idea what she was thinking until Laurel asked, "How do you know when you're in love?"

Was Laurel already in love? Was the dewy film over her eyes, the flush of her skin, her wan manner tonight all signs of honest love? Kathryn felt her blood run hot. What the hell happened on that boat? *You let her, Kay. You let her. Children are innocent of the sins of the father.* Her head was filled with a kind of white noise.

"Never mind." Laurel turned away, her shoulders hunched as if she had been struck.

"Wait!"

Laurel looked back.

"I could tell you that you're too young to know. But you're not." Kathryn spoke from her heart instead of her fears. "I could tell you that you haven't known Cale long enough. But I fell in love with your father in a week." She said no more.

"That's it?"

"I don't know what else to say."

"You didn't answer my question."

"There's only one answer." Kathryn put her arm around Laurel's shoulders and walked to her bedroom door, then told her what she believed to be true. "When you're in love, you won't have to ask me. You'll know it."

CHAPTER

14

April mornings in Newport Beach dawned deep and buttery, as if created by Maxfield Parrish. For Jud, looking out at that golden clarity was part of home. He'd learned to appreciate the Newport house, its uncompromising geometry and minimalist style, expanded over the years into a monolith of glass on the waterfront. With straight lines and wide-openness, the house appeared simple, completely opposite from the complex man who lived inside. It was Victor who had called him back to the mainland, the phone conversation calm and unemotional, a reminder that he'd been the last one to lose his temper.

Jud heard a door close upstairs and checked his watch: 7 A.M. Like clockwork. A few minutes later, he picked up his coffee and took a sip—a distraction when Victor walked into the room—but cold coffee was about as hard to swallow as his pride.

"Let's talk in the study." His grandfather walked to the kitchen door without waiting for an answer and told Maria to bring breakfast into the other room.

Jud dumped his coffee into a potted cactus and poured a fresh cup first, not willing to trail behind, dog-like, and dig the hole deeper. His grandfather hated sycophants and yes-men.

When he walked into the study, Victor said, "I've had seven phone calls from board members since Friday. You called them all."

"Because you told me to find out about Marvetti, and isn't it strange that I haven't gotten one return call? Good stonewalling." He raised his mug in false bravado, while his grandfather's silent presence ate up space. Some people walked into a room and faded into it, some faded before ever coming to the door, and a few, like Victor, owned a room, any room. Jud knew he was not one of the few. But he wanted to be.

"Sit down." Victor tossed the *Los Angeles Times* across the desk. "Read page two." He added another newspaper. "Page five." Another one. "Page three." Another. "Page one."

He'd made his point. Every story broke the fresh news on the investigation of Marvetti Industries, from tax fraud to illegal ties to the mob, and as Jud read each one, his stomach felt like he'd swallowed a rock. He set down the last newspaper. "I'm an idiot."

"If you were an idiot, you wouldn't be working for me."

Jud had no response.

"However"—Victor leaned back in his chair—"every call to a board member showed your vulnerability. You followed up one mistake with another."

"When all I had to do was wait and read a newspaper?" Jud laughed without humor. He hated failing and dealt with it badly, because his life had been a series of successes—school, sports, summer work, college. After grad school, he'd come on board as if the company were a large campus. What had always worked for him before didn't anymore, and he decided at that moment to stop trying to set the world on fire.

"What do you want, Jud?"

"To run this company."

"You don't cut it and I can't advance you."

"I never asked you to push me ahead. No one would respect me. That's something I couldn't stomach." He needed to prove he was something—not Victor, but a different kind of man.

His grandfather was watching him. It was a morning for revelations. He had come into this room—had come back home—fully expecting to see disappointment in the old man's eyes, not something that looked like pride. "I intend to earn my way upward. If you give me something, I'll deserve it."

"The good old Puritan work ethic?" Victor laughed. "Doesn't work, son. The words 'earn' and 'deserve' have no place in business. If you want something"—his grandfather shrugged—"just take it."

Then Maria came in with breakfast and effectively silenced them. Victor had just told him what he wanted him to know.

Cale woke up to the phone ringing. He pulled the receiver to his head, still half-buried in a pillow. "This had better be important."

"Get your head out of the pillow, lazy ass." It was

Jud, Mr. Sunshine. "Tell me again how you make it to your classes every morning?"

"I don't have any classes in the morning." Cale yawned and stretched, still fuzzy and warm with idle solitude. "I schedule them all in the afternoon and evening."

"Did Linda miss me last night?"

"Screw you." Cale sat up. "You know her name. Laurel doesn't know you. She can't miss you. We loved your steaks."

"Well, looks like you'll have Lori and the food all to yourself. I'm not coming back. Victor's leaving early next week and there's too much to do here."

"How is the old shit?"

Jud's laughter came through the receiver. "Surprisingly human."

"Interesting. That's a side I don't see."

"You might if you came home more often."

"Yeah, well, I'll leave Victor to you. You're the one who has to work with him, not me."

"If you don't get into med school, you'll probably find your butt working here, too, buddy, so don't get too cocky. By the way, I've found a summer job for you."

Cale stifled an automatic groan and ran a hand through his hair. Last summer was hell. For three months he worked two offices away from his grandfather, who ran him ragged and never failed to let him know what he did wrong. Most of the time he'd felt like a monkey tied to an organ grinder. Or ball grinder.

"You there?"

"Yeah. I'm here. What kind of job?"

"One far away from the offices. We're taking delivery

on a fleet of tankers. You can drive them in from the factory. A job out from under Victor, where you'll get at least three days off a week. I figured you'd want time off to play with Lucy."

Cale laughed with relief. Sometimes his brother was okay. "Thanks, Jud."

"Sure."

And they hung up. Jud had run interference for him. It was a pattern: Victor-Jud-Cale, Cale-Jud-Victor. Jud stood between them like the Berlin Wall. Cale knew his relationship with his brother was complex, bound by blood and bone and mystic tissue, alike but so different, with Victor pulling them apart and pushing them back together in the oddest but most consistently inevitable ways. He loved Jud but felt deep, invisible scars because he couldn't be like him.

An intense sinking feeling swept over Cale. His hopes and dreams lay before him but looked so far, far away. Med school was fading, the edges of a dream disappearing in clear morning light. He hadn't told Laurel his fears, failures, and doubts, and couldn't. Not yet. He wasn't sure where he stood with her and felt they were on the edge of something, but still a precarious edge. Too many things were crumbling under him. He needed to know something in his life was solid.

The rejections filed through his head in a mantra of mistakes, exhausting him with hard reality, so he lay back down, pulled his pillow over his head, and escaped in sleep.

Friday afternoon, Jud was checking over some figures for a meeting with the finance officer when Victor's secretary called and said his grandfather wanted to see him. He stopped outside Victor's office and sat on the corner of her desk. "How's the weather in there?"

"Clear and sunny, but he's meeting with Rosen in half an hour. It might not stay that way."

"Do you know what he wants?"

She shook her head. "His attorney just left."

Jud went inside and Victor shoved some papers toward him. The documents confused him. "What's this?"

"Just what it says. I'm giving you twenty-five percent of my stock."

So much raced through his head, but all he could say was, "Why?"

"Still worried about earning things? You don't think you deserve it?" Victor handed him a pen. "Sign the transfer and tax papers, and don't ask why."

Jud scribbled his name on all the marked spots and gave his grandfather the papers. But his heart was racing and he couldn't shake the feeling that this was wrong somehow. His brother's face flashed in front of him, his expression frozen when he found out Jud got the MG. *Shut up and take it.*

Victor glanced up. "That's it. You can go."

"I need to talk to you about something." Jud stayed in his chair.

"What?" Victor dropped the report on his desk.

"Cale."

"What about him?"

"He can't get into medical school."

"His own fault."

"You can fix it. A couple of phone calls will get him into USC."

Victor didn't deny it, but Jud could see the wheels turning. Finally he said, "Cale hasn't proven to me he's cut out to be a doctor."

"He made a stupid mistake. You're not going to get perfection from him."

"All I want to see is some amount of control."

"Cale wants to be a doctor. He always has. You know that."

"He got into this mess all by himself."

"He knows that."

"Why should I bail him out?"

"The same reason you gave me the stock."

"And that is?"

"You wanted me to owe you something."

Victor sat back in his chair, thoughtful, then said, "I expect you to not make the same mistake again. Cale jeopardizes his future every time a girl comes sashaying into the picture. He almost didn't get into college. The cheerleader? He has no learning curve, just a pattern of wrong choices."

"Yes, he screwed up, and women are his weakness. But if Cale didn't have such a high draft number would we even be having this conversation?"

"I don't know." Victor's voice was sharp and aggravated.

Jud knew how his grandfather felt about the war. Right now, Cale had almost no chance of being drafted, but if he'd had a low draft number, Jud was pretty certain Victor would pull strings to get Cale into med school. "He scored high on his MCAT, Victor."

His grandfather was silent again and Jud just let him

mull it all over. He'd learned some ways to get what he wanted.

"Why all this sudden concern for your brother?"

Jud didn't answer quickly, but waited before he told Victor what he wanted to hear. "Because if he doesn't get into medical school he will have no choice but to come into the company."

"Worried about the competition?"

"I just don't need the aggravation."

Victor studied him for a long time, then said, "I'll think about it."

Love was on Laurel's mind as she checked her makeup and hair in the mirror. Her mother's answer—that she would know love when it happened—answered nothing. Her mother still mourned her father. Was that true love? Or a complete inability to move on? Elusive love. Something everyone talked about, wrote about, wanted, lived for, mourned, yet no one could really define. Eskimos had hundreds of different words for snowflakes, and yet only one English word existed for love. Would true love just hit her suddenly, or creep up like some dark, liquid alien in a B movie, invade her body, and nothing would ever be the same again?

Maybe she would never fall in love. Maybe she was in love. She gave up and turned out the bathroom light, then headed down the hall, but heard her mother on the kitchen phone and stopped shy of the door, listening.

"I'm sorry. I just can't make it after all."

Silence.

"No," her mom said in a low, firm tone. "I know, but

I can't change that. Good luck, Stephen. I'm going to hang up now."

Laurel heard the soft click of the receiver on the wall phone. When she walked into the kitchen, her mother was dumping a vase of half-dead daffodils in the trash. "Who's Stephen?"

"No one." Her mom set the vase on the tile counter and walked past her carrying the trash can, then cast a quick glance at her and said, "What?" in an annoyed tone.

Laurel remained silent.

"Stephen Randall is just someone from the Chamber." She closed the door harder than normal and a minute later Laurel heard the rattle of a metal trash-can lid in the side yard.

Just then, the doorbell rang and she left with Cale. It was Saturday, and tomorrow they would go back to the mainland on the afternoon boat. Monday, life would begin again, and she and Cale would fit together into each other's old lives.

Across the street she turned back and saw her mom standing in back of the house, watching them, her face and stance unreadable. For a crazy instant she wondered if her mother was envious. Something was wrong. The sharp, monosyllabic answers. Her mother's complete inability to just look at her and smile. Instead, she studied her through troubled eyes, like she was afraid. But Laurel wasn't frightened or scared. She was happy. Finally.

"You okay?" Cale took her hand and she felt that light, queasy feeling, that rush of excitement. Her body came alive.

"I'm fine." Laurel smiled up at him and didn't look back. She'd had her time with her mother. Her lifetime up till then. This was time for Cale and her. This was time for happiness. This was time for love, at last. She was almost certain.

It was late afternoon, but difficult to gauge time by the light coming through the windows of the deserted Golden State Tire building. The glass panes were foggy and ancient; it was like looking through skimmed milk. Traffic from the Santa Ana Freeway, only a few hundred feet away, sounded loud in the vast emptiness of the ground floor, where concrete was too hard to absorb noise. The old freight elevator came to a screeching halt and Victor stepped inside.

On the top floor, he unlocked the loft doors with the anticipation of a man obsessed. Too many emotionless years had passed. Months sped by without him ever coming to the loft. He wasn't even sure when he'd last been there. But the painting was delivered yesterday.

At first, all he saw inside were shadows of huge canvases, until the flick of a switch flooded the rooms with too-bright fluorescent light. Painting after vibrantly colorful painting lined the walls. Too often in the past, he had walked in and expected to see Rachel standing there, commanding attention, wrapped by her work and a crowd. The scent of Arpège was sometimes all too real to him. Perhaps that was why he'd stayed away, just to prove he could. He owned all of her paintings but two. In life, he could never own a single cell of her.

Rachel hadn't liked him on sight, which made her more evocative. A woman who was all light and flame was wasted on his son, a dreamer and a failure. The fire in her was so strong it should have burned her right up. Instead, she burned the men who helplessly loved her, who were bewitched like moths to the flaming sparks of passion all around her.

He was one of them. Rachel Espinosa entered his flesh and blinded him with an intensity that damaged the soul, even though his had been damned long before he ever met her. A black obsession overtook him and nothing mattered, not even that she was his son's wife.

Unpredictable, wild, Rachel was that and more, and some part of him needed to see if he could control her. She struck him breathless, with an alchemy of passion and lust and addiction. Rachel was the one woman he had ever loved. Her elusiveness and mystery fueled the challenge he used to select the women in his life.

He wanted someone who didn't give him a second look. With every elusive woman he conquered, Victor gained what he couldn't in his childhood. He won. He couldn't stay away from Rachel then any more than he could stop his obsession with her paintings. His obsession grew into a living, breathing thing. Throughout the years he stayed away from her for long periods of time, not because the flame burned out but because she scared him, and he needed some control.

She never needed to tell anyone her secrets, least of all him. But Rachel had reasons for everything, dark soul that she was, a powerfully mystic creature who rose from the darkest depths of existence, and no one could read her miasmic thoughts.

Life changed when the truth came out: she and

Rudy were dead; the boys came to him. He saw something of himself in Jud, but Cale was all Rudy.

The temperature in the loft was constant, the air perfect for storing Rachel's work. Victor studied the newest painting. It leaned against a far wall until it could be hung. He moved forward and back, looked at it from all angles, but saw no answers there. Rachel was as unreadable in death as she had been in life.

His thoughts spun back in time, to her face and her voice, to her standing there with an odd, Cimmerian expression, and still, to this day, he would have liked to have heard why Rachel waited so long to tell him that one of the boys was his son.

CHAPTER

15

Loyola University Graduation

It was the third day of a hot spell—something that rattled the natives—so they flocked en masse to the sempiternal beaches of the Pacific, or to the Angeles Forest, where mountain lakes ran cool and clear. On that unquenchable weekend in late May, the families of graduates—those kids schooled as Kennedy's new generation of Americans and now Nixon's lottery draftees—sat on hard folding chairs inside the confines of rumbling college campuses and sweltered.

Jud was running late when he pulled the MG into the crowded Loyola University parking lot, so he parked on the grass and ran, shrugging into his suit jacket. Over the speaker system came the names of the graduates. Near the chapel stood the stage and troops of chairs, the families seated behind rows of black-capped graduates.

"Cutting it close," Victor said when Jud found him.

"Traffic," Jud lied.

A sudden swell of laughter rolled through the crowd,

reaction to a streaker running between the students and the podium, wearing only a cap and all his naked, youthful glory, his hair and face sprayed the school colors. Every grad came to his feet, whistled, and cheered, and the streaker stopped, made an exaggerated bow, and fists raised in the air like a champion boxer, he disappeared between buildings, just ahead of the security guards.

"Tell me that's not Cale," Victor said.

"Can't be." Jud laughed. "There's no girl running ahead of him."

Victor eased back in his seat. "No need to move, my dear. Jud will take the seat next to you. This is a friend of Cale's."

Looking as fresh-faced, striking, and delectable as she'd been on the boat, Jailbait sat next to Victor. First she frowned—she'd obviously heard the exchange about Cale—then appeared as confused and surprised as he was. The clean, fresh smell of her—flowers, candy, and innocence—hung in the torpid air. He sat down hard, but spoke casually. "Laurel, right?"

She looked as if to speak would be a complete disaster, but any number of emotions came over her expression in waves, and her face was reddening. The image of her flaming face at the snack bar came back to him. Her hurt expression when he walked away from her. The sound of crying as she ran down Crescent Street.

"You're Jud?" She found her voice.

"I'm Jud." He started to take her hand but stopped. He couldn't touch her. Victor was watching them. His brother was an idiot. The last thing Victor needed to see was Cale with a girl. And Cale's girl was Jailbait? Hell, the whole day was screwed.

"You look so familiar." Her voice was light; she wore a pasted-on half smile, her eyes dark with meaning beneath a small crease between her brows.

"Cale and I look a lot alike." Jud leaned forward. "All the Banning men look alike." He tapped the program against his leg. "So. You're Laurel. Cale talks about you all the time."

"Does he?" Victor and Jailbait said in unison. She laughed, but Victor didn't. Damn his brother. . . . Damn, damn, damn. It shouldn't matter to him who Cale was falling for. But he cursed his brother for exposing this of all girls to Victor.

Laurel. The name fit her. Long ago, they gave wreaths of laurel branches to poets, heroes, and the victors of athletic contests, as symbols of glory and the crowning prize for the winners.

"You know, I can't help feeling as if I've seen you before," she said casually.

"I don't think so. You're probably thinking of Cale."

She was quiet for a few long seconds, then said, "Wait . . . I know. You look like a fighter I saw once."

Jud laughed out loud, and remembered why he'd first liked her. "I've walked into a few fights."

Feedback spiked out from the speakers. At the podium, they were trying to get some kind of order back in the ceremony, and the chancellor began calling names. When his brother hit the stage, Jud cheered, then said, "Cale said there's a three-hundred-dollar pot going around for the first person who mooned."

"Thank God your brother didn't." Victor was serious.

Laurel looked stunned. "Cale would never do that." Jailbait knew his brother better than his own grandfather, and Jud wondered just how well Cale knew her. It bothered him, this girl and his brother, and for lost minutes his mind went somewhere else.

To overloud applause, Will Dorsey bounced up on stage as if it were a basketball court, inches of his bare legs showing below the gown. He'd do it, Jud thought. He'd moon. He'd flash.

Behind them, Mrs. Dorsey said, "Oh no . . . Someone stop him."

Will took his diploma, walked down the steps, unzipped his gown, and jerked it open with a broad grin. A loud cheer went up. Dorsey stood on the bottom step, wearing basketball trunks and his uniform tank; a placard with big letters spelling DIVISION CHAMPIONS hung from around his neck.

Time moved glacially as the sun bore down onto Jud's head. His sweat was like clothing, covering most of his skin, while thoughts of the girl next to him became a treacherous road his mind had been down before. Victor was talking with her, and it was like watching the spider with the fly, she innocently answering his grandfather's questions about Cale and not knowing that every word was a nail in her coffin.

The graduation finally ended with an abrupt swarm of caps sailing in the stagnant air and enough noise to make the ground shake. Cale came loping up. Victor shook his hand, one palm on his shoulder. "You made it." At least Victor didn't sound overly surprised.

"I made it," Cale said flatly and turned away. "Jud!" He grabbed him in a bear hug and they beat each other on the back.

"Congratulations." Jud ruffled his hair and Cale

swiped at him. "I'm glad it was Dorsey who pulled that prank and not you."

"Yeah, well, I figured you couldn't take it if I did."

"Good thinking," Victor said. "Those classmates of yours are your future. Business connections that could be for life. Years from now you'll be remembered as someone they respected, not the class clown." He was perfectly serious.

Jud exchanged a look with Cale, while Laurel still stood to the side, and Jud thought they must be an odd sight, a family run by a man who had so much and gave so little of himself, and who wasn't exactly the life of the party. Together, none of them were. Too much tension. Too much unsaid. Too much that wanted to be said but never was.

"So what do you think of my girl?" Cale wrapped his arm around Laurel.

Victor merely looked at them. The lapse of silence was not for the faint of heart, and Jud thought Laurel was holding up well.

"Your grandfather and I have been having a nice chat." She smiled up at Cale, their arms linked around their waists, and Jud had to glance away. He looked at everything but what he wanted to look at.

"Yes. We have been talking," Victor said in a tone Jud recognized. But Cale was so high on the day and the girl, he didn't have a clue anything was going on. The dark undercurrent of Victor was there, as dangerous to Cale and this girl as black ice, but then Jud had always been able to see their grandfather clearer than his brother.

"Everyone's heading over to the reception at the

Bird's Nest." Cale checked his watch. "We should go. After that, we have a round of parties."

"When do you have to be out of the dorm?" Victor asked as they walked.

"Tomorrow." Cale and Jailbait held hands, his brother looking down at her often enough to make watching uncomfortable. His brother was in love, and this time Jud's urge was to protect the girl.

Inside the reception, Jud stood in line at the wine table but really wanted something harder to drink. Victor was talking to the chancellor. Cale and Laurel still stood by the door inside a knot of students, most of them lanky members of the basketball team and their dates. A few minutes later Jud settled in behind them. "Laurel?" He held out a plastic glass. "I thought you might like a white wine."

Cale saw him first. "Thanks, Jud." He leaned over her and said, "See? I told you he was okay. Take it. Go on."

She hesitated, then took the glass without looking at him.

Cale laughed, misunderstanding, and squeezed her shoulder. "Laurel, Laurel," he said. "No one here cares how old you are."

The look she exchanged with Jud said it all. And his brother stood there completely in the dark. For a minute, part of Jud was unbelievably angry, yet he knew he had no right to be. That she was with his brother was some kind of stupid fluke. She was just a girl in a world of millions of girls. She was jailbait.

For some perverse reason, he couldn't walk away and stood there longer than he had any right to, talking with Cale about anything he could come up with, watching her because something he couldn't name made him stay. And when she and Cale finally left to celebrate, he followed them to the door, the jolly big brother, and stood there until there was nothing to watch but the empty horizon.

Jud lay in bed that night, the heat and still air creating the kind of dead silence that made sleep impossible. The sky outside his window was moonless and black, the room dark, but Jud knew he wasn't as much in the dark as was his brother. Wisely, Laurel had said nothing, but had looked like a deer caught in headlights whenever he was nearby. Her face and anything else about her should have been none of his concern. Victor, however, was everyone's concern, or should have been. Cale was a fool to believe it would be different this time. Someone had to save her.

"Not me," Jud vowed. "Not me." She was Cale's girl and his brother's newest complication.

Cale was wildly in love, blinded with it. Laurel came into his life at a time when his future had been whittled down letter by rejection letter. When he'd finally summoned the courage to tell her about the rejections, she hadn't thought less of him. She just believed in him. He couldn't believe, so he clung to the girl who could. To be near her and not touch her was agony. An uncontrollable compulsion made him have to watch her, and he always wanted her. It was constant and much more than passion, an innate driving need, as if she exuded something chemically that was impossible for him to resist. The imprint of her body against his stayed with him. At night, he closed his eyes and saw her image as clearly as if in photogravure. Nothing, it seemed, could dull the intensity of Laurel, who had seeped deeply into his tissue until he was incurable.

Together they left the last graduation party on foot, stumbling from tequila shooters, beer chasers, and too much celebration. It was 4 A.M. when they wobbled arm in arm across the grass toward the dorm.

"You drank almost as much as I did tonight," he said.

"Did I?"

"You're supposed to hold me up."

"I am," she said, and he caught her before she fell, both of them laughing like fools. He held her to him and should have recognized the sudden ticking sound, but in an alcohol fog, he merely stood there, looking around.

The sprinklers came at them from six sides. Laurel screamed and tried to drag him away. Hell, it was probably still close to eighty outside, so he pulled her down to the wet grass and they rolled, she screaming, then laughing, each trying to soak the other, kissing sloppily as the sprinklers rained heavily over them and their laughter died.

Wet, muddy, and green, Cale lay on his back, mouth wide open.

Laurel sat up on one elbow. "What are you doing?"

He waited for the sprinklers to pass, then sent a thin stream of water straight up into the air a good two feet. "Spitting water."

"I can do better than that."

He laughed. "Yeah? You're on. Strip spitting."

Laughing, she fell back, took in a mouthful of water, and beat him by a good five inches. "I grew up in Seattle. Take your pants off."

When they were down to their underwear she stood, grabbed her clothes, and ran.

"Wait! You lost!" He went after her, letting her beat him up the stairs of his building.

Inside his apartment they were alone, standing in the dark, the moving boxes stacked like towers around the place. Once they started touching, kissing, he couldn't stop. He never could. Her taste, her skin, her breath all drove him to the edge. She was afraid of going all the way, afraid to let him inside. Even in bed she would stop him. She always stopped. Always. But tonight she didn't.

With school over, Cale could no longer hide in his dorm. Back at Newport, it felt strange to see his grandfather for two days in a row. Avoiding him now wasn't going to be easy. Cale could sleep in and miss breakfast, but not dinner. Tonight, Maria had made tamales and mole, because they were his favorites. With his grandfather's indigestion, the smell was probably enough to put him in a shitty mood the moment he walked in the door.

The old man wasn't scowling when he walked down the hallway toward Cale, sitting in the living room drinking an icy beer. His brother was out, so it was just the two of them home that night. Cale was apprehensive, ready for their usual conflict. But he watched his grandfather, maybe with clearer vision because the emotional scale between them was level. They hadn't had a fight yet.

Victor's hair had grown whiter since Christmas, his face more tanned. The lines of that face were familiar;

he saw them every time he looked at his brother or in the mirror. Clearly, he was looking at himself forty years away. It struck him then that his grandfather didn't move like a man his age. His stride was firm, his shoulders straight, and his step determined. Victor Banning moved like a man who had somewhere important to go.

"Cale," his grandfather said curtly. Like a summons. Or a reprimand.

"Victor."

"Glad to see you remembered where your home is."

"It's good to see you, too." Cale swore he would not get into an argument on the first night home.

His grandfather sat on the sofa and crossed his long legs. It was seven at night and the old man had been working all day, yet he didn't look like it. His hair was in place. He was wearing a silver gray custom suit, paired with a white shirt as crisp as if it had just come out of the laundry box. His cuff links were lapis and he wore a blue silk tie. Victor handed him an envelope.

The return address was printed in the left-hand corner in raised letters: *Keck School of Medicine of USC.*

God . . . They had screwed up and sent the rejection letter here. Cale unfolded the letter, hating the fact that Victor had gotten it before he did, and hating more that he knew what it said. His stomach was somewhere near his throat. This was Cale's deepest shame, exposed to the man who would never let him forget it. His dream would die here and now, and his uncertain future would be sealed.

War raged in Vietnam, stiff-shouldered generals and military advisers were on the nightly news, talking about body counts. Youth rioted and marched, fled the country, and raged at the unfairness. You couldn't legally drink a beer, but you could die for your country. Worse yet, you couldn't vote against the man who sent you to die. In the freest country in the world, no freedom existed for its young men.

"Are you going to sit there, or read it?"

The words on the page were sharp and clear, and all Cale wanted to do was close his eyes. His sorrow at that moment was almost too much to take.

> *Dear Mr. Banning:*
> *We at Keck School of Medicine of the*
> *University of Southern California are happy to*
> *inform you . . .*

In his hand was his acceptance to the University of Southern California medical school and the future he'd had thought he'd lost. Cale felt himself getting emotional. Dammit . . . He could just imagine what his grandfather would say to him if he broke down.

"I made a few calls for you."

The elation he'd just felt, the emotions, the relief, the small inkling of pride—all sank like his stomach. Victor had pulled some strings—or worse yet, written a check—and now he was in. His grandfather wanted him to know he hadn't earned this. The urge to tear the letter up and throw it in his grandfather's face was so strong his hand shook.

"It's yours, Cale. There's your ticket in." Victor studied him in that uncomfortable way—as if Cale were steeped in formaldehyde and Victor held the dissection knife. "There is one condition."

Cale almost laughed. "Of course, there's a condition."

"No girls, Cale."

"It's med school, not the seminary."

"You know what I'm telling you. That's my condition. Take it or leave it."

"You're serious?"

"Perfectly serious."

As usual, Victor had found a way to control him, and a bright red rage hit Cale in his center. "You expect me to be a eunuch?"

"It's medical school. I doubt you'll have much free time. You can sleep with as many girls as you can find the time for, but no getting involved with one girl. No girlfriends. Like the one I met the other day."

His anger was so strong he didn't dare speak.

"If I'm going to put my name on the line for you, you're not going to fail. Every time a girl comes into your life, Cale, for any length of time, your life falls completely apart."

"You old bastard." The letter started to crumple in his fist.

"We'll find out how badly you want to be a doctor." Victor was sitting there as casually as the devil leaning against the gates to hell. "There's no option here. If you want med school, you'll give up your weakness for women and your recurring habit of throwing away your life for some bit of tight pussy."

The words printed on the top of the letter blurred together. Those were the words Cale had wanted to read for so long and the only door open to him. He couldn't close it. Not even for his empty, beaten pride. He slowly smoothed the wrinkles out of the letter and put it back

inside the envelope. He saw no stamp or postmark on
the envelope.

Victor's face was unreadable, his eyes always sharp
and penetrating. They gave away nothing but said everything. Something smoldered in his grandfather, something deep and intense. If you split the man open, Cale
wasn't certain whether he'd bleed fire or ice. Then Victor shrugged as if nothing about Cale was important to
him. As always with Victor, this was a test. "Do you
agree?"

"Yes, I agree," Cale said, knowing he was lying.
Because of Laurel, because of the other night, because of
a thousand cracks in his faith and self-worth, it was a
promise he would never keep.

Laurel walked through the front door of the Planned
Parenthood clinic in Santa Monica and faced a surprisingly empty lobby. Behind a large glass window, a receptionist sat talking on the phone. Nervous, Laurel
adjusted her purse, feeling as conspicuous as huge Alice
in the tiny rooms of Wonderland. The woman opened
the glass and pointed to the sign-in sheet, then went back
to her call. Laurel signed and sat down on a small aqua
chair next to a table with women's magazines fanned
across it.

There had to be some kind of universal rule that
medical lobbies must all look the same: flat, earth-toned,
speckled carpet; leatherette seating on cold steel legs done
in colors from a past decade; and tables made of sawdust,
glue, and photo paper. The rooms typically had an
unreal, movie-set quality about them. So she sat there, as
uncomfortable as the furniture and left to distract herself

with magazines about child rearing, something she was there to prevent.

"Mrs. Peyton." The receptionist stood in the door.

For just a confused instant Laurel thought the woman was looking for her mother. She recovered quickly and followed her down a narrow, warrenlike hallway where the sharp static sound of their shoes on the linoleum matched her heartbeat. The end of the hallway opened up to a larger waiting room with more Naugahyde furniture and bright lights. A woman sat feeding a baby, with three more small children playing on a braided rug in front of her. A young, nervous couple huddled in the corner whispering, and a woman in her forties never looked up from her issue of *Good Housekeeping*.

"Here." The receptionist handed her a clipboard with a black pen chained to it. "Fill this out. No rush. We're running behind today." She disappeared as fast as the White Rabbit.

Laurel filled out the forms with a combination of truths and lies, and wrote the word "cash" in the insurance box, then balanced the clipboard on her knees and tried not to appear nervous. Getting the pill wasn't easy. She'd been warned. There were girls who'd tried and were told no, and to change their sexual habits. Or worse yet, their family doctors called their parents. With her mother acting so dour, so strangely, she didn't want to face that possibility.

An hour later, she was sitting on an exam table with stainless steel stirrups bolted to the end, trying to stay covered in a crisp paper gown the size of four napkins. The door opened and a small, older woman in a lab coat with a stethoscope around her neck came in with Laurel's information sheet and a plain manila folder. "Hello, Laurel. I'm Dr. Davidson. What can I do for you?"

"I'd like to see about getting birth control pills."

The doctor looked at the chart, then up at her again. "You're twenty-one?"

"Yes," Laurel lied.

"Your husband?"

"Vietnam." Her smile felt frozen. "But he's coming home next month."

"Care is free for military families at the military facilities."

"I'm more comfortable with a woman doctor."

After silently taking vitals, the doctor stepped back. "I'll need to do a pelvic exam." The doctor called in a nurse.

Laurel had never had the exam before and lay there, wincing, nervous as she stared up at nothing but the cottage-cheese ceiling and wished the exam would go fast. It didn't, it hurt, and it took forever. She gripped the side of the exam table and closed her eyes.

"Breathe," the nurse said softly. "Just relax."

Laurel wanted to laugh at the impossibility of that. When she opened her eyes, the nurse was watching the clock and wore a look of panicked boredom that said she had a million things to do other than this. No kindness in her, or much understanding in the expression of the doctor examining her.

Was it censure Laurel saw, or was she imagining something that wasn't there? She closed her eyes and just clung to the table. By the time the exam was over, she was half crying.

"You can sit up now. Everything seems fine." The doctor spun away from the stirrups on a rolling stool and the nurse rushed out before the doctor's gloves hit the trash. She made a few notes on the chart and handed Laurel two pink, plastic, pearlized compacts wrapped in plastic and some glossy brochures. "Here are some pill sample packs and information on side effects and venereal disease. You should get in the habit of taking the pill at the same time every day so you build up a routine, either morning or at night. Some women keep them by their toothbrush.

"You'll probably gain a little weight and your breasts will be tender at first. You could have some spotting and you might not bleed the first month or two. These are all normal responses." She scribbled something, then tore it off a pad and handed it to her. "Here's a prescription for ten additional months. Call if you have a problem."

The doctor left her alone, covered in napkins and now painfully aware of the scientific, colder side of love. But the pills were what she came for. Uncomfortable, she dressed quickly, paid cash, and walked outside, where the world looked real again. Hot air and traffic. Sound.

She told herself it was the quietness inside there that bothered her. She dropped the round plastic pill containers and prescription into her purse, and ran down the front steps and out into the sunshine. The bus stop was only a block away. She could ride free all day; it was her eighteenth birthday.

CHAPTER

16

By August, the summer invasion on the island was at a high, and there were more mainlanders per square foot than locals. The same slow, dreaming languor that enveloped the islanders, making them reluctant to leave, drew visitors with manic lifestyles and demanding jobs that lasted more hours than they slept.

After escaping to Avalon, the men fished and lolled in cool dark taverns watching baseball games and drinking beer. Wives and mothers basked under the summer sun, their skin turning the color of wild honey, while their kids played with bright plastic buckets in the sand and along the soft, foamy edges of crystalline blue water. This time of year, the air on the island smelled of Coppertone, cocoa butter, and tourism.

In one two-day period that week, Kathryn sold over five thousand dollars of her work, which filled the front shop and lined the shelves of her studio and the storage room. Last night, like most nights, she immersed herself in her work, using it to purge some of what twisted her all up inside.

Since spring, she couldn't sleep for more than two hours straight. To not tell Laurel about the Bannings was a constant weight, always there, a stone in her shoe she couldn't shake out. So Kathryn knew the sunrises as well as she knew the sunsets. Her new work reflected the dusk and dawn colors of the island, and form came from the dark recesses of an insomniac.

It was afternoon when she moved four pieces from the kiln onto the racks in the back room. A gallery had called her earlier in the week, not about her pieces, or she wouldn't have returned the call, but because someone wanted the Espinosa paintings sold years before to Julia. Kathryn could never allow them in her small house, where like bad fruit they could rot her home from the inside out. Instead they were wrapped and stacked against a far wall of the storage room, barrels of clay and tubs of chemicals for glazing stacked in front of them. There she could forget they existed. But today she couldn't walk by. She lifted the wrapping from one corner. The front painting was the slashed one.

At times like this, when tragedy came roiling back at her, triggered by fate, she doubted she could ever get away from its pain. The past was there, lying in wait every hour of a lifetime, and it came back to remind her that her joy and future were fossilized decades ago in asphalt on some street in Los Angeles.

"Hey, Mom!"

Kathryn covered the painting and entered the studio. Laurel stood by the open door in hot pants, fishnet hose, and a clingy, sheer popcorn top. She'd filled out in the last months, her lankiness turning into sweet curves and her bust now as lush as her grandmother's. The changes were unsettling, because Laurel hadn't been home in weeks.

"Cale's flying in. I need to meet him at the pier in a few minutes." Laurel paused, unable to look Kathryn in the eye, and added, "I just wanted to tell you I won't be home tonight."

"What do you mean you won't be home?" The images in Kathryn's mind sent red flags everywhere. They were sleeping together, a fact that Laurel just used to draw a line between mother and daughter.

"I'm staying with Cale." Laurel stepped outside to leave.

"No." The word was out before Kathryn could stop it.

Her daughter turned around. "Yes. I am." Her expression turned mulish. "I'm eighteen."

"Your age isn't what I'm concerned about."

"What are you so afraid of? You can't keep me close to you forever. I can't be your whole life, Mom."

Was that what Laurel thought she was doing? Kathryn had to bite her lip to keep from telling her the truth. "I don't want you to get hurt."

"So you've told me again and again."

"Think about what you're doing, Laurel."

"No, Mom. No. I don't want to think about life. I want to live it. I'll see you tomorrow sometime." She left.

Kathryn couldn't move or speak. Her arms hung heavily at her sides, and she couldn't pull her gaze away from the empty spot where Laurel had stood seconds before. The begonias and impatiens hanging near the door looked absurdly happy. The roses on the wall trellis were thick and fertile. They should have been wilting. The petals should have been falling and turning brown at the edges.

When she thought about Laurel with that Banning boy, she could almost smell the choking smoke of a destroyed future. Everything, everything she had ever wanted for her daughter was slipping away.

From the seaplane window, sail- and powerboats dotted the harbor as if pieces on a game of Battleship. Luxury yachts, crisp and white, moored outside the snug confines of a half-moon bay flanked with staggered hillsides of stucco homes and ironwood trees. Here and there on the sand, umbrellas cast the image of crouching starfish, and huge striped beach towels spread out in a pattern of solitaire. Near the shoreline, the water was so clear you could see the ocean floor from the air. The entire landscape looked as if it came straight from somewhere in the Mediterranean.

The plane touched down and skimmed the water, motoring up to the pier on pontoons. Cale hadn't seen Laurel in almost a week, because of their conflicting work schedules. She stood on the pier, waving, but he would have spotted her even if she were deep inside a crowd. He grabbed his bag and jumped to the pier. She ran into his arms and kissed him. He dropped the bag. "That felt like longer than a twenty-five-minute flight. I've missed you, babe."

"It's only been four days."

"Five, and we've been playing tag most of the summer."

Her school's internship program had kicked in a week after the term ended and she was working at a chic French eatery in Westwood, the kind of place that was booked weeks in advance and where even Johnny Carson couldn't walk in and get a table. Meanwhile, Cale had been driving tankers along desolate Highway 5 with nothing but the CB radio and an eight-track tape deck to keep him from going nuts.

"I didn't know the internship was going to start in June, Cale. The opening came up and I couldn't turn this down." She sounded defensive.

Cale didn't blame her, or didn't think he did, but knew he resented her work. "I know." He put his arm around her as they walked. "But I start school in two weeks."

"You want school."

"No." He laughed. "I want to be a doctor. School's the requirement."

They passed the candy shop, with a huge taffy wheel in the window, and Cale made a sharp turn, pulling her with him.

"What are you doing?"

"Buying you some taffy."

"No. I've gained too much weight from the pill."

"You look great."

"You just think that because my clothes are a size too small. I'm not Corkie," she snapped.

"Okay, okay, don't get all pissed off." They walked silently all the way to the house. Cale unlocked the door. Her attitude set him off. Inside, he dropped his bag. "I'm getting pretty tired of hearing about my old girlfriend from you. What's the deal?"

"Are you trying to pick a fight?"

He thought he was the one who should be asking that question. She was edgy, touchy. He put his hands on her shoulders and looked into her troubled face. "Is something wrong?"

"My mom doesn't like the idea of me staying over."

"You're old enough to make that choice."

"She's my mom, Cale. In her eyes I'll never be old enough. But she knows now. And I don't care." Her face said she did care.

"Come here. You're plenty grown up for me." He whispered against her lips, "I want you," knowing he needed to persuade her to forget about her mother and to think only about them. He wanted her so badly and touched her in the places he knew made her melt, then watched her sink slowly under his touch. Something inside his head warned him—he was playing her to get what he wanted, but he didn't care. He needed this.

It took Jud only half an hour to get from the steamship to the Island Market, then to the house. He used his key to open the front door, dropped his duffel on the floor, headed toward the kitchen with a bag of groceries, but stopped in the doorway, seeing Cale with a half-naked Laurel pinned on the empty counter, her arms around his neck, her head thrown back, and his brother's mouth locked on her breast. Her hand was massaging deep inside Cale's jeans.

To see her with his brother shook Jud's world, shattered that dark place where he hid his deepest, most secret desire. For a brief moment he tried to pretend what he was seeing was nothing. He didn't want to feel anything, but he did. He wanted to tear his brother away from her. Every breath he took smelled and tasted scorched.

She looked lost in an earthy passion as she jerked Cale's T-shirt up, her hands all over his tanned back, until she broke their mouths apart with a moan to get the shirt over his head. She glanced over his brother's shoulder and saw him in an instant of absolute silence— empty, eerily quiet, but teeming with something vital— the kind of silent stillness that comes just before the biggest earthquakes.

"Oh, no . . ." She shoved his brother away and tried to cover herself with loose pieces of clothing.

Cale stumbled back. "What the hell?"

She was struggling on the edge of the counter to get her shorts up. Cale whipped around. "Jud? Shit!" He pulled up his jeans and fumbled to get them together. "What are you doing here?"

"Watching the show. This is better than a stag film."

"Shut the fuck up, Jud."

Laurel zipped her shorts, her face red as a tomato, then she looked down and silently began buttoning up her shirt.

Jud held up the bra. "You lost this."

Cale grabbed it. "Get out of here."

"It's nice to see you again, Laurel. All of you." Jud's voice was controlled, low, and calm, but his hands were shaking. He was consumed with a red and helpless rage, and all he wanted to do was hit Cale.

His brother came at him. "Stop it!" Cale grabbed Jud by the shirt.

"Let go of me." Jud was so close to losing it. "Now."

Laurel stood in the center of the kitchen, sliding her sandals on. "I'm leaving."

Cale let go of Jud. "No. Don't."

"I'm going home." She walked past them both without looking at them.

"Babe, wait!"

"Let her go," Jud said tightly.

Cale looked at him, then rushed past him. "You asshole."

It took only two strides and Jud grabbed his brother, jerked him back, then swung him around and pinned him against the wall with his forearm against his neck. "I said, let—her—go."

"No!" Cale tried to shove him away.

Jud pressed his forearm deeper into Cale's throat. It was so easy.

"Let me go after her, you dick." Cale's voice was strangled. He struggled, then pulled Jud's arm out from between their bodies and shoved him backward into the dining room chairs. "I want you out of here."

By the time Jud scrambled up, his brother was out the door and gone.

Laurel ran all the way home, taking different streets so Cale couldn't follow her. It was dusky out, not dark enough to hide. She wanted the ground to open up and swallow her. As she rounded the corner of Descanso, the streetlight came on. She raced to the house, stopping just before she hit the steps, using the open gate post to steady herself, then pressed her hands to hot cheeks burning from her own foolishness. All she heard was a ringing in her ears and the pounding of her own heart.

The front porch light was off, but the lamp in the front window was on. She wondered if her mother was still mad at her. What would she say when she walked in?

"Laurel?" Cale stepped out of the shadows between the houses. He was breathing harder than she was.

She turned away. "Oh, God, Cale. Not now. Go home. Please."

He grabbed her arm and turned her around. "Come here. I'm sorry, babe. I'm so sorry. Jud was an ass. I don't know what happened. Maybe he was drunk. Something was wrong. That's not like Jud."

She couldn't tell him she'd met Jud before, and it was becoming her habit, running away from his brother crying and humiliated. Cale tried to pull her into his arms, but she shook her head. "No, please."

"Are you mad at me?"

"I'm mad at myself." The disgust in her voice was hard to miss. It was crazy, this tilted world she lived in. The night air was warm, yet she was shivering, and afraid her teeth would start chattering any second. To her horror, when she took her next deep breath, she began to cry.

"I'm sorry, baby," Cale whispered. "I'm sorry." His face looked panicked. She gripped his shirt in her fists, sobbed into his shoulder, and couldn't stop. Clearly he didn't know what to say or do. It was an immensely awkward moment.

"I don't understand why he was even here," Cale said, as if he were talking to himself.

"Did he know you were coming to the island?"

"We didn't talk this week. But he'll leave." Cale's expression became hard and determinedly thinned. "I'll make certain he's gone. I won't let him ruin the little time we have left together. " He tilted her face up to look at him.

He had the kindest eyes. She remembered thinking that when she first met him. This was a man who wouldn't hurt her.

"I love you, baby."

"I know you do." When he told her that, she felt safe. Someone loved her.

"I have an idea. We'll take the runabout out tomorrow and have lunch at the Isthmus. Okay?"

She nodded.

"Your mother's standing in the window."

Laurel turned and looked, but didn't see anything but the soft yellow light from the lamp.

"I saw her in the back of the room."

Was her mother there watching them now? She had changed that much? Now she was sneaking around to watch them. What happened to the mother she could talk to? What happened to the mother who didn't judge her? "I'd better go inside. We had a fight earlier."

"You're okay now?" he asked.

"Yes." But she was lying. What happened tonight embarrassed her terribly. She had seen a black side to love. It wasn't this beautiful thing that made you fly. It wasn't about the heart. Tonight it was about shame.

"I'll pick you up in the morning. About ten." With a quick kiss and a wave, he walked away.

Laurel closed the front door and faced her mother, standing in a dark corner of the living room.

"What did he do to you?"

"He didn't do anything, Mom. He loves me."

"You were crying. I saw you."

"I know, but I'm okay now. I don't want to talk about it. Please. I'm home tonight. I didn't stay over. You should be happy."

"Laurel please . . . What's happening to us?"

"I'm tired, Mom. Good night." Laurel closed her bedroom door without another word. She didn't want to talk. She didn't want to think. She didn't want to feel. She just wanted to go to bed.

CHAPTER

17

On the eastern side of the Isthmus, lofty date palms lined up like arborous soldiers along a pale, sandy beach, guarding the sleepy blue cove and its long, rustic pier and outbuildings, some dating back to the Civil War. Speeding there in Cale's runabout did much to recover Laurel's wounded spirit. Enfolded by the panoramic vastness of that blue, blue water, everything else in the world seemed suddenly inconsequential.

They picnicked near the water's edge, and ate well—curry chicken sandwiches, crab-stuffed deviled eggs, and peanut butter brownies, foods she'd prepared early that morning—and swam until Cale spotted a leviathan hammerhead, then there was nothing left to do but loll in the sand like indolent sea lions, overly drunk on the sweet addiction of spicy food, sex, and summer sunshine.

It was close to four when they sped around the point toward the cove house. Cale stiffened at the wheel, suddenly looking around, then quickly powered down and sagged back against the seat, swearing.

"What's wrong?"

"Victor's here."

"Your grandfather?" She looked at the silent, crouching house. "Are you sure? I can't see anyone."

"Oh, I'm sure. Look." He nodded south toward a white yacht anchored near the opposite point.

"My God . . ." Laurel looked at him in shock. "It must be close to a hundred feet."

"A hundred and ten." Cale brought the boat closer to the house, where she spotted a white and blue launch docked, the kind luxury yachts carried to motor in from deepwater anchorages. Cale laughed bitterly. "Victor doesn't do anything in a small way." He pulled in behind the launch and cut the motor as she tied off the lines. "We've got trouble, babe." His tone alarmed her.

"Do you want me to leave?"

"I don't know." Cale paused, searching the landscape. "It's too late for that now."

The low roof and planes of the house spread out in wings from a whitewashed deck, where his grandfather—casually dressed in nautical red and blue—stood in relief. In less time than a heart could beat, a riptide of suppressed emotion charged the air, and the world became all too complicated.

"Should we wave?"

"Maybe my middle finger."

"Cale," she whispered. "That's awful."

"I have a feeling you're about to see awful."

"Why? Did you two have a fight?"

"No, but we're about to." He took her hand. "Come on."

Victor Banning let them come to him, standing stone still and so intimidating. Was he even breathing? This was a man who gave little away. "Hello, Mr. Banning. It's good to see you again." She didn't move closer. Victor Banning was not someone you wanted to hug.

"Laurel." He nodded sharply. "I need to speak with Cale. Alone."

"No. She stays."

"Do you think if she stays, I won't talk to you about the reason I'm here?"

"I don't think that for a minute. I want her here. This concerns her. Right?"

Cale's grandfather looked at her. The hard edges in his face melted some. "This is not about you, my dear."

"I think maybe I should leave you two to talk."

"No." Cale wouldn't let go of her hand. "This is because of our past, not you."

Victor directed his words toward her. "I pulled strings to get Cale into USC, Laurel, on his word he would concentrate on school."

"That's not true." Cale was angry. "He said school or a girlfriend. Not both. He made me choose between med school and you. That's why he's here."

Something vital drained out of her. The acrimony between Cale and his grandfather made each breath taste rancid. Cale's hand tightened its hold on hers in a white grip, but even with the bright afternoon sun beating down on them, even with him touching her, she felt a chilly isolation.

"He made me choose two days after graduation," Cale said.

Laurel understood then. His grandfather wouldn't know that that was after they had first made love.

"Whenever Cale has a girl in his life, his grades go down the drain. He consistently chooses women over responsibility. This is medical school. There can't possibly be time for a girlfriend. I'm sorry, Laurel, but you are detrimental to his future."

Overhead, the strangled cries of the gulls seemed like good timing, since there was nothing left to say.

"I won't walk away from her, Victor."

His grandfather grabbed Cale's arm. "Listen to me. I bought your way in and I can buy your way out. Choose. You go back with me now, or you go with her."

What kind of anger and jealousy made men see things in only black-and-white—all or nothing? Neither of these two men seemed able to acknowledge that most of life could be shades of gray. Laurel turned to Cale. "I won't be the reason you don't become a doctor." She pulled her hand away and stepped back, using distance as her armor.

"Laurel, don't." Cale's voice shook with emotion when he reached out to her. She couldn't look at him, and didn't want to look at his grandfather.

"You won't make the right decision, Cale. I have to," she said, and just walked away, so simple an action, so easy, but it wasn't until she was on the road where the gravel crunched brokenly beneath her feet that she realized she was crying.

* * *

For long seconds Cale couldn't move. Laurel's words played out in his mind, one at a time like beads on a rosary. Anger and humiliation and something empty—that she could walk away—left him unable to think clearly. He stared at the place where she had just stood, dumbfounded and aching.

"Well, I guess there is no choice to make." His grandfather hadn't moved.

"I have to talk to her."

"Leave her alone. She's a smart girl. Let her find someone better for her."

Cale rounded on Victor. "I'm not going with you unless I can talk to her, dammit!"

"You have no bargaining power." Victor laughed sarcastically. "I'm making the decisions. Would you really throw everything away now? She left you pretty easily, Cale. You realize that, right?"

Victor could wound with such casual ease; he honed in right to the place Cale was the weakest.

"I'll give you five minutes, then I'm taking the launch back. If you aren't on it, no school."

Cale ran after her. "Laurel! Wait!"

She turned, walking backward and holding her hands up. "Cale. Don't do this. Go back." She was crying. "You have to go back."

The harder he ran, the louder she was shouting, "Go back! Go back!" But he caught her and pulled her against him, holding her even though she hit his chest with her fists. "Don't. You can't do this. You can't do this!"

"I love you. I love you." He leaned down and whispered, "Don't leave me. Don't leave me." He knew when she sagged against him he had a chance. "Listen. Listen to me, baby. There's no way Victor can know what I'm doing at school. We'll be careful."

"You already tried to sneak behind his back and he found out. You never told me, Cale. You hid that ultimatum from me, yet you say you love me?"

"I do love you. I wanted to protect you. Medical school isn't just my future. It's our future. Promise me, Laurel. You have to promise me."

"Cale. Look at the last two days. My mother. Your brother. Your grandfather. The world is trying to tell us something."

"What? That my brother and grandfather are assholes?"

"Maybe we should listen."

"Can you really walk away so easily? I can't, Laurel. I'm willing to fight for you. Today was beautiful. I can't forget it."

"I never thought love could be so hard," she said. They ached together in cloudless gray silence. He understood she must feel the immense, unbearable reality that everyone was against them.

"Trust me." He tilted her chin up so she had to look at him. "School starts in two weeks. I won't be able to see you at first, but I'll call you. We'll wait. We'll be patient. We'll pretend. We'll be smarter than he is. Once I'm there for the first year, he can't stop me. They won't kick me out. I'll have proven myself. I'll get the grades. You can't leave me. I need you too much. We can do this."

"I don't know what to do, Cale."

"Let me handle my grandfather. I have to go back with him. Before I go, tell me you won't leave me."

She seemed to be searching for something in his face, but she took a deep breath and said, "I won't leave you."

"You swear."

"I swear."

"Smile for me, Laurel-Like-the-Tree Peyton, smile for me and tell me you love me."

"I love you."

"Me too." He let her go. "Remember. Me too." He ran back toward the dock and could hear the putter of the boat engine. His tennis shoes thudded on the boards of the dock as Victor drove the launch alongside, almost like he was taunting him. Cale took a huge leap and landed so hard the boat rocked and tilted. He had to grab the side to stay put, and water sloshed up on the deck and soaked Victor, who powered up the boat and headed for the yacht.

Cale boarded the *Catalan* as fast as he could get away. Her diesel engine was running, and he heard the anchors coming up. The two-hour cruise back to Newport would be an interminable hell.

He was already drinking a beer in the salon when Victor came in. "You're a fool, Cale. You thought you could sneak around behind my back? You think I don't know anything about your life?"

He wondered why Victor gave a damn about any of this, including his life and his future, when Jud came up from the cabins below. It didn't take a rocket scientist to understand what had happened. "It was you. You told him about Laurel, didn't you? Damn you, Jud."

His brother didn't deny it.

Cale was so pissed he threw the beer at him and missed, then dove for him and punched Jud hard three times before his brother connected one. Cale tasted the salt of blood in his mouth, tackled Jud, and they rolled across the floor. Cale had him by his hair, pounding him.

Jud caught him with an upper cut, locked his legs around him, and flipped him on his back, so Cale hammered his knee up blindly and nailed him in the kidneys. They rolled into the glass table. The lamp tilted, hit the floor, and shattered next to Jud's head. At one point Cale heard the crew, glanced up as they ran inside, all talking at once. The first mate grabbed his arms. Another grabbed Jud, which helped . . . Cale could knee him in the stomach.

"Stop!" It was Victor's voice.

The crew held them by their arms, so they used their feet. Every foul word Cale knew spilled from his tongue. For every one he shouted, Jud had another more vile one.

"Stop holding them!" Victor shouted this time. "Get back to work and let them fight it out."

Suddenly released, he and Jud tumbled to the floor. Victor stood there like God, watching them beating the crap out of each other. Cale turned back to tell Jud to stop and look at the old bastard, but his brother's fist nailed him on the chin, and everything went black.

During the early weeks of fall, Laurel talked to Cale every night. But with six technical lectures a day, he began to miss nights and often fell asleep on the phone. It became okay not to talk every day, every night, so she worked the dinner shifts at the restaurant and came home after eleven smelling like the night's special.

Soon it was routine: home, shower, phone, bed; life became all about brushing her teeth, grating nutmeg, creating béarnaise sauce, and doing her laundry. She didn't think about the things that seemed so important mere months ago. She didn't wonder about true love and all its mysteries. She didn't go to bed on dreamy what-if's, and when she walked, her feet were planted solidly on the ground, none of that floating along on sheer adoration. No tender mist softened her gaze when she looked in the mirror; everything was sharp, hard, and real.

A rare week arrived when she pulled two golden

lunch shifts in a row, but Cale had lectures both nights, so she came home at four in the afternoon reeking of rosemary, onions, and salmon. Not five minutes later, the doorbell buzzed. Jud Banning leaned against the porch post as if he'd been there for a while. "Jud."

"Laurel." That was all, and the moment stretched out between the two of them, neither moving nor speaking, curiosity and expectation as taut as pulled taffy. "Are you going to make me stand here?"

"I should close the door in your face."

"Probably." He placed one hand on the door frame and looked down at her. His aftershave was English Leather, his sport shirt laundered in Tide, and if she hadn't known better, she might have thought she could smell trouble in his blood.

"Why are you here?"

"I want to talk to you about Cale." On the surface he was cocky and all Jud. Beneath she saw the truth: his frustration, the underlying jitters of someone unhinged. Cale told her they hadn't patched up anything, and when he spoke of Jud, it was with bitterness that echoed more empty than angry.

"Come on in."

He stood in the middle of her small living room, taking up too much space. "Nice place."

"It's a rental apartment. It's all beige."

"I like beige. Too much color makes me nervous."

"I didn't think anything made Jud Banning nervous."

"Then you don't know me very well."

"No. I don't." She didn't want to see him as human and vulnerable. It was better if he was something else altogether. "You want something to drink?"

"Scotch would work."

"I have a bottle of wine, but I'm not offering it," she said in a cranky tone. "I can't buy alcohol. Remember? You can have lemon or peppermint iced tea"—he made a face—"sparkling water, root beer, or Coke."

"I'll have a root beer. Got any ice cream?"

"Yes. You want some?" She opened the refrigerator and took out two long-necked bottles of root beer.

"It was a joke, Laurel."

She popped the tops off and handed him a bottle. "With you it's hard to tell when you're joking."

"I'm lucky to have any sense of humor with Victor for a grandfather."

"Cale's always funny." *Why did she do that?*

"Yes. He is. Has been since he was a little kid." Jud paused and took a drink. "How is he doing?"

"You could ask him yourself."

"He'd have to return my phone calls. I stopped by the dorm, but he's always gone. We haven't heard from him since he packed up and went to school." Jud laughed. "Two weeks early."

"What makes you think I've heard from him? Your grandfather set down the law—he doesn't want me to see him."

"I know my **brother.** He's not going to do what Victor wants."

"And if I have seen him, are you going to tell your grandfather?"

"I'm sorry you were caught up in that." He didn't sound sorry. It had taken time to forget the look on his face that afternoon in the kitchen. Even now, she could feel her skin flush. She picked up the food cartons she'd brought from work and put them in the fridge. "Your grandfather threatened to have Cale thrown out of school anytime. Apparently if you have enough money, you can make someone's life or ruin it."

"Victor would run the world if he could."

"Hand me those last two cartons."

"What is this? Chinese food? I thought you were a chef."

"Well, well . . . You're moving up a notch. You didn't call me a cook."

He finished the root beer and set the bottle down. "I had nowhere to go but up."

"That's true." She opened one of the cartons. "We make experimental meals like this. One of the perks of my job is free food. Chicken ballotine. Sausage and corn-bread-stuffed onions. Fresh river salmon poached in white wine. Julienne carrots with haricots verts and wild mushrooms. Sliced Anjou pears in kirsch and honey cream." He was looking at the food with the same starved look of the rangy dogs at the back door of the restaurant kitchen. *Don't do it, Laurel.*

He took a carton from her. "It smells incredible."

"There's enough for two."

"Are you asking me to stay for dinner?"

"You don't have to."

"I want to."

"Okay. Set the table." She dropped two plates in his hands and put the food in bakeware to heat in the oven, then set two wineglasses on the table and uncorked her precious imported bottle of Pouilly-Fuissé.

"You don't have to open that for me."

She pulled out the cork and sniffed it. "Oh, that's

nice. I'm opening it for me. If you behave, I might let you share."

Dinner was surprisingly comfortable. He was interested in her life, her choices, and her work, and told her funny stories about his antics with Cale. But when the phone rang, the silence between the rings felt louder than the phone. They both knew it was Cale, who sounded exhausted. She felt horribly guilty and staggered her way through a quick conversation, with his brother sitting three feet away.

The moment she hung up Jud said, "I'm not going to say anything to Victor. Cale's dream is to be a doctor. Hell, I'm the one who asked Victor to help him get in."

"You?" It just came out that way, surprised and accusatory, all in one loosely spoken word.

"I love my brother, Laurel."

"Maybe you should tell him that. It could help. I think the reality of school is a lot harder than he thought it would be."

"Ah, the assurance of youth."

"And you're so old."

"In some ways, I'm years older than Cale." His meaning was difficult to pinpoint. There were too many ways she could take that, some dangerously suggestive. She wondered exactly what he'd meant.

"I came here to find out if he was okay."

"He's exhausted, but he loves it." If that was why Jud had come, he had his answer.

"I'd better go." He stood and pulled out his car keys. At the door, he stopped. "Since my pigheaded brother won't call me, would you mind if I call you to check up on him once in a while?"

"Sure."

"Thanks." He walked across the street and hopped in a great little classic red MG, waved, and drove off.

She slept like a log that night and right through her alarm. When she left for work the next day, a large box wrapped in glossy white paper with a big red bow sat on her front porch. Inside was a case of expensive French white wine with a handwritten card.

> *Dear Jailbait,*
> *Thanks for not throwing me out on my ear.*
> *This is for you. So you won't have to lie again*
> *about leaving your license at home.*
> *Jud*

It was another week before Laurel could meet Cale. He didn't want her riding the bus. Although the campus was safe, the surrounding areas weren't, so they chose to meet at the beach.

His truck pulled into a lot and Laurel walked away from the sand. "Well, hello, stranger."

"Hi, babe." His voice was raspy and sounded just as tired and wrung out as he looked—older and thinner, his hair dull and his skin sallow. He hadn't shaved. She was caught off guard when he kissed her hard, harder than she expected or wanted. She couldn't breathe and tried to move, but he pinned her against the fender, her protest muffled by his tongue. When he finally pulled his mouth away, it was only to say, "I want you so badly."

"Cale. Wait."

"What?"

"We're in public here. Come on." She straightened

her clothes, annoyed. His hands had been everywhere. He looked at her like, What's wrong with you? She pulled him toward the blanket spread on the sand. "I packed dinner for us."

"I don't want food. I want you."

"You look like you need food more than you need me. You've lost weight."

He yawned. "I've been too busy to eat."

"When was your last meal?"

"What time is it?"

"Four."

"What day is it?"

"Wednesday." She laughed.

"I ate a banana last night. I think it was last night."

There were fatigue lines on his forehead and around his mouth and eyes, which were bloodshot. He wasn't walking steady and all but fell on the blanket, then lay there with his arm flung over his eyes. Within seconds he was asleep.

Awkward and alone, she sat cross-legged in the sand and watched the gulls overhead. Shouts came from a volleyball game down the beach, and a pair of black dogs raced to catch Frisbees in the air. Near the water, a couple—clearly in love—flew a kite in the shape of a dragon, the long dark green tail rippling over the surf. She wanted to feel that way again, laughing and playful. A cool breeze swept in with a wave. The salt air stung her swollen lips. She didn't like the way he'd touched her, as if love were a necessity instead of a gift. What was wrong? Was it him, or her?

Beside her, he slept soundly. She watched the rise and fall of his chest and remembered resting in his arms.

Today, his touch was brutal, not tender. Desperation edged in his voice and motions. This was not her Cale. This wasn't love, soft and sweet and forever.

She couldn't watch him sleep, this sudden stranger, and unpacked the food. Crab-stuffed deviled eggs, a loaf of fresh bread, some thinly sliced roast beef with slivered horseradish, and fruits with soft cheeses. She opened a beer and set it in the sand next to him. "Cale?" She shook his arm.

He jackknifed up. "What? Laurel?" He groaned, then just looked at her blankly. "Sorry."

"Come eat."

He wolfed it all down with no time for talk. But she didn't feel like eating anything and used her few bites to keep from having to say something. How odd that she had nothing to say to him. When had that happened?

Behind an amber sky, the sun balanced on the water, turning it deep purple and the breeze cooler. The air was thickly pungent with salt and seaweed, and the wind whipped up, spitting sand on them. He lay on his side, one arm propping himself up as he finished off his beer. "We should go soon."

"When do you have to be back?"

"Eight thirty." He yawned, then offered her his hand. "Come on. I'll take you home." A few minutes later they were in the truck, driving toward her apartment. He patted the seat. "Come closer, babe. You're too far away." He swung one arm over her shoulder, the other on the wheel, and the sky was a dark ink blue when they pulled up to her place.

"What time is it?" he asked.

"Seven twenty. Where's your watch?"

"I haven't got a clue. Somewhere between the labs, the library, and the lecture halls. Seven twenty? We have time. Let's go inside."

"Don't you think you should sleep?" She didn't tell him that she wanted to be alone.

"I need you, not sleep." He pulled her up the front steps and unlocked the door. Inside, he was on her in an instant, pulling at her clothes and sucking on her neck and mouth. She closed her eyes, scared, because she started to flinch at his touch. She couldn't breathe. She couldn't feel anything wonderful. He pushed her to the bed and was all over her, in her, on her.

He was on some kind of sleep-deprived edge. What he was doing to her felt panicked, so she lay there very still, and because she had loved him, let him take what he needed from her, while her mind said over and over, *This is not love, this is not love . . .*

It didn't last long. He fell off of her and onto the pillow, sound asleep in seconds while she lay there, an emotional mess. Love had been so easy before. Her passion was gone, lost, and could she find it again? She didn't melt at his touch. Yet he was wonderful, she knew that. What cold, frigid thing possessed her? Her love was suddenly a thin emotion, like smoke from an old fire that dissipates into the air.

At eight o'clock she woke him. From the front door she watched him drive away, aware she was glad he was gone, and wondered what kind of love can just suddenly stop. Maybe it was just time apart. Pressure? The weather? It was painful to think that maybe she needed to end it, and could not imagine saying good-bye to him.

In bed, she slept hard, woke up in a tight ball, her hands in fists. She stumbled to the shower on numb legs, and with the water running over her, she cried for no reason.

Cale studied until his neck ached, his eyes blurred, and his spine felt frozen into the shape of a comma. Through histology and physiology, he drank gallons of coffee and chewed peppermint gum to swipe the fuzz of caffeine from his mouth. He ran on Yuban and Wrigley's, thought axons and glutamine transferase.

Med school was hard—a phrase too simple to encompass his reality of it, which felt as futile as trying to write on water. Even the best instructors crammed every bit of information they could into a slim hour; it was too much to absorb, much less remember. On top of the lectures, labs, and impossibly confusing exams, the powers that be elected to introduce first-year students to clinical experience in a hospital setting at Good Samaritan, to learn from watching how things were accomplished—done well or badly—from simple to life-threatening.

His induction to the surgical ward was put in the hands of a third-year med student, a surgical clerk, with a voice like Minnie Mouse and the bright demeanor of a Miss America contestant. Cale's first visual lesson began with an alcoholic woman who lay moaning on a stretcher as a team of residents tried to insert a central line.

While Minnie narrated this wild ride, the poor patient had curled into a fetal position, dehumanized and still moaning pitiably, as the annoyed resident team concentrated only on the procedure and, once completed, on congratulating themselves. No one thought to touch the woman, the first lesson ingrained into the mind of a med student—make contact, find a reason to touch the patient, take their temperature, blood pressure, anything, but make that contact.

As the residents left, Cale took the patient's hand, brushed the damp hair from her face, and spoke quietly until the nurses took her away. He turned to Minnie: "I can't believe that."

"Wasn't that great?" she said, sans pom-poms. "I'm hoping to get to try one or two lines before I finish here."

I love medicine, whipped cream, and world peace, he thought, disgusted. The cold ugliness of that scene stuck with him all day. Later, he went to a meeting with his clinical tutor, Ed Strovich, a man he genuinely liked and respected. Strovich was standing at the elevator talking to a stout gray-haired woman in a housedress. Back in his office, Ed set down a tray piled with sticky baklava and pushed it toward Cale. "Have some."

"God, that tastes good." Cale ate two more pieces while he told Ed what he witnessed that morning.

"One of the great questions in medicine is how you, as a doctor, will choose to approach it. A couple of months ago, I had to run syphilis tests on that Greek woman who just left."

"She's got to be in her mid-sixties," Cale said. "It must have been a false positive."

"I asked her if she was faithful to her husband, and she swore in God's name she had been, so I asked about her husband, who'd had a stroke four years before and was impotent. I assumed the test was wrong, but before

I retested her, I asked her the tough question: if she'd been sexually assaulted."

"I don't think I would have thought to ask a woman in her sixties that question."

"Sadly, women are raped at any age. It's the hidden secret in too many retirement homes, especially state-run facilities. One thing about practicing medicine is it doesn't take long to see the underbelly of life."

Ed Strovich didn't sugarcoat medicine and didn't malign it. He just gave you the truth.

"She had never told a soul and was deeply humiliated. It happened right after they immigrated here from Greece. She barely spoke English, and was afraid of the police. In her heart, in her head, she wasn't unfaithful. I explained she would have to be retested after treatment. She cried then because she had no money to pay for the first tests, so I told her there would be no charge. She just brought me this." He pointed to the plate.

"Like the country doc paid in chickens and pigs."

"Who probably sleeps better than the rest of us. God knows he eats better." Ed leaned back in his chair. "You don't have to be like those men you saw today, Cale, although you'll get used to seeing that kind of medical practice first-hand. But you can be exactly the kind of doctor you want to be. The best advice I can give you is to try to light your own way."

Ed's words were the first positive ones he'd heard in weeks, and gave him some color of hope and a fresh enthusiasm for medicine, something outside of pancreatic acini and intestinal villi, for what he had always envisioned as his way of medicine. What he wanted to do, he could do.

Later that night, parked outside of Laurel's restaurant, Cale told her the stories and how he felt, the good and the bad. She was his sounding board. He wondered if she knew how important she was to him. He told her things he could never tell anyone else, because she wouldn't judge him.

"Do you think they treated that woman badly because she was an alcoholic?" Laurel asked him.

"I don't know. Maybe. Doesn't make it right."

"No. It doesn't." Her hand was bandaged. He hadn't noticed before.

"What happened?"

"I had trouble concentrating all day. I cut myself, burned the bread, and dropped the soup on the floor. I think Richard would have liked to get me as far away from him as possible."

"Well, I've missed you. Being without you is hell. But someday it'll all be worth it." He turned on the radio to a hit by Jay and the Americans. "Come a little bit closer," he said. "My nights have been way too long."

She moved over and he put his arm around her and began to whistle. He wasn't tired anymore.

"You're really happy, aren't you?"

"Tonight I am," he said. "I'm with you."

Back at the apartment, he carried the conversation for most of the night, telling her about his life at school and relating stories. She didn't talk much. He drank a bottle of wine that slowly put him at peace. He lay sprawled on the sofa, his head in her lap.

"This is our future, babe."

"Cale." She closed her eyes.

He touched her cheek to stop one of her tears from

CHAPTER

19

Laurel understood that the words *I love you* flowed all too easily from the tongue. To say *I don't love you anymore* felt impossibly hard. She had been so scornful of her mother. But now she was just like her mom—without the courage to say good-bye. Wrapped in the warm escape of cowardice, unable to tell the truth to the man who was asleep in her lap, unable to hurt him, she closed her eyes, exhausted by what she did and didn't feel, and when she opened them again, it was morning. She was alone on the sofa, covered with a soft afghan, and sat up, stretching like a cat, before she saw a crisp white note folded tent-style on the smoked-glass coffee table.

> *Sleep tight. Had to run to classes. Will call.*
> > *I love you,*
> > *Cale*

Just holding the note felt traitorous. She was momentarily overwhelmed by a crazy sadness she couldn't shake. Even in the morning, when things were usually clearer, she didn't understand her mixed-up feelings of love any more now than the day she met Cale. She looked down at the note and said out loud, "I don't love you. I don't even know what love is." But empty rooms had no fragile hearts to crush. Empty rooms didn't tell you that you were the reason they could follow their dreams. You could say anything to an empty room, even in the bright light of a new day, and it wasn't the same as saying good-bye.

The day passed with a gray heaviness; time just went on even though nothing was resolved. Cale did call the next day, but warned her he had finals soon, and if she didn't hear from him, not to worry. So his exam schedule gave her a reprieve.

Jud showed up at the restaurant one night for a late dinner and because it was raining, insisted on driving her home. At her apartment, he killed the engine. "How's my brother?"

"Heading into exams. Tired, run down. I think if you tried to call him now, you'd get through. I don't think he has the energy to be mad at you."

The rain stopped and she reached for her purse, and when she sat back he kissed her gently on the cheek in a brotherly way. "I'll call him."

Awkward and feeling all too warm, she left the tight confines of the sports car and could breathe again. "Thanks for the ride."

"Sure."

He didn't drive off, but sat in his car and watched her

go up the front steps. When she opened the front door and looked back, he called out, "Inside safe and sound, Jailbait." Then he waved and drove off, leaving her strangely warm and comfortable, snug in his casual protectiveness.

She grew up with no father who walked nearest the curb of the sidewalk, no father to hold her hand or carry her across busy streets, and learned childhood safety from women who were alone, not from a man's concern for hers. It was a gift she hadn't known she'd missed until that moment. With Jud she was a different person, not insular.

Walking to the bus stop the next day, she was aware of the scent of the air after a night of rain, the warmth and breadth of a giant blue sky, the feel of lazy wind on her skin, and the aromatic, citruslike taste of late fall in California.

Two days later the phone rang and rang. She expected Cale's call and would stare at the ringing phone until she found the nerve to pick it up. "I owe you dinner," Jud said.

She sank into the folds of the sofa, leaned into its arm, relaxed. "You gave me that case of wine."

"You don't want to have dinner with me."

"It's not that. You don't owe me anything, Jud."

"I hate to eat alone." Then he tempted her with impossible-to-get reservations that night at a new restaurant written up in all the LA food columns. "I'll pick you up at six thirty."

Banning men didn't take no easily.

Dinner was exceptional and they left the restaurant at nine. But once outside her apartment, they sat in silence, which was odd, since talked flowed so easily all through dinner. In the pale, true light of a half-moon and the false glow of the streetlights on the corner, shadow defined his angular features and light turned his hair a paler shade of gold. It struck her that Jud looked like a portrait of a man from the past—some aristocrat destined to ascend the throne—out of reach and the kind of man who could be dangerous to the heart.

"Thanks for the company, Jailbait."

"You know my birthday was back in May."

"So you're not jailbait anymore?" He shrugged. "The truth is I like the way you react to it."

"React? How do I react?"

"You get this look like you just ate a lemon."

"I do not."

"Okay, Jailbait. Pucker up and let me see."

She made a face at him and he kissed her quickly, just a soft touch of the lips, as if she were breakable. He pulled back and gave her an easy smile.

That was exactly why she thought he was dangerous. "Pretty sneaky, Jud. Does it work often?" She got out of the car.

"You think I would use a line on a woman now? In this time of great reform? Betty Friedan would cook my goose."

"Women might have changed, but men haven't."

He laughed.

She closed the car door. "Thanks for dinner. I had a good time."

"Me too." He waited till she went inside, and she was smiling when she heard him drive off.

* * *

Jud waited a week before he took her to dinner again. He tried for time and space and still couldn't stay away. They met at a small bistro in Westwood, ate *pintade à la Medici*—guinea hen stuffed with truffles, created for Catherine de Médicis—and Laurel explained the history of truffles when he teased her and called them fancy but ugly mushrooms.

"They couldn't be cultivated successfully, at least not the most flavorful, wild ones. Louis the Fourteenth commissioned a study on cultivating truffles. Some farms in France have used the same forest oaks to grow them, but the experts all claim the product inferior." She held up a fork. "These are the real thing: the flavor is as rich and dark as the forest where they were grown. You can taste the damp earth. Wild truffles from the forests of Périgord in southern France. Hmm. Taste it."

He had never thought fungi erotic.

"Hundreds of years ago, they used pigs to sniff them out. Now, I believe, they use dogs." She laughed. "It's probably easier to hold back a dog from gobbling them up than a pig." She popped a bite in her mouth. "They are quite the delicacy."

Throughout dinner they spoke in the gentle light of table candles flickering over her face. Her sleek brown hair touched her shoulders. She wore brown suede boots, a tight turtleneck sweater, and a long skirt with a slit almost to heaven. Her neck was covered and her thighs showed. When she left for a minute, then walked back to their table, he thought of her story of the dark truffle, thriving only in deep, damp forests where few men had cut a path. Rare, earthy delicacies that gave sustenance unique flavor. Laurel was a delicacy, a prize found only if you search the darkest forest, and her beauty was changeling, as if touched by each second of time passing, a hundred different looks, subtle, perhaps undetectable to most, but he caught the smallest nuance and thought he could fill a lifetime just watching her.

Tonight he saw the slow and complete abandonment of her fear of him. Gone was the wary look of an animal about to be cornered. Her manner was easy, her voice keen with natural emotion, no invisible barrier to protect her and keep him at bay. Every time he was with her, he was reminded that he had lived most of his existence in a man's world, where things were what they were. No women to give his life flares of emotion, highs and lows, and another pair of eyes, more sensually refined, with which to tenderly view the world around him. Later, Jud sat in his car studying her profile. It was difficult to look at her and not see what was missing from his life.

"Look at all those stars," she said, her head back against the seat. "When I was little, I used to sit in my grandmother Peyton's lap and she would tell me that the biggest, brightest star I could see was my father looking down at me."

He had to trace her jaw with his finger.

"What are you doing?" Her voice was charged, as if it was caught in her throat, shaky and vibrating.

"Touching you."

"That's dangerous."

"I know. The best kind of danger." He rubbed his index finger over her bottom lip. He was re-creating the delicate lines of her face on a blank page, or maybe tracing it into his memory.

"You're too old for me, remember?"

"I know, but I don't care."

She looked down, then pulled away, her hand on the door handle. "I'd better go."

"I'll walk you up." Once there, he leaned against the post and watched her.

Before stepping inside, she paused and looked at him. "I can't give you what you want."

He didn't push. He didn't speak. At that moment he felt what she was feeling, thought what she was thinking. The face he was looking down at was one that had haunted him.

"I'm sorry," was all she could say.

"I know you are."

"Good night."

"Good night, Jailbait." He walked away, courageous; it was such a hard thing to do when he was consumed with the most overwhelming feeling of regret. Inside his car, he just sat there, then glanced back at the closed door. Holding on to the steering wheel with both hands, he tried and failed to will away the longing, then put the key into the ignition.

Laurel stood in the kitchen, washing down three aspirin with a large glass of water. The knock on the front door startled her. She flung the door wide open.

"You shouldn't do that," Jud said.

"What?"

"Open the door like that. Someone could just barge in."

"Someone like you?"

"Someone like the Manson family."

"Okay, point made. Should I close it now?"

"Here." He held out her wallet. "I found it on the floorboard."

"It must have fallen out of my purse. Thanks." She didn't close the door, didn't want to. What was it about desire that made you unable to function?

He wasn't making any kind of move to leave. "When you look at me like that," he said, "I wonder what you are looking for."

"Oh, Jud." She glanced down at the floor, then back at him. She closed her eyes and took a deep breath. "I'm not looking for anything. I think I've already found it."

"Cale?"

She shook her head. "No."

The truth was out there, hanging in the air between them. He studied her face, searching too, then stepped to the edge of the door and rested his arm on the frame, looking down at her. "I won't come any closer than this unless you ask me to."

"I don't know if I can."

"You want to."

"Yes," she admitted and could feel tears in the back of her eyes. Her heart pounded in her chest and she was struck with the first feeling she'd ever had that she was exactly where she was supposed to be.

"I don't want any regrets."

Now she was the one that stepped closer, until they were separated by just a few inches, the width of the doorjamb, and she was standing on the edge of something vital.

He wouldn't move. "You can step back, Jailbait, and close the door in my face, and this moment will be over."

"Over," she said, "but not gone."

"No. Not gone."

Everything up to that point in her life became this one, single, living, breathing, naked moment. Human drives and wants and needs. Life's choices were the hardest things to live with. She saw what she was feeling reflected in his aquiline face and the blue flare of his eyes, then a pale, regretful look of lost time, missed opportunities, if only's blurred his expression. He was about to give up. So she grabbed his tie and pulled him inside.

CHAPTER

20

A trail of scattered clothes marked a path to Laurel's bedroom, where moonlight came through the window and spilled over the bed, turning her white sheets and their naked skin pearlescent. Rising from the deepest places in the body came the powerful scent of the sea, and the sublime, peaked awareness of the senses, the true sensual: on their tongues, the taste of salt and each other; their legs hopelessly tangled, sleek against rough; arms that held each other tightly; and the wild, slow, honeyed words whispered when someone was moving deeply inside of you.

Laurel had no fear, no worry, no thought of anything but there and then, and who. Certainly no regret. She flew wherever his clever hands and body took her. Completely lost in abandon, she followed him naturally. His thrusts were measured and slow, his motions easy; it was something he seemed to want to make last.

Every kiss, every touch, every second together felt so

right. A hundred years from then, another whole life-time away, she would remember each moment as if it were yesterday and would know on that singular night, the stars fell to the earth, the ground shook, and the impossibly unknown became real.

He took her to orgasm on a higher plane than the physical, her shudders like little earthquakes, her heart beating so fast she couldn't keep up. Her mind was nothing but the sweet, warm, white fog of spent desire. When her head cleared, she opened her eyes to find him watching her. Silently, he took her head in his warm hands and kissed her forehead, her cheeks, her chin, then her lips. They lost themselves again, and again.

The sun was warm and high when she awoke, naked and sleek between warm sheets, and to the spicy scent of someone else's skin. Jud lay next to her on his stomach, sound asleep. To her, love had always been myth and magic, a bedtime story told inside her head every night until she had become love's proselyte. Love was the end-all and be-all.

Yet here she was, so inexperienced she didn't trust what she felt now, even though it was there before her, a neon-lit billboard: This is love. This *is* love. Even if she could trust what was in her head and her heart, she had to face the awful truth that she was still tied to one brother and in love with the other.

"I'm a mess," she said aloud.

"Well, if you are, then you're my mess." A long mas-culine arm slid around her. Jud was looking at her with a sleepy smile, eyes so blue in the morning light it was like looking through fine crystalline glass at the expanse of a summer sky. "You look beautiful to me," he said.

How strange that she was thinking the same thing. She didn't explain her mess was on the inside.

"I like you tousled and naked." He pressed his lips to her bare hip, then shifted and tossed aside the sheet. "I want to see you in the sunlight."

Strangely, she didn't feel exposed, but revered, and when he touched her, when he whispered he wanted her, she lay back into the safety of his arms and the sweetness carried her away.

After only two hours sleep, Jud stood in the kitchen, drinking strong, black, eye-opening coffee and talking with Laurel, so soft and lovely, a woman radiant in the morning after. From the window, the sun painted the day with its warm amber glow. The earth was a wonderful, quiet place, and he felt solidly grounded in the last ten hours. The coffee was pungent, espresso black, and bitter when it cooled, so he poured another cup, thinking that his past experiences, his judgments of women and sex and matters of the heart, had just been wiped out in a single, shattering night.

The doorbell rang, and he started to stop her. "Laurel?"

But she swung the door wide open. Cale walked inside as if he owned the place. "What's Jud's car doing out front?" Cale looked at him, still in the kitchen. "What are you doing here?"

Laurel's expression turned pale and bloodless, the warm glow gone and the white glint of fear and horror in her eyes. Jud took a sip of coffee and said to her, "I warned you about the door."

"What's going on?" Cale wanted his answer from Laurel and stood between the two of them, but Jud knew his brother had been between them for a long time.

Laurel placed her hand on Cale's arm. "I tried to tell you."

"What?" Cale's voice rose, high emotion in it. "When?" He wasn't shouting, but almost. "Tell me now." He looked at both of them, but neither spoke.

To Jud, he asked, "Have you slept with her?"

"No."

"Yes," Laurel said at the same time.

The sound that came from his younger brother said it all, the kind of anguished sound no human can control. Cale seemed to shrink as if he were falling into himself, maybe crumbling inside, and looked at Jud in complete disbelief. "You're my brother. You're my brother."

Saying it twice made the words cut deeper. Jud didn't move.

"It's my fault," Laurel told him.

Cale's expression turned ugly for an instant, then seemed to collapse as he shook his head. "Oh, Laurel. I wonder if this has anything to do with you."

"What do you mean?"

His younger brother looked at him, eyes wild and burning with condemnation, and Jud thought he looked just like Victor.

"You bastard." Cale gave a sharp, achingly pain-filled half laugh that hit Jud square in the deepest part of his guilty heart. "You explain it, big brother." Then Cale walked out the door.

Laurel moved first. "Cale! Wait!" She stopped at the edge of the door. "Please. Don't leave like this."

"Good-bye, Laurel," he said and didn't look back.

She hung on to the doorknob because if she let go, she'd sink into the floor. When she found the strength, she faced Jud. "What have we done?"

"Don't do this. After last night, he was going to find out, Laurel."

He sounded too casual, too flip. Cale was his brother. She remembered the look on Jud's face in the kitchen in Catalina. She closed the door with a soft click. A simple sound in a situation that was anything but simple. "He said this had nothing to do with me. What did he mean?"

"He thinks I slept with you because you were his girl. He's always had this idea that I'm competing with him."

"Are you?"

"No," he said sharply. "You and I have nothing to do with him."

"You actually believe that?"

"Yes." He came toward her.

She held up her hands. "Don't. Please. This is all my fault." She felt nauseous. "Didn't you see his face? Oh God . . . I wanted to break it off with him the other night, but he fell asleep in my lap. After he told me I was the reason he could get through school. I'm a coward. I could have told him I didn't love him anymore. Instead, I fell asleep and he was already gone when I woke up."

"You're not a coward, Laurel. You're human."

"Am I? It doesn't feel very human, what I've done. It feels cruel and inhuman. I've made this so ugly." She couldn't look at him. But there were no answers in the fibers of the apartment carpet, no answers across the room or outside the window, where the sun shone brightly and seemed a ludicrous thing. "I can't do this. I won't come between you two."

"There's no good way to break off a relationship." He crossed the room and put his hands on her shoulders. "Look at me. He was going to get hurt either way. We can't help how we feel."

"We did it badly, Jud. Really badly."

"It's too late. I won't let go of what I feel for you."

"What exactly is it that you feel for me?" She thought perhaps he had to choose his words carefully. "You can't say it?" She searched his face for answers, escape, relief. What she saw was only Jud, the same look on the boat before he said I'm sorry and walked away.

"I can say it, Laurel. You want me to say I love you. What about you?"

"I don't know what I feel."

His hands fell away, dropped to his sides, and he looked as if she had hit him.

"I'm sorry, but that's the truth. I thought I knew what love was. I thought I was in love with Cale. I was wrong. How can I trust what I feel for you?"

"You don't feel anything for me," he said flatly.

"I feel everything for you."

He reached out to her but she stepped back.

"I just need time to understand it."

"How much time?"

"I don't know. I have to stay away from you, Jud. I have to understand what's happening to me. I can't think if you're here."

"That should be a big clue, Laurel." His voice was bitter and sarcastic.

Seconds turned into minutes before she said, "Please give me some time to clear my head."

He stood there, stewing, hands in his pockets, looking everywhere, then at her. "Okay. I'll back off. One week. No more." He grabbed his wallet and keys from the end table and walked to the door. He stopped, searching her face for something. "I do love you, Jailbait."

She started to cry.

"Just remember that, okay?"

"Talk to him, Jud. Go talk to him. Please. I can't come between you. I can't."

"I've given you enough promises for one day."

"He's your brother."

"I'll think about it." He left just as his brother had, without looking back.

Laurel closed the door, feeling weak and Tilt-A-Whirl queasy, because life could change with the speed of a carnival ride. She took deep breaths between her tears, trying to hold back the guilt and shame, wounded by what she had done. At that moment, she could not have looked in a mirror. Cale's betrayed expression swam before her eyes, and she ran into the bathroom and threw up.

CHAPTER

21

Cale walked through the hallways of his world with no direction and little memory of his actions. Like surgery gone horribly wrong, he was mutilated inside, and nothing, not copious amounts of liquor, not shapely women, not even the escape of sleep could wipe away the fact that Laurel had chosen Jud over him. His wounds ran deep and bloody and his self-worth plummeted. Again he faced failure, and worse, that Laurel didn't love him. The past flew back to remind him: the women he loved had left him.

He had been living on the edges of solitude for months, maybe years, and his phone calls to her had been an infusion of strength. Without them, without her, who was he? Was there anyone left who would believe in him? It destroyed him cell by cell to think of her and know they wouldn't be together forever. Even worse, to think of her with Jud. Love was a terrible world to inhabit. Love lulled you into feeling safe, but it was all a fantasy, like some dark comic-book story where the villain who threatened to destroy the world was both friend and foe, wore a mask half dark and half light, and time was the only thing holding back the sad truth that betrayal was inevitable.

Each day, concentration become more impossible. Even Dr. Strovich had to call him on stupid mistakes and told him it was a good thing his exams were over. Cale had drifted mindlessly through time, until the afternoon he came out of the lab building to find his Judas brother standing on the front steps.

Jud came toward him. "Cale!"

"Go to hell."

Jud grabbed his shoulder.

Cale swung away from him. "Leave me alone."

"Wait. Listen to me."

"No." He kept walking but Jud dogged his heels.

"I met her first."

He faced his brother. "What are you talking about?"

"Laurel. I met her first."

"I didn't see a flag sticking out of her that said *Jud Banning*." Cale trembled with the pain of suppressed, raging anger. He met her first—what the fuck did that matter? Then something inside him, something he thought was dead, began the slow, painful act of dying all over again.

"Laurel was the girl in Catalina. The one I was in the fight over."

Cale started walking again. "I have newfound respect for the guy who beat the shit out of you."

"Stop." Jud came around in front of him, blocking the way. "Go ahead. Hit me."

Cale's hands were in rock-tight fists. He wanted to smash Jud's face in. "I'm not going to give you an easy out."

"You want to. Come on, hit me." Jud wouldn't move.

"Go away, Jud. Run to Laurel. You wanted her badly enough to take her." He looked Jud in the eye. "Or maybe it isn't about Laurel any longer. If it ever was."

"You think I don't care about her?"

"I have no idea. The conquest is over. You won. I lost. Funny. Isn't that the way it always is? I want something and you get it." They were still brothers, bound together by blood and parentage, conceived by the same bodies and born from the same womb. But Laurel wasn't a basketball game or a sports car. She was his heart. Jud took her, and Cale didn't think he could ever forgive his brother for that.

"I can't change how she feels. I'm here because she wanted me to come talk to you."

Cale laughed caustically. "Oh, that's sweet. Did she want me to hit you, too?" He shook his head and looked past his brother at nothing. "You just don't get it, Jud. You never will. Because you're you—the golden boy—and I'm me, the fuckup."

Jud didn't follow him after that. When Cale was a few yards away, he looked back. His brother was standing under a pepper tree near the Norris Library. You bastard . . . Cale took a few more steps, then called out, "Run, big brother. Run. So you don't waste time away from her."

After that, time, like everything else in his life, lost value. Nightly visions of Laurel rose before him. Sometimes he woke to the scent of cinnamon taffy, the taste of honey, or the clear bell sound of her laughter. Sometimes during the day and always at night, he would close his eyes. Darkness was easier, an escape, because life without her meant he would have to learn to light his own way.

A bank of opaque fog floated just off the San Pedro coast, silent, still, and eerie when it cloaked the SS *Catalina*. Laurel sat in a red leather window seat in the hollow, open galley and looked out at nothing but white mist. A deep, plaintive foghorn sounded every few minutes, buoy bells clanged with each swell, and the steamer's engine rumbled away, leaving the real world and the mainland behind.

It had all started here, in this galley, and the months since played out in her head, scene by scene, an exposé of how she'd gotten to this point, a mental game of "What might have happened if?" Every choice she'd made, right and wrong, was there for her to question. Why did she sleep with Cale? Because she was in love? Because he was in love? Because she wanted him— someone—to love her? Because Jud hadn't wanted her? The inescapable truth was, she chose to finally sleep with Cale the night she found out Jud was his brother. It was clear now. She'd fallen head over heels in love with Jud the moment he brought her that first glass of wine. Now she wasn't certain whom she had betrayed more, Cale, Jud, or herself.

No solid answers came to her in those hours. The ship moved into Avalon harbor, where the water was gray-green and the sky a dull pewter, the air briny, humid, and as thick as the fog they had passed through earlier. At home on the island, she hoped to find some kind of clarity, some way to rebuild the shambles she had made of three lives. Home was safe and the place to run. Now she ran to the island she had run from a few months ago, which pretty much defined her undecided life—a zigzag of mistakes. But the one constant in her life was her mother, the person who loved her without any demand.

Laurel had been sitting and waiting for over an hour when her mother came home from the shop and she told her about Cale and Jud. Her mom's reaction was hellish.

Kathryn paced the living room. "I knew something like this would happen, Laurel. You wouldn't believe me, but I could feel it coming."

"How could you know? You don't even know Jud."

"I knew they would hurt you. They're Bannings. How could they do anything else to us?" Her mother's voice changed pitched. "They destroyed our lives." She was gripping the back of a chair with white-knuckled hands. Her mother cried as she spoke, the kind of crying you can't stop and sometimes don't even realize is there, crying that comes from someplace desperate. Clearly what she was feeling burned her up. "Those two brothers will ruin yours. You say you love Jud and not Cale. Well, I say you shouldn't go near either of them."

It had been a mistake to come there. "Mom. Please, I'm sorry. You don't understand. It was me. I'm the one who came between them."

"You? Hardly. This started years ago."

"What are you talking about?"

"They killed your father, Laurel."

Her mother had flipped out. Panic swelled out from

her voice. So mad, the crazy way she was reacting, the things she was saying, like some pot boiling over. Her own desperate search for love had driven a spike between them, too. "Mom? You're not making sense."

"Wait here." Kathryn left. She came back in the room, a pale woman carrying an old blue shoe box under her arm, and handed her a yellowed newspaper clipping.

Laurel read it and slowly, horribly, she understood. "Their parents were in the other car?"

"They weren't just in the other car. Their father was drunk and driving like a madman. He ran a light and slammed into your father's car. The accident and the reason your father was killed were all Rudy Banning's fault."

"You've known this? You knew Cale was their son?"

"Shannon told me his last name was Banning after you brought him to meet me. I tried to find you. I went to the house at the cove and found his brother instead."

"Do they know?"

"No."

"Why didn't you tell me?"

"Would it have changed how you felt?"

The small black type on the yellowed page began to blur. Light-headed, she took a deep breath and closed her eyes. "I don't know." By some strange destiny, she'd brought her father's death and that relentless, black morass of pain back into their lives. Her mother's face was almost unrecognizable, her eyes those of an insomniac, her skin bloodless. She had lost weight, her chin was too pointed, and her mouth as thin as someone a decade older. Standing before Laurel was one more broken person.

So this is love.

Jud kept his word and didn't go back for a week. On the seventh day, he was at her place at eight in the morning, determined to make her understand that this was real. After taking what he wanted, he would now have to fight for her. The morning he'd left her, he bought a ring. Every day since, the velvet box stayed in the pocket of his suit jacket or sport coat—the inside pocket, just inches from his heart. He walked up the steps looking downward, mentally practicing his words as he had been for days. He knocked on the door and turned, his hands in his pockets, until no one answered. He pounded on the door. "Laurel! Laurel! Open up!" He stepped back.

In the front window hung a small black-and-white For Rent sign. It was suddenly difficult to breathe; a sinking realization paralyzed him, and his only thought was he was a fool—one who now regretted ever giving Laurel even one more day.

After an interminable minute, he hopped over the railing and pressed his hands and face to the glass. The furniture was there, but the stereo was gone, and the knit throw on the sofa back, her mother's pottery, and the photos. The strongest sense of panic he'd ever experienced came over him. His hand shook as he wrote down the rental number, then drove for the nearest telephone. Her number was disconnected. At the rental number there was no answer.

The sweat of fear with its metallic smell poured from his head and body. He ran to his car and drove to find her. When he needed air, he had to heave great breaths, and driving in a straight line took two hands on the wheel. He went to her school, because the restaurant wasn't open yet. They told him she had left. No transfer. No forwarding. He waited outside the restaurant until someone let him in. Laurel had telephoned two days ago, apologized, and said she wouldn't be back. Every hour he called the rental number until that night when he reached her landlord and was told Laurel Peyton had given up her deposit and said only that she was leaving.

At midnight he fell into bed, drained and desperate, and slept the quiescent, dreamless sleep of a man who couldn't face his transgressions. The next morning, Jud took the first seaplane to the island.

Kathryn sat in a corner chair, a box of Kleenex in her lap, an old blue shoe box open at her feet, a cup of cold tea in her hand. No amount of sugar could smother the bitter taste of lemon. Outside, the early-morning world seemed empty of humanity and fooled you into thinking there was a safe place to hide. She wondered if Laurel could find a hiding place.

The sight of Jud Banning walking up to her door came as no surprise. His appearance seemed the appropriate black moment, considering the last forty-eight hours. Her daughter had run away from all of them, even Kathryn, especially Kathryn.

Behind him, the sky still held smudges of pink from the morning's sunrise. The Westminster clock on the table chimed eight times, each note just a second off from his knocks. She opened the door. "I knew one of you would come," she said in lieu of niceties like hello. "I was right to be worried that day."

"I'm looking for Laurel."

"She's not here."

"Where is she?"

"She called me two days ago to tell me that she had to get away from everyone." The sound she made should have been a bitter laugh, but it sounded like glass breaking. "She even had to get away from me."

"I have to find her. I love your daughter."

"So did your brother. I think you are both using her. It's not love, but a bad case of who wins."

"Is that what she told you?"

"She told me what Cale said when he found you two together. There is something between the two of you."

"My brother was wrong."

"Still, she's now caught between you both and doesn't want to be there."

"It's not like that. You have to understand. She has to understand."

"Go away and leave us alone." She started to close the door.

"Wait! Please. I know she's probably in Seattle."

"Then why are you here?"

"I need to explain to her. I can't lose her."

He couldn't lose her? She wondered if he even realized what he'd just said. Winning and losing and destroying. She opened the door wider. "Come inside." He was silent, looking out of place. She handed him the box of clippings and watched him read the top one, watched the same pale, blood-draining realization come over him that had come over Laurel. One ruined life for another. "If you love my daughter more than yourself, Jud Banning, you'll walk away. You'll love her enough to allow her to put together the pieces of her life, a life that doesn't include anyone named Banning. Your family has done enough harm to us."

"Does she know?"

"She does now. She didn't last week."

"Then that's all the more reason I need to talk to her. I'm sorry about your husband. But this was my father, not Cale, not me. We are just as much victims of that accident."

"Stay out of my daughter's life."

"You want to punish me, but you're punishing Laurel, too."

"If she loved you, she wouldn't have left you. And I don't want to punish anyone. I want to protect her."

"She doesn't need protection from me. I would never hurt her."

"You already have." Her voice cracked. "Go. Just leave." All she could do was hold out her hand to keep him away. Here, inside her home, he was even stealing the air she needed to breathe. "Please. Get out of my house."

She was still crying when he shut the door behind him, and she fell into a chair, head back, eyes closed, with Laurel's words on the phone haunting her. "I won't come between two brothers. And Mom, I just can't forgive you for not telling me the truth. I'll call you in a few weeks and let you know where I am. Good-bye." With those simple words, her daughter was gone.

The clock chimed the half hour before Kathryn could move. She showered and went to work, sat down at her desk, and called the gallery in Seattle. Two phone calls later, she had the contact who represented Victor Banning and told the man she had one Espinosa to sell. The arrangements were made and she hung up. Easy as that. It was done.

In the storage room, she struggled to pull out an Espinosa painting and spent the rest of the afternoon tightly rewrapping it, before calling the movers to come the next day and crate it for shipping to the mainland. The island hardware store was only a short stop on the way home. Thirty minutes later she stood in her bedroom, where the overhead light shone so bright she could see all the cracks in the plaster of those old stucco walls, all the false gaudiness of the loud yellow color she'd tried to live with. She wasn't Evie. Her sister's life didn't fit her any better than Julia's had, so Kathryn shoved all the furniture into the center of the room, picked up a roller, and painted her bedroom blue.

Two uniformed men removed a crated canvas from the delivery truck parked behind Victor's Town Car as

Harlan gave them directions to the loft. Victor turned and faced the only blank wall left on which to hang Rachel's two lost paintings. His heart was pounding and his blood felt hot, almost making him light-headed, the way he'd been whenever they were together. Time couldn't erase the bell-like memory of what it felt like to be with Rachel.

They had rendezvoused in a building like this one, with a rattling freight elevator and the bleak skeleton of LA's industry for miles in all directions. But from inside that reclusive flat, no outside world had existed, because there had been no exterior walls. A square room with no windows, just a bed without a frame on the hardwood floor and an open, spare bath with a steel shower, toilet, and standing sink, all appropriately cell-like. For more than a decade they had fucked in a room with no true light, blue skies, or sunshine to make it clear they had so much to lose.

Rachel had been both his passion and poison. They were two souls driven by lust and power and something neither could name, each struggling to control the other, both unable to walk out and stay away.

"It's done, Victor." Her voice had always been emo-tionless when she said those resolved words, a cool Rachel so unlike the burning body that had been under him only moments before. His heart still pounded in the aftermath of sex. But she lay next to him, turned away, her skin as white as the sheets and walls, the defined bones of her long, lithe spine snaking up to her neck, where she had smelled like Arpège and paint, her hair in sharp contrast and black as the thing between them. He could see the violent imprint of his fingers on her buttocks, and when she sat up and lit a cigarette, red-orange paint showed under her nails, a slash of yellow on her elbow, green on a thumb.

Rachel was the only color against the room's blank canvas, staring away from him and looking distantly alone. It was there—the wall she erected to keep them apart—but it always crumbled. Smoke pluming from her cigarette dissipated into the air. It struck him that passion was always described in the terminology of fire—white-hot, smoldering, blazing—but fires could be put out.

Rachel leaned over him and pressed the cigarette to his mouth, then stood and slipped her dress over her head.

He hated the taste of tobacco and dropped it into a glass of watered whiskey on the floor. "You're leaving."

"Yes."

"I see. Then you got what you came for."

"So did you." She stepped into her heels, looking down at him.

"I suppose I did." A lie spoken aloud sounded closer to the truth. He was an accomplished liar.

She picked up her purse, dropped her cigarettes and lighter into it. "I wish I could stop this."

"Only because that would mean I have no power over you. You shouldn't worry, my dear. It's human nature to cling to something."

"I'm clinging to the wrong thing."

"Then go. But you can't stay away."

"Neither can you, Victor." She opened the door to leave, but turned back. "I don't love you."

He had perfected the art of hiding soft emotions. "I know. We're a pair, you and I, because I can't love anyone," he'd told her, and for one naked moment, they looked at each other, the truth plain and real despite all their lies.

His doom was to long for a love too destructive, and necessary as air. Not a day had passed since her death that he didn't crave another day with her. Even now, so many years later, as he stood in the loft surrounded by almost all of her work, part of him was missing. He didn't regret that he'd told his son the truth—he couldn't open that door—but he regretted that in doing so, he'd lost Rachel forever.

Reliving history, he stood before that last blank wall until the freight elevator rattled to the top floor. He held the door open as they delivered the painting, uncrated it, and leaned it against the empty wall. Not until the truck's gears sounded from the street below and the engine droned away did he tear off the wrapping.

Alone, he stared at the canvas with a huge X cut through the middle so the painting collapsed in its center. He couldn't have named what single emotion ran through him: shock, rage, puzzlement. Reeling and silent, he rushed from the loft, so hot his head and hair felt on fire and he could swear he smelled smoke. He crawled into the backseat. "Take me home, Harlan." By the time they were on the freeway, Victor had contacted his attorney on the radio phone. "Who sold you the painting?"

"Is something wrong?"

"I'm not certain."

His attorney came back with the information. "The owner wanted the money to go to a charity. The Jimmy Peyton Memorial Fund."

"I'll call you later." Victor hung up, his breath shallow, a sick feeling in his belly. "Jimmy Peyton and the Fireflies," he said aloud, a name he hadn't thought of since the first days of the accident, then never thought of again. Peyton. Peyton. That last girlfriend of Cale's was Laurel Peyton. Jimmy Peyton and the Fireflies. Laurel Peyton. Couldn't be. Her family would never let that connection happen. He hadn't bothered to check her out because the girl was inconsequential. What an irony if her name alone would have been enough to split them apart.

But the damaged painting was clearly vandalized, a visual of their damaged lives. Their damaged selves. The shreds of lies they lived and spoke and told themselves were truths. He rolled down the rear window, because it was so stuffy, stagnant. "Harlan. Turn up the air." A strange, sharp sensation shot down his right cheek, circled until his face felt numb, then was gone. His mouth tasted metallic.

"What did you say, Mr. Banning?"

"Turn up the air. I can't breathe." In his brain he said those words, but what spoke from his mouth was muffled gibberish. Harlan's name was "Shhhhluban." The edges of his vision turned white and began to disappear, so he closed his eyes. Everything was hot and spinning.

When he opened his eyes again they had pulled over and Harlan was leaning inside the backseat with a hand on his shoulder. "I can't understand you, sir."

Air, he thought. It's so hot. I need air. But his mouth wouldn't move.

On a Friday afternoon, Cale received a call from Jud that Victor had had a stroke. It took him over an hour to get from school in LA to the hospital in Santa Ana. Cale went from the nurses' station straight to ICU, where his grandfather lay hooked up to monitors and an IV. The old man's face was a grotesque pale mask, half the Victor he knew—sharp bones and angular muscles—the other half slack, as if the muscle and bone were crushed. His skin was gray, his hair matted with sweat, and he wasn't conscious.

Jud stood at the window, hands in the pockets of his suit pants, looking at a loss for words, his expression strained. Cale didn't know if that was because of him or Victor. He hadn't seen his brother since that day at school when Jud came to him for some kind of absolution. "What happened?"

"They were on the freeway. Harlan said Victor wasn't making any sense. He was rolling down the windows and talking gibberish. Harlan called his doctor, who told him not to bother with an ambulance and to drive straight here. They need to do more tests once he's awake. He can't speak, but the stroke didn't kill him."

Cale said nothing. Jud stood at the window. His grandfather lay in the bed. A canyon of pain stood between them.

"Now that you're here, I need to go make some calls." Jud walked toward the door.

"To Laurel?" He couldn't stop himself.

"No." Jud faced him. "I don't know where she is. She's left. Her apartment, her school, the restaurant. Her mother says she doesn't know where she is. Claims Laurel didn't want to come between us."

"Too late for that."

"There's a lot more to this than you think." Jud

looked like a loser, and it was strange because it was a look that didn't fit him.

"Did you try Seattle?"

"I have someone looking now. But I think she wants to stay gone." Jud opened the door. "I'm going to find Harlan."

Alone, Cale scanned Victor's chart. Results from the CAT scan were there. The stroke was severe, but he would make it. Cale used a corner of the bed sheet to wipe the saliva from Victor's mouth. The old man would hate this.

Whether he would be the same was the question. His grandfather had been vital and always willing to make everyone's life hell. Cale wanted to despise him, but it was easier to hate him when he wasn't pitiable, unmoving, like one of those stunned gulls from his childhood. Cale touched his hand and the old man opened his eyes, tried to speak, and winced at the guttural sounds.

"Don't, Victor. I'll get someone."

His grandfather gripped his hand and wouldn't let go, so Cale reached over him and pressed the call button. When they came to take Victor away for tests, the nurse had to pry his grandfather's fingers loose, then Cale stood in the empty room, his knuckles red and hand throbbing. To his horror, he began to cry. Deep sobs he couldn't stop. His despair swelled up and out from some lost, empty place; it racked his frame, stole his breath, and possessed him. He sank into the chair by the bed, his face in his hands.

The minutes disappeared until Jud touched his shoulder. Cale needed more time to control himself, and when he did, they didn't speak, a couple of busted veins bleeding in silence. Finally he wiped his eyes, embarrassed. "I don't know why that happened."

"I'm sorry about Laurel, Cale." Jud didn't understand.

"It doesn't matter. I don't care anymore." The words slipped out of his mouth so fast, as all lies do. Cale knew he would care for a long, long time.

PART THREE

2002

When the fight begins within himself,
a man's worth something.

Robert Browning

CHAPTER

23

Newport Beach, California

One afternoon a week, Cale Banning escaped his surgical practice for eighteen holes at Harborview Country Club. Taking up golf had been his wife Robyn's idea, some twenty years ago, back when the long, consecutive hours of surgery drained his concentration, when he came home antsy and on days off hovered distractedly around the family.

"Cale, darling. We know you love us. Your colleagues respect you, your patients trust you, but your intensity is about to eat you alive. For God's sake go play racketball, soccer, tennis. Bang the heck out of a golf ball. Do something for you."

On his birthday she and the boys gave him a set of clubs, and Jud joined forces and handed him an expensive golf membership, telling the boys, "Your dad spent half his childhood searching for injured seagulls. Now he can spend his free time chasing after birdies and eagles."

This week, like most, he played with Lofty Collins, a cardiologist and med school buddy from USC whose real name was Karl, but "Lofty" had stuck years back because he could send a golf ball off a clubface so high and long it seemed to hang there in midair, waiting for applause before it dropped onto the green.

Collins used his club to point toward the rough. "A hundred bucks says you cut right and end up in the trees."

"You're on." Cale swung, and five minutes later he stood beside a giant eucalyptus tree with no view to the green.

"Hey." Lofty was laughing. "Looks like you have a clear shot to the trap."

"Trap, my ass, and stop crowing." Cale whacked the ball a good three shots from the hole. By four o'clock, he was into Lofty for six hundred bucks.

"I'm going to give you a break, Banning. Double or nothing. You make par and you won't owe me a thing."

Cale looked down at the foreign implement in his hand. He had a bagful of clubs, but he would have been better off throwing the ball toward the green. "Screw the money. It's my game that's gone to hell."

"You just like to win. Or you don't like to lose. Tell you what. I'll bet on my good game against your lousy one. I eagle this hole and you have to agree to look at that patient of mine."

"I leave my scheduling up to Sharon."

"Bullshit."

"Call Madison. He's a good surgeon."

"I don't want Brad Madison on this one. I want you."

"Why?"

"Because you're the best, asshole."

"I'm the best asshole?" Cale eyed the fairway. "I've had a lot of practice."

"Glad to see you haven't lost your sense of humor. Just your guts."

It wasn't about the game any longer, not about two friends giving each other a hard time. Cale faced Lofty. "What the hell is that supposed to mean?"

"You've changed since Robyn died."

"We were married for almost thirty years. Yes. I miss my wife."

"That's not what I'm talking about and you know it. The fire in you is gone."

"There must be some unwritten law that people who haven't lost a spouse will tell those who have how they should feel, act, and recover."

"I'm a good enough friend to ignore that and point out you were one of the best cardiothoracic surgeons around. I never thought I'd see someone with your ability to save lives actively choose not to."

"Ask my patients about their lives. I haven't lost anyone in a long time."

"Not since Robyn died."

"Yeah, well, medicine turned out to be a waste of time for her." The air was a calm seventy-eight degrees, no breeze, no marine layer, no fog. All blue sky and sunshine. In a world without his wife? It just felt all wrong. "I choose my surgeries. Everyone chooses their surgeries."

"Robyn was proud of your work."

"If you weren't one of my oldest friends, Karl, I'd put my fist through your nose so even Evanston couldn't reconstruct it." Cale swung and watched his golf ball sail off to the right. "I'm in the trap."

"I think you've been there for a long time, buddy."

"I'm one hell of a surgeon." He sounded embarrassingly defensive.

"Yes. You were one hell of a surgeon."

"Okay, okay." Cale held up his hand. "You're a hard-headed bastard. Send the records over. I'll take a look at them. Now, will you shut up?"

"Sure." Lofty lined up his shot, drew back.

"What's the patient's name?"

"King." Collins resettled into his stance and eyed the green. "Her name is King."

Santa Ana, California

Annalisa King loved her father, but sometimes he wasn't an easy man to love. Like now, as she drove along the freeway with her cell phone to her right ear, listening to him go on and on.

"You have talent, Annalisa. You are *my* daughter," he said for the thousandth time in the last year, his voice loud over the cellular waves and his accent getting stronger. "I tell you this before. You work with me, in a few years I will give you your own restaurant. Annalisa's. Can you not see your name on the awning? See the windows etched with the *A*?"

"I don't want my own restaurant."

"You think you are too good to be a chef?"

"You know that's not true."

"It is in your blood. You throw your talent in the can."

"Trash, Dad. In the trash."

"Trash can. It is the same thing. You change the subject. Just like your mother. Designing kitchens. You are both crazy."

"King Design has a solid reputation. Mom designed all your restaurants."

"You must listen to me, *ma petite jeune*."

She wanted to say, "I'm not your little girl anymore! And you can't tell me what to do." But he was still talking, pushing, pushing, pushing to get his way. He could not forgive her for choosing her own career over the one he wanted for her. In his mind, she was choosing her mother over him.

He finally stopped talking and she had no idea what answer he was waiting for. "Love you, Dad. Lots of traffic. Gotta hang up. We'll talk later. Bye." She turned off her cell phone and tossed it into her open briefcase on the passenger seat. But his words, created solely to make her feel guilty, echoed like a hard-rock beat in her head, so she rolled down the window and turned up the radio.

Fifteen minutes later she stood in an elevator speeding upward ten floors to the top of the BanCo Building. Dizzy, she braced her hand on the wall. A little sweat broke out on her brow line the way it did when you had a low-grade fever. That's what nerves did to you.

Unlike her mom, she refused to sit quietly and wait while the Del Mar Company picked the winning bid for the Camino Cliff project, so without her mother's knowledge, she made an appointment with the man in charge. The elevator doors opened to a softly lit, plush lobby with a polished receptionist behind a half-moon desk made of brushed chrome and burnished mahogany.

"I'm Annalisa King. Of King Design. I'm here to see Mr. Banning."

The woman checked her appointment book. "I'm sorry. I don't see your name for today."

"It's regarding the Camino Cliff project."

"You want to see Matthew Banning." She flipped open another leather-bound appointment book. "Here it is. Have a seat. I'll let him know you're here."

Annalisa sat down on one of the cushy sofas and crossed her legs, tapping the red sole of her designer shoe against a chrome-and-glass coffee table spread with glossy issues of *Orange Coast* magazine. Murano glass wall sconces provided soft light on sueded walls, and the sofa fabric was expensive mohair. She leaned to the side and looked behind her, where a original Miró rose a good seven feet upward. Money, money, money.

Three months ago, King Professional Design had submitted plans and a bid for a new resort with seven restaurants and ten professional kitchens, which meant a five-million-dollar contract. Camino Cliff would cover thousands of acres of Southern California's prime coastal real estate, just a few miles from Pelican Point and from the luxurious Ritz-Carlton. The golf courses would be designed by Arnold Palmer's company; the hotel and condominium projects were upscale, with staggering Pacific views, and the Swiss spa world-class. The restaurants spanned everything from an authentic Japanese tea room and sushi house to a marble dining room with a glass-domed ceiling, expansive ocean views, and the finest in California haute cuisine.

She hoped to edge in front of their competition by meeting with the man in charge. Not the head of the Del Mar Ranch Company, to whom they had submitted the bids, but with the corporate owner and parent company, BanCo.

"Mr. Banning will see you now."

Annalisa followed the receptionist down a long hallway flanked with offices and an elegant glass conference room, before they stopped in front of a massive rosewood door carved with the image of a wind-swept Monterey pine. Annalisa followed her inside.

"This is Ms. Annalisa King of King Design."

Hand extended, Annalisa stopped when she saw the man who came from behind the desk. He was younger than she expected, late twenties, and somewhat devastating.

"Matthew Banning." He took her hand and stood there, looking as if he'd walked out of a love song, deep voice, dark hair, blue eyes, and a good six inches taller than she was in her three-inch Louboutins. She glanced at his left hand. No ring.

"Is something wrong?" he asked.

"You're so young," she blurted out.

He laughed genuinely. "I was just thinking the same about you."

"I'm a child prodigy."

"Good. I like working with brilliant women. Have a seat." He didn't return to his desk as she expected, but leaned back casually against its edge and crossed his feet.

"You know, if I sit down in this chair and you stay like that, I'm going to feel like I'm talking to God."

"Good. I'm glad we've established our relationship," he said, deadpan.

"So do I have to pray to get the Camino Cliff contract?" She tried for a relaxed look and laughed, thanking God she hadn't said anything about getting down on her knees.

"There's strong competition."

"I know. Cuttler did the Ritz, the Palms in Indio, and the renovation for the Ranches at Santa Ynez. Riverton's company did Pelican Point and the Inn at Cote de Casa. But we did Megryl's Del Sol, Jonathan's, Tommy Bahama's, and Cutter's." She reached inside her briefcase for the King portfolio, but when she looked up she saw the remnants of surprise on his face. "You aren't familiar with our jobs."

"No."

She stood a little taller when she said, "You weren't considering us for this job at all."

"No."

"Funny, you don't look like a man who makes mistakes." He didn't move or speak. "I want this contract, Mr. Banning."

"Tell me why I should give it to you." He was good. His expression gave nothing away.

"Because my mother understands the function of the restaurant kitchen better than anyone. She can work with even the most demanding chef. She was a chef at Camaroon."

"Beric King's LA restaurant?" He paused. "King Professional Design," he repeated slowly. "I don't suppose that's a coincidence."

Annalisa smiled. "My mother handled my father for a long time. Still does, though they've been divorced for years. We Kings know the restaurant business and we know design."

"Cuttler and Riverton have more experience. Both companies are well over twenty years old. They do the majority of projects this size. "

"When I walked in here you said I was young. I'm twenty-two. Inexperienced maybe, but I grew up in this business. It's in my blood." She quoted her dad. Matthew Banning was listening. A good sign on a day for big risks. "We're a small company," she continued, "but that works to your advantage. You'll have our complete attention until this job is done. Our focus will be solely on your job."

"Riverton's bid is lower."

"And you believe that bid?"

He didn't respond.

"There's no deal cutting other than the standard volume discounts. No trick sales. We all pay the same price. But I expect Riverton will tell you he can get a discount, then just make up the dollars in another area. Stainless steel at fifteen percent more a foot, a little more here in the lighting, a little more in stonework. Your contractual allowance for overages is ten percent over bid, right?"

"Right."

"Riverton and Cuttler will come in over, as close to that ten percent as they can. You'll want to call their past jobs and ask if they were on or under bid. The answer might surprise you."

He still looked nonplussed.

She handed him the glossy portfolio she'd put together. "Here's a list of the jobs we've done. You can call and ask every single one of them about us. We have never once gone over our initial bid." When he took the portfolio she could see she had him thinking. "Neither my mother nor I will make promises we cannot keep. You won't need your ten percent overage allowance." She knew it was all or nothing. "You give us the deal and you can remove the allowance clause from the contract."

"That's half a million dollars."

"Yes it is."

"Risky."

"I don't make promises I can't keep." She picked up her briefcase, pulled out her card, and handed it to him. "Please call me if I can answer any more questions."

He took the card and straightened. "Well, you've certainly given me something to think about."

"I'll bet I have," she said with bravado that came from having nothing to lose. She gathered her things and shook his hand. "I want this job."

"I can see that."

"Then I needn't take up any more of your time." She walked away, but stopped in the doorway. He was looking at her legs. If a pair of costly shoes and a short, Italian-designed skirt would get the job, they were worth every penny. "Don't make the wrong decision, Matthew."

Without looking back, she headed for the elevator. The door opened and shut behind her before she sagged against the wall, her heart pounding, clammy sweat on her hairline and under her arms. Going after what you wanted was not easy.

Surfside, California

Laurel Peyton King understood that no marriage was a straight line and time tested the truths in any relationship of the heart, but her divorce had left her with a flayed feeling. She was a helpless failure at love who married for the wrong reasons, too inexperienced and wounded, and stayed married long after she should have picked up her pride and left. Après divorce, her life was less complicated, and she realized staying together for their daughter had been another lousy choice in the name of love. Beric King was a master chef, the man who created those extravagant post-Oscar meals, an energetic TV charmer when he cooked for the morning shows, a name scrawled across green awnings on famous boulevards called Hollywood and Fairfax, and a husband who made life like water constantly boiling over.

The only material thing she had wanted from the divorce was their beach house in an enclave that straddled a strip of land between the sand and the Pacific Coast Highway, where homes were stacked together like books on a library shelf and were as diverse as the people who made up California.

She and Beric happened upon their gray bungalow with white trim only hours after the For Sale sign went up, and had bought the house immediately. Before long, the crisply painted porch anchored with giant pots of fat geraniums and lush impatiens became her safe haven, barely inches from the toasted California sand, where she could feel the waves hit shore, taste the sea in the air, and watch a neon sunset with the moon already high over her shoulder. Nights there were cool and dark, no line of streetlamps to outshine the stars, and the sky was deep and indigo; it started at sunrise and didn't end until it reached the place where the sun set.

In a land of sameness, days constantly seventy-eight degrees, neighborhoods of two hundred homes (four models and five phases), and too many white, German-made convertibles on the endless miles of Pacific Coast Highway, her small slice of coast didn't look or feel homogenized. With the wide blue Pacific spread out before her, Laurel found her center there and lived alone with her mistakes.

Most days for lunch she left the office to go home to a sandwich, a breath of salt air, and a quick look at the early news. Today lunch was late; it was midafternoon when she sat across from her TV in the kitchen corner eating a tuna sandwich. A thin blue ribbon of news stories ran across the lower screen while the station's legal journalists and experts discussed a death-penalty murder case of national attention. The defendant, a high-profile Seattle executive accused of killing his wife, had been captured near the border. No white Bronco footage replayed again and again, but courthouse clips of family, children, and alleged mistresses filed across the screen in a kind of grisly cartoon.

A defense expert's familiar face flashed on the screen. "This is a circumstantial case. No murder weapon. No concrete forensic evidence. The prosecutor has his work cut out for him."

"But we all know he's guilty," an ex-prosecutor and analyst jumped in, disgust and judgment in her voice. "The man called his mistress and pretended he was in Hong Kong the day after his wife was found dead."

"Just because he's a liar doesn't mean he killed his wife. The assistant DA will have to keep the jury focused on the victim." The TV screen filled with the young prosecutor's image. "Greg O'Hanlon has a ninety percent conviction rate. He's the son of Judge Patrick O'Hanlon, proof the apple doesn't fall far from the tree."

Laurel turned off the TV. She should have never turned it on. She tossed her tuna sandwich into the garbage disposal and drove back to the office in Irvine Business Park, where King Professional Design occupied the southwest corner of the fourth floor.

"Your mother called about her new show," her assistant told her the moment she came through the door. "She wanted to make certain we had the right dates. Why won't she let any family come to opening night?"

"Superstition of some kind. I gave up trying to understand my mother years ago."

"Annalisa called a few minutes ago. She'll be here by four thirty. And I took care of the airline tickets and hotel reservation for the trade show."

"Fine," Laurel said distractedly and put the bank receipt on Pat's uncluttered desk. Inside her office, she dove into a set of project plans. Eventually she stopped trying to make herself work and unlocked the filing drawer in her desk. A thick manila envelope in the last file hadn't been removed in over a year, a record for her.

The letters inside were from an investigation agency, the large photo of a tall young man with sandy hair whose face was part of her youth. A sudden, bitter taste filled her mouth, as if she had bitten her tongue. All these years and she still couldn't let go. The paper shredder was behind her, the trash can next to her. She looked at them both before she locked up the envelope again as she always did.

Moments later the door burst open. "I don't need an appointment. She is my wife!"

Pat blocked the doorway. "Ex-wife."

Beric King stuck his head inside. "Can you not stop this woman?"

"It's okay, Pat. Let him in."

"Of course it is okay." Beric looked at her assistant as if she were a fallen soufflé.

Pat rolled her eyes and closed the door. Her ex-husband straightened his jacket and scowled, then faced her, pulling down the ends of his sleeves with sharp little jerks. "You should fire that woman."

"Why? Because you don't like her?"

"Yes."

"Well, you're out of luck. She does a great job."

He made one of those scornful noises in the throat the French make instead of calling you stupid.

"Maybe I'll give her a raise."

"Everything you do is to spite me."

"I have more important things to do in my life than to spend my days thinking of ways to annoy you. Besides, annoying you is so easy."

He sat down in a chair and leaned back comfortably. "I do not know what I ever did to make you so angry."

Laurel sank her head into her hands. "Oh God, please, not today."

Beric was silent, his arm slung casually over the chair back, one leg crossed, an ostrich leather boot resting on his knee. His deep red hair was slicked back in a low, long ponytail, his silk and linen jacket open over a thin dark T-shirt and jeans.

For so many years she had tried to love this man. "Why are you here?"

"I want to talk to you about Annalisa."

"You should talk to Annalisa. She's twenty-two."

"She will not listen to me."

"You mean she won't do what you want."

"She should be working with me. I am her father."

"And I'm her mother. She's working here and doing quite well."

"She is wasting her talent."

Laurel stared at her ex-husband. He could hurt her so easily. "Our daughter has more than one talent."

"When she was a little girl, she would always say, 'I want to be a chef, like you, Daddy.'"

"When I was six, I wanted to be Karen, the Mouseketeer. When I was ten I wanted to be Gidget. When I was twenty-two I didn't want to be either."

"No, you were a chef by then, like Annalisa should be. You. Me. My father. My mother. My brother." Beric moved his hands in the air and his voice grew louder. "I tell her it is in her blood! The fruit in the dirt is like the tree."

"The apple doesn't fall far from the tree," she said. *Like the O'Hanlons.*

"That is what I meant. Annalisa is my apple. I want to stop her from making the mistake of her life."

"Really?"

He looked at her stubbornly.

"I think you just want your own way."

"This is not about our marriage, Laurel."

He could twist anything. "No, it's about our daughter. You have to stop hounding her. She loves you, but she wants to work with me. I'm not forcing her to be part of my company."

He leaned forward and poked the desktop with one finger. "You have this company because of me."

She leaned forward and placed both hands on her desk. "And you have Annalisa because of me."

Now he looked as angry as she was. He pushed the chair back hard and stood. "I can see coming here was a mistake."

"It usually is."

At the door he stopped. Beric loved parting shots. "You do not care about your daughter."

"Go away, Beric. Please." She waved her hand. "Go . . . go . . . cook something."

He made that noise in his throat again before he left.

Laurel popped a couple of antacids, then spun the chair around to face the windows. The freeway interchange looked like a concrete knot in the distance, and behind it, tall steel-and-glass buildings framed South Coast Plaza. Overhead the sky was that vibrant California blue, the late afternoon sun reflecting gold off the mirrored skyscraper windows. She had worked in the kitchen of the restaurant at the top of the tallest building, months after they moved back from France, and had earned that job herself; no one knew who Beric King was in those days. But he changed that dynamically by branding his world. He put his name on everything—

the Donald Trump of haute cuisine. And she had used that brand in naming her business. When she had first told him she wanted to start a design business he'd laughed at her. Now he was taking credit for it. The possibility she was riding on the glamorous coattails of her ex was like a pail of cold water in her face.

A light tapping came from the door and Annalisa stuck her head inside. "Daddy's gone, right?"

"The coast is clear."

"I heard him when I came in, so I went straight to my office. I had to listen to him on the cell phone all week."

"Let your voice mail answer it."

"He calls until he fills my mailbox."

"No one can ever accuse your dad of not going after something when he wants it."

Her daughter made the French throat noise perfectly. Annalisa was everything good about her ex. "Your father doesn't believe in taking a backseat." Laurel paused, then said what she was thinking, "Maybe I should have named the company Peyton Design. "

"No. My name is King," Annalisa said simply.

Laurel merely stared at her daughter. Tension she hadn't even felt drained from her body. One of the problems with her marriage was Beric could so easily make her doubt herself. "Sorry. Fresh wounds and too much of your father's fly-by drama."

"Good. You're mad at dad, too."

"Actually, I'm working hard not to give him that much power over me."

Pat interrupted them with a fax still warm from the machine. "Good news from Jack Colson. I thought you'd want to read this."

Laurel read the fax in disbelief. "They're checking our references." She looked from Pat to Annalisa. "Jack says Del Mar called him about our work. They are actually considering us for the Camino Cliff project. My God."

"Of course they are. We do the best work," Annalisa said with all the creamy assurance of youth.

Laurel expected the contract to go to one of the larger, older firms. Camino Cliff was pie-in-the-sky, like buying a lotto ticket for a megajackpot. "I don't believe this."

"You can't keep thinking so small, Mom."

"I'm realistic. Makes for a safer existence."

"Safe, maybe. But I'd rather win and you can't win without taking a risk. Makes life more interesting." Annalisa stood up. "I have to leave early. Dinner plans tonight."

Laurel continued to study the fax. Jack implied it was a done deal, that Del Mar would take their bid, but Laurel didn't want to believe it was possible and was afraid to want it. She had stopped dreaming a long time ago.

"Mom?"

Laurel looked up.

Annalisa stood in the doorway. "Daddy is never realistic."

For the last three, poststroke decades, Victor Banning
went to every mainland opening of Kathryn Peyton's
work. First in a wheelchair pushed by Harlan, later with
a walker, and eventually, like tonight, leaning on an intri-
cately carved silver cane some might consider a work of
art. A phalanx of people flanked each lit niche, examining the twisted glazed pots that were actually clay sculptures, some close to life-sized. The collection was titled
Dark Places, with individual names like *Night Sky, Jungles,
Closet Time,* and *The Heart.*

Victor thumbed through the brochure before reading
the artist's statement.

> Artists live twice. Once in real time and
> again in each work they create. I've been an
> artist for over four decades. I use the pain
> of life to create works with meaning. Art

isn't art without meaning, and meaning
can come only from human experience.
                                    K. PEYTON

She stood outside the crowd, wearing something
bohemian. Music piped through corner speakers was the
Irish folk kind played in three-hour movies, and the bar
served only wine. She said nothing when he walked up to
her, and looked resigned. He used his cane to gesture
around the room. "You're trying too hard, Kathryn."

Her next breath was long. "I disliked you less when
you couldn't speak." She always crossed her arms when
they faced each other. Protective gestures he noticed.

Their conversation had grown into an artistic en-
deavor, perfected over the years, its silent seeds beginning with his first appearance, when his mouth was
numb, his arm and leg cursedly limp, and coherent
speech impossible. But for years now their short
exchanges had more meaning than any work of art. "I
can't get a scotch," he said.

"You don't need a scotch."

"Alcohol makes people put aside their inhibitions.
Cocktails will make people spend money."

"It's sold out, Victor."

He didn't try to feign surprise and held up the
brochure. "I read your statement."

"It's new."

"I know. It takes a long passage of years to see the world
clearly. This sounds as if you want to live in a garret."

Small frown lines creased her face and golden skin.
She wasn't an easy woman to read, but she looked
thoughtful and didn't respond. No comeback.

"The classic image of pain and the artist. I knew someone once whose art could only come from scandal." For one brief moment Victor felt something close to sorrow. He nodded at the nearest piece, then at the room in general. "This collection is impressive. You've grown, Kathryn."

She looked him straight in the eye. "Am I supposed to thank you?"

"No, but looking at your work makes one wonder how tortured your life is."

Her laugh had a humorless sound. "I think you know all about torture."

He could look in the mirror every single day—had for most of his life—and see no cure for unhappiness. "I know the dark places of the heart."

"I imagine you do, Victor. Excuse me. I'm sure you'll want to go where they serve scotch. Alcohol is supposed to soothe a tortured soul, and I need to mix." She left him standing there, and tonight, like all the other nights, she never asked why he was there.

The only photo in the room was of a woman who would never grow old. She stood on a sandy beach with her sons, caught laughing in a clear blue instant of her slim lifetime. The picture anchored the corner of Cale's desk, there to jog his memory. So much of the time now he stumbled through his days like someone hit in the head and unable to remember the past.

He washed down a couple of naproxen with some cold decaf coffee—possibly the worst drink in existence—and studied the King woman's history a second time, making notes until the ink ran out on his Mont

Blanc, a gift from Robyn. He slammed drawers and told himself it was because he couldn't find an ink cartridge. Finally he dropped the pen on his desk and rubbed a hand over his face.

His wife was diagnosed with cancer early, a small, pea-sized tumor. No chemo. Lucky lady, Robyn only needed radiation. Until another tumor appeared, then another and another. In the end, they fed her enough chemo to kill the cancer, or what little was left of her. After she was gone, he would glance up from the newspaper and speak to her out of habit. He'd catch a flash of a bright color from the corner of his eye and look up, sure she was coming into the room. In the middle of the night he'd turn over and reach for her as he had for so many years, only to find himself alone with pillows that smelled like laundry soap instead of the tropical scent of her shampoo.

Soon death and all those percentages and statistics associated with it became a weight on his back every time he examined a patient or walked into the OR. His desire to tackle any high-risk surgery was shot, gone. Surgeons might take a lot of flak for their arrogance, but only an enormous ego had the confidence to believe you could beat death.

"Hey, Pop." His younger son, Dane, strolled through the door as if he owned the office, and maybe the world. A gift of youth.

"You're going to make one hell of a surgeon," Cale told him.

"Probably, if I can ever grasp the technique for a central line. I blew it again this morning. I wouldn't want to be my patient."

"You'll get it."

"So they tell me whenever I hit bone."

"Go deeper under the clavicle. I couldn't tie a suture knot for the life of me. Keep trying. Medicine is more practice than talent."

"Thank God, else I'd be drummed out of the brotherhood."

That wasn't true. His golden son was one of the gifted ones who had an instinct for medicine, a mind for diagnosis, and usually grasped complex skills with ease.

Dane picked up the photograph. "I remember this day. Mom was mad at you because you were trying to get the right camera angle and stepped on our sandwiches."

Cale laughed, but only because his son did. He had forgotten about his heel prints in the bread, and his wife's reaction. Only their perfect moments ever seemed to come to mind.

Dane set down the photo and studied the film display. "What's this?"

"Here are the records." Cale stood and gave Dane his chair. "You tell me."

While his son read over the patient history, Cale sat on the corner of his desk, where bright spring sunshine shone in from the south window, turning everything the color of old newspaper. He adjusted the photograph away from the light.

"Looks like she's had aortic valve replacement." Dane thumbed through the records. "Seven years ago. Possible arrhythmia just discovered during a routine check."

"Here's the video of the latest echocardiogram." Cale explained the results.

"I don't know how you face this kind of challenge day in and day out."

He didn't admit to his son that his hands sometimes shook, that he didn't know when he had stopped needing to hold a frail and damaged heart, or how one day the OR suddenly felt like a Roman arena.

"What are you going to do?"

"I need more tests."

His office manager came in. "Matt called. He's changed your lunch to Tommy Bahama's."

Cale checked his watch. "Did he change the time?"

"No. You're going to be late."

"Damn." He shrugged out of his lab coat, while Dane turned off the video. Cale handed the office manager the files. "Call Dr. Collins's office and have them schedule a TEE. I'm not sure what we're looking at." He grabbed his keys. "Let's go, son."

Forty-five minutes later they walked into Tommy Bahama's, a trendy Newport Beach restaurant off Pacific Coast Highway, the kind of hip young place that served fruit-sodden fish and reggae chicken.

Dane groaned, looking around. "Palm trees and parrots? All I wanted was a good hamburger that doesn't scream I-was-made-in-a-hospital-cafeteria, an icy Coors, and a little ESPN."

Matt was in the back of the restaurant, talking to a man in a tropical shirt. Cale nudged Dane. "There's your brother."

"Who's that with him? Gilligan?"

They didn't stop laughing until they were in a booth

with Matt and had ordered. Dane slapped a palm frond out of his way and swore.

Matt looked at him. "What's wrong with you?"

"If they put a paper umbrella in my beer, I'm leaving."

"Change your order to a martini, little brother, and maybe they'll skewer the olives with a plastic monkey."

"You're living in a time warp. I stopped collecting swizzle sticks when I was ten. What are we doing here? I wanted a pound of sirloin and a pile of fries. If anyone I know sees me here I'll have to hide behind this menu. Wait"—Dane turned to Matt—"I know what this is. You're going to tell us you're gay. I always thought you were too pretty."

"Funny," Matt said, then paused as the waiter brought their food. "We're looking at bids for work on the Cliff project. One of the commercial design companies is local. This kitchen is one of their projects. I wanted to take a look at it."

"Has Jud seen this place?" Dane scanned the room. "I'd like to be here when he does."

"I'm overseeing the project and have to pick the subs. I'm interested in the kitchen design, not the restaurant design. I'm leaning toward giving the contract to a smaller company."

"Jud had a reason for giving you control." Cale knew his brother didn't do anything lightly. "And you wanted your own project."

"A baptism by fire," Matt said, but Cale knew this was a big deal to his son.

Dane laughed. "You told me you hated feeling like a yes-man."

"I did. When he gave me carte blanche, he said I

wouldn't have anyone to blame but myself when all hell broke loose, which it would, weekly, maybe daily."

"Be thankful he's your boss, son. Jud learned the business from Victor. You're luckier than he was."

"Speaking of our illustrious patriarch"—Dane scraped tropical fruit relish off his hamburger—"a hundred bucks says Uncle Jud's date to Victor's birthday bash is under twenty-five."

Matt laughed. "Another sweet young thing for you to steal away, Dad."

"She was thirty and I didn't steal her away."

"Once she heard about Mom she spent most of the evening talking with you." Dane stuck the paper umbrella garnish from his lunch in Matt's sandwich. "Here. I hate pineapple."

"It had only been a year since she'd lost her husband. I understood what she was going through." Cale hated that he sounded defensive.

"Yeah, but Uncle Jud was pissed," Dane said.

"He was a bear at work for a week," Matt added. "I couldn't blame him. He walked in with this drop-dead knockout of a woman, someone every man there would have given their left nut for, and she spent the entire night talking with you in a dark corner. While he spent most of the evening pacing at the bar and trying to pretend he didn't care."

"He took her out to dinner once. There was nothing between them." Cale signaled for the check, then caught a look his sons exchanged. "And there was nothing between us, either."

"Too bad," Dane said. "You just might have to get a life, Pop."

Cale had a life. He just didn't know how to survive it. When his sons finished their food, he said, "I need to get back to the office."

Matt put his hand on the bill. "I'll get the check, Dad. And I'll take that bet, little brother. A hundred bucks. On Jud's date."

"You're on." Dane stood.

Matt slid his arm around him, laughing. "Jud's been back with Kelly for a while. You want to pay up now?"

"Screw you, Matt."

Outside was too warm, the Southern California heat baking in waves above the asphalt; it aged skin, bleached hair, faded paint and photographs on office desks. Cale put on his sunglasses and headed for his car, his sons walking ahead of him, tall, grown, and on their own. For a moment he felt old just looking at them, until they started a mock fight, socking each other in the upper arm, laughing and egging each other on as they'd done when they were young teens with big feet and long thin bodies they hadn't grown into yet.

Though men now, they still liked each other. Cale made a mental note to call Jud, then leaned on his car, watching his sons horse around in the parking lot. Everything about the moment seemed wrong without Robyn there to rest his arm around. He played the mental game of those left behind: the memory test. What would she have said if she were next to him? With the deepest of sorrows, he realized he didn't have a clue.

Jud Banning only heard half of what she was saying, something about buying a condo. Kelly was a leggy brunette, a magazine editor with one failed marriage and no kids. They'd met years before through Robyn, dated, broken up, met again six months ago, and fallen back into an easy, comfortable relationship. With his work so demanding, Jud preferred easy. What he had wished for in his youth didn't feel like much of a gift at middle age, when in a single week he'd been in Alaska, Nevada, and Louisiana, and had come home only to have to put out a corporate fire in Santa Barbara that morning. The term "bone-tired" had meaning now.

Through the restaurant window came shades of pink and gold from a Pacific sunset, highlighting engraved silver, thin crystal, and Kelly's precise, classic beauty. Surrounding him were all the trappings of a romantic dinner, the kind they'd had more and more of in the last month. He took a deep drink of whiskey.

"The condo I'm considering is in your building."

"Why do you want to move?" He set down his glass and the waiter brought a salad he didn't touch.

"Change is good." Her voice was overly bright and gave him a heavy, sinking premonition.

"You're in a great house. Great neighborhood," he said. "You've lived there how many years?"

"Ten."

"It's home for you, Kel. You're there every night. You have those kids next door you take everywhere. I barely know my neighbors. The condo works for me. The only yard I want is my dock."

She wasn't eating either and stared down into her champagne glass, the lemon twist curling on a delicate crystal rim, the kind that sang under your finger and could break from a harsh sound.

"You like your neighbors, your space, your lawn, the flowers."

"Flowers can grow just as well in pots on a balcony."

Running through his head were a hundred reasons why her plan was a really bad idea.

"This isn't about growing flowers," she said finally.

"And it's not about buying a condo." He finished off the scotch.

To her credit, she didn't flinch, but shook her head. "You'd think I would have learned the first time around."

A car horn honked in the distance, laughter came from a nearby table. The clink of silver on bone china. He heard the piano music from the bar, a Billy Joel song. "I like you in my life, Kel."

"I know you do. But I want more. I'm in love with you."

He reached across the table and took her hand, genuinely sorry. He'd never reacted well when cornered. "You know I care. We have time. Is something wrong at work? Maybe I can help."

She only looked at him, a little startled, then laughed as if he were a lost cause. "Robyn warned me. I thought you were only a workaholic who made no time for anyone else."

"I run the family business."

"I'd hardly call BanCo a family business, Jud."

"The company has always been demanding. I don't understand why Robyn would warn you."

"She didn't warn me about your work. She told me you couldn't commit to a relationship, any relationship. She called you a classic Jack Nicholson."

He hated being called a classic anything, even by the dead sister-in-law he had adored.

"I had hoped it would be different with us." Kelly stood up and dropped her napkin on her plate. "I want commitment and a life spent with someone who loves me as much as I love them. I deserve that, Jud."

He stood up, too. "Kelly, wait. Let's talk about this."

"Do you want to marry me?"

"I don't know. Maybe. Someday."

"Jud, please. I deserve the truth."

It was a few seconds before he answered her. "The truth is I don't want to marry anyone right now."

"I know." She picked up her purse. "Don't worry. I won't buy the condo. But please don't call me again."

He watched her walk away from him, tall and elegant, her slim spine and square shoulders bare in a black cocktail dress, her dark hair glossy. He knew it smelled like Hawaiian flowers and her skin like baby powder. Kelly slept on the right side of the bed. She used his athletic socks to keep her feet warm and drank milk with Pepsi. She loved him, but for the life of him, he couldn't go after her.

A realist never dared to dream because a lost dream felt like something of a nightmare. Living with one hope after another was crippling. Snippets of what-if crept into your days. Your mind wandered down paths not taken. Too soon your world stopped being real and you looked only for the impossibly perfect.

All the temptations of a perfect world hit Laurel when King Design won the Camino Cliff contract. On the tails of the news came a vellum invitation with a gold-lined, embossed envelope announcing a cocktail party for all the project contractors. A quick trip to the salon for foils. Shopping with Annalisa for the dress, the shoes. Now, in a classic black sheath and designer heels, Laurel felt a realist's sense of irony as she added the perfect accessory—ridiculously expensive diamond drop earrings she'd bought after Beric had had his third affair.

"Mom?"

Laurel heard the front door close. "I'm coming." She met Annalisa at the bottom of the stairs. "These shoes are going to kill me."

"You needed something sexy."

"What I'll need is my health insurance when I face-plant somewhere. Come to think of it, these shoes cost more than my health insurance." Laurel went into the garage and paused. "I'm walking like Anna Nicole Smith."

"Mother."

"I'm going to change into pumps."

"Stop it. You look great. You walk fine. Are you really going to let four little inches keep you from looking twenty years younger?"

"You are a cruel, cruel child." Laurel took off the shoes and got in the car. "I'm not driving in these. They're for women who ride in limos."

The restaurant in Laguna was beach chic, with stone columns, glass, and tumbled marble floors. They followed Private Party signs into a bar and terrace overlooking the pale sand and blue water, with the callow green shadow of Catalina on the horizon. Waiters served hors d'oeuvres and champagne from crystal trays and people milled around in groups, while men at the bar stood two deep.

A tall, good-looking young man in a custom suit left one group and joined them. "Annalisa." Her daughter looked oddly nervous when he took her hand. He turned, a telling little moment, since he hadn't let go of Annalisa's hand. "You must be Laurel King. I've seen your work. It clinched the contract. Annalisa was right."

Without missing a beat her daughter said, "Mom, this is Matthew Banning."

And it was like a vampire had just sucked Laurel dry. One deep breath and she recovered enough to make small talk, to grab a glass of champagne and sip it, while in a room suddenly filled with white noise.

Annalisa explained BanCo's connection and Matthew Banning told her about his meeting with her daughter. The walls felt as if they were closing in, air seemingly nonexistent. She wanted to place the cold glass against her forehead, but all she could do was look into his face and see another one. This was Jud's son.

He had very dark curly hair, nothing like the sandy blond hair of the Banning men she'd known. But with that one word—Banning—his eyes and features, the jaw, the slashes when he smiled all took her back to 1970. Laurel wondered what his mother was like. When he laughed, she remembered that sound. How odd it felt to be standing here so many years later, like someone on the outside looking in, and watch her daughter talking to Jud's son.

When she glanced over Matthew's shoulder she was thankful for every inch of her heels. Jud was standing in the doorway looking toward the opposite side of the room. At that moment, she was not a strong woman. She had no preparation. No time. With a plastic smile, she said, "Excuse me. I'm going outside and get some air."

On the terrace, she turned her back to the room and gripped the railing tightly, aware of her heart pounding. She took long, deep breaths of cool, sea-washed air. The sun was slipping down the sky and wouldn't set for about another hour. She put on her sunglasses, then sat at a table in the far corner, which was a good spot to hide. Time moved with each crash of a wave. She drank the champagne too fast and set down her empty glass. A few people walked by. She was looking out at the sea when the coolness of a shadow fell over her. Jud stood barely a foot away, discolored slightly from her dark lenses, holding an amber cocktail and a champagne. He set the champagne in front of her, and she was struck by an almost comical sense of déjà vu.

"I saw you through the glass," he said. "And I asked myself why a beautiful woman was out here alone." He paused, then added, "I'm Jud Banning."

There was a beat of silence, an instant of discovery when she wanted to laugh or cry or both, because she realized that he didn't have a clue who she was.

CHAPTER

25

Jud pulled out a chair. "Do you mind if I sit down?" The blonde hesitated long enough for him to wonder if she was going to send him packing.

"Interesting, Jud Banning, how your pickup line hasn't changed over the years."

Shit. He'd slept with her. She was looking down to remove her dark glasses, and her hair hid her face. Then thirty years fell away.

"Jailbait?"

She gave a short laugh. "We have a problem. I'm not even close to jailbait age anymore."

"You changed your hair." He sat down and took a long drink.

"Yes." She touched her hair in a self-conscious motion. "Quite a few years ago. After my divorce I needed a change."

She was still lovely, softer, a little heavier in the way that gave older women lushness, the kind of figure that made you want to stay in bed. She was divorced. Another fool who had lost her. And he didn't know what to say.

"Awkward. Isn't it?"

"What are you doing here? This is a private party." He sounded like a bouncer, territorial and ready to throw her out on her ear.

"I was invited. My daughter and I own a professional kitchen design company. Your son hired us for the project restaurants."

"I don't have a son."

Frowning, she looked at his left hand. "I thought Matthew was your son."

"He's Cale's oldest son."

"Cale has sons?"

"Two."

"Is he here?" She looked around.

"He's a doctor, Laurel. A cardiothoracic surgeon."

Her face was colorless. "You're kidding."

"No. He finished medical school at the top of his class." Since she was that surprised by Cale's profession she didn't remember much about them. He felt betrayed. "All he ever talked about was being a doctor."

"I remember," she said softly enough to make him forgive her, then feel a pang of envy for his brother.

He wanted to say more, but it was one of those moments when sound grew louder, when a million things to say slipped your mind.

She stood up. "I think I should leave."

Suddenly her image and Kelly's melted together. She started to walk away. He grabbed her arm. "Wait, Laurel."

Startled, she stared pointedly at his hand, then up at him. "What are you doing, Jud?" He wasn't holding her hard, but he refused to let her run away.

"Mom?" A stunning young woman with long red hair came up to her, and Jud let go of Laurel's arm. "I've been looking for you."

"This is my daughter, Annalisa King." Laurel stepped back out of his reach. "This is Jud Banning."

"You're Matthew's uncle. It's good to meet you." She had vibrant coloring, the kind that turned heads, but it wasn't her coloring that caught him off-guard. Her face was Laurel's, soft and young, with that rare promise of a woman who would be beautiful for an entire lifetime. Laurel's mother had looked the same when he'd stood on her doorstep and begged her to tell him where her daughter was. It struck him that Laurel was much older now than her mother had been then. So many years had passed, and still, a singular time so small on the scale of a life never lost its importance.

Annalisa grabbed her mother's hand. "You need to come inside. The architects for the restaurant projects are waiting. They're familiar with Megryl's and Cutter's and want to meet you."

Laurel looked at him, then said nothing more than "Good-bye."

Her daughter stopped a few feet away and turned. "No, Mom, wait. Mr. Banning should come, too. He certainly has an interest in King Design, in how we work and who we are."

He caught the pleading in Laurel's eyes and turned to her daughter. "You two go ahead. I trust Matthew to have chosen the best companies for the job. I think I'll stay here and watch that sunset." He gestured toward the horizon with his glass and the ice rattled like loose bones and broken skeletons.

"Good-bye, Jud." Laurel walked away with her daughter and didn't look back, even after they disappeared through the open glass doors.

The gulls wheeled and cawed noisily overhead and the water splashed against the rocks below the stone terrace. The sky was brilliant—red, purple, and gold—and muted everything, even what he was feeling. At that moment the sky was not much different than it had been a long time ago, from the deck of the SS *Catalina*. Funny that he could remember so clearly a sunset over thirty years old. He turned, leaning against the cement balustrade, and sipped his drink while he watched her through the softly tinted glass. He'd let her leave, but this was a woman he wasn't going to let go.

Matthew Banning held her hand too long, brought her the right drink without asking, brushed against her in a crowd, then placed his hand on her bare back while he apologized, and seemed to have a devastating smile meant for only her. It was killing Annalisa. If this kind of attraction game were happening in a bar, they would go home together.

So she did her damnedest to keep her mom nearby as a deterrent, until she came out of the rest room to find him standing in the hallway, over six feet of dripping sex appeal and surefire trouble. He was talking to one of the project contractors, an opportunity for her to whip by him and get out the front door.

"Annalisa, wait. Excuse me." He turned back to the

man. "We'll talk Monday." Matt jogged over to her. "I've been looking for you. Things are winding down here. Would you like to get something to eat? I know a quiet place near here that serves a great steak."

"I came with my mom. I was just going to meet her at the valet, but if some of the group are going out to eat, I'll tell her."

"Look. I'm trying to ask you out."

"On a date," she said flatly.

He laughed and looked away, then rubbed the back of his neck with a hand. "Yeah, on a date."

"Do you think that's a good idea?"

"I've thought it was a good idea since the day you walked into my office and told me why I should hire you."

"And now that you have, I don't think dating is a good idea."

"Tell me if I'm wrong, but I sensed there was something going on here. Between us."

He was a foot away from her, but she could feel him on her skin, small pinpoints of energy, like the air during an electrical storm. "I won't deny there is something, but your contract is the biggest we've ever had, and frankly, just too important. You should be happy it's that important to me."

"I am glad you take the job seriously, but that has nothing to do with dinner."

"I think we both know it does. Dating at work? That's asking for trouble."

"We don't exactly work together."

"I'm not buying that argument."

"You should. Nothing will change on the job. My

private, social life is completely separate from my business."

"Only in a perfect world, Matthew. I'm sorry." She stepped away from him. "I can't. My mother's waiting. I'll see you later." The hallway felt a mile long, longer with him watching her walk away. A couple of the contractors had heard and were watching her walk away. Outside, the air was cool against her hot cheeks. She closed the car door and buckled up.

Her mom didn't look at her—a bad sign—and rested her arms on the steering wheel. "Okay, young lady," she said with perfectly bad timing. "We need to talk."

"You have a captive audience. Fire away, Mother." Her daughter stared out the window.

Ten feet more and Laurel stopped the car. "You drive. I've had champagne." She was fine, actually, but let Annalisa drive and answer her questions, instigate an argument and try to make this her fault. They were two signals away from the restaurant before Laurel spoke. "You should have told me what you did."

"Meeting with BanCo got us the contract. Why are we rehashing it?"

"Why are you biting my head off?"

"Because someone in there hit on me."

"And that's a bad thing?"

"Just annoying. I don't want to talk about it. Look, Mom. We'll never get anywhere sitting around and waiting for the world to come to us. We have to fight to get ahead. We have to take risks. Would you have ever even thought to go higher than Del Mar? To even fight for the job?"

The truth hurt, spoken in such a derisive tone, and more, the idea that Annalisa thought she was so passive. It took so few words for mothers and daughters to hurt each other. And seeing herself from her child's truth didn't match the person Laurel thought she was. "No," she admitted, "I wouldn't have done it. But I don't think I need to. Apparently I have you to do that."

"I'm not sorry. One of us had to do something." A truck cut them off and Annalisa hit the horn.

"It's a lot easier to jump headlong into trouble when you don't have a lifetime of mistakes clinging to your back."

"Where's the mistake? We had absolutely nothing to lose. We were either going to get the contract or not."

There was no risk. Her daughter was right. How often had she looked for risks where there weren't any? She had become the kind of person afraid to move forward, and—damn—where exactly had she buried herself? Laurel sat there in silence, mired in a chasm of doubt while lights from the roadside businesses and passing cars flickered inside, creating colored shadows on the windshield, the mirror, and their profiles, a kind of surreal, carnival atmosphere of a Fellini film or that confusing instant when you first wake from a dream.

By the time they turned into the colony road, you could have cut the silent air with a knife. "I'm glad you fought for us," she said to Annalisa. "But we need to tell each other what we think, and what we're doing. This is a business partnership. You should have told me what you did as soon as you did it instead of sending me in there tonight with no clue. I was blindsided. That's not good business." Facing the Bannings without warning. A nightmare. But her daughter knew nothing about her past. Secrets were heavy black burdens weighing you down throughout life, often the very things that kept you from moving forward or looking for happiness.

Annalisa pulled into the alley behind the beach house. "I should have told you. But sometimes, well, I don't know, it seems as if you are afraid, Mom. Not just in business, but like you're afraid of life." Inside the garage, she got out of the car and faced Laurel over it. "You said it took your heart surgery for you to finally leave Daddy. You started the business in spite of him, but it's as if you're afraid to take the next steps. Like you're frozen in time, not moving forward or backward. I don't mean to criticize you, really I don't, but you're not happy."

"You make me happy." Laurel took the keys.

"Even when I sneak behind your back?"

"You won't do it again." Laurel eased up the steps to the kitchen door still uneasy in her shoes. "I think happiness might be overrated, and certainly it's fleeting, not exactly something to hang your future on."

"Oh, Mom. What's the big deal about making mistakes? You have to live."

She looked at her daughter, so young, oozing confidence, standing on one foot in even skimpier stilettos and easily tapping the other, while glibly instructing her about risk and mistakes, about life and happiness.

Laurel spoke from the raw pain of experience. "Mistakes can change lives forever."

"But change isn't a bad thing."

"I'd like to be young again and so self-assured." She shook her head and laughed a little, maybe with a bit of longing. "I'd love to race into life with my arms wide open, ready for all of it, with the idea nothing bad would ever happen to me or those I've loved."

"Then do it. Run. Like this . . ." Arms outstretched, Annalisa ran—actually ran—in those shoes to her car. "Night, Mom."

Laurel watched her pull away and closed the garage door. Inside, she headed for the stairs, hit the tile floor, caught her heel, and fell flat on her face. Pain rang through her arm, chin, hip, and knee. Stunned, she lay there for a second, then started to laugh, alone, still embarrassed. But a minute later she was crying, head buried in her arms, face to the damned cold floor, sobbing. It was a while before she sat up, pulling off the stilettos while she sniffled, a silly fool.

Being unhappy was a difficult thing to admit, when you suspected the reason you were in such a miserable place was your own fault. Like someone lost in the woods, she was going in all the wrong directions. Her dreams felt so far out of reach. She'd faced one of them tonight, faced him in four-inch heels.

But four-inch heels didn't make her any younger. She couldn't click her four-inch heels together and find her true way home. Four inches didn't bring her any closer to happiness. Four inches didn't erase the past.

Seattle, 1970–1971

For those months after Laurel left Cale, left Jud, left her mother, and left LA, her life became nothing but lies. The lies started with the idea that the Pill was foolproof. Ninety-eight percent. Laurel was in the two percent, and pregnant. Panicked, she went back to Seattle, because once it had been home. She lied to her mother about transferring schools and found a job at a restaurant in the kitchen instead, lied about the father of the child when she couldn't hide her pregnancy any longer. She lied to the doctor at the clinic where they treated her, lied to the adoption attorney who set up the adoption for her—told him she'd had multiple partners and didn't know who the father was. In that time of free love, partner swapping, and communes, girls went for abortions in dirty rooms in the backs of bars and markets in Tijuana. But a girl from school once bled to death after a botched abortion, and another had to have an emergency hysterectomy.

As afraid as she was of her pregnancy, she was more afraid of ending it, and she honestly didn't think she could do it. Life grew inside her. Some other woman could choose that way, but she wouldn't. So instead, she lied to survive; because she was scared and young and she knew if she ever let either Banning brother know the truth, it would shatter them all for a lifetime.

She even lied to herself as she tried to distance herself from the baby, tried to pretend it wasn't as terrible a time as it was, that what she was doing was for the best. But the best answer wasn't always the easiest one. At night she lay in bed, the baby kicking inside of her, and wondered which mistake was worse.

The adoptive parents were a nice couple, a district attorney and his wife in their thirties who had tried and tried to have a baby, but the woman had almost died with the last miscarriage almost five months into her term. Laurel met them once and saw something in the woman's eyes when she looked at her distended belly. She saw a longing so intense, it was almost unbearable to watch.

Laurel worked at the restaurant kitchen up until the last few weeks, when she sat alone in her apartment and talked to the baby inside her. She told it how good its life would be with the O'Hanlons, all the while trying to really convince herself.

The delivery was long—a punishment for her sins?—twenty-one hours of labor. There were marks on the wall from her fist, marks from the fake wedding ring she'd bought herself and wore in public until the last month of her pregnancy, when it stayed on her finger only because she was so swollen she couldn't get it off.

The baby was a boy, nine pounds. He came out quietly, eerily so, almost as if after all the punishment, God was being benevolent. She would never have the memory of his cry. She put her hands over her ears so she couldn't hear his cooing noises. They asked her if she wanted to see him, but she closed her eyes and turned her head away, afraid that if she looked at him, she would never give him up. She loved him enough to do this. He deserved the O'Hanlons, who had been through so much and wanted a child in a way she couldn't. Not now. Not here. Not this way. He deserved a mother who could look at him the way Barbara O'Hanlon did.

After she signed the papers, her belly and between her legs still sore and tight from the delivery stitches, her signature safely made, the attorney handed her an envelope. "It's from Barbara," he said.

Laurel turned it over in her hands.

"You don't have to read it."

Detached, she studied her name beautifully written in indigo blue ink from a fountain pen. She could see the small bleeding vein marks on each letter of her name. The envelope was thick, cream-colored expensive paper. It wasn't sealed closed. The flap was tucked inside.

> *Dear Laurel,*
>
> *I don't know if I can tell you in this letter what it means to us to have this wonderful gift of life. We named him Gregory Patrick O'Hanlon. We will cherish him.*
>
> *When the time is right, I will tell him it takes a strong woman, one who loves her child more than herself, to give him up to a better life and let someone else love him every single day of his life.*
>
> *And we will.*
>
> > *Barbara*
> > *O'Hanlon*

Laurel curled into a tight ball as she sobbed with the letter in her hand, and the nurses left her alone. One brought her hot chocolate and a copy of the latest issue of *Glamour* magazine. She opened the magazine and cried because she felt so much older than the models inside. The things they wrote about, college dates and parties, long hair versus short, my day at an antiwar rally, hot pants and suede boots, didn't matter to her anymore. But she wasn't certain what did matter.

That first day after the birth, she got up so many times

and started for the nursery. Perhaps she just wanted to say good-bye. But she never made it there. Once, she made it to the end of the hall, where she could see the nursery viewing window but not the babies inside. The O'Hanlons stood there, arms wrapped around each other, both of them laughing and crying at the same time. She turned around and went back to her room, then went home the next day.

A week later she left Seattle. She packed up what she wanted to keep, not much: a fringed shirt, two sweaters, an alpaca poncho, and her patchwork jeans. She left the key to her apartment with the manager, gave her old maternity clothes to a shelter in the U District, sent money from her trust to an international bank account, and left.

At the airport, she flew standby on a plane to the East Coast, spent eighteen hours on a hard chair at JFK, uncomfortable because she was still bleeding. She went into the women's room and changed her pads dispassionately, her back ridged, her eyes closed. At 11 P.M. she took a Pan Am flight to Paris. From her window seat she watched the lights on the ground disappear, leaving everything behind her as though it were someone else's life.

CHAPTER

26

Cale had never thrown a surgical instrument in his life, but a few days before, he'd lost control in the OR. Complications weren't unusual—surgery was seldom routine. He had always had some kind of innate ability to switch gears. Enter an adverse event? Experience and calm method always kicked in.

The heart valve replacement hadn't carried heightened risk: Dan Hardt wasn't old, the organ wasn't in failure, it wasn't a second open-heart surgery. But a mere artificial heartbeat or two on the machine was time that could have saved the patient. Cale had felt his freeze happening as if he were separated from his own body. After fighting the monster in his head for months, he'd carried that monster on his back into the OR on Tuesday, and a thirty-nine-year-old father of three died.

In the three days since, he did five successful surgeries. But yesterday, he walked in on a candid conversation among his team.

"Poor man," one of them said. "He's a lost soul."

"Me?" he asked, interrupting them. "Or Dan Hardt?"

The women blushed and lied, the men grew stoic. But he'd heard them talking about the surgical tray crashing against the floor, months of his moody commands, the day he'd been so angry about rock music on the private sound system and ordered it turned off. Dr. Banning, who used to scrub to Janis Joplin and Joe Cocker.

He had never thought of himself as one of those physicians with behavioral problems, the men who were known as tyrants but geniuses. The world of medicine—even the laity—often believed temperament was tied to genius, so unacceptable behavior became acceptable.

Now Cale sat on a chair in the waiting room of a colleague, staring at the floor and seeing only that moment of devastation overcome the wife of the patient he had lost. Sally Hardt's expression haunted him in the rearview mirror as he drove home from the hospital, on the backs of his eyelids when he tried to fall asleep, and he even saw it reflected in his dining room window while they okayed the catering menu for Victor's birthday celebration.

"Come on in, Cale." Rick Sachs held his office door open. The In door. The Out door led to the parking lot, so clients could come and go with anonymity. Sachs was tall and trim, a respected psychiatrist specializing in troubled physicians. Burnout, addictions, illness, senility, and some patients sent by their administrative boards because they were just plain bad doctors with too many lawsuits and complaints.

Rick sat down across from him. "So what's this about?"

"My private M&M," Cale said. Morbidity and mortality conferences were a weekly ritual at every academic hospital in the nation. During an M&M, all in the department discussed cases that had been problematic, had unfortunate outcomes, or were caused by procedural or diagnostic error. "I lost a patient on Tuesday, and blew up in the OR. I threw an instrument tray."

Rick wrote on a notepad. "Is this something you've done before?"

"No."

"You've lost patients."

"Yes, but not for a long, long time. A few years."

They talked about the procedure, about the circumstances, about his private life and more private pain, and Cale cried openly. Even if he could have stopped his tears he didn't try. Tears were proof he still felt something. Eventually, he'd eaten up over an hour with Sachs and discussed another appointment.

"You don't have a reputation for problem behavior," Sachs told him. "You're well respected. But this incident can't help the self-doubt you're feeling."

Cale listened to Rick's assessment, and it almost killed him to ask the question he was most afraid of. "Would you recommend I stop practicing . . . at least, for a while?"

"The fact that you're here on your own says enough for me. Certainly something has to change, but you've had subsequent surgeries this week. It's not a skill issue, Cale. And you aren't Jacob Wilson." Wilson was a once well-respected local physician who refused to stop doing surgery and had his license pulled when his deteriorated mental state led to three deaths. "You aren't taking drugs or drinking," Rick said. "You've had a tough loss and feel your profession let you down."

"Not me. Robyn."

"Your profession let you down, Cale, when medicine couldn't save your wife. Clearly depression is a problem here, and I'm not telling you anything you don't understand. Depression isn't something you can self-diagnose. We expect more from ourselves. But today's world is one of Prozac, Zoloft, and Wellbutrin. You're human, even though so often your patients look to you as more, and sometimes you ask yourself for the impossible. There's a clear reason they call it medical practice; even the word suggests we're far from perfect. Mistakes happen, but your reaction to them is what's changed. And that's what we need to address."

They set another appointment and Cale stood to leave.

"There's one important question I need you to think about and we'll discuss your answer next week."

"Sure. What is it?"

"Ask yourself if you're upset because you lost the patient, or because you ruined a statistic."

Sunday night Kathryn dropped her suitcase on the entry floor of Laurel's beach house and slumped into a chair in the living room. "It'll be nice to not sleep in a hotel for a change. I always forget how much work these shows are."

"I don't know why you keep doing them," Laurel called out from the kitchen. "I'm making us some herbal tea. The galleries would take your work sight unseen. You're getting older, Mother."

"Thank you for pointing that out. I couldn't tell from my sore feet, bad eyes, gray hair, and crooked fingers." She laughed to soften the edges of her words, but it was true. Her glasses were stronger, her hands often ached at night, and she made mistakes in glazes she'd been mixing for years. "I constantly lose my studio keys and sometimes I'll just stare at the phone because I can't remember your phone number."

Annalisa touched her shoulder as she walked by. "I'm twenty-two and I walk into my kitchen and forget why I'm there. You're not old, Mamie. The show was fabulous. It wasn't even the opening, and yet tonight there was this energy in the room, almost as if the work vibrated toward you. I saw the sense of awe on people's faces, the way your pieces make them think. They discuss the work." She kicked off her shoes and hugged a throw pillow to her chest. "Think about it. You live alone. You create alone. The shows are the only place where you can actually see your work through the eyes of the outside world. Besides, I love this collection. It deserves viewing."

"I'll admit there is an addicting kind of energy to having a show," Kathryn said. Which could have been the thing sapping something vital from her lately, because she didn't get the same euphoric feeling she used to. Too often she felt empty and wrung out. Laurel could be right. She was old. "Maybe I'll cut back. I don't know."

"And maybe you should do them more often," Annalisa said with a lovely bit of stubbornness.

"Good God, don't encourage her." Laurel set the tea tray down but didn't sit. "Shoot . . . I forgot the lemon."

Over her shoulder she said, "Your grandmother will wear herself out."

Annalisa winked at her. "Mamie doesn't look used up to me."

Her granddaughter was the first person to get the meaning of a piece; it was like watching the workings of her own mind. Some people ascribed to the theory that certain traits skip a generation—genetic hopscotch—and Kathryn liked to believe she and Annalisa were most alike, and that her granddaughter's red hair came from her and not Beric King.

Certainly there was little friction between the two of them, and a bit of hero worship on her granddaughter's part. No judgment. Laurel was a completely different story. Too often they tiptoed around each other. And Kathryn still had trouble forgiving her for running off to France, marrying, and raising Annalisa those first years in a place so far away. Lost years were evaporated time. You couldn't open a can and pour the years back into your life.

Laurel handed Annalisa the lemon dish and sat down. "I wasn't trying to be critical. But you look tired."

"I am," Kathryn admitted, her voice sounding as brittle as her old bones. Victor Banning's comments had her tossing and turning, annoyed and running on no sleep. She didn't like to think of herself as a stereotype. Her art did come from pain. Pain equaled art equaled meaning, and art without meaning was nothing but medium. The best work was organic.

But the idea that she could produce only from self-infliction disturbed her. It said something awful about her choices. Sipping her tea with lemon, she sank farther into the couch cushions. Pieces of her art were scattered around the room, on tables, on the mantel, in lit niches. A huge, more recent piece dominated the corner. "Interesting that I can sit here and see how my work has evolved. I've never kept enough pieces over the years to view it like this." Before her was a retrospective of K. Peyton's work. "He was right. I have grown."

"Who was right?" Annalisa and Laurel were watching her.

She'd spoken aloud. "Just a critic on opening night," she lied. "I wasn't good in the early years."

"That's not true, Mother," Laurel said quickly and with surprising vehemence.

It was so unexpected Kathryn gave pause, then laughed sharply. "Of course it is. I was talking about my earliest work. You were too young to remember anything I did before your father died."

Laurel stood abruptly. "Follow me."

Kathryn and Annalisa exchanged a puzzled look, but Laurel was already marching up the stairs. They caught up with her in the master bedroom, where the sharp scent of roses hung in the air.

"Look at those flowers. The roses are the size of my fist." Annalisa moved toward a table. "Is that a Baccarat vase?"

"Looks like it," Kathryn said. Dozens of white roses and deep greenery fanned out from a large vase on a table near the corner window. "I can barely see the beach."

Laurel pulled a narrow piece of white pottery from the bookshelf and confronted them with it. "I wanted you to see this."

"Who gave you the flowers, Mom?" Annalisa picked up an empty florist's envelope.

"I ran into an old friend."

"That's some friend. What did the card say?"

Laurel froze, then spoke in a rush. "Good luck on your business venture."

A mother could always hear her child's lie. Kathryn understood that her daughter wasn't going to discuss the flowers and she would snap at Annalisa if she asked another question.

"I hope it's a man, Mom. You need some romance in your claustrophobic life."

Laurel turned as pale as the glaze on the piece she held.

"That's my work," Kathryn said, somewhat astonished. It was an early vase and one Jimmy had liked. She could have walked right past it anytime over the years. In those early days she'd seldom sold much and was an artist dealing with failure and still searching for discovery.

"I love this piece," Laurel said quietly. "Don't tell me you had no talent, Mother. I've never seen anything equal."

"It's so different, Mamie." Annalisa took the vase from her mother's hand. "Even your signature is different."

"My early work wasn't well received. One critic— the kindest of the group—called me too sleek and easy." She'd cried in Jimmy's arms that night, when four years' worth of work was slammed in the press. She was young and inconsolable, her skin thin and her wounds deep. Eventually he'd gathered a bunch of his negative music reviews, which were snobbish and caustic, read them aloud, acting them out until life seemed something ludicrously funny.

But now, all Kathryn felt was terribly confused. The vase was sleek, but never easy. She doubted she could produce something like it even with her years of technique and experience. The Kay Peyton who signed the vase could no longer experience a youthful purity of innocence and happiness. She was now K., not Kay, and she knew simple was the most difficult to create. Simple was, in truth, minutely complex.

Her earliest work flooded through her memory in a montage of forgotten, veristic images. A part of her past cracked open before her in a clarity that left her sinking with dread. She longed only to discuss Laurel's flowers, but instead said, "I'm not that artist anymore."

The ruined look Laurel gave her almost brought her to her knees. And Kathryn understood in that single, raw moment that this exchange had nothing to do with art.

Late that night, after her mother had gone to bed and Annalisa had gone home to her own place, Laurel dressed for bed and turned off the bathroom light. One foot into the bedroom and she could smell the spice of the roses over the herbal scent of her soap and shampoo. A surge of something really unfortunate hit her again. Longing, thrill, excitement. The feelings she'd had when she was seventeen, eighteen, the same feelings she'd had that afternoon when Jud's flowers were delivered to her office. But she had no right to those feelings. There was so much between them, too much in the past.

There was a knock at the bedroom door. "Laurel?"

Her mother stood in the open doorway, her robe tied tightly around her waist, making her look smaller, older, and more frail than Laurel could ever remember. The florist's card was in her hand. "This was on the kitchen counter."

"Thanks." Laurel took the card.

"What's going on, Laurel?"

"What?"

"Don't play dumb with me. 'One flower for every year. Thirty years is too long,' signed Jud."

"I'm not seventeen, Mother."

"You're forty-eight and I would think you'd have learned by now not to go backward in life."

"Well, I guess I could just live my entire life in the past like you." Slapping her mother in the face would have been kinder, but the words spilled out and she couldn't stop. Everything she was feeling took over. "Look at what we've become. With all that vitriol, there's no room for me, Mother. There was never any room for me because you wrapped yourself in grief and anger and pain, locked yourself away in your studio and inside your work. You know why I love that vase? I love that vase because there's joy in it. It's not some twisted piece representing the dark side in life. It is simply beautiful." She paused. "I would have liked to have known you then."

"I was a different person living in a different time. Happiness, joy, don't last long. I know. The last time you were mixed up with that family, Laurel, I lost you." Her mother's voice caught and she looked away, seeming to shrink even more. "You went to live in France. You got married. You had Annalisa. All of it, all of a woman's most important life moments, were six thousand miles away from home."

"You were there for the wedding."

"As a guest. I flew in at the last minute because that was when you told me about it. I've wondered if that was the point. And then the wedding was in a pasture."

"It was a lavender field, not a pasture. In 1974 I thought it was romantic. In retrospect, a lot about that day was a mistake. But none of it has anything to do with now."

"It does for me. Every time someone named Banning comes into our lives we lose something, something we can't get back."

Laurel walked around the bed and put the card on her nightstand. "I had to get away, Mother."

"Because of them. Because of those two brothers. You were caught in the middle. It was their fault."

"It was my fault. My fault."

"You had to get away from me." Her mother was crying and Laurel hated that she was again the cause of all this pain.

"Look. I'm sorry this hurts you. I'm sorry it reminds you of things in the past that are difficult to remember. I wouldn't bring you any more pain over Daddy's death for anything. But it's over. It's done. It was so long ago. We can't change any of it. You have to understand this is about business."

"What business?"

"BanCo is the parent company for Del Mar and the Camino Cliff project. I didn't know that when we bid the project, but this is a chance for King Design to take off. A once-in-a-lifetime opportunity, and Annalisa went after the job and got us the contract. A five-million-dollar contract."

"Five million dollars," Kathryn repeated flatly. "I can't compete with five million dollars."

"It's not about you. This is as important to Annalisa as it is to me. She's a smart kid and I'm proud of her. She doesn't know about my past or yours with the Banning family, and I'm not going to let your fear take from her what you took from me." She sounded so rigid and bitter, almost as bitter as her mother.

Kathryn walked out the door, but stopped and turned back. "All I wanted was to protect you."

"Let it go, Mother." Laurel took a long, deep breath. "Please. Let it go."

CHAPTER

27

The next morning her mother was gone with only a note saying that she was going to stay in LA, close to the gallery, for a few more days. Laurel's night had been pretty much sleepless. Guilt was an ugly thing, and the relationship between women often a complex knot of emotional reactions. The things she'd said she couldn't take back. Nothing felt simple anymore. The office elevator closed behind her before she noticed the two single-tubed roses—each the size of a fist and with its own card—on the floor in front of the office door.

Lunch. Call me when you're ready.
                            Jud

The rest of the day was a mess, with Pat on vacation and Annalisa meeting with Del Mar and running errands. The phone rang off the hook most of the morning and into the afternoon; the project plans had been delivered to the wrong company, so Laurel had to spend time stuck in traffic to pick them up; and all day, every hour, the florist delivered a single rose of a different color: flame red, sunshine yellow, wine red, light orange, pink—bright and soft. Each card came with a local phone number and read the same.

Near the end of the day, she had lined up the cards like Roman soldiers along the edge of her desk, the stemmed roses flanking the corners. "I'm not going to call you." She aimed a pen at the cards, and one by one shot them off the desk, then gathered the cards and flowers and dumped them in the wastebasket before she went to work on a project appliance list.

A few minutes later the florist delivered her favorite rose, a lavender gray called sterling silver. "Damn him," she said under her breath and sagged down on Pat's desk.

"He sure is persistent," the delivery girl said, then explained, "I took his order and filled out the cards."

Laurel checked her watch. "How many more?"

"Two. I have them in the van."

"Could you go get them now?"

"Sure."

When the girl came back Laurel handed her a slip of paper with her credit card number. "There's still time for a local delivery?"

"Another hour."

"Do you have any cactus at the shop?"

"We have everything."

"Then send him the biggest, thorniest cactus you have with a card that says, 'No.'"

The girl was still laughing as she closed the office door.

But back in her office, Laurel took one look at the flowers in the trash and decided she was a weak, weak woman. The only vase in the cabinet was oversized, but she filled it with warm water anyway, and while cutting the ends, she noticed all the thorns had been clipped off. Life should be so simple. Just clip off the thorns along the way.

"I'm back!" Annalisa came down the hall with a box of coffee and supplies and disappeared into the small kitchen, then flopped down in a chair across from her, kicked off her shoes, and crossed her feet on the rim of Laurel's desk. "That vase is too big." She used a piece of red licorice she was eating from a tub to point at the vase.

"It's the only one we had here. How'd things go today?"

"Fine. Slow. But that's probably just as well. I want to wait until we get back from the Chicago show before I make a list of possible fixtures. Those flowers from the same guy?"

"I'm not going to discuss the flowers. We'll need sample drawings, but we shouldn't lock in any configurations yet either. I picked up the plans today. Also, I'll need to meet with the chefs involved pretty soon."

"Get this. They aren't contracted yet."

Laurel dropped her pen. "You're kidding?"

Annalisa shook her head.

"Talk about cart before the horse. Can you imagine your father coming into a place where the configurations and appliances had already been selected?" Laurel laughed. "They'd have to start all over just on principle. He would rant about everything, even if it were exactly what he wanted."

"I told them. Then they dropped a bombshell. They're talking to Dad about the cliff restaurant."

Laurel swore and rested her head on one hand.

"You would have washed my mouth out with soap if I'd said that word."

"I learned it from your father."

"It's not French."

"Your father swears in Anglo-Saxon English. He just doesn't do it around you, his little girl." Laurel sat back in her chair and thought for a moment. "At least I understand your father. My biggest problem will be keeping him from telling us how to do every kitchen on the entire job."

Annalisa slumped lower in her chair. "Dad's going to hound me all the time about working with him."

"Maybe not. When he sees how good you are at what you do, he might finally leave you alone."

"Sure. And I'm going to win Lotto and not gain any weight from eating half a bucket of this candy." She held up the red licorice and bit off the end. "We can hope he turns it down."

"Your father? No way. Is that your dinner, or do you want to come over?"

"Sure. Let me put this candy away."

A few minutes later, Laurel was locking the office door and the elevator bell sounded. Beric rushed out waving a manila envelope. "Oh, there you both are. Good. Good. I have a surprise for you. Guess what this is?"

"A contract for the cliff restaurant at Camino Cliff," Annalisa said flatly.

"Yes! How did you know?"

Annalisa looked at her, then back to Beric. "They told me today you were talking with them."

"At first I thought, no. But they convinced me. So now I have the very best news." He stood there, laughing, cocky, arrogant, his hands on his hips. "I have all the restaurants on the project. They will all be Beric King restaurants."

Laurel couldn't stop the small groan that escaped her lips, and Annalisa looked pale as flour.

"It is good. Come, come. We will celebrate." Her ex-husband slid his arm around her shoulders and Annalisa's and squeezed them both close to his body with all the Gallic enthusiasm of a Frenchman hugging two buoys to stay afloat. "Maybe, and I'm only suggesting a possibility"—he squeezed Annalisa hard—"we will call one of them Annalisa's and *ma petite jeune* can design her own place. Then she will work for her *maman* and *papa*."

"Dad. Please."

"I know, I know, I know. It is all too much. We will talk later. All the Kings will be working together again." Beric herded them toward the elevator. He looked at her and she wanted to flinch. "This will be great fun, Laurel, no?"

"Great fun, Beric. Just great . . . like our marriage."

Dinner with her parents was always interesting to Annalisa. Though they'd been apart for years, her father still loved her mother, and sometimes it was painful to watch, because he had a complete inability to understand what had happened, along with trouble letting go of what he thought his life should be. Annalisa loved them both, but she had been an innocent, unknowing bystander while her parents' marriage deteriorated the more and more they worked together.

Alone, her mom wasn't lost anymore. But their divorce had crippled Annalisa; she lived the Sturm und Drang of guilt and anger, sorrow and blame. For a while, she took everything out on her mother the way teenage girls could do when they understood their own emotional power: mothers would always love you no matter what horrible things you said when the pain was too much to live with.

Tonight, though, her mother suffered through her father's exuberance and assumptions, his energetic need to tell both the women in his life what they should do—the world according to Beric King, chef, father, husband, ex-husband (which was worse), and pain in the ass.

After her parents left, together and still arguing over the width of stainless counters, Annalisa didn't feel like going home to an empty condo. She wandered into the bar, where a popular local jazz group played, and sat on a bar stool, sipping a drink, which was better than sitting at home alone, watching hopelessly romantic movies and eating microwave popcorn or, worse, that pint of cookie dough ice cream she'd bought during a weak moment.

The room grew crowded and noisy, with others leaving dinner and wedging their way to the bar, and soon the band took a break. Some of the tension from dinner drained away with people all around her. In a body of perfect strangers she was freed from the terrible fate of a single woman at home alone—the clear expectation and despair that no one would ever love her, and the world would go on, everyone falling head over heels but her. She turned around to set her drink down and came face-to-face with Matt Banning. "Well, hello," Annalisa said.

"I saw you sitting here." He leaned against the bar, close enough to wish she could move her stool.

"I like jazz," she said. "Did you come to see the band?"

"No. We just had dinner."

She looked around. "Who?"

"My dad just left. We try to have dinner every week. Male bonding," he said with a laugh, but he wasn't insincere. Something told her she might envy his relationship with his father.

"I had dinner with my parents, but I didn't see you."

"We ate upstairs, where it's quieter. My dad doesn't like noisy restaurants."

"Restaurants are home territory to my parents. They usually make up a large part of the noise." The squeeze of lime in her glass was a distraction for an awkward instant of silence, because his impact on her was unsettling, alarming, like a siren only she could hear. Around him she grew warm with desire she was powerless to stop. It rose from a secret place so new to her. He sat only a foot away and still the air vibrated; she could feel his presence in those sensitive places: the back of her neck, along her arms, perhaps from some butterfly feeling deep inside her heart. Such unfamiliar territory, and she thought herself too lonely a creature to trust those kind of unexplainable feelings.

"Let me get you another one," he said. "What are you drinking? Vodka?"

"Club soda with lime. I like to know what I'm going to say next." As he ordered from the bartender, she regretted what she thought her words revealed about her. "I drink sometimes, but seldom during business hours, and not when I'm driving."

He handed her a fresh club soda. "You like to be in control."

"No more than you do," she said, laughing. "You drank Coke at the cocktail party the other night. I saw you order."

"Can't take your eyes off me, huh?"

"That's it. You have me so infatuated I will do anything to be near you. I'm obsessed. Every time you look over your shoulder, I'll be there. I live you. I breathe you. I dream you."

"I wish that were true."

She stopped laughing abruptly and could see his expression turn serious. "Please—don't, Matt."

"I was being honest. Would you want me to lie?"

She thought perhaps at that moment she would prefer the lie. "Why me?"

He shrugged. "I don't know."

"There are thousands of girls in Orange County, and plenty in this room who would jump at the chance to meet you. Pick one of them."

"One of the women in this room?"

"Yes."

"I did. She won't go out with me."

"No. She won't," Annalisa said firmly. "So what's your alternative?"

"Staying dateless and lonely and unattached." He leaned closer. "Don't you feel sorry for me?"

"You're not going pin your dateless state on me."

"So explain your dateless state."

"I never said I was dateless."

"You're right. This will be our first date."

"No. It won't." She set her glass down hard. "I'll find a girl for you. There. See that blonde over there? She's very pretty."

"She has a tan."

"Every blonde in the room is tanned. Since when does having a tan bother men?"

"Wrinkle city."

"Matthew . . . Matthew . . . Matthew . . . Men don't think about women and tomorrow. Only what they want now."

"You make us sound like two-year-olds."

"I'm not going to argue that one."

"Who have you been dating?"

"The wrong men."

"Did they all act like children?"

"No."

"Just most of them?"

She took a drink and wished it was vodka, sorry she'd led the conversation down this road.

"Tell me about the last guy you went out with."

"I don't think so."

"Why not? Are you still dating him?"

"God, no." She wasn't seeing anyone, but to admit that to Matthew Banning might make her look pitiable. Something in his expression told her he would sit there until she answered him. "Okay, the truth is"—she winced—"the last guy I went out with was a blind date."

"No one should ever go on a blind date."

"I was doing a favor for a friend." She paused, then added, "He told her later he thought I was too big."

He choked on his drink, then looked at her as if she were lying.

She held up her palm. "I swear. It's the truth."

"Was he short?"

"No. Tall, blond, and a stockbroker."

"He was a blind man, not a blind date."

She stayed silent because what the guy had said about her still got to her a little. Too big, and she had a carton of ice cream in her freezer and a tub of Red Vines at work. Her willpower was nonexistent, even now when she should get out of the bar and leave temptation while she could. It wasn't easy to walk away, because she liked talking to Matt, was flattered by the way he looked at her and teased her, the way he stood close without touching her. He was dressed casually in a polo shirt, jeans, and moc loafers with no socks, and used her silence to study her long enough that she wondered what he was thinking.

"You must be what? A size eight, about a hundred and twenty-seven pounds."

"How did you know that?"

"Lucky guess."

"You can look at a woman and nail her weight and dress size? That was no lucky guess. You must have sisters."

"One brother. Back in college the guys had running bets on girls' size and weight. There was money involved, so I won a lot."

Warning bells went off in her head. This was a man who could accurately guess a woman's weight, a knowledge that told her one thing: he knew women too well for a man raised without sisters. Bill, the blind date, drove a black Carrera. This was Southern California, land of the automobile, where you were defined by what you drove, and everything about Bill had screamed player. Annalisa told herself Matt could be like Bill, who wanted an arm ornament, who cared more about what the woman he was with and the car he drove said about him. She didn't think that kind of game was a substitute for love. Sadly, she shook her head. "You men are shallow beings."

He just gave her a narrow-eyed look that promised he'd get even.

"I don't want to talk about me or my weight or my dress size. I want to find you a date so you can stop looking at me with that hangdog, I'm-lonely, please-love-me look."

He laughed then. "Is that how you see me? No wonder you won't give me a chance."

She reached out and gently turned his face toward the opposite end of the bar. "Look at that blonde on the last bar stool. See? She has chin-length hair and she's wearing red."

He studied her for a moment, then made a face. "Too skinny."

"Good thing you don't work in Hollywood. Okay then, someone different." She scanned the bar, then leaned in closer. "The one with the brown wavy hair. Over there by the telephone." She gave a nod in that direction. "She looks like Drew Barrymore."

"That is Drew Barrymore."

Annalisa studied the woman, then shrugged. "Well, go for it."

He shook his head. "High maintenance."

"I've always wanted to know what a man's definition of high maintenance is."

"Anyone who is on the news."

"You're awfully picky."

"Why do I get the idea that you would like to have added 'for a man' to that last statement?"

"Unfair." She held up her hand. "You didn't hear me say that, did you?" He just looked at her, reading her too closely to the truth. She had trouble hiding her cynicism. "You're putting words in my mouth to distract me."

"I know what I like. I'm selective."

"You're a man. You can't be that selective."

"See? I was right. You have a chip on your shoulder."

"That was a joke," she lied. "Now stop trying to antagonize me." His expression told her she hadn't fooled him. "What about the brunette three stools down from her?"

"Now you're changing the subject."

"I'm trying to find you a woman. Pay attention, please. Look. She's gorgeous, voluptuous. Men like that, right? And see her laugh?"

"I like redheads."

"Do you expect me to believe you only date women with red hair?"

"My tastes in women changed recently."

"I'm not going to go out with you, Matt."

"I'll wait."

"God, you're stubborn. You have to be crazy. This project will take almost two years."

"I'm a patient man."

"That's an oxymoron."

"Funny. See why I like you?"

"You're nuts. That's what you are."

"Nuts about you."

"You don't stop, do you?"

"You can't blame a guy for trying."

Time to go. She stood and grabbed her purse. "Thanks for the drink. It's getting too loud now for me."

He set down his glass. "I'll walk you to your car."

"That's not necessary. Stay. Listen to the band. They're good."

He reached behind her and took her sweater off the back of the bar stool, but didn't give it to her. "I'll walk with you. The parking lot is dark."

"I know self-defense."

"I've seen that tonight, Annalisa."

"No, really." She looked over her shoulder at him. "I'm a black belt."

"Good. You can protect me, then." He placed her sweater over her shoulders and paused for just a moment with his hands on her. It was a simple thing, an old-fashioned courtesy, but it felt intimate and sexy. He just touched her shoulders, then gave them a small squeeze. For a heartbeat she forgot how to breathe. Outside they stopped, and she turned to tell him good night.

"I'm over there." He pointed west with his key remote.

Damn, so was she.

"Where are you?" He waited a beat, then asked, "What's the matter? Did you forget where you parked? Hit the alarm button."

"No. I'm over that way too."

He easily guided her with his hand on her elbow. "Good, then you can't run away from me or from any potential carjackers."

She had to laugh. "Okay, I'll walk you to your car and beat off any criminals you might attract."

"Funny."

"You poor, frail man, you. What are you, six inches taller than me?"

"I'm six two."

"Eight inches. I'm five four."

"I know," he said with a self-assured grin.

They crossed the parking lot, neither of them talking anymore. She hit her key remote and the lights flashed on her car.

He started laughing.

"What's so funny?"

He raised his key remote, pressed it, and the lights went off on the white truck parked next to her.

"You are obsessed with me," he said, still laughing.

Over a hundred parking places in the lot, and they were parked next to each other. The word "fate" flashed though her consciousness. She believed there were reasons for the things that happened in life. She believed in patterns. Her feelings were so strong. Every time she looked at him she felt something, which was why she tried to keep things light. She wasn't ready for a relationship that might burn her. Matthew Banning would set her on fire. And she couldn't date a man she worked with—a surefire way to destroy love.

He opened her car door for her. She got in, put the key in the ignition, but he didn't close the door, and leaned on it instead. With her hand on the steering wheel, her other hand on the key, ready to make a clean getaway, she paused for a heartbeat, then made the mistake of looking up at him.

He said her name softly. "I meant what I said before. We're alike, you and me. We go after what we want."

"I can't do this, Matt."

"Yes, you can."

She started to say something else completely futile.

He held up his hand and stopped her. "I want you. But I'm willing to wait until you're ready."

The moment he said it, she melted. He was wearing her down. Matt was wealthy, smart, successful, and too good-looking. If she were him, she would play the heck out of life. Maybe that's what he's doing, she thought. Maybe this is his line, his method, this flattering, single-minded pursuit. She let that thought digest, scared and confused. Self-preservation told her she couldn't start anything with this man she sensed could really break her heart.

"Good night." He stepped back away from the car.

"Good night, Matthew." She pulled the door closed.

He shoved his hands in his pockets and she watched him get in his truck. Not a Porsche. Not a Viper. Not a Ferrari. Not a player's car. It was shiny. It was spotless. And it was a white Chevy truck.

Jud walked into the offices of King Professional Design more determined than confident. Laurel's daughter sat on the front desk, the phone against her ear as she scribbled on a notepad. She glanced up at him, smiled exactly like her mother, and raised one finger to signal she'd be a minute.

Along the walls were suede sofas flanked by glass tables. Soft light spilled from the ceiling and wall fixtures, and light from a corner window lit a section of the room, which was painted a warm sand color, a soft backdrop for black-framed, white-matted photographs. Next to the industry awards, plaques for outstanding workmanship, and local business commendations hung finished shots of King Design projects: slick stainless steel kitchens with walls of steel cabinets, heavy-duty refrigeration coolers, and multiple cooking and preparation stations. Some of the photographs focused on the chef in the forefront of his streamlined, sleek work space. Written in script on the matting was the name of the restaurant, the chef, and the date.

A matted collage made of a glossy magazine spread hung nearby, from an industry journal called *Professional Cooking Now,* and it focused on an interview with Laurel. He'd always thought of her as a girl of solitude. Something about growing up without a father left her adrift and formed in her a deeply emotional concoction of doubt and agony. In the photo he studied now she appeared open, confident, proud; the lens had captured her in a genuine moment. It was a strange kind of exposure, because the Laurel he remembered exposed so little of herself.

"Mr. Banning." Annalisa walked toward him. "I'm sorry for making you wait."

"Jud. 'Mr. Banning' makes me feel old." Old enough to be her father.

"You certainly aren't old." There was heavy pause while she stood there a little awkwardly, watching him with a questioning look. "Did we miss an appointment of some kind?"

"No. No." He waved a hand and the lie came so easily. "I'm meeting your mother for lunch today."

"Really? She didn't say a word to me. Our assistant is out on vacation and the place falls apart when she's gone, especially Mom's schedule. She's in her office. It's this way." Annalisa walked down a short hallway past another office, a planning room with a drafting table, bookcases of catalogs and heavy binders, and a small coffee room with a compact kitchen area. She knocked and opened the door. "Mom?"

Laurel stood at her desk, the bright light from the window around her silhouette. "What, sweetie? I—" Her eyes went to him for an empty few seconds, before her mouth clamped shut.

For an instant he felt panic in his heart, and it took him by surprise. He had forgotten how, whenever he saw her, he felt something strong and indefinable.

"Jud's here for your lunch appointment." Annalisa turned to him. "It was good to see you again. Bye, Mom."

Laurel crossed her arms, her stance and expression mulish. "Just what lunch would that be?"

More telling than words were all his roses in a vase on her desk. He touched one and said, "You never called, so I came in person. Thanks for the cactus."

"This is ridiculous." She sat down in her chair, then started to say something, but her gaze went past him to where Annalisa walked across the hall, waved at her mother, and disappeared in the other office. A second or two later, he heard the copy machine. Frustration was all over Laurel's face when she leaned toward him and whispered, "Why are you doing this?"

"What?"

Annalisa poked her head inside. "I'm off to the job site. Enjoy your lunch."

He waited until he heard the front door close. "I want to take you to lunch. We have an unresolved past. Now we're doing business together. We should bury the hatchet."

"Why do I have the feeling you're going to bury it in me?"

He held up his hands. "Truce."

"I don't trust you."

"That should be my line."

Her face fell and she looked as if he had slapped her. It was a sad thing, the way a man's ego could balloon over time. He had a bad case of wounded pride, which had just boiled to the surface. Rather than apologizing, he said calmly, "Let's talk over a sandwich."

"Talk about what?"

"Your business. Your daughter. Your life since 1970."

"You're not going to go away, are you?"

"No."

She studied him, her expression taut while she tapped her fingers against the desktop, either angry or nervous. But within seconds he could see her come to a decision. "Okay. Let's go." She grabbed her purse.

Outside, the bright sunlight bounced off the building's metal pillars and mirrored glass and caught the pale gold highlights of her hair. "I like you blond," he said, and she stopped to touch her hair as she had before. She wore it in a length between her shoulders and chin, and the ends curled softly under, framing and amplifying the loveliness of her face like parentheses.

"Change is good," she said briskly. "Letting go is even better."

That was how the conversation went on the drive to the restaurant. She said little, gave him one- or two-word answers heavy with innuendo, and he thought he might never get through to the Laurel in the photograph.

After a few tense minutes, she sagged back against the seat. She didn't wear the same deer-in-the-headlights look from the cocktail party and the office. "This isn't much of a truce, is it?"

"No. I know I forced you to do this," he said. "Believe it or not, I didn't plan it. Annalisa asked me why I was there."

"Why were you there?"

"I wanted to see you, then the opportunity for lunch presented itself."

"So you lied."

"You don't get what you want in this world by letting opportunity slip by."

"You know, you are the second person I've heard that from. Do I look that passive?"

"I wasn't talking about you. I was talking about me." He pulled up to the restaurant and her mood switched and she was laughing.

"Do you come here often?" she asked.

He rested his arms on the steering wheel and said, "You don't like this restaurant."

"It's great. Can't let opportunity slip by," she said brightly. "Let's go." Then she was out of the car.

He caught up with her inside. "What's so damned funny?"

"Laurel!" The maître d' enveloped her in a bear hug, and suddenly they were talking a mile a minute about his daughter and hers, last month's menu, the fresh flowers, lobsters, while Jud stood there feeling foolish and completely useless.

The host caught his eye. "Mr. Banning. I didn't see you."

"We're together, Thomas," Laurel spoke first.

"Then I have the best table for the two of you." Thomas took them to the same intimate spot where Kelly had walked out on him. Through the polished windows the great wide Pacific spread out before them, sunlight catching across its blue corrugated surface. The skies were even bluer, the kind of day that could lull you into thinking falling in love was easy.

Within seconds, waiters and busmen buzzed like hovercraft around their table. Their ice water was poured instantly, napkins were placed in their laps, and the first few minutes were made up of small talk between Laurel and almost every employee there.

When the last one left, he said, "Okay. I got the joke. This is one of your design projects."

"Never been here in my life," she said with a straight face.

"Why do I think the chef is going to come out here and take your order?" He glanced at the menu, then it hit him, one of those moments when you feel like a real stupid ass. "This is a Beric King restaurant, as in King Professional Design."

"He's my ex."

Jud wasn't exactly prepared for how that news hit him. He had met the man, had eaten his exquisite, unparalleled cuisine at entertainment balls, and often favored his local restaurants, where like here, they knew him by name. But imagining Laurel married to the enigmatic Beric King struck him hard. After so many years he had forgotten what the hot flare of jealousy could feel like, although common sense told him that feeling anything was plain stupid. So he ordered a single-malt scotch to her viognier. "You know Matthew just signed him as the chef for the Camino Cliff restaurants."

"I know," she said. "Boy, do I know."

Her tone said more than anything about the state of her relationship with her ex-husband. He knew then that she had divorced Beric King, not the other way around. Some part of him hoped her ex was a lousy husband and Laurel wasn't one of those people who always left. He wasn't sorry he ordered the scotch. He wasn't one to sort out his feelings on the cuff.

"Beric's been waving the contract in our faces. He never does anything halfway. He'll create havoc in the planning, want to run the whole project, will tell you everything you are doing wrong, and change his mind over and over again." She raised her wineglass in a mock toast and took a drink. "Welcome to my nightmare."

"Matt's running the project, so he'll be the one to deal with Beric. But"—Jud shook his head, laughed slightly, because what else could you do when coincidence made the world suddenly so much smaller and you found yourself caught in the ever-shrinking consequences?—"I'm the one who suggested him."

"You might want to take my knife away before you admit to something like that."

He set down his menu and braced his elbows on the table, looking her square in the eye. "Tell you what. I'm going to let you order for me instead. It's your chance to get even."

"Damn you, Jud. You know I can't use food as a weapon. My culinary pride won't let me order anything but the best. Stop grinning, you bastard," she said sweetly, "or I might order you calf's brains. They are quite a delicacy. And God knows a serving of brains would never hurt a man."

"Ouch," he said, taking a drink. "You don't need knives, Jailbait. Your words are sharp enough."

She leaned forward and whispered, "You should probably stop calling me that."

He shrugged. "We had a past. You can't hide from that fact. It won't disappear just because it makes you uncomfortable." He set down his drink and asked, "Why is that?"

It took a long time for her to answer. "The truth is I'm not sure what you want from me."

"Neither am I," he lied again, and the waiter came over, listening while Laurel began the order. Jud took a moment and thought about why he was here. Their intimate connection had never faded for him, and he was loath to admit he carried her memory with him—exquisite and painful, confused. Sometimes over the years a thought of her would spread darkness over a great moment. An eerie sense of unfinished business had followed him all the days of his life since.

The waiter said something that made her laugh

again, in that husky kind of sound nature created to propagate the species of man. Jud leaned back in his chair and relaxed. When the waiter left he said, "You gave him the order without ever looking at the menu. Impressive."

"I know food. I just don't know why I'm here." Something dark crossed over her features, the kind of bleak pain that was difficult for anyone to hide.

"When you look like that I can't believe life has hurt you so badly, Laurel."

She closed her eyes as if she could hide that way. He imagined her hands were knotted tightly in her lap. Her breaths were long and measured, then she asked, "Why did you come? Why the flowers?"

He thought about it for a moment, then admitted, "I'm a bad loser."

"You would have lost more had I stayed and continued to come between you and Cale."

"You know what I don't understand?"

"What?"

"The damage was done by then."

She looked down at her hands, then drank her wine. She poured another glass. "How long did it last?"

"For Cale?"

"Yes, for Cale."

Jud shrugged. "He was angry for about six months, then he met someone else." Although Cale and he were close, the most painful events couldn't be taken back, and the betrayed seldom gave second chances. There were jagged edges both he and his brother felt; the remnants of lost trust stood between them, never going away completely even as the years passed. Some lessons learned in life stayed buried underneath the flesh, scars so sharply and permanently damaging that even the bond of blood couldn't heal what had happened.

He recognized how guarded she was from the way she spoke, in fits and starts, as if she needed to fill the awkward void of silence they fell into when his gritty questions asked for answers that mined too deeply. So he plied her with expensive wine he didn't really drink and watched and listened until the salads came, then time and the courses flew by.

The wine loosened her up. Soon she talked freely about restaurants and cooking, about places they both knew well and the menus, about each dish, the piquant sauces, the smoky or pungent flavor of fresh herbs, and the difference between food here and food in France. He wondered why she'd had to run to another continent.

"After living abroad for so long, you come back and things here are so different. I don't understand it," she said. "We have so much wealth and science in this country, yet we drive-through for hamburgers made from beef injected with hormones. The fruit in the market can have the right color, especially if you put enough wax on it and grow it under lamps in hothouses, but never the succulent, ambrosial taste of fruit grown on green vines rooted inside the earth and ripened in honest sunshine, strawberries you can eat from the vine without washing, cream separated from that morning's milk, butter churned an hour ago, a yeasty baguette still warm from the oven, and eggs so fresh and bright you see nature's true colors are never diluted." She stopped abruptly. "Why are you smiling?"

"A meal with you is always original." He poured her

the last glass of wine from a second bottle. On the wine-glass was the clear red imprint of her lips. Listening to her took him back in time, to another meal, and for an infinitesimal moment he was thirty years younger, infused with the warmth of something lost to him. She talked about food to a man who hungered for something else. "Time doesn't change everything." He raised his glass to her, because she looked suddenly uncomfortable. "To old friends."

She drank but grew quiet, stared at the empty glass with her lips still caught in relief on its rim, and he remembered that years ago he could look at her and feel crazy things. Pleasure was all he could name, and he understood because the years had made comprehension clear as looking through fine crystal—his lifetime was entwined with hers. She was his first true love and he had never mourned the death of that singular love because it had never died.

Her nervousness, the need to avoid him, the look that crossed her face made him believe she might be fighting the same feelings. But he could be a fool. Could be she felt nothing. Could be he was running down the road straight into a cement wall. With nothing to lose, he said, "I never would have thought to look for you in France."

"It was a spur-of-the-moment decision."

"What brought you back?"

"Beric's ambition, Annalisa," she answered quickly, then after a moment added, "and eventually my mother begged me to come back. She had strong reasons. Our lives had changed, so we came back." She set her napkin on the table and nervously glanced around. "The place is empty. My God . . . the sun's setting. What time is it?"

"After five."

"We have to go." She stood up quickly, then sat down and put her hand to her head. "How much wine have I had?"

"Almost two bottles, but I'm driving." He took her arm and they left. As he started the car, she looked at him and said blankly, "I can't drive."

"You don't have to. This is my car."

"I know that. You don't understand. My car is at the office."

"I'll take you home, Laurel. Just tell me where I'm going."

To his surprise she lived maybe ten miles from his condo in Balboa. He wondered what kind of fate made their lives cross now. How many times had they passed on the streets, been standing nearby, at a gas station, the market, the theater? Today he discovered he had eaten almost exclusively at the same restaurants she frequented. He'd met her husband before. Barely a foot away from him sat the woman who taught him life was benign and monopolistic. She was the person who had created in him his decades of blinding ambition, which kept time for the softer things in life safely out of his reach. That, and an affinity for poets from centuries before who wrote verse about love and the women who left them.

> But we by a love, so much refined,
> That our selves know not what it is,
> Inter-assured of the mind,
> Care less eyes, lips, and hands to miss.

"Turn here . . . Jud?"

He came back into reality, but found himself looking at her eyes, lips, hands. "What?"

"You missed the turn."

"Sorry." He turned the car around and from her taut directions eventually pulled into a parking place in the alley behind the houses on the strand. "I'll walk you to the door." She didn't argue but carried her shoes as they walked, his palm resting on the small of her back. While she looked for her keys, he stood on her porch with his hands in his pockets, surrounded by pots of bright flowers and looking across the sand to the soft heartbeat of waves on the shore. "I'd bet it gets pretty crowded in the summer and weekends."

"It does. Beric complained of the crowds. Said it was like living in a bowl of fish. But I love it here. I like activity around me. Some professional volleyball players are locals and they'll practice here. For the most part, people are friendly or keep to themselves. When you live alone, sometimes it feels good to have people around. Noise means life. I can sit here and tune it out when I want to. Nights are always quiet." She shrugged. "It works for me."

He leaned against the railing, watching her.

The front door was open and she stood in front of it, a bit defensively. "Thank you for lunch . . . and dinner." She laughed.

"You okay, Jailbait?"

"I'm okay. Home safe and sound." She stepped inside and looked back.

He didn't move. "Good night."

"Good night." She closed the door.

He walked down the steps, around a patch of pickle-weed with yellow flowers, and onto the brindled sand. The wind came in smelling of the sea and blowing his hair and collar back. A few miles away his condo faced a boat-filled marina, mirror calm and placid from the breakwater. Here he could feel the rush of the waves, taste the salt in the air. A group of surfers coated in seal-like wetsuits and sand carried their short boards down the strand, and soft jazz trumpet came from a nearby patio where a couple sipped drinks and talked. A small blond woman walked a pair of retrievers on the sand while gulls floated noisily overhead, their heads turning pink from the setting sun.

He looked back at her house from a distance, maybe fifty feet away, the wind at his back, the moon overhead, and the sky losing color. A warm light came on upstairs and the strangest sense of peace inexplicably came over him.

> Our two souls therefore, which are one,
> Though I must go, endure not yet
> A breach, but an expansion,
> Like gold into airy thinness beat.

He stood there ignoring time until it was dark, and he walked to his car and left. Later that night, he lay in bed and asked himself the singular, elusive question: why this woman? Even more elusive was the answer, but then no man could ever understand his own obsession.

At the job site, Annalisa avoided Matt Banning for most of the week. So when both he and her father walked into her meeting with the contractor, she said the first thing that came into her head. "What are you doing here?" Matt seemed startled and she wanted to take the words back.

"Is that any way for a daughter to talk to her father?" Beric said, annoyed. "Can you believe how she speaks to me? You get this from your mother." With three sentences he had just reduced her to his little girl in front of the men she had to work with, and whose respect she was fighting so hard to win. He turned to Matthew. "Did you hear that?"

"I sure did," Matt said, half laughing, because he knew she'd been talking to him.

She sat on the corner of the worktable and took a second to set down her pen and notepad. "You caught me unexpectedly," she said without apologizing. "Why are you here?"

"I need to talk to you immediately about the plans for the Cliff restaurant."

Matt stepped forward. "Beric tells me he needs more footage in the kitchen."

That was weird. They hadn't done the kitchen configurations yet. She faced her dad. "Why? There's plenty of room."

"No. No." Beric shook his head, walked around the table, and collapsed in a leather executive chair. "It is much too small."

"But we haven't decided on the actual kitchen configurations. The trade show is only a week away from now. You cannot possibly have a problem when all you've seen are the initial blueprints."

He swung around in the chair and leaned over the table, where the plans lay spread from end to end. "There is a huge problem already. I know. Look at these." He poked his finger at the blueprints. "I just know. I have a feeling for these things."

The moment he spoke about feelings she understood he was doing this on purpose and couldn't believe he would try to undermine her this blatantly. She glanced from the contractor and job sup, to Matt and back to her father, who was frowning at the blueprints.

"Show us where you feel there's a problem. Here." She faced down her father, looking into his eyes for something other than what she was seeing: that they were both running neck and neck toward a finish line in a race he had started. "We can't fix it if we don't know what's wrong."

The seconds ticked by without him saying anything. He looked back at the plans in silence.

"If you can feel something is wrong, study it and tell us where you feel it."

The moment she said it he slowly lifted his gaze to hers. "I don't think I can put it into words."

"You don't have to. Just point."

The job sup coughed but she kept her father pinned with a glare.

"Let me finish . . . please," her dad said with an annoying tone of patience mixed with condescension. "Words that you will understand, *ma petite jeune*."

She was so brittle at that exact moment, if someone had touched her, she would have shattered into pieces.

Matt put his hand on her dad's shoulder. "You know, Beric, Annalisa is one of the smartest young women I have had the pleasure of working with. Jim and Peter— the architect—and I were just talking about it in a meeting a few days ago. We trust her to be able to address any issue or problem you will have with the project."

She didn't know if she wanted to smack Matt or hug him. What she did know was that she wanted the men in that room to understand that she could stand on her own. "Jim?" She faced the contractor. "How difficult would it be at this stage to change the size of the kitchen?"

"Well, there are two possibilities." Jim studied the blueprints. "We can move the freezer unit here and expand out eight feet. Here. That would give us almost another hundred square feet. Or we can expand the wall out and eliminate this patio area between the west corner and the trash container area. This will give us another hundred and fifty."

"Which is the most expensive?" she asked.

"Eliminating the patio, because we're dealing with the outside lines of the building."

"Then we'll move the freezer units. I'll check with the manufacturers and do several CADs. I can see what's new at the trade show." She didn't ask anyone his opinion, especially her father, who leaned back in his chair and watched her, his expression unreadable.

He stood abruptly. "I believe my daughter has found the perfect solution."

His daughter. It was all she could do not to rest her head in her hands and groan. It was always about him.

"I will leave you to your work." He waved at Matt. "Stay. Stay. I can find my way out." But he came over and kissed her on the cheek, because Beric King was the kind of man who marked what was his—names on awnings, branding on cookware and appliances, packages in the frozen food sections, and daughters who tried to stand on their own. "I shall call you later, *ma petite jeune.*" Then he left the room.

For a few heartbeats no one spoke. "My dad could rival Garbo for an exit." She braced her hand on the table and added, "My mother is a saint."

Jim burst out laughing and stood. "My heart goes out to you, kid. We're going to get a coffee. You two want to come?"

"No," she and Matt said at the same time.

When the others left, she crossed her arms and looked up at Matt. "You don't have to defend me to my father."

"Everything I said was true."

"I'm glad the men on this project trust me. As you pointed out before, I'm young."

"I heard grousing about it when they first met you,"

he said with the frankness she liked in him. "Some thought I hired you for other reasons."

She laughed facetiously. "Three of them saw you asking me out after the cocktail party."

"I don't usually behave that badly. The point is, in a short time you've won over everyone who had doubts."

"Thank you for telling me." She relaxed. "You should be aware that my dad has another agenda here. He wants me to be a chef—a little female clone of himself. And I refused and work with my mom. I think that was what today was all about."

"If it was, you handled it well." Matthew Banning stood two feet from her, close enough so she could smell his cologne. There were moments when she wanted to reach out and touch him. Glancing down at her feet was safer. She brushed imaginary lint from her skirt, then crossed her arms. Self-preservation.

"I was impressed with the way you handled your father."

"I've had a lot of practice, and I watched my mother for years. What my father doesn't know is that the cost of his changes are going to come out of one of his other budgets. I won't go over the bid, especially not for his precious ego." She hadn't realized how hurt and angry she was until she said those words out loud. "I will find a way to offset the cost once I've been to the trade show."

"I'm not worried, Annalisa." His cell phone rang. For just a moment he looked sorry, then he excused himself and walked away to answer it.

She put some distance between them, too, made a few notes in her Day-Timer. He was talking quietly across the room and said, "Me too."

She felt a sharp pang of disappointment. "Me too" was the universal answer to I love you, I want you, or I miss you.

The others came back in with their coffee, and Matt pocketed his phone, then gave her a quick glance. "I need to get back to the office. We'll talk later."

She stared at the door long after it closed, heard his truck start, his tires spit on the gravel outside the work trailer, and the distant sound of John Mellencamp singing "I Need a Lover." In her car CD, she had the Pat Benatar version. She wanted to laugh, or maybe run. Jim asked her a question about the plan changes and she went back to work, but every so often, she would glance out through the metal blinds at the dissected landscape and wonder if Matthew Banning was playing a game.

Cale saw Rick Sachs a few more times, each session answering questions that needed stronger answers. Human ego was endemic to the art of medicine. But no statistic was more important to him than a patient's life. He made that bluntly clear to Sachs.

All that they spoke of he knew, but it was no longer clear-cut and he had trouble making sense of everything on his own. He couldn't think in terms of the practical—something that made a surgeon able to work around his innate empathy and compassion and to make all those incisions and never allow himself to bleed.

"You open them up and find the unexpected," Cale said. "There was never a clue. Later you can go over it, reexamine all the tests and your notes, replay every motion in your mind, and still feel confounded."

Rick set his glasses down. "Patients die of complications."

"Exactly."

"I understand that, Cale. But do you?"

The question echoed in his head long after he left Sachs's office. How the hell had he gotten to a place where everything he had learned about his medicine was jeopardized? He had to pull himself out of this. He was no different than his patients, and expected his doctor to say exactly what he needed to hear and—voila!—gone would be his illusionist's existence, pretending a magic that was lost to him. Some way, somehow, he had to find it again.

It was appropriately dark outside by the time Cale walked into his Harbor Ridge house from the garage, frustrated, unsure, angry at himself.

"Pop! There you are." Dane came toward him from the living room unshaven, wild-haired, his clothes wrinkled and his shirt buttoned wrong.

"Are you okay?"

"I was in on an ASD repair today. She was thirteen years old. The real deal." Red-faced, pacing and antsy, his eyes moist, overcome with excitement, and on an emotional high, Dane spoke of his first heart surgery, sometimes choking up as every moment of those intense hours in the operating room spilled from him in a tumbled rush of med terms and surgical images that Cale knew so well.

Back when his boys were very young—so easily fascinated by something as simple as a sand crab burrowing, a seashell tangled in kelp, a pelican diving for food—one blond-haired toddler chased a butterfly across the backyard, laughing and seeing only the joy of its winged flight when it slipped from his reach. Each everyday moment that time and age, life and stress had blinded from Cale was a single new miracle in the eyes of his small child. Now Dane stood before him, disheveled, bright-eyed, born of a penultimate and passionate instant Cale had had with Robyn, now a young man overwhelmed with disbelief at what he had just done and seen; it shone from every part of him, eagerness, passion, and something Cale might have felt another lifetime ago. God, he wanted to be his son right now.

"At first it was strange. You know? I was nervous. Felt like I was trespassing. Then I held that human heart in my hand and it was like holding a captured bird. After that, everything went perfectly. God . . . Pop. To do this for a lifetime? You are so lucky." Dane stopped pacing, hands up in surrender, and faced him with a sense of awe that made Cale feel like an imposter. "I have to do this, too. I have to practice cardiac surgery."

Cale couldn't say exactly when he had heard the call. It was always there as if whispered by God, and he had wondered once about Dane's decision to study medicine, whether it was his son's choice or he was merely following in family footsteps. But before him right now, he saw his son's calling—the honesty and the wonder of it—and he put his arm around Dane. "I have no doubt you'll do better than I have."

His son embraced him hard. "Impossible."

Laurel heard from her mother a couple of days later about plans to meet Annalisa for dinner before she went back to the island. As always, what had passed between them that night in her bedroom wasn't brought up. Why change a lifetime of ignoring the truth? All that invisible emotion was still there; it stood between them as surely as the name Banning.

Her daughter came rushing to the table all out of breath. "I'm sorry I'm late." Annalisa collapsed in a rattan chair between the two of them. "What a week!" She dropped her purse on the floor, then looked at them before she leaned forward, searching the restaurant. "Where's the waiter? I want a glass of wine. If I weren't driving, I'd order a whole bottle."

"That bad?" Laurel asked.

"Daddy showed up in the middle of my meeting with the project contractor."

"Oh, God. It's started."

"What's started?" Kathryn asked.

"Beric."

The waiter interrupted and Annalisa ordered her wine, then explained. "After we won the design contract, Mamie, they began negotiating with Daddy for all of the resort's restaurants."

"I can only imagine how that news must have hit you both," Kathryn said. "Beric has always been a handful. He never liked the idea of your company."

Annalisa sipped her wine. "He wants me to be a chef."

"He wanted the same thing from your mother."

"I was a chef for a long time," Laurel said. "Until he drove me out of the kitchen and out of the marriage."

"Remember that Thanksgiving? You and Daddy were arguing about something and he got mad and threw your turkey across the room."

"The food fight at Cameroon."

"I'll never forgive myself for visiting Evie that year," Kathryn said. "I missed the chance to give Beric a little payback for some of the drama he gave us for years."

"Nothing stopped him." Annalisa was laughing. "He stormed around the kitchen with mashed potatoes on his head, directing everyone on how a bird should be seasoned and garnished."

"Those potatoes were a direct hit." Laurel had just found out Beric had been sleeping with his television producer for six months. He was throwing a fit because he'd been caught, not because of the turkey. "I think I gained more satisfaction out of throwing that spoonful of potatoes at him than any meal I ever cooked."

"I would have liked to pitch a pot of potatoes at him the other day. Daddy is so pigheaded. You know, he was trying to make me look bad." Annalisa's disbelief and hurt were there in her words. "And when that didn't work, he took credit for my ideas and designs and my very existence."

"That's your father."

"It's all about him," they said in unison.

Kathryn looked to Annalisa. "Sounds like you could use a break. You haven't been to the island in months. I'll be done with the show early tomorrow. Come back with me for the weekend."

"I don't know, Mamie. This project is so demanding."

"Do you have to work on weekends, too?"

"No, but—"

"Annalisa," Laurel said. "Is that Matthew?"

"Where?" Her daughter whipped around.

He had been standing alone near the front door, but

a leggy blonde walked over and hooked her arm in his. Laurel started to raise her hand, but looked at her mother, realized what a stupid thing she was doing, and froze. *Why didn't I keep my mouth shut?*

Matt waved, said something to his companion, and walked toward them.

Annalisa finished off her wine and set the glass down. "I need to go to the rest room." She grabbed her purse and stood, but she couldn't get out from behind the table before he was standing there.

"Laurel." He nodded once, then said, "Annalisa."

Her daughter was pinned between him and the table and she looked none too happy about it.

"Matthew," Laurel said, "this is my mother, Kathryn Peyton."

Kathryn put her hand out and smiled. "Hello, Matthew . . . ?"

He smiled and took her hand. "Banning, ma'am."

Kathryn paled, but to her credit didn't pull her hand back.

"Matthew is in charge of the Camino Cliff project, Mother," Laurel said.

Annalisa hadn't moved and looked annoyed. "Excuse me," she said, and rudely stepped around him and left in the direction of the restrooms.

He glanced in her direction, frowning, then turned back. "It was good to meet you, Mrs. Peyton." He smiled at her mother and said, "See you later, Laurel."

As he walked away, Kathryn leaned across the table and harshly whispered, "Another Banning?"

"Cale's son."

"My God." Kathryn rested her head on her hand.

354 - JILL BARNETT

"Both of us are working with him. He's in charge of the project. He gave us that contract."

Before her mother could speak, Annalisa walked up and put her hand on Kathryn's shoulder. "Mamie? You're right. I haven't been to the island in a long time. I think I'll go with you tomorrow, if we can take the later boat. I have some work to do in the morning."

"We can take any boat you want," Kathryn told her.

"Well, that was certainly a quick change," Laurel said.

Annalisa shrugged and she looked tired. "Why don't you come too, Mom?"

"No. I can't," she said too quickly, panicked as she searched for an excuse. "The nursery is delivering some Japanese maples on Saturday." *Make a note to call the nursery tomorrow and order trees.* As the waiter took their orders, she wondered if she were going crazy. Imagine how her mother would have reacted if she had known that three hours ago, Laurel had agreed to go to dinner Saturday night with Jud.

Friday night, Kathryn slept through the night for the first time that week and awoke the next day feeling less antsy. To not brood over her argument with Laurel was easier when she was with Annalisa—their relationship was never strained, bitter, or filled with resentment. The shop was dead, so she flipped the Return sign and went out the back. The air was warm and tasted like gardenias. A shot of island sunlight hit the flagstones in the atrium garden between the buildings, and when she stopped to water the deep magenta bougainvillea blooms trellised up the walls, the pots of flowers and miniature citrus trees gave her a moment's pleasure. Intricate pottery bird feeders she made on sunny days hung from the eaves, where a hummingbird with red feathers flitted in and out, and she could hear laughter in the courtyard nearby.

Her studio smelled earthy and burnt inside, the scents of damp clay and kiln firing. Glass covered the whole south side of the studio and the light was always good, so good that sometimes entering the studio was like walking from a deep cave into the noonday sun.

Along the wall shelves was her latest collection of pottery. All of it was fired in the vibrant shades of the island, which were her signature—the aquas and tourmaline of the water, the deep amber of a Catalina sunset, the verdant greens of the hillsides, and the brilliant pink-magenta of the bougainvillea growing everywhere.

Annalisa walked out from the back room wearing a heavy brown canvas potter's apron with the chalky remnants of dried clay on her face and hair and spattered all over the apron front, her thick red hair pinned up and half falling out of a sloppy topknot.

Kathryn took one look at her and said, "Looks like the clay won."

Annalisa looked down at herself. Her shoulders sagged in defeat and she used the back of her hand to swipe the hair from her face. "I'm a lost cause. I've forgotten everything you taught me."

"I told you it had been too long since you'd been here."

"Every time I get the wheel spinning the stupid clay flies off."

"Show me."

"Okay, but don't laugh."

And Kathryn laughed before she even started.

"Oh, God." Annalisa dropped her face into muddy hands.

"Sit."

Annalisa unwrapped a clump of clay the size of a small head of cauliflower and dropped it in the center of the wheel.

"That's your first problem."

"What? It's in the center."

"They call it throwing for a reason. Scoop up the clay. Now throw it."

Annalisa tossed it on the wheel like a softball pitcher with a broken arm.

"Are you feeling all right?" Kathryn placed her hand on her granddaughter's forehead.

"Why?"

"You have all the energy of a dying sloth."

"Thanks."

"It's true."

"What do you want me to do?"

"Put some emotion into it. This is art. Art is emotion. It's feeling. It's passion, good or bad, elation or anger."

Annalisa picked up the clay and slammed it onto the wheel so hard the sound exploded like a gunshot. She looked startled for an instant, then started laughing.

It was the first truly free emotion Kathryn had seen from her since she came. "That was an improvement. I don't know what brought that passion on, but it worked."

"I just had to picture his face in the center of the wheel and it was all so easy."

"Whose face was it?"

"Matthew Banning."

Kathryn felt the floor come up to meet her. She reached out and grabbed Annalisa's shoulder. "Not you too."

"Mamie? What's wrong?" Annalisa stood up quickly and grabbed her arm. "Sit down before you fall down." She opened a bottle of water and handed it to her. "Drink this. Your skin is absolutely gray."

Kathryn sat there feeling overcome by dread. It was happening all over again, only worse. Some angry, mean God destined all the women in her family to be destroyed. His tool was the Banning men.

"Tell me why you're so upset. What did you mean, 'Not you too'?"

Kathryn was no good at lying about this. The name Banning was a trigger. It all spilled from her mouth like locusts. "I hate that name. Hate it. Your mother was almost destroyed by the Bannings."

"I don't understand."

"Jud Banning was the reason your mother ran away to France."

Jud found that everything was easier for the next two days. He whistled at work, which drew a few confused stares, walked faster, and wiped up the floor with his squash buddy at the health club. He sang in the shower. Saturday morning, outside in the driveway of his water-front town house, he washed and waxed his cars, a white Suburban, a black Mercedes, and the MG. That evening, when he was taking a shower, it crossed his mind that

Victor's parties weren't casual. Cale's wife, Robyn, had taken them over years ago and no one had changed anything since she died. So it had become a tradition for them to be held at Cale's place, a rambling, open home on Harbor Ridge with great views and a pool and basketball court.

Jud drove to Laurel's place too early, stopped and had a drink at a small bar near the Huntington Beach pier while he watched the clock, the people flying kites in the evening breeze and walking their dogs on the beach as the sun set.

Her porch light was on but it wasn't really dark yet. A pair of gardening gloves and rubber clogs caked with sand were next to the mat, and a gray tabby rubbed up against his slacks, whining impatiently at the door.

"Hello, fella." He scratched the cat's ears. "Locked out, huh?" Jud straightened and hit the doorbell, then shoved his hands in his pockets and waited.

Through the etched glass he saw her silhouette, and when she opened the door he was damned glad he'd found her again. "Hey, girl."

"Not likely. I'm forty-eight."

"What am I supposed to say, 'Hey, middle-aged woman'?"

She laughed then. "Just let me grab my purse."

"I'll wait here." He stood at the railing as the horizon melted to deep, dark blue; it was one of those nights when a sliver of a moon was already halfway across the sky and you could taste the salt in the air and feel the waves pound the sand a short distance away. He realized then his heart was pounding almost as loudly.

"I'm ready."

"You look incredible, Jailbait."

"You really can't keep calling me that. What's wrong with using my name?"

"Too impersonal." He put his hand on her back as they walked toward the MG.

"You still have this car."

"I'm not sure I could ever give this baby up." A few minutes later they sped down Pacific Coast Highway. She wore the same perfume. The scent of years past filled the small confines of the car and was there in every breath he took. Songs on the radio filled the silence, and they didn't talk for a few miles. When he turned onto Cale's street, she was staring out the window, her hands folded tightly in her lap, hugging her purse against her stomach, and she looked uncomfortable. "You're awfully quiet."

"I can't believe you talked me into this."

"It's just a dinner party." He pulled into the driveway, but stopped before pulling up to the valets they always hired.

"Who are these people? I guess I should know a little about them so I don't make a complete idiot of myself."

He wasn't certain how to tell her where she was.

"Before we go inside, shouldn't you tell me something about this dinner party?"

"Tonight's my grandfather's birthday celebration." Jud tightened his grip on the leather steering wheel. "This is Cale's house."

"What?" She was white. "You told me it was a dinner party."

"It is. Would you have come if I told you what it was and where it was?"

"No. And I'm not certain whether you're trying to manipulate me or patronize me."

"You always were too smart." There was beat or two of strained silence. "I'll take you home if you really want me to."

"Okay," she said, holding her purse tighter, eyes straight ahead. "Let's go."

He didn't do anything but sit there and let her think about it, then gave it one last shot. "It won't be that bad. You'll have fun. You're going to have to see them all at some point. Why not get it over with?"

"Why would I have to meet them if I never go out with you again?"

"Do you really think that's going to happen?"

"Would you leave me alone if I told you I never wanted to see you again?"

"No. Would you really tell me that?"

"No."

"Come on, JB. No one's going to eat you alive in there." She said nothing. "Okay, I'll take you somewhere else." He put the car in reverse.

She placed her hand on his. "No."

Before she could change her mind he pulled the car up to the valet.

CHAPTER

29

One of life's supreme ironies was not lost on Laurel: we run from the people and things we should face, and we face head-on what we should run from as far and as fast as we can. So it was hard to know what made her walk through the door of Cale Banning's home. People walked in and out of one another's lives all the time without questioning or justification. But she was a runner, at least that was what she believed in those rare moments when she looked back on her life and questioned all her beginnings and endings. Life was all wrong; it would be simpler if she could just start with the end.

She expected the elegance inside, the limestone floors and custom furniture, imported rugs, the subtle alabaster fixtures, even the fine art. But it was the wall of glass overlooking an expansive view of Newport's lights and the dark Pacific sea and sky that gave a feeling of vast endlessness, as if they were floating above the world.

Couples danced to a band on a large terraced patio where tables were placed under strung lights and tall stainless steel outdoor heaters, and servers dished from a buffet near a bar, where Jud stood ordering their drinks.

"Hello, Laurel."

His voice took her back thirty years and she turned around.

"It's been a long time."

"Cale." The first time she ever saw him, he epitomized all those vibrant colors of youth—trouble, hunger, a combination of eagerness and that innocence we have until life proves us naïve. She could only imagine how she had changed in all those years since. If experience sapped the color from your life, she was a black-and-white photo. And although he was even better-looking now, with some silver in his time-darkened hair and creases of experience in the corners of his eyes and mouth, the Cale that stood before her had no edges, just a sense of something innately lost about him.

"I like your hair."

"Thank you." She laughed nervously. "Jud didn't recognize me." They both looked toward the bar, where Jud's back was to them. He leaned against the bar waiting for their drinks, foot resting on a stool while he talked and laughed with some people nearby.

"Then he's a fool. I saw him walk in with you—Jud is always full of surprises—and I probably would have recognized you with blue hair."

"A Smurf."

"A Smurf." He smiled then. "Can I get you something? Blueberry Slurpee, Pepsi Blue, Bombay Sapphire?"

"Maybe a quick flight to Mexico."

"Feeling out of place?"

"A little."

"I should have a talk with my brother."

What passed between them was oddly easy. That same old repartee. She should have felt uncomfortable, on edge, ready to run. Two minutes with Jud caused more turmoil inside her than she felt now standing there with Cale for the first time.

"Laurel?" Matthew joined them. "This is a surprise. Is Annalisa here?"

"You know my son?" Cale said.

"Laurel and her daughter are doing the kitchen designs for the Camino Cliff project, Dad."

"Annalisa isn't here, Matthew."

Jud walked up and handed her a glass of wine before he looked at Cale and said, "Just like old times."

She wanted to kick him, but Cale only laughed. "Once an ass, always an ass. Why do you go out with him, Laurel?"

"I'm not sure right now. He's a bit of a pest. Doesn't take no easily."

"I'm missing something." Confused, Matt looked back and forth between them.

"We're old friends," Cale said.

"What's going on over here?" Victor Banning carried his years as elegantly as the cane he used to join them. He was smaller, thinner, the bones in his face more pronounced. One side of his mouth and eye drooped slightly and his speech was not sharp. The conversation came to a halt.

For an instant they stood there like cats with a cornered mouse, and she wondered who would pounce first. "Happy birthday, Mr. Banning."

"Thanks. Just glad to be still breathing. I remember you. You're that Peyton girl." He looked from Cale to Jud. "When was that?"

"Nineteen seventy," Jud said.

"Your mother still lives on the island?"

"Yes. Her studio has been there for years." She was careful how she spoke of her mother with someone like Victor, who Cale swore all those years ago could smell the aroma of dissention a mile away.

"I'm familiar with her work. Impressive. The new show was a success."

She could only imagine how her mother would react to Victor Banning complimenting her work. To Victor Banning knowing her work. To Victor Banning walking in on one of her shows. Her mother would take one look at him and run away on fire. Another Banning to blame for their own mistakes.

"I'm so confused," Matt said under his breath. "So how do you know each other?"

Cale held up a hand. "Stop. Someone has to save her from the Banning inquisition. There's food by the pool and over there near the bar. Jud, if you're not going to take her outside, I will."

"Find your own date," Jud said.

"You're not Jud's date," Matt said to Laurel.

"Yes," Jud said pointedly, "she is."

"Who's Uncle Jud's date?" A young man with the Banning good looks walked up, chewing on a chicken wing. "I was hoping for last month's centerfold."

"You're your father's son," Victor said.

"Why would you say that, Gramps?"

"I hate it when you call me that."

"Why do you think I do it?" He grinned at Victor, then winked at her. "Hi. I'm Dane."

"Hello, Dane. I'm sorry I'm not a centerfold."

"This is Laurel," Jud told him. "And it would be great if all of you would stop giving her a hard time. She's an old friend."

"Whose friend?" Dane asked. "Uncle Jud's, Gramps's, or Dad's?"

"Who knows? I'm completely in the dark. I thought she was a business associate," Matt said.

"Of course you would, big brother. Everything with you is business."

Jud looked at Cale. "They're your sons. Do something."

Cale glanced at Laurel and a heartbeat later they both burst out laughing. "Aren't you glad you came?"

"Well, I'm not nervous anymore."

"Good," Jud said. "Because you looked like you wanted to shoot me when we pulled up and I told you where you were."

"You're not off the hook." She poked his shoulder with a finger. "He told me we were going to a dinner party."

Jud took her hand and threaded his fingers through hers, apparently something of note by the looks on the others' faces. "I didn't lie. We are at a dinner party. I had enough trouble just getting you to go out with me. And you admitted if I had told you where we were going you would have never said yes."

"Why did I say yes?"

"I gave you no choice."

"So where's your hot date?" Matt asked Dane.

"She couldn't get off work." He shrugged and picked up another chicken wing from a passing tray. "Looks like I'm all alone."

"The woman I wanted to ask refuses to go out with me," Matt said.

"Who is that smart woman?" Dane said.

"Probably a friend of your date—the one who used the excuse that she had to work."

"This is a sad state of affairs," Victor said. "Jud's the only one with a woman."

"Well," Dane said. "We all know Dad, here, doesn't have a date."

Cale faced his sons. "You two laugh all you want. This year I might steal Jud's. What do you say, Laurel? Dump Jud."

"Fat chance," Jud said.

Laurel looked at him. "Don't be so sure of yourself, Jud."

"I like you," Dane said. "You're perfect for my dad. Beautiful, smart, and you put Uncle Jud in his place."

"She's great," Matt added. "You ought to see her daughter."

"What daughter?"

"Forget it, little brother. I saw her first."

"Let's go outside, Laurel," Jud said quickly. "There's food and a band. I can keep you to myself and protect you from my obnoxious family." Jud put his hand low on her back and propelled her forward to the sound of Victor Banning laughing.

But Victor wasn't laughing later, when Laurel spotted

him sitting alone in a chair and staring out at the party. He turned. "Come sit by an old man on his birthday."

"You look like you've had enough of your birthday."

"That obvious? I'll have to work on my poker face."

"I think you've had years of perfecting a poker face."

"Smart cookie. Robyn was a smart cookie, too. These things aren't the same without her."

"Cale's wife?" When he nodded she said, "You approved of her."

"She was good for him. Kept the boy focused. Gave the Bannings a little class, kept us in line."

"I can't imagine anyone keeping you in line."

He laughed. "Even me. Matthew is impressed with your company. We talked about it earlier. And your daughter."

"Annalisa wanted the contract badly. She's a lot smarter than I am, but young, only twenty-two. I think she feels pressure to prove herself to the contractors on the job."

"Drive is a good thing."

"I suppose it is, unless it becomes the be-all and end-all. There are things more important."

"Perhaps." He shrugged. "To be successful, you have to make sacrifices, hard choices, be willing to do almost anything to get ahead." Here was the Victor that Cale told her of all those years ago. Beric too had an obsessive drive. It was hell on earth to live with someone who pushed that hard and wanted success and power more than anything else in the world. Values and family went out the window.

"Here you are." Jud joined them. "I thought you disappeared on me. We haven't had a dance."

"Thanks for humoring an old man," Victor said, then looked up at Jud. "You can stop scowling at me. She's all yours."

"Oh, no she's not." Dane almost picked her up and carried her away. Laurel was laughing when they were on the dance floor. "I'm the youngest. I hate feeling left out. Besides, look at how irritated Uncle Jud is. He thinks we've been monopolizing you all night. But he won't admit it."

"He was fairly stubborn when I knew him years ago."

"Jud? No." Dane grinned. "Matt and I have a bet going on how long it will take him to blow."

"You're trying to make him mad?"

"Sure. These family events can be deadly dull. We have to put some spice in the night."

"You should be ashamed of yourselves."

"You're probably right. But we Bannings don't like to acknowledge our own faults, just each other's. We all can be pretty pigheaded. But I'm the most charming."

"You know, I think you are."

"Ah. Too bad. Song's over." Dane leaned closer and said, "Watch this as we walk back toward Jud."

They were probably six feet from Jud when Matthew stepped in between and cut him off. "My turn." He winked at her and pulled her back toward the dancers without looking back.

"You're terrible."

"Me? What did I do?"

"Just how much is this bet you have going?"

"What bet? I know nothing about a bet."

"Dane told me."

"The kid never could keep his mouth shut. A hundred bucks," Matthew said, grinning. "Two hundred if Jud gets angry enough to challenge Dad to one of their one-on-one games." When she didn't respond, he added, "Basketball."

"I know what one-on-one is."

"Around here it's an old Banning family tradition of rivalry, superiority, and dirty play." He spun her around and she laughed. "So how's Annalisa? You have the same laugh."

"We do? She went to Catalina with her grandmother for the weekend. She's been working pretty hard. The big commercial trade show is the end of next week in Chicago. We'll be ready to start the kitchen configurations afterward."

"That's what she said." He seemed to hesitate for a moment.

"What's wrong?"

"I think her father embarrassed her the other day."

"He can do that pretty easily."

"She didn't have to worry. I was sold on her the first time I met her. She impressed me."

"I had no idea she was going to push for acceptance of our bid."

"What she did was perfectly ethical." Matthew began moving her in a specific direction, then stopped. "So how do you know my dad?"

"I met him and Jud in Catalina one summer. It was a long time ago."

He stopped. "Here, Dad. Dance with Laurel. My feet hurt." He handed her off to Cale, then went off to waylay Jud.

Laurel almost felt sorry for Jud, but he had tricked her into coming, so she didn't worry much. And she was having a good time. "You have a lovely home here. It's a great view."

"I ramble around in it most of the time, with Dane interning and Matthew having his own place. I've thought about selling it, but I'm too lazy."

"I don't think anyone would call a doctor lazy. I've always heard their time isn't their own. Is medicine everything you thought it would be? Was it worth all the hard work and time?"

"I think it was. I'm a surgeon."

"I know. Cardiothoracic. I couldn't believe it when Jud told me what field you'd gone into. It's really a strange world, Cale. I don't really talk about it much, but I had valve replacement surgery seven years ago."

Cale missed a step. "What?"

She nodded. "I had rheumatic fever when I was a toddler. The valve problem didn't surface until I was forty."

"Who was the surgeon?"

"Dr. Sussmann at UCLA."

"He's good. I know him. Who's your cardiologist?"

"Karl Collins."

Cale began laughing then.

"Of course you know him, too. He's local."

"I went to school with him. We still play golf a couple of times a month. His wife was good friends with Robyn."

She could see him close off, like saying her name was sin. She searched for something to say. "Robyn was your wife."

"Yes. She died a couple of years ago of breast cancer."

"I'm sorry, Cale." The comment sounded trite to her ears and she wished she hadn't said anything. "Your sons are wonderful. Dane is quite the charmer, and a joke-ster."

Cale shook his head and laughed. "Now what's he cooking up?"

"I'm not telling."

"He keeps everyone on their toes. He always has."

"He's very confident, and Matthew is great." The fact that he had sons was her gift and why she could even be there. One of those justifications you used to balance life. "You should be proud of them both."

"I am. Most of the credit goes to my wife. The boys were very close with their mother."

The song ended before she could say anything else, and the band said good night.

"I guess that's it," Cale said. They were the last ones on the dance floor. In fact it looked as if everyone had left. Laurel turned just as Jud walked out through the patio doors. He didn't look very happy when he saw the band packing up.

"Looks like it's time to call it a night," Cale said.

"Victor's seeing the last of them out," Jud said. "Where are your sons? I'm going to kill them with my bare hands."

"Hey, Dad! Uncle Jud! Down here!" Dane's shout came from a distance. Then she heard the repetitive sound of a ball bouncing on the basketball court at the bottom of the property. Matt hit the court lights and it was lit up like a ball field, with Dane in the center shift-ing the bouncing ball from one hand to the other.

Cale elbowed Jud in the side. "A hundred bucks say Dane wins." He took off for the court.

"You got it, buddy! Matt will clean up the court with him." Down on the court, Jud shrugged out of his coat. "Get that ball, Matt! Come on. Don't be a wuss!"

Dane scored and Cale shouted from the sidelines and clapped his hands. "That's it, son! Keep your rhythm going!"

Jud paced like a caged cat. "Matthew. Damn. Are you gonna let your little brother beat you?"

"Shut up, Jud," Matt called back, then stole the ball and pitched it high, right into the net.

"All right! That's the way!" Jud whistled so loudly Laurel winced.

"Go, Dane! Get 'em! It's your ball!"

Dane scored the next two points and his father shouted, "Whoa! That's my son!"

Matt stopped, tucked the basketball under his arm, and looked at his dad. "Last time I looked I was your son, too. Is there something you want to tell me?"

"Don't take it personally. I have a hundred bucks riding on this game." Cale cupped his hands around his mouth and hollered, "Clean his clock, Dane!"

Victor walked up to Laurel, watched for a minute, then asked, "Who's losing?"

"Jud and Cale," she said dryly. An older man they'd introduced as Harlan brought some folding chairs and they sat down.

Jud was shouting and running along with Matthew. "Get loose! You're too stiff. He's got the ball. Dammit! Stop him, Matt! Are you listening to me?"

The ball sliced though the basket.

"Shit! Shit! Shit!" Jud punched the air and twisted around.

Cale crowed and punched Jud in the arm. "You're going to lose."

Jud loosened his tie and unbuttoned his shirt, then he rolled up his sleeves and bent down, hands on his knees. "Okay. You can do it, Mattie boy. Let's go!"

"Here he comes, Dane!" Cale shook his hand in the air. "Look out! Stay with him! Stay with him!"

Matt scored and Jud whistled even more loudly.

"You can do better than that, son. What's wrong with you!" Cale called out to Dane. "You took your eye off the ball!"

It looked as if both Matt and Dane were getting more frustrated with Jud and Cale than with each other.

Laurel turned to Victor. "Is this normal?"

"No. They're calmer tonight than usual. Probably because you're here."

From what Laurel could tell, neither brother remembered she was there.

It was wild, an uncontrolled man-eat-man competition that went on until Jud called Matt a pussy. Matt turned, red-faced, and threw the ball at his uncle's head.

Jud ducked. "Damn . . . Hit *him*"—he pointed to Cale—"not me. I'm on your side!"

"Like hell. You get out here and play if you know so goddamn much." Matt was disgusted.

A minute later Jud and Cale were on the court in their street clothes, paired off in teams, Cale and Dane against Matt and Jud. That lasted about five minutes. Matt walked off first, Dane right after him. Matt used his shirt for a towel and dried off his face and neck. He looked at Dane. "You owe me two hundred bucks. Jud lost it first."

"I know. I'd have thought he'd have had more control tonight." He looked at the court. "Did Dad just take a swing at him?"

"Yep. Too bad he missed. Shoot . . ." Matt slung his shirt around his neck. "Hey, Jud! Stay with him! Keep your eye on the ball! Don't lose him! You can do better than that!"

Jud flipped him off, then almost tackled Cale to steal the ball and score.

"I've never seen anything like this," Laurel said.

Dane turned, clearly puzzled. "You haven't?"

"Well, I take that back," she said, watching Jud trip Cale and run for the net. "Maybe when I was changing channels and hit the WWF." It exhausted her to watch them and she stifled a yawn. This wasn't the way she imagined ending the first date she'd had in almost two years.

Matt looked down at her. "This could go on for a while. You want me to take you home?"

She looked at the court, where Jud slammed the ball into Cale's back. "This is painful to watch. You two should be ashamed of yourselves."

"Nah," Dane said. "They like it. I'll go with you. I have early shift tomorrow."

She said good-bye to Victor and followed Matthew and Dane up to the house, but paused at the patio doors and looked back. From everything she could tell, Jud hadn't even noticed she'd left.

It was a short drive home and they kept her laughing, and argued good-naturedly over everything from who was the better player to who would walk her to the door, settling only when they both did. Inside in her kitchen, she could still hear them egging each other on as they walked along the side of the house. She poured herself a glass of water and listened until their voices faded and the car pulled away. It was a long time before she turned off the lights and walked upstairs. She didn't turn on the light in her bedroom, just kicked off her shoes and curled into an overstuffed chair near the windows. She had not run this time. She'd faced her past, faced Cale and Jud together, even faced his two sons, all the time knowing Cale really had three sons.

Cale lay sprawled in the middle of the basketball court he had built for his sons, the overhead lights glaring into his face and blinding him, his heart pounding in his chest, clothes torn, sweat dripping off his temples and down over his ears, his body feeling pretty much as if it had been beaten with a two-by-four. He took two long deep breaths that burned in his chest, and he was just getting the feeling back in his feet and legs.

"I'm too old for this," Jud groaned next to him. "I need CPR."

"Call an EMT, asshole. I'm struggling enough for my own air." They both were panting like bulldogs. "Did I win? I never saw the last shot."

"You didn't see it? In that case, I won."

"Bullshit." Cale found enough air to laugh.

"Who wins the bet?"

"Do you need the money?"

Jud laughed. "No. Do you?"

376 ~ JILL BARNETT

"No."

Jud flung his arm over his eyes. "Those lights are murder."

Cale grunted something, then lifted his head off the concrete.

Victor was sitting on a chair alone. Cale sat up, resting his arms on his bent knees, and looked down at Jud, who hadn't moved. "You can turn out the lights, old man. Your fun is over."

Jud raised one arm and waved it in the air. "Happy birthday, Victor!"

"Oh, shit."

"What?" Jud turned to him just as the lights went off.

"Your date's gone."

Funny how Jud was on his feet a second later. "Laurel?"

Victor was walking away but stopped. "Matthew took her home about forty-five minutes ago."

Cale limped off the court behind Jud, who was suddenly very quiet. They moved silently toward the house and met Dane and Matt at the door, each holding an extra beer.

"Here, you look like you need this," Dane said. "Can I borrow two hundred bucks?"

"What for?"

"I lost a bet with Matt."

Cale turned to Jud. "Pay up. I won. You owe me two hundred bucks."

Jud opened his wallet and handed Cale the cash, which he gave to Dane, who handed it to Matt. He folded it and tucked it into his shirt pocket, and looked at Jud.

"You owe us big-time, Jud, for taking home your date," Dane said.

"The date you monopolized all night along? You're turning out to be worse than your father." Jud walked inside and flopped down on a chair, and some part of Cale hoped he'd blown it with Laurel.

"Don't worry so much," Dane said. "She was just tired. She didn't seem upset."

"Just amazed by your deftness with sportsmanship." Matt laughed.

"Who?" Victor walked out of the kitchen.

"Mrs. King," Matt said.

Cale thought he heard wrong. "Who?"

"Mrs. King. Laurel," Matt said simply.

"She was married to Beric King." Jud sipped his beer.

The King woman's records . . . Call and set up a TEE for the King woman . . . I don't talk about it much, but I had valve replacement surgery seven years ago. Conversations ran through his mind with the realization that Laurel was Lofty's special patient.

"Hey, Pop?" Dane called him into the kitchen and said quietly, "Isn't that the name of that heart patient whose records I looked at the other day?"

"Yes, but you can't say anything."

"I know that," his son said with irritation. "Why do you think I called you in here?"

"Sorry."

"What are you going to do?"

"Help her."

"Hey, what's going on in here?" Matt asked with Jud on his heels.

"They're probably cooking up some new bet." Jud

tossed his empty beer into the trash. "Like your father doesn't make enough money."

"And you're so poor."

"Go home. Both of you," Cale said, only half joking. "Take Victor home. He's beat and so am I." It took time to get rid of them all, for Matt and Victor to drive off, for Jud to stop pacing and finally leave, and Dane to go to bed. At half past two Cale sat down in his study and stared at the phone for a minute, then called Lofty Collins anyway.

It was about five forty-five on Sunday evening, damp and cold because the fog had rolled in about three. Laurel stood at the open refrigerator, her cat, Henry, weaving in and out between her legs. "What do we want to eat? Chicken in peanut sauce?" She looked at the cat. "Maybe? Okay, how about lamb chops? No, huh? Sun-dried tomatoes and spinach pasta with goat cheese?" She paused, then opened the freezer. "This blissful carton of Ben & Jerry's ice cream?"

Henry whined.

"Good idea. No dishes to clean. Just a spoon and your bowl. We can eat in front of the fire." She grabbed a spoon, took out a small Pyrex dish for the cat—it took an act of God to separate Henry from his Ben & Jerry's—and reached for the ice cream.

The doorbell rang.

"Right at dinner time. Perfect timing. What will they be selling tonight? Wrapping paper? Coupon books? Chocolate? Henry, get ready to attack. Someone is coming between us and our Chunky Monkey."

Laurel flung open the front door and stood face-to-

THE DAYS OF SUMMER ~ 379

face with Jud. She took a long breath. "I knew I shouldn't have shown you where I live."

He shifted and looked past her. "I heard you talking to someone. Am I interrupting?"

"Yes." She used the spoon to point at his feet. "A vitally important conversation between my cat and me." Apparently Henry's idea of an attack wasn't the same as Laurel's. He was rubbing up against Jud's leg. "Okay," she said, waving the spoon in the air. "The truth is out. I've become one of those women who lives alone and talks to her cat. Tomorrow I shall wear purple."

Jud rubbed Henry's ears and looked confused.

"Never mind. You'd have to be a woman to get the joke." She leaned against the door and crossed her arms protectively, tapping the spoon against her side. "Why are you here?"

"I owe you an apology. I don't usually abandon the women I take out."

"You were busy." She was glad she sounded flip.

"Yeah, busy making an ass out of myself." He looked honestly contrite.

"That's true. At least you can admit it. Some people would blame everyone else."

"Some people?"

"My ex was never wrong."

"As I get older, I find I'm wrong more than I want to be." He laughed a little. "Hell, I think I knew the game had gotten carried away when it was happening. Old habits, I guess."

Hesitating for a second, she looked down at the cat, a discerning creature who always ignored strangers and her ex. She opened the door wider. "Come on in."

"Wait. Give me a minute." Jud turned and ran to the alley.

She heard the tweet of his remote, then looked down at herself. She was wearing black yoga pants, a white sports tank, and a gray zippered sweatshirt. She stepped out of her old pink flip-flops with their dirty imprints and kicked them into the corner behind the door. Henry sat on the brass threshold. Both of them were obediently waiting. What was wrong with this picture?

A car door slammed and Jud came back around the corner with a bottle of wine and a white plastic sack from Chang's. He held up the takeout. "Peace offerings."

"Well, that was worth waiting for. I'm starving." She closed the door behind him. "It smells wonderful. Come on in the kitchen."

He followed her inside and set the food on the island while she took down plates, serving spoons, and a tray. She tossed him the wine opener, set two wineglasses out, and opened the food cartons. Inside were chicken lettuce wraps, steamed vegetable dumplings, honey crispy shrimp, brown rice, and spicy green beans.

"Okay." She planted her palm on the island and the other on her hip. "This is no lucky guess. These are all my favorites."

"I called ahead."

She stuck spoons in the cartons. "How did you know I eat there?"

He tapped his head with a finger. "Great mind."

"I don't think so. I didn't just fall off the tuna boat, Jud."

He handed her a glass of wine. "I saw the cartons in your office kitchen the day we had lunch."

"You were there what? Five minutes?"

"About."

She picked up the tray of food and started for the front room. "Well, that was observant," she called out over her shoulder.

"I'm always observant."

She set the tray down on a low table and tossed a couple of floor pillows down on the rug for them to sit on. "Sure. Really observant. That's why you never saw me leave with Matthew last night."

"I owe Matthew for that."

"Yes, well, it gave me the chance to find out all kinds of things about you."

"Like what?"

"This is great wine."

"You're changing the subject."

"Yes. I am."

"Tell me."

"I love Pouilly-Fuissé."

"I remember."

Time and the years disappeared, replaced by the image of the crooked front stoop of a small apartment building in LA, where a case of expensive French wine sat with a note that started *Dear Jailbait*. She felt something deep and elemental, the jagged edges of feelings she couldn't control, even though she tried. She couldn't even turn away, and she knew everything she was thinking was raw and open and there for him to read if he looked for it.

Forgetting about that case of wine didn't mean she had forgotten what it had led to. What good did it do to lie to yourself? His image had always lingered in the back of her memories, in that safe dark place where she could hide everything so she wouldn't have to think about why she hadn't been free to love him. What did that say about the two of them, that she had forgotten so much while he remembered so much?

She set her wineglass down and he poured her some more. "Thanks." She paused, then looked at him. The man on that basketball court last night did not think about things; he ran on sheer instinct and huge emotion. That was Jud. "You were set up, you know."

"What was set up?"

"Dane and Matthew set you up last night. Those two worked you like precision machinery."

He just stared at her.

"They had a bet going. That's why they kept cutting in and interrupting us." She saw the realization hit him.

"They are dead men. Damn . . ." He wasn't really angry, didn't look dark or glowering but as if he wanted to laugh, and she remembered why all those years ago she had fallen so fast for this man. "That's pretty inventive of them," he said. "Why do I have the idea that this wasn't the first time?" Then he did laugh. "I'm impressed. Hell, I wonder exactly how long they've been doing that to us."

"I think for a long time."

He shook his head. "That explains a lot of things."

"Like what?"

"Like why you let me in here so easily tonight after what happened."

"I've always had a soft spot in my heart for a sucker."

They both laughed, then in the lapse of silence that followed, Laurel stood and picked up the dishes. He took the tray into the kitchen but brought a new bottle of wine back with them. She sat on the sofa, pulled her knees up, and tucked her feet under her.

As if they had done this a hundred times, he walked right over to the fire, squatted down easily, and poked at it, then added more wood. He sat with her, poured the wine, and kicked off his shoes, then crossed his feet on the coffee table and looked around the room. "This really is a great house. Those high ceilings and the crown molding. You don't see Heatilator fireplaces much anymore."

"I love the detail."

"I'm surprised your ex didn't fight you over this place."

"He didn't dare."

"That bad?"

"It's too long a story to tell."

"I have all night."

The images that flashed through her head were unwelcome and X-rated. He could say a few words and get her all twisted up inside.

"He seems to be a man who knows what he wants."

"Yes, well, he always has. Confidence is not his problem, just the opposite. The French are a very determined people. Stubborn."

"You're a stubborn woman."

"I lived in France for twelve years. No one is more stubborn than the French, especially if they're wrong."

"But you married one of them."

She looked into her wineglass, as if there were magic in there that would hide her from the truth. "Yes. I did. He is a dramatic man and a brilliantly talented chef." Her marriage to Beric had been painful, his constant need for attention a strain on their marriage. Over and over he put her in a position to chose between Annalisa and him. Too often he would run to someone else, using the excuse that he didn't get what he wanted and needed from her. "He taught the sauce class."

Jud laughed. "The sauce class?"

"Beric is a master at sauces." She smiled. "He's actually a master at everything. Just ask him. He can talk about himself for hours."

"And that was why you married him?"

"No. Of course not. I was kidding, somewhat. I was his protégée. He was a master chef. It didn't take long for things to become more complicated. In many ways, it was quite wonderful. His family took me in. They were, are, all quite the strong personalities. I'd never been around a big, loud family like that. It was like being surrounded by a bunch of helium balloons, so different from the life I had known. I think at that age I was young and free, and being in France was wildly romantic."

"How long were you married?"

"Too long. But I would do it all over again for Annalisa." She faced him. "I'm not proud of my mistakes."

"You're too hard on yourself for the choices you've made."

"So say you." She laughed. "You don't have to live with them."

"I live with more mistakes than you could ever know, Jailbait."

And she understood he was talking about her. "So what about you?"

He shrugged. "What do you want to know?"

"You never married?"

He shook his head.

"Never came close?"

"I've had some long-term relationships. I lived with a couple of women. One for over four years."

"What happened?"

"She wanted to get married. She was a great girl, in corporate finance. Sharp as can be. I think I really cared about her." His voice drifted off.

"What happened?"

"I couldn't commit to her the way she wanted. I tried in the end, but I kept postponing the wedding." He took a sip of wine and said, matter-of-factly, "BanCo has been my life for a long, long time. She knew that going in, but it got old for her. She finally gave up and married an English professor who writes poetry. I went to one of his readings in Westwood a few years back.

"I think in the end she wanted to get far away from the corporate world. I get a Christmas card every year. Jan is a bank manager in a small town in Washington and apparently quite happy."

"Do you have any regrets?"

"A whole lifetime of them." He laughed. "The latest one being that I didn't bring you home last night."

"You're forgiven."

"Good." He finished off his wine, set the glass down, sat back, and then turned to her.

Neither of them spoke. The silence was fast changing from awkwardness to something else, a taut line of emotion between them. She wanted to speak, to be bright and funny, with words to make them laugh and that would quickly cut off this complicated thing that was spiraling between them.

But she couldn't think when he looked at her that way. In the back of her mind was a vague sense that this was what she wanted. This was why she had opened the door.

"I don't want to regret not doing this." Jud slid his hand behind her neck.

She didn't know until the moment he touched her that she had been holding her breath. He slowly pulled her forward until their mouths touched. The taste of wine was in his mouth. His tongue licked her lips and the kiss turned deep and free and sexy; it went on for a long, long time before he pulled back.

It took her a moment to realize he'd stopped. She had forgotten how this man could control her physically. Amazing how some things didn't change. There had always been a hint of desperation in Cale's love for her, and maybe that had been why she couldn't break it off all those years ago, why she couldn't tell him that she loved his brother.

Jud was different—raw, dynamic, and confident. He didn't look at her and sit there wanting her. He looked at her and took what he wanted from her.

"You look so serious," she said. "What are you think-ing about?"

"The poetry of us."

"What?"

He smiled as if he were laughing at himself and

shook his head. "I was thinking how much I want to do that again."

"I never thought you were the kind of man to hesitate when you wanted something." She spoke with authority, as if in her mind the decision were crystal clear. How very far from the truth.

"I don't want to scare you off," he said.

So it was up to her. He had done this before, so many years ago, pushed and pushed and then dumped the decision in her lap. For some reason she couldn't explain, that appealed to her and forced her to admit that her attraction to this man had never changed. It felt as overwhelming as love did at seventeen, and she hadn't felt that way in a long, long time. She knew he would have to leave now. The fire was just embers, the wine bottles empty. But she could taste him on her tongue. She wondered what kind of world, what kind of almighty power sends your life spinning in such circles. Without meeting his eyes, she inhaled deeply and said, "You should probably go."

"Yes." He paused, watching her. "I should." But he didn't make any move to get up, so she did. He hesitated for only an instant, then stood, his expression taut with regret.

A lifetime of what-might-have-beens flashed through her head as she walked to the front hallway. His shoes on the tiles sounded hollow as he followed her, the familiar loneliness of one set of footsteps. She hesitated for only a heartbeat, then turned away from the door and walked toward the stairs, stopping halfway up. She looked down at him. "The bedroom's up here."

CHAPTER

30

Jud followed her as if there had been no years in between, no other lifetime, followed her like a man caught by a Siren and without a single thought or fear of what might lay ahead, because she was Laurel and with her everything was different. Nothing else mattered now and never had, not even trust between brothers.

By the time they reached the upstairs hallway, she looked scared, second-guessing herself, so he pulled her to him and kissed her to completeness, until her body was pliant against him, until there was no physical sign she mentally struggled with this, until her desire turned ripe and equaled his own. He walked her toward the front bedroom, through wide double doors, shrugging out of his sweater and shirt, barely breaking apart to do so, while she pulled clothing over her head, kicked it off with her feet, and stood at home in his arms without reticence.

> *If they be two, they are two so*
> *As stiff twin compasses are two;*
> *Thy soul, the fixed foot, makes no show*
> *To move, but doth, if th' other do.*

The bedroom was dark, all shadows and silhouettes, cocooned by bookcases and furniture, windows and walls limned with only the soft buttery light from a distant streetlamp. Bathed in that light, her skin lambent, she drew him down to the bed. Under his famished hands her body was his, softer, fuller, belly and thighs lush, different from years ago, better than his memories. Perhaps for all the years apart, or because of them, he loved her long and easily, slowing down countless moments to savor what was between them—something different from fire and passion, something even time couldn't extinguish. And when it was over, when their sighs quieted and hearts slowed down, when their breathing was close to normal and life after ecstasy fell back into the ordinary, he closed his eyes, sultry sleep engulfing him.

But in that last instant of consciousness, when the world and its edges began to fade away, before conscious reality completely disappeared, he understood that together they were anything but ordinary.

Laurel was making breakfast the next morning when Jud came downstairs, his hair damp from a shower and he needed a shave. She flipped a breakfast crepe. "I have some disposable razors under the bathroom sink."

"That's okay. I'll shave at home. I'm not going to the office. I have to fly to Denver this afternoon for an annual board meeting at one of our subsidiary companies. I won't be back until Thursday." He poured a mug of coffee and stood just a foot or so away, watching her while drinking it. "What smells so good?"

"Spinach soufflé crepes with honey bacon and cheese sauce." She set out plates and a dish of sliced melon filled with raspberries.

"You didn't have to do this for me."

Laurel laughed. "I didn't. I eat a huge breakfast most mornings. Breakfast is the most important meal. It fuels your heart."

He leaned forward. "My heart got plenty of fuel last night. I have a full tank, sweetheart."

She smiled up at him as if they had been doing this for thirty years. The most natural thing in the world was the kiss they fell into, the way her arms went around his neck, his hands warm and familiar on her back and bottom.

"Mother!"

They broke apart like guilty teens.

"Annalisa. What are you doing here?"

Her daughter stood in the doorway looking as if someone had hit her.

Laurel turned to Jud, not knowing what to say. He reached out and squeezed her hand, then looked at her daughter. "Good morning, Annalisa."

"Jud. Mr. Banning." Her voice was icy. "What are you doing here? It's eight in the morning."

"Jud spent the night last night."

"No kidding."

"Stop it, Annalisa." Laurel was angry and embarrassed.

"I care about your mother. This isn't something

sleazy. Don't make her feel like it is. I've known her for a long time."

Annalisa looked from him to Laurel, then her face crumpled. She burst into tears and ran out the door.

Laurel felt completely nonplussed. "Well, that was interesting."

"Shouldn't you go after her?"

"Probably." She didn't move.

He hooked his arm around her waist and pulled her to him. "You okay?"

"I don't know. But I don't regret last night."

"Thank you."

She smiled against his lips. "You're welcome."

"Do you want me to stay while you talk to her?"

"No. You go ahead."

"I'll call you later." He kissed her.

Laurel followed him outside and down the stairs. Back at the alley, he paused before he got in his car, so she waved and waited until he had driven away. On the beach she spotted her daughter near the water, standing alone and staring out at sea. Laurel walked through the cool sand, sidestepping chalky cracked shells and dirty green kelp ropes left from the high tide. Her footsteps made a grainy sound in the deep sand, so she knew Annalisa heard her walk up, but she didn't turn around. "Annalisa? I don't understand. Why are you so upset? You've been trying to get me to date for years."

"You didn't tell me you knew him before." Annalisa's face was tight and emotional. "He was the one who was sending you the flowers, wasn't he?"

"Yes."

"You could have told me, Mother."

"It's a long story."

"Mamie told me."

"What exactly did she tell you?"

"That years ago he hurt you so badly you ran away to France."

"That's not true. But even if it were, would it matter now? He hasn't hurt me now. Our past is complicated."

"Are you in love with him? Were you in love with him?"

To Laurel last night had been wonderful. Standing there now with Annalisa was so uncomfortable. She had no idea how much she should say or how true her feelings were at that moment. She wasn't ready to share them with anyone, not even Jud. It took her a while to answer. "He's just come back into my life. I care about him. Is that what's bothering you?"

"No." She looked down at her feet. "Yes. Oh, I don't know. Mamie said the Bannings destroyed us. She told me about the accident. She said I shouldn't care about Matthew. That he would only hurt me."

A single conversation from all those years ago came flooding back, almost real enough for Laurel to feel the pain all over again, her mother telling her how Cale and Jud's father had killed hers. That she wasn't safe. Her mother's once-calming maternal voice suddenly high-pitched, transformed by anger and grief, the fear and bitterness her mother carried in her damaged self like some hierophant.

She could see what Annalisa was feeling—scorched and terribly mixed up if she had any feelings for Matthew. At that moment she wanted to forever silence her mother. Laurel put her arm around Annalisa's shoulders. "I'm sorry, sweetheart."

Her daughter began to cry. "She's right. Matthew already has hurt me." Then Annalisa blurted out her whole story, then added, "And after all that, 'I'm a patient man, Annalisa. I'll wait. There's no one else I want.' He's with that blonde at the restaurant. You saw him. Men are jerks."

"Well, yes, they are sometimes. We women confuse them, which doesn't take much in some cases." Annalisa didn't laugh. "The good news is you never went out with him."

"I just wasted night after night dreaming about him, worked twice as hard trying to impress him. Can you believe I almost threw away my principles for him?"

"Which principles?"

"I told him I had a rule not to date anyone I worked with."

"Principles are wonderful things to have." She tucked Annalisa's hair behind her ear. "But principles won't keep you warm at night."

"You think I'm wrong? Oh, of course you do. You're sleeping with Jud Banning."

There were times, like now, when being a mother wasn't all it was cracked up to be. Times when you could actually slap your child. Instead she took a long breath and chose her words carefully. "Love is difficult enough to find without putting restrictions on it. Work is part of life, and life is where we form our relationships. Falling in love at work might not be ideal, but people have been doing it for centuries."

Annalisa didn't respond. She just looked miserable.

"You wouldn't be in the world, sweetheart, if I had lived by those rules."

"True, but you and Daddy divorced because you worked together."

"Is that what you think?"

"It's true."

"The truth is that I divorced your father because of his infidelity. I forgave him and forgave him. That didn't stop him. He was having an affair when I had my heart surgery."

"Daddy?"

She hadn't told her daughter the truth behind the divorce to protect her from all the ugliness of it. Annalisa had been a teen then, angry anyway, heartbroken their family was falling apart. Now Laurel saw that the only person she was protecting was Beric. Without the truth, her daughter had drawn her own conclusions, wrong ones that had just affected her life in a bad way.

This was one of those times when the truth needed to come out. But she was afraid of the truth; that happened when you had too many secrets. There were some truths that should never be told. She couldn't tell her biggest secret. Maybe she was the one who should have been slapped.

She took Annalisa's hands and explained, "After the surgery, when I came home from the hospital, I decided I wasn't going to take it anymore. I wasn't going to live another day in a marriage that was so unhappy for me. I just couldn't do it, not even for you."

"I didn't know. I wouldn't have wanted you to stay for me. Dad makes me so angry. Did you know he cried and cried about how much he loved you? He talked about the strain of working together. He made it sound as if working together caused the divorce."

"Your father is high-strung. He needs things to go his way."

"But it was all his fault."

"No. No. That's not true. Divorce is seldom all one person's fault."

"What did you do?"

Laurel hugged her arms to her chest and stared out at the horizon. "Sometimes I wonder if I loved him enough."

"You are the most loving person I know." Now Annalisa was the one who wrapped her arms around Laurel. "I have never doubted that you loved me."

"You're pretty easy to love yourself. Matthew is right."

"I don't want to talk about him."

"Why? The blonde?"

"Yes."

"Annalisa."

"What?"

"You told him you wouldn't go out with him."

"Yes."

"Just once?"

She shook her head miserably. "About twenty times at least."

"Then don't you think it's unreasonable for you to be angry because he dates someone else?"

"I'm not really mad at him, Mom. I'm mad at me." She smiled thinly and linked her arm in Laurel's. "I'll be fine. I'm sorry I made such a mess of things a while ago. I was just . . . oh, I don't know . . . surprised to see Jud there. Especially after what Mamie told me."

"Yes, well, I'm going to have a long talk with her. She didn't know what was between us then and she doesn't know now. She cannot hear the name Banning without getting so upset she isn't rational."

"Don't be mad at her."

"I'm not," she lied. She was truly angry at her mother for telling Annalisa things that should have come from her, things that weren't colored with her mother's vitriolic anger at the Banning family. They walked back to the house arm in arm, too many questions still unanswered. Laurel stopped to wash her feet off at the sand shower near the porch and heard the phone ringing, so she ran inside. It was Dr. Collins's office calling about some appointment mix-up and they wanted her to come in tomorrow.

"I'm supposed to be flying to Chicago tomorrow," Laurel said into the phone. "But the flight isn't until four thirty. Yes. I can come in at ten." She hung up and walked into the kitchen. The last time they had called her in it was because they had forgotten to draw blood.

The cold, congealed breakfast crepes lay on the counter. Annalisa poured herself a cup of coffee and sat down, picking at the fruit.

"You want some breakfast?"

"No. I need to drive to Laguna and pick up new specs for the project, then go home and pack. Are you going into the office?"

Laurel checked her watch. "In about an hour." Her daughter looked as if she carried the sins of the world on her shoulders. "You okay?"

Annalisa finished off the melon, wiped her hands on her jeans, and gave Laurel a hug. "I'm fine, Mom. You can't mourn what you never had." She set down the coffee mug. "I'll see you later."

* * *

When the phone rang, it didn't take caller ID for Kathryn to know it was Laurel.

"Mother, what did you do?" Her daughter's voice over the phone was almost as angry as it had been the night they argued.

"She's making the same mistake you did. Someone has to stop her."

"You had no right to tell her anything about me. I'm her mother. I should tell her. You have no idea what happened between Jud and me. None."

"I know he's the reason you left me. He and that brother of his. You think I could ever forget that? They used you before, but you're willing to forget it so easily."

"Believe me, I don't forget anything."

"I can't save you from going down that road again, but I can stop her. She was already upset. That Matthew fellow has already hurt her. She needs to know what happened. She needs to understand what they did to us. I won't stand by and watch her destroyed because you refuse to talk about the past."

"I don't have to talk about the past, Mother. You've never stopped living in it."

Those bitter words just hung in the air and neither of them said anything.

"You've hurt Annalisa, Mother," Laurel said in a quiet tone.

"Matthew Banning has hurt her."

"I don't know if I can forgive you for this."

"You never have forgiven me, Laurel."

"Then we're a pair, aren't we? I've seen firsthand how hard you work to keep your grief brutal and unforgivable."

"I think we've hurt each other enough for one phone call."

"Good-bye, Mother." Laurel hung up and Kathryn stood there for the longest time, the phone in her hand, the words so hurtful and hateful they burned her up inside. She couldn't cry anymore. She'd cried too many times over Laurel.

Laurel walked into her cardiologist's private office at 10:05 on Tuesday. Karl Collins carried his good looks in the tousled, gangly way of a seventeen-year-old boy who never outgrew his awkwardness. His nut-brown hair, empathetic brown eyes, and strong hands were features his patients appreciated, along with assets like an acerbic wit and an ungodlike manner and willingness to joke in the face of sometimes frightening diagnoses. His reputation as a cardiologist was arguably the best. Dressed in a shirt and tie, pen in his pocket, with that familiar broad smile, he stood as soon as she walked in, but Laurel looked past him toward the tall shadow at the window. "Cale? What are you doing here?"

"Hello, Laurel."

"Have a seat." Karl gestured at the chair in front of his desk. She knew then something was going on and sank down as if her legs had given out.

"I asked Cale for a second opinion after your last appointment."

"Why? What's wrong?"

"You have an arrhythmia."

An irregular heartbeat? "Is there something wrong with the valve?"

"We're not certain." Cale put his hand on her shoulder. "We want you to get a TEE. A transthoracic echocardiogram. The images of your heart and blood vessels will give us a clearer view."

"We want to know exactly what's going on, Laurel," Karl added.

"What do you think it is?" She could see neither of them wanted to speculate. "Oh, for crissakes, you two. Stop being doctors and tell me what's going on here."

Cale spoke first. "It could be a problem with the valve. It could be an infection."

"We don't know because of your past surgery. It could be any number of things, Laurel." Karl paused, then asked, "Have you been to the dentist lately?"

"Yes, for a cleaning and chipped filling, but I took my antibiotics. I know better than to miss those. What if the valve is bad? It's only been seven years." The words came out rushed and panicked.

"Don't do that to yourself," Cale said sternly. "We don't know what's wrong. But we'll find out and fix it."

She thought she might cry and felt overcome with the swelling feelings of weakness and loss and sudden fragility. She just wanted it to be yesterday, forever, like Bill Murray in *Groundhog Day*.

"I want to do a quick exam, Laurel." Karl came around his desk.

She stood mechanically and followed his nurse to an exam room, where she stuck a thermometer in Laurel's mouth and took her blood pressure, then marked the charts and handed her a paper gown. "Strip to the waist. You know the routine."

Laurel set her purse down on a chair, put on the gown, and sat stiffly on the edge of the exam table, feeling every single heartbeat in her chest. After a sharp knock on the door, both Karl and Cale came in, stethoscopes hanging from their necks and with those doctors' smiles meant to put you at ease, which usually did just the opposite.

Karl read the chart. "You do have a slight fever." He handed the chart to Cale. "Ninety-nine. How have you been feeling?"

"A little tired, I guess, but I wasn't sleeping well last week."

Karl listened to her chest, pushed back the paper gown, and moved the steth around her back, then stepped aside and Cale did the same exam. She looked up at him as he listened to her heart. His expression was taut and serious and gave nothing away.

"I'm scared," she whispered and felt as if she might cry.

He dropped the steth and took her hand. "It's going to be okay, Laurel."

"I didn't know what to expect the first time around. I do now. I know too much. I know second surgeries carry a high risk."

"Your friend here is the best." Karl looked as if he sincerely believed that and stepped out to check with his nurse about the test schedule.

"Can we do this?" she asked Cale.

"What do you mean?"

"Should we do this? We had a past."

"It might not seem like a perfect situation to you. Look, you need me and I want to do it." He paused. "But it's your choice."

"I've always felt very badly about what I did to you."

"Laurel." He laughed and shook his head. "Afraid I'm going to get even on the operating table?"

It was so stupid she laughed, too. "No."

"We were a long time ago. I was young and in love. You hurt me. Jud crushed me. I felt deeply betrayed, so I stopped caring about anything and focused only on medicine. But if it hadn't been you it would have been someone else. I came out the winner here. I found exactly what I wanted to be and do, and after that, I found a woman I could love in the same way I loved medicine, and I did love her for almost thirty years." He tried to cover his pain with a professional smile, but Laurel recognized the emotion that crossed his expression.

"I'm sorry you lost her."

"They were good years that I wouldn't change for anything. So in a way, I need to do this, Laurel. You had valve surgery and now you might need something more. And here I am a cardiothoracic surgeon. It seems to me as if this is the way things were supposed to turn out."

Karl came back in. "The test is scheduled at UCI Med Center for tomorrow at eleven."

"Tomorrow?" Laurel didn't think it would be so soon. "So fast?"

"My office was supposed to get you in here ten days ago." Karl made it clear he wasn't happy with his staff.

"We need to see what's wrong." Cale's voice was gentle. "And as soon as possible."

"I'm supposed to leave for a trade show in Chicago today."

"Not now you aren't," Karl said.

So she dressed and took the appointment information and left, numb. She was almost to the front door of the medical building when Cale called her name and came running up to her.

"You okay?"

She nodded first, then shook her head, afraid if she spoke her voice would crack. He put his arms around her. "It's going to be fine."

She was crying by the time they sat down on a bench near an atrium water feature, surrounded by lush plants and spilling into a granite-edged pond with spotted fish and butterfly koi the colors of a sunset.

"Talk to me," he said.

"For years I never worried much. I had a murmur. I'd heard about it since childhood. Then when Annalisa was maybe thirteen, I started getting so tired and run down. Going up stairs was a problem. I went to the doctor, he sent me to a specialist, who said I needed surgery, so I just did what they advised. They were so matter-of-fact. I don't know if I was just naïve, or unwilling to really accept what was happening. Only afterward did I understand what I had gone through. I didn't face my mortality until I was in recovery. It was much tougher than I'd thought." She stared at her hands. "Now I know what to expect. I'm scared. It's risky, if it's a second heart surgery. The fact that you are here tells me I should be worried."

"Don't jump the gun, Laurel. I can't tell you it'll be a breeze. But I can promise I will do everything I can to make this as easy as I can. Even stepping aside if you want another surgeon."

"I don't want anyone else."

"Just have the tests and we'll take this one day at a

time." He stood. "Come on. I'll walk you out. I'm head-ing for the hospital."

At her car, she paused. "Thanks, Cale."

He reached up and brushed her hair from her face; it had stuck to her tears. "I'll be there tomorrow and we'll see what's going on."

"Here you are, back in my life when I need you."

"Maybe we both need each other."

She laughed then. "Oh, right. I'm sure you have no other patients."

He didn't laugh, but just said, "I'll see you tomorrow, Laurel-Like-the-Tree."

Laurel made a vague excuse to Annalisa about a forgot-ten appointment she couldn't change and promised she would fly to Chicago the next day. Tuesday night, she let the machine pick up Jud's two calls from Denver. The only person who knew what was happening was her überdiscreet assistant, Pat, who picked her up Wednes-day morning and drove her to the outpatient wing of the hospital. Pat would then wait and drive her back home.

Both Cale and Karl were there for the test—two men she trusted—yet she lay on the table feeling shaky at best. Getting a tube stuck down your throat and hav-ing to swallow it didn't sound easy. But the sedative helped and the nurse numbed her throat. As with most medical tests, the idea of the procedure was worse than the actual test. She lay there with the tube in, trying to breathe calmly. A nurse leaned over and wiped the saliva from her mouth, and the tech talked to her in an even, easy tone, which made her breathe a little easier. But she watched their faces, searching for meaning in every expression. Cale stepped closer at one point in the test and placed his hand on her shoulder. "Close your eyes and relax. It won't be much longer."

A medical minute always felt like an eternity, and the prep and test had taken the better part of an hour before they moved her into a bed in the recovery area. When she looked at the wall clock, she saw she'd been there for almost two hours. They gave her juice with a straw and a cup of hospital pudding, but she wanted answers, not cafeteria food, so when Cale and Karl both walked in together, she searched their expressions for an early answer, but found none. "Well," she said brightly, "if it isn't the Blues Brothers. The least you could do is smile and lull me into a sense of security before you give me the bad news."

Cale gave her a small smile then.

"Too late. I can see something is wrong." She stared at her hands folded and white knuckled.

"How are you feeling?" He sat down on a stool and rolled over to the end of the bed.

"Okay."

"We have the test here." Karl held up a video, then slipped it into a machine. "I'm going to play it so you can see what we found."

Cale used a pen to point at the back-and-white sonic images of her beating heart. "You have a tear right here, in the graft valve. It's leaking."

"So what does that mean? Another valve? More surgery?"

"The valve looks to be strong. It's working well, but we'll know more when we go in. The best-case scenario means we might only have to repair the tear."

"How complicated is that?"

"Any heart surgery has its complications."

"Don't do that. Please. I want to know exactly what I'm looking at."

"There's another complication we have to address first. You have endocarditis."

"An infection?" She knew that was not good. They'd given her the lectures after her first surgery and at almost every yearly checkup. Like Pavlov's dog, she heard the word "infection" and reacted with panic. "How does that affect the surgery?"

"We have to clear it up before we can operate, which means you'll need antibiotic treatment."

"So you give me a prescription and schedule the surgery?"

"No. You'll need intravenous antibiotics," Karl told her. "I'm admitting you to the hospital now."

"Oh God—for how long?" Chicago. The show. Annalisa. Jud.

"A few days." Karl scribbled on her chart and didn't look up. "Then you can administer the antibiotic yourself at home."

"Once the infection is cleared up," Cale added, "I can go in and see what we're looking at."

"What's the risk factor?" she asked.

"Less with your old friend here." Karl opened the door and called for a nurse. His beeper buzzed. He checked it impatiently. Laurel took that instant to watch Cale. He was so serious. That alone scared her more. Karl handed the nurse her chart. "Let's get Mrs. King into a room."

"Wait," Laurel called out to her. "My assistant, Pat, is

waiting for me. She was going to drive me home. Can you send her in here?"

"I'll send someone to find her." Karl left with the nurse.

"Still scared?" Cale rolled the stool over and took her hand in both of his.

"Of course." She smiled too brightly. "So these are a surgeon's hands."

He laughed. "Good thing they aren't shaking or you'd be out of here all too fast."

"I trust you." It was strange, the expression he gave her, and something passed between them that was from long ago. His manner softened and he was the old Cale, looking at her as if she were something special. At that moment, she might have done anything he asked. "I do have a problem. I didn't tell Annalisa what was going on. I didn't want to worry her. She was pretty shaken through the last surgery. I'd been home for about a week when I woke up one night and she was standing over me, watching me breathe." Laurel could still remember the sheer terror on her daughter's face, even in the shadows of darkness. "I'm supposed to fly to Chicago to meet her."

"Do you want me to call and talk to her?"

"God, no. I'll make some excuse. I want to tell her at the right time. Not when she's out of town. Not over the phone. Not when she has so much on her plate." She paused, then added pointedly, "I just don't want you to tell anyone."

"I wouldn't do that. Your medical condition is private."

"Not even to your brother?"

"Especially not to my brother."

She laughed. "Okay."

He looked like he wanted to say something else, but Pat came in then, her face creased with worry. "They wouldn't tell me what was wrong."

"Don't start crying. I have an infection and they're going to give me some antibiotics."

Pat looked at Cale.

Laurel introduced them, then Cale left, saying he would check on her later.

"Banning? Another one?"

"Yes. Another one. Jud Banning's brother. Matthew Banning's father."

"It's raining Bannings."

Laurel laughed. "Yes, disco mama, I guess it is. There's also another son and a grandfather."

"My doctors never look like that." Pat sat on the edge of the bed. "Now what's really wrong?"

"I told you I have an infection."

Pat merely looked at her.

"It's in my heart, so they are making me stay a few days on antibiotic IV."

"I'm so sorry."

"I know. Me too. I'm not going to tell Annalisa yet. I'll tell her there's a problem on the job and I have to stay to solve it, that we need her to handle the equipment decisions and to make the orders. I know she can handle it on her own, and she should, but I'm afraid she'll fly home if she knows what's happening with me. I need you to back me up on this."

"Okay."

"And if Jud Banning calls—"

"*If?* He's called twice today."

"Okay, okay. He's out of town until Thursday, I think. I want you to tell him I'm in Chicago and I'll call him when I get back. Same with my mother."

"Besides lying to everyone, is there anything else you want?"

"I just need you to protect me for a little longer. I don't want everyone hovering around me, and that's what will happen if they find out. This came on so suddenly and right now I'm just not that strong."

"You rest. Lying is part of my job description. 'Ms. King is out to lunch, Ms. King is away from her desk, Ms. King is in a meeting.' Now, tell me what you need from home." Pat made a list, then said, "I'll take care of Henry. If you think of anything else you need, call my cell."

Laurel sagged back against the pillow. She could feel her frustration and emotion all swelling up inside her. Her throat was tight. Her eyes burned. She was going to cry and she was afraid if she started she wouldn't be able to stop.

A cell call wouldn't help her. She needed a miracle. And she hoped to God her miracle was Cale Banning.

CHAPTER

31

Even in slacks, Victor felt overdressed walking down the streets of Avalon, where bikini tourism was now the island's gold standard. But this piece of paradise was a place of contradictions, where someone once built a casino that was never used for gambling. The island was just a distant suburb of Southern California, yet a place you couldn't walk or drive to. Once Spanish land, which lost its piousness when it first became a smugglers' haven, it then became a romantic idyll tempting sport-fishing movie stars and chewing-gum magnates.

A purple haze hid the shadowed profile of the mainland toward the east, while the late island morning was warm and sullen, heavy with the promise of a flawless afternoon, the kind that made people leave their cold, gray lives behind for the chance to sink shallow roots in balmy Southern California.

Yet for all the promise of the sun, there was no promise left in Victor's days. He didn't live his life in sunshine seasons or pacific years, but in weeks and hours. Time mattered only when he realized it had passed. Should he chance a glance into any of the storefront windows along the walkways of this tourist town, a stranger slouching with age and walking with a limp would have stared back at him. Who was that old man?

Now his birthday celebrations marked his life passing and everyone acted as if the fact he was still alive needed to be ritualized. The funny thing about aging was you could never go back. Your choices were done and made, the roads chosen, rocky or not.

It was early when he entered Kathryn Peyton's shop. The dark corners of the room still carried the chill of night. Art pieces more commercial than at her shows lined shelves of random size and placement, each painted in complementary colors to best display the piece—a blue flutelike vase, a green shallow bowl, or an elongated red pitcher, Modiglianiesque in design.

"Can I help you?"

There was some irony in the fact that the young woman behind the counter had hair the same ebony as the woman whose painting he sought. "I want to see Kathryn. Tell her it's Victor Banning." He leaned against the counter, cane hooked on his forearm, his feet aching the way so much of him ached nowadays, and watched the motion of the second hand on the wall clock. Time was fickle; it could rocket by and suddenly one day you were old, or in moments of tension, time moved like a glacier.

The Kathryn Peyton who emerged from the back room carried herself with the singular quality of a woman who had lived too many years alone—that osteal sense of sheer determination that guarded the broken spine of only the loneliest of souls. Funny how you could see in others your own weaknesses.

"Victor." She approached him alone, a whitewash of dried clay on her arms and hands, her smock spotted with chalk and color. The young woman with Rachel's hair had completely disappeared. "Why are you here?"

"We've spoken at every one of your shows and you never asked me that question. Why is that, Kathryn?"

"I doubt you're here to rehash the past. I care about here and now."

"That's not true. You care more about the past. We care because we live with it. Maybe more than most people."

"What do you want?" she asked sharply, her spine straight, her manner cool.

"You seem certain I want something."

She laughed. "Oh, Victor, you always want something. I just never cared to know what. You would think a man who had so much would be content."

Something in her laugh took him back to a time when he almost had everything, but a woman's brittle laughter made him understand he had nothing. "I cannot imagine living a more boring existence."

"Why are you here?"

"I'm old."

She said nothing.

"You have something I want."

"So you're here to buy art."

"Yes. You sold me something like it a long time ago, but it came damaged."

"Appropriate, don't you think?" Her words were meant to cut painfully, her façade almost Calvinistic, a

412 ~ JILL BARNETT

thick, colorless glaze to protect the friable clay beneath. Warfare came to him naturally, and he understood her dark and secret weaknesses as he did his own. He considered them his catalysts, what made him strong.

He slumped toward the counter, not looking at her. "We both lost everything a long time ago. I thought perhaps we might stop destroying our lives over it." He closed his eyes and spoke softly. "Put them to rest."

A few heartbeats of silence passed before she moved. "Maybe you should sit down. Here, in the back room."

"Give me a minute." Perhaps over the years he had perfected this duplicity. Maybe there was more of his father in him than he liked to admit. Or his childhood had forever branded his memory with exact images of the way a weak man looked and moved. When he sat down, her manner had changed as much as her voice. To get what he wanted, he needed to touch something essential in this woman, a place he sensed was locked down to everyone, including herself.

"Here's a glass of water." Her voice had turned supple, the defensive edges dulled by concern. "You look like you could use it."

"I could use a scotch."

She left and came back with glasses of ice, offered him a small, airline-sized bottle of single-malt scotch, and poured vodka into her glass of V8.

"All the comforts of home." He looked around. "Do you ever go home, or is this your garret?"

"I don't live in a garret, Victor. You've said it before. You are wrong."

Her denial cinched it. He was in. "You think so? You're an artist. I'd say it comes with the job."

"But then you aren't an artist, are you?"

"No, I'm an observer."

"You know what I see? Two people drinking at nine thirty in the morning," she said all too brightly.

"Two people who have lived our lives poorly."

She took a drink and said, "Speak for yourself. My life is exactly the way I want it. And if I lived in a garret, it would be because I chose to live that way."

"How did you picture your life when you were young?" It was a simple trap, the way he maneuvered her into talking about the past, then about the pain of losing someone you loved, children and childhoods. The more she spoke the more open she became, the more animated and easier to read. He told her about his mother's coldness, his inability to capture even a single moment of her approval. He had never spoken to anyone about his soulless mother who made the penultimate mother's sin of loving one child over another, and who then went on to commit herself to eternal damnation by taking her own life.

When he was done, the silence felt heavy but right, as if someone had peeled away a dead layer of life. He knew what it was like to withdraw when pain became more than anyone could bear. Sometimes the only safe place left was inside, aloneness. You escaped, or you became a man who destroyed everything around him.

"I almost followed in your mother's footsteps the night of the accident," Kathryn told him. "There are times when living seems harder than dying."

Did all women have something innate inside them that made them give up so easily? Why give up, when the fight was the best part of life? Not for the first time, Victor wondered what happened inside that car between Rudy and Rachel, and if one of them decided they should die. The pain he felt at that moment was genuine enough to make him for a brief instant forget about the painting. He was too old to go down this road. Kathryn Peyton with all of her pent-up emotions, her need for vengeance, and her ice façade had not killed herself. "What stopped you?"

"Laurel. My child stood there while I held a handful of pills. The choice was no longer mine." She spoke of Laurel, said she was her reason for going on when the world suddenly ended. Yet something in the way she phrased things told him she had not been successful in her relationship with her daughter. It made him think of the father he was and of his sons. One of them was dead because of him and the other didn't know him as his father. A role he understood. His sole mission was to hammer out the innate Banning weakness from his male progeny. He used every stratagem, even cunning, to keep his father's flawed genetic legacy from destroying the Banning men.

She touched her mouth as if she wanted to take everything back, then faced him squarely. "I never wanted to think of you as someone with a childhood, with a mother, and a sister, and a son. I didn't want you to become real or human to me. The moment you do, I might have to understand you."

It was done. Now she saw him in a different, humane light, one he had created with the truth, but for inhumane reasons other than the pouring out of souls. Had he been less driven he might have felt bad for using her as he was, but he didn't live his life with regrets. He took her hand, then stood. She would expect him to deal for the painting now. "Thank you, Kathryn. I'm going to leave."

"You didn't get what you came for."

"Yes. I think I did." He left, knowing he had gotten exactly what he wanted. But still he left the envelope on the counter.

Annalisa checked into the Chicago hotel, went to an early cocktail party, then to dinner with the team from one of their bigger suppliers. Back in her room, she tossed and turned all night, haunted by silly, recurring images of Matt Banning with a dozen different blondes. Yet she was the one who had said no, no, no when she wanted to say yes. She didn't want to make the mistake her parents had. What a joke . . . Damn you, Daddy.

At 3:43 A.M., she threw back the covers, took a bottle of water from the minibar, and swallowed an Excedrin PM. Her eyes burned and were probably puffy and bloodshot. No man was worth this. She fluffed the pillows, settled back, and turned on the television, flipping through the infomercials.

The sound of the alarm woke her, and startled, she sat up, shoved her hair out of her face. The TV was still on. Well, hell . . . she had crashed before she learned how to make a million dollars buying houses with no down payment.

It was 8 A.M. when she left the cool confines of the hotel and walked into the sweet sunshine on her way to the convention center. Cars, delivery vans, and cabs crowded the lanes of Lakeshore Drive. Two blocks down the street, her cell phone rang and she checked the ID

416 ~ JILL BARNETT

screen and flipped open the phone. "Hey, Mom. I'm on my way to the show now."

"Good." There was silence.

"Is something wrong?" Annalisa asked.

"There's a problem with the plans on the Tea House and I'm going to have to stay here and resolve it. The meeting is scheduled for Saturday morning."

Annalisa stopped, then sidestepped the people on the sidewalk. "Do I need to fly back there?"

"No. You need to handle the show orders."

"Alone?"

"Yes. You probably know better than I what we need. Sweetheart, this is easy for you. If I were there, I'd probably just be standing behind you for the next three days."

"That's not true."

"More true than you know. And there's nothing we can do. You'll have to handle that end. I'll take care of things here. We have no choice. It's time you do this part of the business alone anyway."

"I don't want to do it alone." I don't want to be here alone, she thought.

"Think of your father. If you come back with everything together, he won't be able to say it was me."

"That's unfair. You know I would do anything to prove to him I'm doing what I should be doing, anything to get him to let go and treat me like an equal."

Her mom laughed. "Your father would have a difficult time treating any woman as his equal."

"Are you okay? You sound tired."

"I am. I didn't sleep well. How are you?"

"Standing in the middle of the sidewalk in morning traffic."

"Okay. I'll let you go."

They said their good-byes and hung up. She dropped the phone back in her bag. "Great," she muttered and checked her watch. Ahead of her, a traffic signal was broken and a patrol officer stood in the middle of the intersection directing antsy, congested traffic. Everything would be so much easier if someone would just step in and direct your life when it became too complicated to understand.

She swung into a Starbucks, left with a vanilla latte and a reluctant determination to do what she needed to do. Outside the doors to the McCormick Place complex, she strung her name badge around her neck and went into the show solo. Today, she was King Design.

Laurel hadn't watched a soap opera since Luke and Laura were married. But there was little else to do in the sterile cubical that was her hospital room. Watch TV, read, sleep, eat elastic Jell-O and thick, tasteless tapioca pudding, or walk around with her IV pole.

Cale walked in and saved her from going comatose. "Hey there, gorgeous."

"Me? Hardly." She wanted to leap from the bed and fling her arms around him she was so glad to see someone.

He glanced up at the TV.

"That's Sam, short for Samantha," Laurel explained. "Sam loves Sonny, but he's supposed to be dead because he has to hide from the Mafia so his wife, Carly, won't be killed by the Casadines."

"Who are the Casadines?"

"A fabulously wealthy but evil family comprised of mad scientists, conniving women, and young, handsome rogues and thieves who happen to fall for—and impregnate—only the women in Port Charles."

He laughed.

She turned off the TV.

While Cale read her chart, he asked, "How are you feeling today?" He didn't look up.

"Bored." She set her tray aside. "Not to mention I'm ready to walk down to the kitchen and take over. You could play racketball with the lime Jell-O." She paused. "Do you actually eat here?"

"Anything I don't have to cook works for me."

She rested her hands on top of her blanket. "So. When can I go home?"

"Soon."

"How soon?"

"When your fever goes down."

She leaned forward and tried to steal a look at the chart he was holding. "What is it?"

"Let's see." He stuck a thermometer into her mouth.

She rolled the thermometer to one side of her tongue. "You did that to shut me up."

"I wouldn't do that to you."

"Wouldn't do what?" Karl Collins walked in.

"Stick the thermometer into her mouth to shut her up."

"Cale?" Karl shook his head. "Nope. But I would."

Cale removed it and checked the reading.

"What is it?" Laurel asked.

"A thermometer." Cale didn't look up from his scribbling.

"Great," Laurel muttered. "I've put my life in the hands of Abbott and Costello."

"Doctors are so unappreciated." Karl gave Cale a hangdog look. "And here we are just trying to make Laurel Hardy."

Cale threw his pen at him, but he was laughing. "At least you didn't say 'Hearty.'"

"Do you two treat all your patients this way?"

Karl said, "Only the ones we like."

"How did you ever graduate med school?"

Cale laughed. "A love of abuse, bribery, bullheadedness, and the ability to get by on an hour's sleep." Karl left then, with another joke, but Cale was still sitting on her bed. "Your fever is down. But wait. I know you want to go home but I think you need to stay a little longer. You'll do that for me, won't you?" When he looked at her that way, spoke to her in a soft voice she didn't remember him having, she thought she would do anything he asked. And the realization startled her. All she could do was nod.

"Good girl." He patted her hand and then, as naturally as if he had done so a hundred times, he reached out and tucked her hair behind her ear. It was an intimate touch. The touch, the voice that could talk you into anything—she wondered if he had cultivated those in med school. He was good-looking still, had the same smile he'd had all those years ago. Maybe he was better looking, actually, because now he wore some of life on his face, those indescribable things that give a really wonderful face character. She could almost forgive herself, or at least understand why everything happened all those years ago. Why she had thought she loved this man. He checked his watch. "I'd better get out of here before the nurse comes in and throws me out." He put her chart back. "I'll see you tomorrow." At the doorway he paused. "Good night, Laurel." Then he added, "Like-the-Tree."

She watched him disappear down the hallway, then sagged back against the pillow and fiddled with the tape on her IV. Sitting alone in a hospital bed was a constant reminder that she had a life-threatening problem with her heart. At night, she was still aware of the medicinal smells in the air, the noises in the hallways, the bell on the elevator, someone's quiet laughter, the way the nurse would come in the middle of the night and wake you to change your IV or take your temperature.

All of it brought back the frightening little experiences from seven years ago she had forgotten. The way she could feel every beat of her heart, extreme, like some old cartoon where the character meets his love and his heartbeat is exaggerated and pounding so hard it moves his whole chest. Her heart beat in her neck and throat, as if she'd been running for hours. She hated that fluttery feeling. It made her dizzy, so she closed her eyes and saw Cale's image. For survival and her own sanity, she had never let herself think about Cale Banning. Jud sometimes, on those lonely nights when she tried to imagine what would have happened if her life had taken a different path. When Beric had affairs or after the divorce. She tried to think in terms of her life, her choice, her decision. How else could she live with herself?

From the day she walked out of that Seattle hospital, she refused to let Cale live for one second in her memory. Because she would have had to face the truth that she had given up their son. There were no happily-ever-afters for them. There never could be; going into that particular past at all was like wanting the impossible.

But now the impossible was happening, and she had no control over it. A strange, grand irony brought her back to this moment, to this truth, where the young man whose heart she had broken became the doctor who would fix her own broken heart.

CHAPTER

32

Matthew Banning was standing in the lobby under a warm circle of light when Annalisa returned to her hotel. One look and she was struck by a deep, primal hunger she couldn't explain, and she didn't know if she wanted to run toward him, away from him, or run something through him. His expression was strained when he spotted her, as if someone had pulled his skin so tight he'd never smile again. She composed herself and tried to build a protective wall in less time than it took to breathe.

The noise in the lobby faded to background the moment he called out her name. He came toward her. "I've been looking everywhere for you."

"Why?"

"I need to talk to you."

"Is this about the job? Mom said there were problems—"

"My coming here has nothing to do with the project." There was something probing in the way he studied her face, and she wondered what he was looking for. She kept walking, with him dogging her steps. "I've flown all the way here to talk to you. Are you going to send me packing without hearing what I have to say?"

She stopped, conflicted, knowing she really didn't have the strength to tell him to go away. With her arms crossed protectively, she said, "Okay. I'll listen. Talk."

"Not here in the lobby."

The bar was loud and filled with people watching a game on TV. She'd eaten earlier and the restaurant had a line anyway. He took her arm and walked toward the doors. "Let's get out of here."

"I'm tired, Matthew." She pulled away. "I've been up since six. My feet are killing me. If you want to talk to me, then you can talk to me upstairs, where I can put my feet up, have a drink, and relax."

He followed her inside the elevator, which had a mirror on the back wall, so she caught a glimpse of them as a couple—his GQ cover looks, the crazy thought that her hair matched the stripes in his tie and he could rest his chin on her head while holding her. The elevator filled quickly, making small talk unnecessary. The idea crossed her mind that taking him to her room was stupid, or manipulative, she wasn't sure which. Inside her suite, she kicked off her shoes, tossed her bag on a chair, and headed for the minibar. "You want something to drink?"

"A beer."

She poured some Jack Daniel's into a Diet Coke and handed him a Heineken, then felt the need to put some distance between them, so she walked away and sat on the sofa.

He stood in the middle of the room looking as if he didn't fit his body.

"So talk. What was so important that you flew to Chicago to say?" She sounded petty and didn't mean to.

He took a draw on the beer. "This seemed like a good idea a few hours ago. I thought it would be easy. I thought I would walk up to you and just say, 'Your mother is dating my uncle.'"

"I know."

"You know? Great." He swore under his breath. "Now I feel like an ass. This wasn't exactly the way I imagined it."

"My mother and your uncle are seeing each other, therefore you think we should do the same thing."

"It seemed like a good argument at the airport. Sounded better in my head. Now it sounds stupid. Your whole theory is damned stupid. We don't meet many people in our lives that we truly want. Not the way I want you, Red."

Dream words. The things she wished for, the thing she almost threw away.

"Look. This doesn't happen to me." He paced back and forth, while his voice grew louder. "I'm not some drip. I don't look at women and fall in love, dammit!" he shouted at her.

"You think you are in love?" she shouted back. "What about the blonde?"

"I knew you'd bring that up. I went out with her to show myself that I could. That you were not important. That I could lose myself in someone else. And then there you were, sitting in that same restaurant as if the world were laughing at me. After that, when I looked across the table at her, I couldn't see anything but you. I took her home right after the longest fucking meal of my life, then I ran on the beach for two hours. I couldn't run away. I couldn't run free." He shook his head and laughed in disgust. "I tried."

"So you ran here?"

"I've never done this before. I don't know how it happened, just that I can't take it anymore."

She closed the distance between them. "Me either," she said so quietly she wondered if he heard her. Then he was kissing her, his hands in her hair, her clothes, and on her body, and she wondered why she had ever said no. She pulled off his tie and shrugged out of her suit jacket, he unbuttoned his shirt and she pulled at his belt and pants.

Their mouths never lost contact, but it wasn't enough. She wanted to crawl inside him. Their clothes flew everywhere. As if it were second nature, they fused together. She looked into his face, and saw exactly what she was feeling: that moment of mutual vulnerability undefined by gender, powerless and powerful, the deepest anyone can get inside this thing called love.

The board meeting in Denver dragged out for another day, then snow closed the airport, so Jud sat in the airport bar, waiting with other frustrated people, drinking warm beer and eating the only food left—popcorn and pretzels—until they finally began to call flights and a cheer went up in the bar.

A guy sat down on the seat next to him and grabbed a handful of popcorn. "You been here long?"

Jud checked his watch. "Six hours. How 'bout you?"

"The same. Where you headed?"

"LA."

"I'm waiting for a Chicago flight, then on to Boston."

Laurel was in Chicago now. Through another beer, he talked with the guy, who then stood and grabbed his laptop case. "There's my flight. Good luck, buddy."

Jud cupped his hands around his warm beer. The snowfall had slowed, the flakes still the size of popcorn, but he could see activity out on the runway, deicing trucks and lights. He was antsy, wanted to get home, although she wouldn't be there. In a mere three days his life felt different, as if it had just begun. He'd talked to Laurel Monday night, heard she and her daughter had worked things out, but wondered what kind of reception he would get the next time he saw Annalisa King.

A long, long time ago, he had let Laurel get inside him and had lost his mind, or at least his common sense. She had passed through his life all those years ago and left everything broken and shattered in pieces he couldn't seem to put back together, so he never tried again. He'd thought it wasn't in him to love someone; it had been burned out of him long ago. But they met again and life felt different, as if it were starting all over again. Some things, some people, they just stayed with you forever. He and Laurel were different now. People changed, life changed, nothing was ever exactly the same again. His hair might have gray in it now, he wasn't so naïve and eager, but what he was feeling was anything but old. Maybe, he thought, maybe, it would be better this time.

He paid his check, slung his garment bag over his shoulder, and headed for the gate. Another hour-long delay was posted on the board and there were no seats at the gate area, so he walked down the concourse. A woman's voice announced the last call for Chicago flight 447. Jud went up to the desk. "I'd like to switch tickets. Is there any room on this flight?"

"We have seats open in first class." She took his ticket. "You're a platinum member. I can exchange it for you. What about the return?"

"Just leave it open."

A few minutes later she handed him his boarding pass and Jud walked down the jetway.

Laurel dropped the plastic hospital bag on the floor by her front door and knelt down and picked up a purring Henry. The sound came from deep in his chest as if his heart were working overtime. She flinched then and switched arms. Henry's weight put pressure on the shunt in her arm that was slowly dispensing even doses of the antibiotic drug for a required number of days. In the kitchen she took a root beer and a glass of ice from the fridge, then went outside on the porch with the cat in her lap. Some kids with hard, tanned bodies played volleyball on the beach in front of her. A dog chased a Frisbee down near the water. People enjoying the sun and sand, and she wondered if any of them were listening to their hearts beat.

All around her were laughter and voices and the sound of music from radios on the beach, the distant rush of the waves. The sky was unnaturally blue. The air was still and warm. An alkaline ring from recent watering marred the clay plates beneath her pots. On impulse, she leaned over and pinched off a dead blossom from the impatiens in the deck planter, first one, then another,

another, another. Soon she was moving from giant pot, to planter, to pot, pulling off dead flowers and leaves until she paused on a single pink and white blossom, the color of a baby's skin. In the middle of the petal was a dirty brown spot, the beginning of the end and a sign it was going to die. She couldn't pull it off. She couldn't finish the job. It still had color and moisture and life. She pulled back and swept up the dead flowers into her shirttail, then dumped them in the trash.

Inside her small garden cabinet was a box of fertilizer called Miracle-Gro, and for a stupid moment she wondered what would happen if she drank it. Feeding her plants was habit; holding her cat, walking on the beach, loving her daughter, and now, after so long, making love—all those were normal moments in a healthy life. She set down the watering can and stood there, the beach spread out like desert before her, her fear so real it was difficult to even breathe.

If the girl in the red bikini spikes the ball, I'll fix pasta for dinner. If that seagull lights on the telephone pole, I'll have white wine tonight. If that flower doesn't die in the next two days, then neither will I.

Annalisa opened the hotel room door expecting the room service she'd ordered, and her father walked inside. "Daddy? What are you doing here?"

"Why do you think I am here? The restaurants have my name on them. I need to make certain the job is done right. Where is your mother?"

"She's not here." Annalisa could hear the bitterness in her voice.

"You mean you are here alone? What is that woman

thinking? You cannot do this." He shook his head. "It is a good thing I have come. Do not worry," he said with such condescension Annalisa had to close her eyes for a second. "I am here, *ma petite jeune*."

Matthew walked out from the bedroom dressed only in his slacks, his hair freshly damp from a shower, a towel slung around his shoulders. "I'm starved, Red." He stopped the second he saw her father. "Beric? Mr. King."

Annalisa stood there as silent as the two men in her life. She was too angry to speak.

Her father looked from Matt to her. He drew himself up and said, "Just what are you doing here with my daughter?"

"Daddy, please."

"I care about Annalisa." Matthew put his arm around her and her father's look narrowed.

"That isn't what I asked," Beric said stubbornly. "You are sleeping with her."

"That's none of your business, Daddy."

"Yes, I'm sleeping with her," Matthew answered at the same time.

"Are you going to marry her?" Her father spoke to Matt and ignored her.

She laughed caustically. "You sound like some actor from a bad period piece."

"Shut up, Annalisa," Matt said.

"What did you say to me?" She looked at Matt.

"I love your daughter." Now Matt was ignoring her.

"I'm not asking what you feel. It's my little girl I am worried about. You are having sex with her. Sex means commitment."

"Only in 1950," Annalisa said, but neither of them was listening. If her mother had heard that she'd have laughed herself silly before she chewed out her father for what he was doing and saying.

"What do you want from me, Beric?" Matt cut to the chase.

"I want to know you will marry her."

"That's it!" Annalisa stepped between them, waving her arms. "Do not answer that, Matthew. You don't have to. And don't ever tell me to shut up again."

"She is just like her mother," her father said over her head.

"Yes, I'm like Mother. Thank God, because if I were more like you, I'd be a jackass. When are you going to understand that what I do doesn't reflect on you? I'm a grown woman. I can make my own choices and my own mistakes."

"I know that."

"Then why are you here?"

"You are *ma petite jeune*. I am here to help you," he said simply.

"I am twenty-two years old. Just what is it about me that makes you assume that I cannot do anything without you?"

He didn't answer.

"You don't know, do you?"

He was still silent, but his mouth thinned and his expression was frustrated.

"I'll tell you exactly what it is. Everything is always about you, Daddy. Well, this time it isn't. What's between Matthew and me is about us, not you. He's someone I want to be with and I think we will be good together, but we don't know yet. I'm happy, but you feel your pride is at stake. The great Beric King's pride is more important, so to hell with his daughter's happiness."

"That is not true. I am protecting you. I don't want you to get hurt."

"You are the one hurting me. You won't let me go. You call me your little girl and you continue to treat me that way. You won't listen. I am happy working with Mom. You don't understand that I didn't choose her over you."

He stood stiffly. "You should be a chef. You are wasting your talent just like your mother."

"Bull! This is what I want to do. And I'm damned good at it. But you don't trust me. You don't believe in me. You rush here to do the job because you assume I can't. Well, I can. Sit down."

"You are shouting and cursing at me, Annalisa. Daughters do not shout and curse their fathers."

"I said, sit down, Daddy." She gathered together the restaurant diagrams and plans and printouts she'd worked on so late every night, the specs and the product lines, everything to make the kitchens state-of-the-art. She moved to the seating area and shoved the plans at him. "Look at these." She set her laptop on the table in front of him and pulled up the CADs. "Here's the Tea House. Here's the Diner. The Bistro, the Patio Club, and the Cliff House. Look at them, Daddy, and tell me I don't know what I'm doing."

A knock came from the door.

"I'll get it," Matthew said.

"That's probably room service," she said, then faced

her father. "I'm tired of being treated like I have no mind, no pride of my own, no intelligence. I'm tired of you treating me as if I'm a stain on your clothing."

"I do not do that."

"You do." She insisted. "You do." She could see in his face what she'd just said finally made him think.

"Matthew? What are you doing here?" Jud Banning walked into the room, frowning, a garment bag slung over his shoulder. "Do I have the wrong room?"

"You have the right room." Matt closed the door behind him.

"I need to talk to Laurel." Jud looked at Annalisa. "Hello, Annalisa. Where's your mother?"

"She's not here."

He dropped his garment bag. "Okay, I'll wait. Beric." He crossed over and shook her father's hand. "It's good to see you again."

"Laurel's not here," Matt told him.

"I said, I'll wait." Jud dropped into an easy chair and crossed his feet on a stool.

"My mother isn't here, in Chicago. She stayed home."

Jud swore under his breath, then rubbed a hand over his face and gave a short derisive laugh. "I haven't talked to her since Monday, when she said she'd be here for the show. I flew here straight from Denver."

"There was some problem at home," Annalisa explained. "Something with the job site."

Jud looked at Matt. "Then what are you doing here?"

"Sleeping with my daughter."

Matt swore.

Jud looked from Beric to Annalisa to Matt. "You think that's a good idea?"

"You're going out with her mother."

"He's sleeping with my mother."

Beric shot Jud an odd look, sizing him up. "You're sleeping with my wife?"

"Ex-wife," Annalisa said.

Matt walked to the minibar. "Does anyone else want a drink?"

"Jack and Coke," Annalisa said. "Strong."

"Anything but beer," Jud said.

"I'll have a vodka straight. Absolut." Beric turned to Jud. "Have you seen these plans? Look at this kitchen. It is better than Camaroon." He opened the Cliff House plans. "Look here. My Annalisa did these."

"I'm not surprised." Jud took his drink from Matt while looking over the sketches. "I've heard nothing but praise from everyone on the job, all the subs, and especially from Matthew. But that was before I knew there were personal complications."

"Nothing is complicated," Matthew said. "You can't criticize me when you're doing the same thing."

"I'm older and have more experience."

"Apparently not," Matt said. "You're here and Laurel isn't."

"What I do with my personal life is my business," Jud said pointedly.

"Ditto." Matt shot an annoyed glance at Annalisa. She knew exactly what he wanted to say. And she thought perhaps Jud was a lot like her father. She merely smiled encouragingly, a look she hoped said that she understood.

Matt shook his head a little, then winked at her and headed for the bedroom. "I'm going to go put on a shirt."

Her father studied Jud with new interest. "So you are one of the brothers. Which one are you?"

"The oldest."

Beric nodded, then silently sipped his drink. He was quiet and Annalisa wondered what he was thinking, what exactly he knew, and how he felt about Jud and her mother. If he was really hurt, she was certain she would have seen it. Her father looked at her for a speculative moment, then held up his glass and gave her a silent toast. To Jud he said, "It is good you know my daughter is so talented. Together, we are going to make your resort restaurants the best on the West Coast."

Annalisa drank half her drink to keep from laughing out loud and was going to say something when someone knocked on the door.

Matt came out of the bedroom buttoning his shirt. The knock came again and he glanced from the door to her, his expression uneasy.

She shook her head and held up her hand. "Whatever you do, don't answer it."

CHAPTER

33

Laurel sat on the overstuffed linen chair by her bedroom window, her feet on the ottoman and Henry wedged between her and the chair, snoring. The crystal vase Jud had given her was filled with clean white spider mums, even whiter lilies, and frost green eucalyptus. She'd bought them that morning when she went out for the Sunday paper. The flowers were signs of life, the box of warm Krispy Kremes was pure what-the-hell, and the envelope of photographs and investigative reports was her past chasing her down.

One look at the front page of the Sunday paper with its side headline about the Wardwell trial in Seattle, and she'd swung by the office before she drove back home. Greg O'Hanlon was quoted repeatedly in the article, his name, the things he said, how he said them. Her curiosity had started in the hospital, when the trial was on the news constantly. Now as her mortality hung heavily on her back, she questioned the choice she'd made so long ago.

The doorbell caught her off-guard, and she quickly shoved the photos back in the envelope and stuck it under the table skirt. From halfway down the stairs, the tall silhouette visible through the frosted glass warned her it was Jud. Of course, in that way life could thumb its nose at you, she opened the door to Cale.

"Good morning." He held a box of Krispy Kremes and the same morning paper tucked under one arm.

She burst out laughing. "Great minds, Doctor. Come in."

"What's so funny?"

"I have a box of those doughnuts upstairs. I was already drowning myself in fat, sugar, and white flour instead of egg whites, dry toast, and skim milk."

He raised the box. "These are the only way to spend a Sunday morning."

"So says the heart surgeon."

"I took a chance and I looked up your address in the files," he admitted as he followed her into the kitchen. "Nice house." He set down the box and paper on the island and planted himself on a counter stool. Cale and his ease. He never looked uncomfortable no matter where he was. "How are you feeling?"

"Fine," she said too brightly. "You want some coffee?"

"Sure." He opened the doughnuts and ate one with his coffee. He reached for another doughnut. "What kind of decaf is this?"

"Decaf takes the whole point out of the drink. I can't swallow it. Like a few cups of caffeine here and there actually do any damage."

He grabbed a fourth doughnut. "Remember. Moderation."

"Like four doughnuts in three minutes?"

He grinned. "Five. How's the IV shunt?"

"It's difficult to sleep with. I roll on it."

"Let me see." He touched it. "Does that hurt? Sometimes they can go bad. Watch for swelling or discoloration."

She pulled a doughnut from the box and dipped it in her coffee. "Okay."

"I've scheduled your surgery for Thursday."

"Oh." She dropped the doughnut on the counter. The bite she took was already halfway back up her throat.

"I know you're worried. We need to do this, Laurel."

"You said second surgeries carry a higher risk. That would worry anyone." She braced her hands on the countertop. "Exactly what percentages are we talking about here?"

"It's not a good idea for you to go into this thinking the worst."

"God, I hate it when you avoid the answer. I'm already a worst-case-scenario kind of gal, especially because I went into surgery so blindly the last time."

He stood and took her hands in his. Again she looked down at those hands, the ones that would hold her and fix her heart. She wondered if Greg had Cale's hands. "You have to trust me." There it was again, that calm voice, combined with a long-ago familiar look that could get her to do anything, from actually considering decaffeinated coffee to giving up her virginity.

"I'm so damned scared."

He put his arms around her. "Don't be. Trust me."

She closed her eyes and just let him hold her. When

she opened her eyes, Jud was looking at them through the front window, roses in his hand.

"Oh, God." She stepped out of Cale's arms. "It's Jud." She ran to the front door.

"What the fuck is going on?" Jud walked right past her toward Cale. "What the hell are you doing here?" He turned to her. "What is he doing here?"

"I've only been here a few minutes," Cale said evenly.

"Long enough to move in on her, from what I saw in the window."

"Is that what you think?" Cale sounded genuinely surprised. "You think I would do that?"

"We did it to each other thirty years ago."

"You're being an ass."

Jud dropped the flowers and moved dangerously toward his brother. Laurel stepped in between them. "What are you doing, Jud? This isn't a competition. You're acting like this is that stupid basketball game." And then she had the awful thought *What if I am?*

"She's right, Jud. You're trying to make this into something it isn't."

"It looks like something to me."

"Everything looks like something to you. That's your problem," Cale said pointedly. "Yes, I have feelings for Laurel, but it's not what you think."

"Then why are you here?"

Cale didn't speak. He just looked at her.

"I asked you a question," Jud said. "Why are you here?"

"He doesn't deserve the truth," Laurel said stubbornly.

"No, I don't suppose he does."

"I want to punch your lights out." Jud's voice was tight.

"Why?" Cale asked.

Jud said nothing.

"What's wrong, Jud. Say it. Come on. Say it."

Jud stood stonily silent.

"Okay, I'll say it. It's an old habit that started a long time ago, Laurel, long before you ever came into our lives, wedged between us by Victor. You see, Jud has to win." Cale squared off with him. "Even when everything about Victor and you, Victor and me, Victor and us was eating me alive, Jud, even when I took myself out of the competition, you always had to create something where there was nothing. Just so you could win. Why? It's so fucking nuts. When are you going to learn you don't have anything to prove?"

Jud faced her. "You told me you were going to Chicago. You told Annalisa there was some problem with the job. There was nothing wrong at the job. No one called you. You lied. It looks to me like you lied to be with Cale."

"I didn't stay here to be with Cale."

"A nice little postcoital breakfast like we had Monday?"

She saw red. She was shaking.

"Easy, Laurel." Cale stepped toward her.

Jud punched him so hard Cale stumbled back and hit the wall.

"Cale!" She ran over to him.

"I'm okay." He rubbed his jaw.

She faced Jud. "He just came here a few minutes before you did. And yes, I lied. To my daughter. Which has nothing to do with you. Sometimes a lie is safer and less painful than the truth. I've lied a lot in my life, Jud. I used to feel guilty about it. But someone told me once that everyone lies. It's true. Can you possibly imagine having to tell the absolute truth for your whole entire life? Who could do that? We lie to protect the people we care about. We lie to bring joy to those we love. We lie to our children about Santa Claus and the Easter Bunny and the Tooth Fairy. I'd be willing to bet you've lied on your taxes."

"That's not the same thing."

"Only the pompous and self-righteous rage about lying. Because the truth is, everyone does it. Do you want to know why I lied to Annalisa?"

"No. It doesn't matter anymore. You said it, Laurel. This has nothing to do with me." Jud walked out.

Tears ran down her cheeks and she was panting, her hands tight-fisted.

"Go after him, Laurel."

"No."

"Tell him what's going on. You know I can't."

"No."

"You're being as stubborn as he is."

"I don't want to talk to him right now. He doesn't trust me. He needs to cool off." She saw Cale's mouth was bleeding. "Let me get you some ice."

Sunday night, Laurel called Pat after the *60 Minutes* exposé on the Wardwell case to tell her she wouldn't be in the office until Tuesday. The next morning she took a seven o'clock flight to Seattle. On the flight, the shunt began to swell and discolor. Laurel left the plane and went straight to Swedish Hospital emergency. Twenty minutes later a woman named Donna sat down on a rolling stool and took Laurel's arm in her hand. She removed the IV shunt and replaced it with another. "Whatever it is that brings you up here must be pretty important."

Laurel watched her tap for a vein. "It is."

Donna looked at her expectantly.

"I'm here to see my son, before I have surgery," Laurel admitted.

"What? He can't come to you?"

"No. He's an attorney and has an important trial. He can't leave."

"Your patient history says you had valve surgery seven years ago."

"I did." Laurel said. "But there's a tear. They have to see if they can repair it."

"When?"

"Thursday. I need to see him before—" Laurel couldn't say it. She didn't want to voice it. "Before I go under the knife." She laughed nervously.

"You'll do fine, honey." But the look the nurse gave her said she understood. "How long has it been since you've seen him?"

"It feels like a lifetime."

"Kids." Donna shook her head, disgusted. "My son at college never calls. Unless he needs something. The older one is in the marines, stationed at Camp Pendleton. He calls me every week." She stood. "There you go. All fixed up. You tell that son of yours when you see him that he needs to call you. You're his mother."

What would she say to him—*Hello, I'm your mother*? Morally, was she really his mother?

It was eleven o'clock when Laurel left the hospital for the courthouse downtown. The cab pulled up behind a white news van with the station call letters KOMO TV painted on its side. She paid the cab and walked past the camera and news media milling around the front steps. A line of people at the metal detector inside the front door held her up, and it was eleven fifteen when she sat down on a hard bench in the hallway outside the courtrooms. Opposite her were long glass windows and a lushly planted garden on the other side.

Some people stood in the garden, smoking cigarettes and talking casually, and she was swept with a feeling of sadness and resentment. She had never smoked. She had never done anything she knew would damage her heart. But the reason she was even standing in that courthouse came screaming into her mind and forced her to question how she'd lived her life. Maybe her choices—so many of them wrong—had damaged her heart from the inside out.

She checked her watch too often, every few minutes. It was eleven twenty-three. She studied the people who walked by. Two men and a woman talking as they walked briskly, briefcases in their hands, and they wore trim-fitted dark suits and expensive shoes. Attorneys. A woman in a dark red dress with a gold name badge and flat shoes rushed down the hallway, slipping into a white sweater. A clerk late for lunch? A young couple with a baby that looked just under a year walked with a woman dressed like an attorney. As she passed by, she said, "I'll send you the adoption papers as soon as they are recorded." The couple was laughing. The way the mother held the child, the looks of joy and wonder on their faces and in their voices. She had heard that laughter, had seen that look thirty years ago.

Eleven thirty-six.

She opened her purse and took out a photograph, then asked herself why she had brought it. Did she really think she wouldn't recognize him? Greg O'Hanlon. Even if his image hadn't been there on her TV, even without her own investigator's photos over the years, even if they had even been in the same room, she believed she would have sensed it on some innate, cellular plane of recognition.

Down the hall, the door to Courtroom No. 3 swung open and people flooded out. Laurel stood, holding her purse tightly in both hands. The noise level grew and sound echoed up off the marble floors. He was taller in person, cleanly groomed, and dressed in a gray suit and pale blue tie. He looked Banning through and through. She walked toward him, her head buzzing, not knowing what she would do or say, just walking, walking. Someone shouted his name and he turned so suddenly he ran right into her, knocked the breath from her. She started to fall. He grabbed her shoulders to steady her. "I'm sorry!"

She looked up into his face and for just an instant saw her mother there in his expression.

"Are you okay?" He was honestly concerned.

Was she okay? Could she say it? *I'm your mother . . . birth mother . . . some kind of mother?*

The son she gave up had his hands on her shoulders and was waiting for an answer.

"I'm fine."

"You're sure? I'm so sorry, ma'am. I didn't see you."

"It's okay. Really."

Someone called his name again. Closer this time.

He released her and turned, grinning. "Hey, Pop!"

A tall, elegant man with a face she'd seen years ago through the nursery glass clapped him on the shoulder. "Let's hit Smarty's for a sandwich. When do you have to be back, son?"

"I've got until one," Greg said.

"Good. Let's get out of this zoo."

She watched them walk away, talking in the too-perfect image of a father and son. But Greg stopped and turned around, looking at her to see if she was still okay. She, who was a stranger to him. What swept through her at that moment was something intimately profound—love, warm and golden, different from the kind of love that melts you from the inside out, different from passion and desire, but pure, instinctive, something only a woman had the power to feel. One of the biggest secrets of life—this natural maternal emotion lost to men—came over her sweetly. She felt it in every pore of her body, and understood it was eternal.

Laurel raised her hand to her son and smiled. He smiled back at a stranger, turned, and walked on with his father. She stood there long after the hallway was quiet and empty. A sense of peace like none she had felt before completed her—one of those rare times in life when everything was right with the world. She walked outside under a clear Seattle sky, stepped into a cab, and headed for the airport.

Annalisa opened the front door to the beach house at seven thirty Monday evening and called out, "Mom?"

She found her in the living room, poking at the fire, where a large yellow envelope curled and disappear in the flames. "What are you doing?"

"Burning some old papers I've been meaning to get rid of for a long time. Get yourself a Coke. Have you eaten?"

"I had pizza," Annalisa called out from the kitchen, and a few minutes later she walked back to the living room with a mug of tea. Her mother had settled on the sofa, her knees drawn up, and was huddled in the corner hugging a silk pillow. "Here." Annalisa tossed her a throw. "You look like you're freezing. Should I poke that fire?"

"No," she said quickly. "Please. Just sit."

Annalisa kicked off her shoes and spread the throw over both of them the way they always did when she was young and they sat together on foggy nights drinking hot mint chocolate with homemade marshmallows, and even a few months ago, when they spent the night curled together eating microwave popcorn and watching long hours of *Pride and Prejudice*.

"It didn't take you long to get here."

"I flew back this afternoon. I was at a friend's place in Huntington Harbor when you called." She was with Matt when her mother called. What was between them was all so new and consuming and wonderful.

"How was Chicago?"

Blissful was her first thought, but she said, "Chaotic."

"It always is. But I knew you could do this. Did you have any problems?"

"Not with the show or the suppliers. I'll go over the lists with you at the office. The plans are there."

They lapsed into silence. I'll tell her now, Annalisa thought, but looked at her mother and her words disappeared. The fire snapped and crackled. She sipped her tea. Outside, the view of the water had disappeared into thick white fog that condensed on the windows.

"I have to talk to you about something," they said at the same time, then both laughed nervously.

Her mother adjusted the throw and sank farther into the couch. "You first."

"Daddy showed up in Chicago. He said he was there because he knew I needed his help."

"I hope you told him off."

"I'd already done most of the work by the time he got there." She set her tea down on a clay coaster. "I think he was really looking for you, but I'm not certain. And Matthew was there."

"Sounds rather convenient."

"Not really."

Her mother was no fool. "What are you trying to tell me?"

"I'm seeing Matthew. It just happened. There. I mean he came there and I remembered what you said about life and relationships and I stopped fighting it . . . him. Then Daddy came to the hotel and figured out what was going on. He gave Matthew a pretty hard time. Archaic ideas about marrying me. All he needed was a shotgun. Stop laughing."

"I'm sorry. But that's so like your father. How'd Matt hold up?"

"Pretty well, actually. Until Jud came."

"Jud was in Chicago?"

"He flew in from Denver. He was definitely looking for you."

"And instead he found you and Matthew and Beric."

THE DAYS OF SUMMER ~ 447

"It felt as if the hotel room had a revolving door."

"No wonder he looked so burned out when I saw him."

"He handled Daddy beautifully, especially after I told Daddy you were sleeping with him."

Her mother groaned. "Oh, shoot. Annalisa."

"He was going to find out, Mom."

"I would have liked to have kept that information private. For a while."

"Well, he knows now. Besides, you implied Jud was important to you."

"I did?"

"Yes. On the beach that day. You wouldn't say much. You wouldn't be evasive if you felt nothing for him." Annalisa shifted her feet under her. "Don't worry. I'm glad you're finally seeing someone. Now what exactly did you want to talk to me about?"

"There wasn't any problem with the job while you were in Chicago. I stayed here because I had a doctor's appointment Tuesday."

"What kind of doctor's appointment?"

"With my cardiologist, Dr. Collins. You've met him. He called in a specialist. An old friend actually." She gave a short laugh. "Matthew's dad."

"You're kidding?"

"No. I knew him when he was just going into med school."

Now Annalisa understood her father's comment about "the brothers."

"I had a test on Wednesday, which revealed some problems."

Annalisa's stomach sank and she felt suddenly sick.

Her mind filled with the vision of her mother looking gray and pale and the nightmares she had all those years ago when she would wake up afraid that her mother would die.

"They think I have a tear in the valve and they need to go in and see what's wrong. And fix it." Her mother's voice was strong and even, for her sake. "Cale Banning is a heart surgeon, apparently quite a good one."

"When is the surgery?"

"Thursday."

"It's going to be okay, Mom. It's going to be okay." She was trying to soothe her, but like a little girl fell into her arms instead.

"Are you crying?"

"Yes."

Her mother let her cry, then said, "I didn't want to tell you about this over the phone, when there were so many miles between us. You understand that, right?"

"I would have been hysterical."

"You're stronger than that."

Annalisa pulled back. "Look at me now. So stupid. This is happening to you and I'm crying. I wish I were more like you, Mom. You're the strongest woman I know."

"I'm glad you're here. I'm glad you're older because I can tell you the truth this time. I don't feel very strong right now, honey." The expression on her mom's face said it all. Annalisa remembered the look from years back, when she was small and wandered away, lost in the meandering retail miles of South Coast Plaza. Hours later, reunited, her mother looked just like she did now.

Now, suddenly, life just switched. Her mother was breakable. From somewhere deep and instinctive she moved out of her mother's arms and held her instead.

"And next comes the hardest part."

"The surgery." Annalisa said knowingly.

Her mother laughed softly. "That too. But worse. I have to call Mamie and tell her Cale Banning is my surgeon."

"No, Mom." Annalisa straightened. "We have to call Mamie."

Kathryn listened to the news from Laurel with a numb feeling, until she realized there was a horrible, almost frightened reluctance in Laurel's voice when she told her Cale Banning was the man in whose hands she would either live or die.

Before Kathryn could find a single right word, Annalisa cut in, her voice harsh and warning. "Don't be an idiot, Mamie, just because Cale's name is Banning. He's her surgeon, and apparently a damned good one."

The rest of the conversation was oddly emotionless: she would take the first boat over; Annalisa would pick her up; the surgery was the day after tomorrow. She hung up the phone saturated in sweat that came from a natural, cold fear that she was helpless and could not protect her child. She sat down hard on a chair in the middle of her studio. The surgeon's name didn't matter. She held her pounding head in her hands. It didn't matter. It didn't matter.

The angry things Laurel had said so often lately haunted her nights. It was difficult to understand what had gone so very wrong. How could she have been so very wrong? It had become clearer and clearer to her: the Bannings were pawns of fate, while the real danger, the real villain, was how she had chosen to live her life, the singular vindictive focus that turned her into someone her daughter couldn't be around. What she had refused to forget turned into an obsession. Her artist's statement had said it all. She used the pain of life to create works with meaning. Art wasn't art without meaning.

And that was what Victor Banning had meant. If she could have lived in a garret, she would have. Instead she made her home into a garret, her life into the embodiment of human pain. She lived in blue rooms because then she wouldn't forget the festering emotion that fed her art. K. Peyton, the artist who threw herself upon the thorns of grief and never got up, the same woman who lived only in a small, confined world so she could control her life.

Artists and writers locked themselves away for a reason, some odd kind of agoraphobia at its core, cocooned away because when you stepped outside into a huge, wide world everything bad could happen. When you left yourself to fate or God you could be driving down an LA street one minute and dead the next. So Kathryn spent years living other people's lives, then created one where there was room for her art but nothing else. Not even Laurel.

All her mistakes played out before her, like some macabre documentary on how to ruin a life. She couldn't scream, she couldn't speak, but Kathryn lost it and ran through the studio breaking pieces of art, which felt good when she heard the crash, even better when they shattered against the wall. She threw her work away, her art—the things that had become her life, the only things outside the cancerous vengeance she carried.

When there was nothing left to break, she stood in

the aftermath of her own battle, panting, and began to count. Twenty-five pieces had left marks in the wall, like that alarm clock the night Jimmy died. Proof of grief. Proof of anger. Proof she had wasted a lifetime and alienated her own daughter.

By sheer adrenaline, she dragged the huge Espinosa painting out from the back room, tearing off the protective wrap violently. She hadn't looked at it since it hung between the windows in Julia's bedroom. Now K. Peyton looked at it, seeing the work through an artist's eye. The meaning was all emotion, tangled dark lines and waves of turmoil, color so strong it was almost uncomfortable to look at. Unforgivable.

She had not known or cared about its title, but it was written boldly in the left corner: *Obsession*. She backed away from it, understanding all too well the message, and could have stood there facing the painting and the truth for a minute—or half an hour. Time held no consequences when you faced a ruined life.

The envelope Victor had left that day was in her desk, the check uncashed. She wrote a note to him, put it into the envelope, crossed her name off the front, and wrote his, then she called the movers.

It had been more than two days since Jud had walked away from Laurel. Tuesday night about midnight, he shrugged out of his suit jacket, pulled at the knot on his tie, and played his messages.

"Jud? This is Laurel. Would you call me when you get this? I need to talk to you."

Call her when he got the message? At twelve fifteen? He lay on the bed and picked up the phone, hesitating.

Hell, he was in so much trouble with her now, what did it matter if he called at midnight?

Her voice was almost a whisper when she answered.

"Laurel? It's Jud. I just got your message."

"I need to talk to you," she said. "But Annalisa is staying here tonight and I want to speak to you alone. Can you come over in the morning?"

"When?"

"About ten?"

"Okay." He didn't say good-bye because he was searching his mind for the right words of apology, and when she didn't say anything else either, he asked, "Are you okay?"

"I need to explain about Sunday."

He still wanted to strangle his brother. "I'll be there at ten."

"Thank you, Jud. Good night."

He hung up when he heard the click on the other end, folded his arms behind his head, and pushed off his shoes with his feet. He'd gone bugshit the night before and ended up at the twenty-four-hour gym playing racquetball for hours. Still he couldn't let go of the anger. He felt so damned helpless. Whenever he closed his eyes to go to sleep, he saw the expression of condemnation on her face when he'd hit his brother. After so many years, now he stood in Cale's shoes.

At five to ten the next morning, he pulled up to her house and sat in the car for a few minutes, resisting the urge to merely drive away and keep driving. His palms were sweaty and his stomach in knots when he knocked on her door.

She answered quickly.

He'd forgotten in the short span of angry days what he always felt the moment he looked at her.

"Hi." She opened the door wide. "Come in."

He followed her inside toward the living room, where a tray of coffee sat on the table in front of the sofa. She handed him a cup and sat down. "I want to tell you why Cale was here Sunday."

"Look, Laurel, I know I was an ass."

"Wait. Please. Let me talk. This is difficult." She held up a hand. "You owe your brother an apology. He's my doctor, Jud."

That was the last explanation he'd expected.

"He's going to do surgery to repair my heart valve. He came by Sunday morning to break the news that he had scheduled the surgery and to see how I was feeling. I wasn't in Chicago because I was in the hospital for tests, then intravenous antibiotics. I'm still on them. This is the shunt." She held out her arm. "The surgery is Thursday."

"Tomorrow?"

She nodded. "I have to check into the hospital tonight."

"But Annalisa didn't say anything."

"She didn't know until late Monday. I felt I needed to protect her. I had valve replacement surgery seven years ago. It wasn't easy on her then, and I was afraid if I told her before the show she'd fall apart. I only found out the day before. My doctor had called Cale in for a consult and I had no idea. I went to my appointment and there he was."

All he could see was the image of Cale with his bleeding mouth. Jud set his coffee down with a sick and guilty feeling. "Cale couldn't tell me, could he?"

"Professionally? No, and frankly, after you jumped to the wrong conclusion I was too angry to tell you. I hated that you thought I would make the same mistake I made years ago. I'm older and I'd like to think I'm smarter now. But more than that, I hated that you didn't believe in us. Then you hit him."

"I'm a weak man. When it comes to you, I run on emotion. I don't like that about myself, but I can't deny it exists." When she didn't say anything, he apologized. "I'm older, too, and I can't lose you again. I won't lose you. Come here, Jailbait." He pulled her into his arms and across his lap.

"I should have been honest with everyone, but that's easier said than done." She laid her head on his shoulder. "You must have been exhausted. Annalisa told me about you flying into Chicago."

"I was going to surprise you."

"Instead you got Beric." She gave a short laugh. "I wish I had been there."

"He and I understand each other. We both lost you. We have more in common than in conflict."

"You haven't lost me, Jud. I would never run from you again."

"Just how serious is this?"

"Second heart surgeries are always more difficult."

"That sounds like a canned answer, Jailbait."

"It is. But still true."

What neither of them said aloud hung heavily and unspoken between them. Irony was often cruel. What if they had finally found each other again and she didn't make it through the surgery? All he said was, "I do believe in us."

She put her fingers against his lips. "You don't have to explain. I should have told you what was going on."

"Where's Annalisa?"

"She went to pick up my mother. She's coming in from the island on the next boat. I have to check into the hospital later this afternoon."

He understood they had only hours and not much of it alone. But he told himself it was enough for now, sitting together on the couch, his chin resting on top of her head. Each breath wasn't about the scent of her shampoo, but just Laurel. "Tell me what you're feeling. Talk to me."

And she poured out everything, what happened before, the risks, why she was afraid to tell anyone, that she had talked it out with Cale but somehow that was different from talking to him, not safe, but more like speaking to a friend. What she never said aloud was her strongest fear and his: that she could die.

> Dull sublunary lovers' love
> —Whose soul is sense—cannot admit
> Absence, because it doth remove
> Those things which elemented it.

The words fit and gave a timelessness to the pain of human feeling. He knew them by heart, the poetry of love and loss that always reminded him other men felt the same things.

When she was quiet, he said, "Let's not do this to each other again, sweetheart. Lean on me."

"I will. Just hold me, Jud. I want to feel alive."

CHAPTER

34

His practice of medicine had become less about a shot in the dark and more about instinct. Cale's lab coat didn't feel like another team's uniform, and he'd pulled into his garage twice and found his steth still hanging around his neck. Wednesday evening, the night before Laurel's surgery, he left the hospital elevator and passed Elizabeth Madison, a colleague and the anesthesiologist he'd worked with for close to eight years.

"I just left our patient. Your turn, General." She gave him an irreverent salute as she passed by.

"I want you on time tomorrow, Doctor," he said, mimicking the unyielding, erudite voice and words every surgeon heard while in training. "And be sure to genuflect when I walk into the OR."

"What?" She turned around, walking backward as she spoke. "I don't have to kiss your ring this week?"

"No, but you can kiss my ass."

"Everyone kisses your ass, Dr. God."

"Everyone but you."

"Someone's got to keep you humble." She laughed and paused in the elevator. "See you in the morning, Cale."

The elevator doors closed and he continued down the hall on the habitual path he'd taken since he was a surgical resident, to visit his patients the night before surgery, answer questions, ease fears, even the unreasonable ones, and especially when their fear was justified. He found Laurel was justifiably scared; her daughter and mother were, too; and he talked to them, answered honestly, and tried damned hard not to be evasive, since he knew vagueness bothered her more than the truth ever could. But it was the silent terror he saw in his own brother's eyes that haunted him even into the morning of surgery.

At 5 A.M. Cale opened his front door to get the paper and found Jud sitting on the ground, leaning against a potted hibiscus tree, and wearing the same clothes he'd worn the night before, his knees drawn up, his chin resting on them. When he looked up, the ravages of worry sapped any life or color from his face.

Cale was so surprised to see him there he lost his words.

Jud handed him the paper. "Got any coffee?"

"Yeah, but I'm not going to bring it to you. You'll have to get up off your ass." Cale went back inside but left the door open. He was eating a piece of toast and reading the headlines when he realized Jud was standing in the middle of the kitchen like a man with amnesia. "You know where the mugs are," Cale told him. "Get some coffee and sit down before you fall down."

He was still mad at himself for Sunday's events, blaming Jud aloud for what were really his own mistakes. Why he had chosen to not see the truth in their relationship before was a hard question he'd asked himself. For as much as he had always felt trounced by his older brother, the truth was he was too busy trying to catch up and be like Jud to see who and what his brother really was, which wasn't his brother's problem, but merely himself trying to walk in Jud's shoes.

After marrying Robyn, he hadn't wanted or tried to be Jud. But now Robyn was gone and he was back living life in his brother's shadow. No wonder he had doubts in the OR. He had lost himself. Who was Cale Banning—surgeon, father, brother? The husband Robyn left behind? He'd been thinking about little else until he realized it took Laurel and Jud and all those screwy moments in the past to bring him back to the present, and maybe give him back his future.

A few minutes later Jud sat across from him, uneasy, watching him the way a cat watched the neighbor's dog. "How's your jaw?"

"Sore, you asshole."

"I'm sorry about the other morning."

"Forget it."

"No, I mean it, Cale. I was out of line."

Cale set the paper down. "When it comes to Laurel, you always have been."

His brother dropped his head into his hands and didn't say anything for the longest time. When he looked up again, his face was taut and he choked out the words "I love her."

"I know you do, moron. It's torturing you. It tortured you thirty years ago. I was glad then because I wanted to hurt you." Until Laurel came back into their lives, Cale had never seen so clearly the emptiness deep inside his brother and understood what losing her all those years ago had done to him.

Jud rubbed his eyes and pinched the bridge of his nose. "What is the truth about this surgery? What are her chances?"

"I can't tell you."

"Screw that professional shit and tell me."

"It's not confidentiality. I don't know myself until I get in there. Her kind of surgery can be tough. I lost someone less than a month ago. It's like operating blind."

Jud swore and sat there, obviously hurting. "You have to save her." Then Jud did something Cale had seen him do only three times. He broke down crying— loud, hoarse sobs like those when their parents were killed, like those when cancer devoured Robyn from the inside out, and now, when the woman he had loved since he was twenty-five was facing death.

In that moment Cale understood the gift of Laurel, that she had come back into their lives when they all needed something. She was as striking and appealing to him as she had been all those years ago, back in the days of summer, and there were moments—just one or two, at Victor's party or in her kitchen before Jud showed up—when he could have fallen for her all over again. But Jud? Jud was locked in a kind of thirty-some-odd-year hell. He could love only Laurel, and that was the difference between them.

He let his brother cry it out. Men cry, but they don't want anyone to acknowledge it, so he waited for Jud to get under control and said, "Go take a shower. Get something to wear from my closet. I'll fix you breakfast and we'll go to the hospital together."

Two nurses and an attendant rolled Laurel and her IV pole from the hospital room toward the bank of elevators. She lay looking up at the anxious faces of her daughter, her mother, and Jud as they walked alongside. The nurses were angels, making small talk, silly jokes, and trying to ease the tension everyone was feeling. On the fifth floor they stopped near the surgical waiting area. Time to say whatever needed to be said at moments like this.

Jud leaned down and kissed her. She had asked him the day before to take care of her mother and daughter if she didn't make it, and trusted he would. Nothing had to be said now. "I've always loved you, Jailbait," he whispered in her ear before he stepped away from the gurney.

Her mother's face was a stoic mask as fragile as the delicate clay pieces she created. She put her hand on Laurel's forehead, exposed from the surgical cap that contained her bangs and hair.

"I'll be fine, Mother."

"I know you will."

Even now they couldn't speak the things they had to say to each other. Her mother just looked old, her pale mouth thin, her eyes darting and anxious.

Annalisa gripped Laurel's hand so tightly it hurt her fingertips. "Mom. Listen. If anything happened to you, I would miss you, like my hands, like my feet and my heart." The words, innocent and true, tumbled out rushed, as if in the only moment Annalisa could ever speak them.

Such words so profound from her child caught her off-guard, and all Laurel could do was reach up and place her hand on Annalisa's hot and flushed cheek, knowing this beautiful young woman was the reason she existed, the most important thing she would leave behind if she died.

Your child . . . children gave life its most essential meaning. Perhaps she had not thought of this before because of what she'd given up all those years ago. Avoid thinking about what defined mothers, because what kind of mother gave her child away? She started to cry, knowing it was too late and stupid, that she'd made her decision, but no one would know the real reason she was crying.

"Mom." Annalisa touched her hand.

"I'll see you in a while," she said evenly, but had to close her eyes to all she saw on her daughter's face, and when she opened them, she was staring at her mother over Annalisa's shoulder. It took a minute to speak. "My God, Mother . . . how hard I've been on you." She reached out for her hand.

"Laurel." Her mother was at her side, sobbing in bursts of "I'm sorry" and "My fault" until Annalisa pulled her away from Laurel and tried to calm her.

Her last glimpse of them was the image of Jud with his arms around both women, then the bright fluorescent lights in the hall ceiling bled by on the way to the operating room, a red-and-white exit sign, a wall-mounted fire extinguisher, just flashes of things, like looking from a train window, a train traveling someplace she'd been before but never wanted to see again. Once inside, she had the absurd thought that the room looked like a professional kitchen: pendulum lights, an expanse of easy to disinfect and workable stainless steel surfaces, white walls, sinks, appliances, and rolling carts. The floors were truly ugly, though.

"We need to move you onto the table." The nurses helped her and she lay there taking deep breaths, trying to be calm and brave and whatever else you were supposed to be. From somewhere outside the room came the diluted sound of the sixties. "I hear Janis Joplin," she said.

Someone laughed. "Yeah, he's back."

She didn't understand, but before she could ask what they meant, Cale was there dressed in green scrubs, staring down at her—the face she had believed she loved once a long time ago.

"How are you doing?"

"I've been better."

He squeezed her arm, looking so at ease. Cale, who was never nervous. No wonder he was so good at his job. It probably never crossed his mind that he could fail.

"You will be better when we're done," he said. "We're going to fix you all up so you won't have to do this again." He winked at her, exuding confidence, so she let go of everything else, because even if he hadn't spoken with such authority, she still had to believe him.

The long hours of waiting tested even Jud's patience and left him raw and restless. He didn't leave Kathryn, Annalisa, and Matthew except to get coffee, and felt in a constant state of nausea, while Annalisa ate her way through the hours. Matthew brought her chips and Cokes, candy and pretzels. She chewed gum and drank thin hot chocolate from a machine. At noon she ate turkey, dry mashed potatoes, waxy gravy, and institutional peas.

Kathryn barely moved, sitting in the small confines of the waiting room surrounded by Bannings, probably her worst nightmare. He was there and back in her daughter's life, which was in Cale's surgical hands, and Matthew had joined them around nine and hadn't left Annalisa's side. Kathryn didn't cry again, but read magazine after magazine and said little, slowing fading into the silhouette of herself. At one point, Jud handed her a bottle of cold water. "You look like you did the first time I met you."

Her blank look told him she didn't understand, then, remembering, she nodded and took the water. "Thanks."

"You okay?"

"I don't know." She seemed to have trouble finding her words.

He believed her much stronger than he was, until he realized she was reading *Outdoor Fishing*. Only a blind man could not see the importance of what had passed between her and Laurel just before the surgery. A complexity existed in female relationships he thought he might never understand.

"It took all the wrong things to finally bring her home from France," she said finally. "Sit. Here. Please. I shouldn't have blamed you and your brother. Why Laurel left had just as much to do with me. I'll always regret that." She took a drink. "And more."

Across the room Annalisa and Matthew sat together, his arm around her, listening when she needed to talk, silent when she didn't. Poor guy was gone over the girl. Jud had been there himself a long time ago.

464 ~ JILL BARNETT

"They have their whole lives ahead of them." Kathryn shook her head. "However you measure a whole life. God, I hope they make all the right choices."

He didn't say what he was thinking: that the wrong choices only seem wrong when you looked back on them.

Then Beric King walked into the room exuding his television image, long auburn hair falling in a single braid over a cashmere jacket worn with custom slacks, an Italian belt and shoes, a basket of signature gourmet sandwiches held out before him as if he were ready to feed the five thousand. Hard to miss the way he carried himself, like a man who knew his place in a room of strangers and who would seize his own perceived position among those who already knew him.

"Jud." Beric sat down comfortably after catching enough of the nurses' attention. He watched Annalisa eat her sandwich and Jud's, spoke to Kathryn awhile, and when the silence grew too heavy and long, he called his daughter's name. "I want to talk to you about the width of the stainless steel counters."

"What?" Annalisa looked ready to eat him.

"The counters."

"I thought you and Mother worked that out."

"We disagreed."

"Dad," she said evenly. "Mother is lying in there somewhere close to dying."

"Very well. I can see you are too emotionally upset to handle your job right now. I will wait."

The break of silence said everything about Beric and his daughter. Perhaps Beric and his women.

"Come with me, Red." Matt pulled her with him.

"I'll get you something to eat. We'll be right back," he called over a shoulder.

Beric picked up a magazine and said nothing else. While no small part of Jud resented him for marrying Laurel, he pitied the man more, for failing, and asked himself if all the bravado of Beric King was only clothing designed to hide the naked truth that Laurel didn't love him anymore, and that he couldn't control the most important women in his life.

The time ticked by at glacial speed and reading couldn't distract Jud. Before coming that morning, he grabbed a book from the backseat of his car. Aside from the fact that it was small and fit in his pocket, the idea that a volume of Metaphysical poets would help distract him was a testament to his inert state of mind. He would find no comfort in the words of mourning from other men in other lifetimes. He couldn't sit as part of a vigil and read about love and death, sonnets to dead women whom men had canonized with words of souls and hearts, sigh tempests and tear floods. He couldn't make himself think of his love for Laurel in the form of words.

So the longer he sat there, the more familiar he became about stupid details of a room he wanted to never see again. The black-ringed clock on the wall must have been broken, or kyped from a Lewis Carroll book. Only the second hand ever appeared to move. The walls needed paint, something other than diluted green, and the linoleum was the color of wet cement, topped with chairs made for someone with a twenty-six-inch inseam.

His brother sent no one with news, which was annoying, but then, this was Cale's territory and Jud felt lost here, so he spent his time on an internal roller coaster, riding hills of anger and nervousness, while mentally making enough deals with God to change the path of his life forever.

Waiting for hours on end meant there was time to think, about things like the incident Sunday in Laurel's kitchen, an example of what kept him and Cale from being as close in blood as they were in looks, and it brought to mind the patterns their lives took, moments so similar. The last time he'd been waiting like this had been in a hospice, with the family, while a silent and dark Hadesian cancer stole their sweet Robyn away. The unacceptable pain of losing her crushed Cale in those last hours he spent bent over her bed, and Jud wasn't certain his brother had stood straight since that day.

Here Jud was in a vigil for the woman he loved without question, though Laurel had a chance Robyn never had. He looked up for another wasted glance just as Cale, in scrubs, walked through a set of doors. The triumphant smile on his face told Jud everything. He jumped up, whooping like a sports fan, fist in the air, and scared Kathryn, her face turning pale. For all her stoic silence in the long waiting room hours, she now looked ready to sink into the floor. "Kathryn. I'm sorry. It's okay." Leaning on him, she felt too frail to stand as she was, then she broke down, gripped his shirtfront in her fists, and sobbed, speaking incoherently.

"Mamie." Annalisa took her grandmother by the hands and made her sit down.

"It's all good. Everything went well," Cale said, looking at each one of them. "She's a tough one." He was still grinning. "You can go in soon." And at that moment, Jud thought his brother finally looked taller, and maybe stood a little straighter.

A huge elephant was sitting on her chest, choking her with its trunk. Laurel couldn't swallow. Her eyelids wouldn't open. Voices came from somewhere. Unfamiliar voices. The only sound she could seem to make was a low growl deep in her throat or the rasp of her own breathing. Under her fingernail she felt a flannel bedsheet, scratched it, then managed to open her eyes. The edges of her vision were cloudy, like beach fog. Her world turned from milky gray to color. The ceiling overhead was the mint green of a hospital room. Tubes came out of her mouth and she remembered it all from before. There was a sudden beeping sound next to her, which sped up, beeping faster. This was life.

She heard footsteps. "Hello, Laurel." A nurse's face came into her line of vision and the woman touched her hand.

Laurel could feel tears slip down the sides of her face and into her hair.

"It's okay. You came through the surgery just fine. Dr. Banning will be here in a minute."

Laurel held her hand tighter.

"I'll stay right here. I won't leave."

Then Cale was there telling her what he'd found, what he'd fixed, and that she was going to be okay. "Jud might have killed me with his bare hands if I didn't pull you through this. He doesn't have a clue it was you who did the pulling. But then you probably don't get that either, do you? He loves you, Laurel. All these years there's been something missing in my brother. I didn't

know what it was until you came back into our lives."
He gave the nurse some orders, then turned back. "I'm
going to let your family and my brother in now, two visitors at a time, then you need sleep. I'll be back later."

Her mother and daughter cried, holding her hand
like the nurse told them to, so she could squeeze in
response while they talked about all the things they
would do together until they ran out of promises and
said reluctant good-byes. They looked so much alike,
perhaps were alike, one woman young and old. A quietude, arcane and rare, settled over her in that bare
moment when the two of them walked away together.

The screens around her and attached to her sent signals and readings that were foreign and meant nothing
to her. Eyes closed, she felt HAL-like, computerized
instead of human. The coldness of the room didn't help.
But she was alive and fine, according to Cale, even if
some machine was helping her breathe.

When she opened her eyes, she realized there was
something completely laughable and surreal about seeing
the man you love walk in with your ex-husband. Her
first thought was vain, that she must look like hell, tubes
running out of her arms and body. She probably had
Fisher King hair. All around her were machines and
monitors, beeps and buzzers and strange wheezing
sounds, nurses moving efficiently around the open room.

Beric took her hand first and began spilling his guts
about everything he had ever done wrong in their marriage. Hearing their history aloud made it sound like a
lesson in stupidity, and Jud smiled at her a few times,
then finally stepped in. "Beric, she can't respond. Why
don't you wait and talk about this later?"

Beric looked at her, then bellowed a laugh. "I know what she would say. That I love a captive audience. See? She squeezed my hand."

Laurel had come to a point in her life where she no longer regretted her marriage, or him, only perhaps the time gone. He left as he always did, ever the big personality, and Jud took his place. No, that wasn't right. The truth was clear to her now. Beric had been taking Jud's place for years.

Closing her eyes was okay. With Jud she didn't have to stay awake to reassure him. He knew. The pressure in her chest and her head was getting worse. She began to shiver and heard him ask a nurse to bring her a warm blanket. The woman adjusted an IV and told her she had injected some pain meds, said she should sleep.

"I'm here, Jailbait." His voice was like bourbon—a silly thought she blamed on the drugs. But she was certain she felt him press his mouth to her palm, kiss it, before the medication sent her far away, to some strange dream world where she heard Jud Banning reciting love poetry.

CHAPTER

35

His cars had changed over the years, still sleek, still black, but the building was the same as it had been when Victor first purchased it back in 1960. The City of Industry hadn't changed much, was just what its name said it was. The Golden State Freeway, old, narrow-laned, and all concrete, still cut through its heart, surrounded by paint factories, canneries, packaging houses, and an oil refinery in the distance that pumped steam and fumes into the air. There was no gentrification here, just time almost at a standstill, and the bad side of what California industry used to be before environmental causes and agencies, so you didn't want to breathe too deeply.

Victor got out of the car more slowly than he'd have preferred, his old body slow to react nowadays. Harlan closed the car door and leaned against a front fender as he had for too many years to add up. A scruffy orange tabby, thinner than he remembered, lay curled and sleeping near the front doors.

"How long has that cat been around?" Victor faced his old friend.

Harlan's craggy ex-boxer's face had wrinkled like a prune, and he was shorter. His head was barely over the top of the Town Car. "That old thing? Too long, like us."

Time and life had just disappeared into thin air like those fumes from the factories. Victor was looking around him when the moving truck pulled up, and he told them to use the freight elevator. On the top floor, he unlocked the door and flipped on the light with traitorous fingers bent like commas. The windows were covered with metal blinds to block out the damaging sun, and the place was kept spotlessly clean by people who would never know or understand what was in this room.

Huge canvases with slashes of bold color hung from high near the ceiling to the floor, under expensive gallery and museum lighting. Harlan had asked him once if he was going to keep them locked up here, and why. Even now no sane answer came to mind. He had lived with Rachel's shadow for more years than he could remember. He raised her sons, his penance for betraying and killing his own. He tried not to admit he could have easily lied to Rudy all those years back and changed the course of things. When he started buying the paintings, it was out of a need, never a plan.

He heard the elevator doors squeak open and two men came inside carrying a huge crated painting. "Where do you want it?" one of them asked.

"There against that wall." The bolts to hang it from were in place. The movers removed the crating. A familiar envelope was taped to the wrapping with his name

written on it. Victor tipped the men. "You can go. I'll
unwrap it."

Inside the envelope was a folded note and his check
for two million dollars, which wasn't torn into pieces.
He wondered if the painting was, and pulled off the
wrapping. The canvas, stark white, a good eight feet by
five feet, was undamaged, and a riot of bold color—
orange and blue and red, black lines, and vibrant emotions painted by the woman he loved enough to betray
his own son.

Rachel had been life and breath to him. He loved her
to the exclusion of everything. Nothing else mattered.
There were no morals involved in what he felt for her,
something even her death couldn't change. Would he
have done things differently? Probably not. He didn't
think regret existed in him since that day he cried uncontrollably over his dead and heartless mother. When he
glanced at the title of the painting, he didn't think much
about it, until he opened Kathryn's note.

> *They say obsession is about the things we
> cannot forget.*
> *But that's wrong. It's about what we cannot
> forgive.*
>
> K. Peyton

Victor tore up the note and the check. Inside
another room in the back of the space, he turned on the
light. Years of clay art and sculptures lined the walls and
stood in corners, starting with the earliest Kay Peyton
works, purchased anonymously in the early years, then
the few K. Peytons he'd bought since, whatever num-

ber was needed to sell out her shows—a rare occurrence now since she sold on her name and talent.

He turned off the light and pulled up a chair in front of the last painting leaning against the wall, and he sat. After a while the air in the room grew thinner. It was hard to breathe, so he stopped trying.

Governors past and present, senators, and congressmen came to Victor's funeral, some to eulogize. Eloquent and politic, they talked of raw land and Pacific hillsides covered in wildflowers, told stories of the coast after the war and a city of growing suburbs so sprawling you had to have cars, oil, and gas to exist, of industry and those who changed the landscape of the state. In paying tribute to the man, they christened him one of the last visionaries to give California its history, and spoke of him in godlike terms. Victor would have loved the implication but hated the pandering.

The service was more about money and power than anything religious, the way he would have preferred: some music, a crowded church, and the family dutifully sitting in the front row. Jud listened to men lionize a Victor Banning from magazine covers. But he and Cale knew the grandfather who made a home in which the three of them formed an odd family, devoid of estrogen, thriving on conflict and dysfunction yet fused together by some moral and genetic bond. No one was certain what made Victor Victor. Certainly not the men who spoke as if they had known him. Not Jud or Cale. Most of his story and any reason why he was who he was went to his grave with him.

Dane was the one who mourned deepest when he'd

heard. He adored the old man in ways that baffled everyone. The mysteries of kinship could skip whole generations. Watching Dane struggle with his grief took Jud back years to an empty hospital room where Cale was crying uncontrollably over things Jud could only guess. Now Cale was composed and even, controlled, like Jud. They were men who stood on their own and didn't show what they were feeling.

To the sound of a single trumpet and through church air pungent from the aromatic perfume of California wildflowers, they bore Victor outside, the Banning men, Harlan, and Victor's longtime attorney. Jud passed faces, blurs of familiarity, until in a moment of clarity he spotted Kathryn Peyton sitting in the back of the church.

The grave site was for family only and Harlan, who chose to say good-bye and leave with the minister. Jud, Cale, Matthew, and Dane, all dressed in dark suits with simple boutonnieres on their lapels, stood in a silent line staring awkwardly down at the coffin inside an open grave. A ceremonial shovel with a brass handle was stuck in fresh brown soil piled next to them.

"Aren't we supposed to throw some dirt on it?" Matthew asked finally.

"Flowers." Jud unpinned the flower from his suit and tossed it in the grave.

"*On* the coffin, Jud."

His boutonniere landed under the casket platform. "Too late. Throw yours."

"The old man wasn't a flower kind of guy," Cale said.

Matt picked up the shovel. "I think we should do the dirt thing. After all, he made his money from the ground."

"Good one." Jud had to laugh and noticed Cale

shook his head, but he was smiling. There was something eminently freeing about laughing in the middle of all this odd seriousness, which felt wrong. Victor loved theater, but he preferred the dramatic moments he himself staged.

Matthew poured dirt from the shovel along the top of the coffin. "Good-bye, Victor. I forgive you for giving my little brother the motocross bike I wanted for Christmas in 1988."

"I loved that bike," Dane said, taking the shovel. "Best surprise I ever had." He poured his offering of dirt. "Thanks, Gramps."

"I had forgotten about that night," Jud said.

"I haven't. We left Victor's and I dropped you kids off along with your mom, then Jud and I drove all over trying to find the same bike so you wouldn't be disappointed."

"I didn't get the bike for a month." From the tone in Matt's voice, Jud doubted he had really forgiven the old man.

"I know. I had to order one. Give me that shovel." Cale dug into the dirt pile. A huge clump of dirt hit the casket with a loud thud.

"I wonder if he heard that." Jud took the shovel.

"Wait a minute." Dane raised a hand. "Don't do anything." He ran back to the limo and came back with a rare and hugely expensive bottle of single-malt scotch. "Gramps's favorite." He started to pour it on the coffin.

"Are you nuts?" Matthew snatched it out of his hand, holding it protectively to his chest. "Don't waste it."

"Give it to Jud," Cale told him. "He's the oldest. You start. Say something and take a drink."

Jud loosened his tie and raised the scotch bottle. "To Victor. Who taught me all about competition." He took a swig.

"The hard way." Cale took the bottle, braced his feet, and said, "To Victor. Who treated me like a bastard son and made me think I was never good enough."

"Did he do that, Pop?"

Cale lowered the scotch bottle and swallowed. "Ask Jud."

"He was a tough old bird. Even when we were kids. Scared the hell out of me the first time I met him."

Matt stared at the scotch with a bewildered look. "I don't think I have anything horrible enough to say."

"I'm not going to say awful stuff about him," Dane said.

"You've always been a wuss."

"Like hell, Matt. Victor just liked me best. You've known the man your whole life and can't talk about anything but that bike?"

Matt took off his coat and hung it on the shovel handle. "Give me the bottle, Dad." He stared down at the grave for a long time. They all looked at him, waiting. "Okay. To Victor, who—"

"—was an asshole." Cale sat down on the grass. "Now take a drink, son, and pass along the bottle. I've got a list long enough for all of us. This might take a while."

By the time the scotch was near empty, it was almost evening, and the limo driver had been asleep for an hour. They lounged on the ground in front of the grave in their shirtsleeves, their ties draping the casket.

"To Victor, who adored my wife." Cale drank, set the

bottle down, and leaned back on his elbows, feet crossed.

"He did love Mom."

"She had a long talk with him after the bike fiasco. He never pulled a stunt like it again."

Dane sat up with his arms resting on his bent knees. "Has anyone noticed we're saying nice things about him?"

"Yeah. About half an hour ago," Jud said. "After you lost the bet over the tie toss."

Matt picked up the bottle and eyed the contents. "Looks like two more, which is good because I'm getting drunk. To Victor, my great-grandfather—not a great grandfather—who took me into the company the day I graduated." He swallowed more scotch. "I've always felt good about that."

"You should," Jud told him. "Victor said you were the best thing to happen to BanCo. Said 'that kid has the balls for business.'"

They laughed because the old man wasn't one for long speeches and big words, but Jud would have bet that Matthew had forgotten and forgiven Victor for the bike, and anything else he had done wrong. Even Cale had mellowed and talked about him with humor instead of bitterness. The last rounds became more about memories and funny stories than purging dysfunction and motivated irreverence.

"This is it." Dane stood up, holding the bottle in the air.

Once on their feet again, they were all back where they had been to begin with—a line of men in front of Victor's grave.

"The last good-bye," Jud said.

Bottle held high in a eucharistic gesture, Dane said, "To Victor. A man larger than death." He finished the scotch and christened the casket, glass shattering in a strange, final communion. No one said anything else. Instinctively, together, they observed a minute of silence as the sun set over the coffin, catching the fragmented glass of a family's life, and Victor Gaylord Banning came to his end.

Turning away, each volleyed for the right jacket, and with their arms around each other, paired in brothers, the Bannings stumbled down the grassy hill of a quiet cemetery and piled into the limo.

Some time passed before Victor proved Dane right. Via his will, the old man came roaring back from the grave and into their lives. His attorney sent the documents to Jud's office, where, as executor, he would take care of the necessaries. He'd been in Alaska, then New York, and flew back in time to take Laurel home from the hospital. So it was late afternoon the following day before he had waded through mail and messages, done urgent business, and finally had a moment to look at the will.

The document open on his desk, Jud read the words twice before he picked up the phone and called Victor's attorney. "I'm reading the will, Tom. It says, 'To my *son,* Cale Banning.' Is this some typo?"

"Victor was specific in the wording, Jud. I asked, too."

"What do you know?"

"Only that Rachel was Cale's mother, too."

Jesus . . . Jud took a second to garner this thoughts.

480 ~ JILL BARNETT

"There's something in here about art valued at over fifty million dollars. I've been in Victor's home. That's a hell of a lot of art, or at least a few single works so valuable I'd have known about them."

"Much of that figure is for your mother's paintings, Jud. He bought them all over the years. Along with the will is a set of envelopes with copies of deeds and keys for all the properties. The art is stored in the warehouse with the City of Industry address. You want me to meet you over there?"

"Yeah." Jud stood, grabbed his suit jacket, and thumbed through the envelopes. "I'm leaving now. I should be there at four."

At seven o'clock, Jud pulled out of his garage and headed for Laurel's. He wasn't certain what he was going to do—talk to her? But he couldn't sit home rehashing this mess any longer. As he drove along Pacific Coast Highway, he tried to make sense of what he'd discovered today. Damn Victor for leaving him with this time bomb in his lap.

He could change the will and Cale would never know. That option came up with Tom, who said he would stand by his decision. Or he could tell his brother—shit! uncle and brother—the truth: that Victor had had an affair with their mother. But he would hate it if someone knew this kind of thing about him and never told him.

Traffic wasn't the best, and he missed the colony entrance road and had to backtrack a mile. He knocked on her front door before he opened it. "Laurel?"

"In here."

He found her in the kitchen cooking something that

smelled like the best of Paris, and put his hands on her shoulders and kissed her neck. "Shouldn't you be resting?"

"I slept most of the day and I'm starving. I can't seem to get enough good food. Sit." She pointed at a bar stool with a wooden spoon, then paused and studied him. "You look like the one who needs sleep. What's wrong?"

My grandfather slept with my mother, and my brother doesn't know he's Victor's son. He couldn't say the words aloud and walked around the island to avoid any more questions. "Bad day. Long day. I'll open a bottle of wine." He didn't want to tell her the truth, and had pretty much decided in the car he shouldn't. Women weren't big on lies and secrets. They always wanted to tell the whole truth, overdiscuss, and speculate on all the emotions and motives behind it. She would have no idea how to deal with this kind of thing. The moral dilemma he had to settle was his alone, and as easy as it would be to hide the truth, knew he couldn't do that to Cale.

From the time their parents died, maybe earlier, Jud had tried to protect his brother, and he'd made a mess of it most of the time. Cale had the right to know the truth, so it was his brother's decision alone to tell others or choose to never say a word.

The problem was, he was the one who had to tell Cale. So he needed to be with her, wanted to be there, even if she didn't know why and never would.

After dinner, they sat on the sofa together, listening to music playing softly on the stereo and the occasional distant break of a wave. She tilted her head back against his shoulder and asked him if he wanted some coffee. "Hell, no . . . I feel like a fatted calf."

"Ready for slaughter?"

"You slaughtered me a long time ago, sweetheart." He looked down at her to see her smile. "You feel all right?"

She settled deeper into the sofa and his arms. "Wonderful. Tired, maybe a little sore. Taking deep breaths is tough. No long sighs for a while."

"We've got plenty of time. I'm not letting you go anywhere."

"I'm not leaving. You couldn't throw me away. Besides, this is nice. Us together. Feels comfortable with you here."

He waited awhile before he said what was on his mind. "Maybe we should make it permanent."

She sat back and faced him. "What exactly are you saying?"

"Maybe we should get married."

"Are you speculating, or asking?"

"Depends. Are you saying yes?"

"It would make my mother happy. She's never forgiven me for getting married in a lavender field in Provence. She would finally get the wedding she wanted."

"I was thinking we could get married quietly in Vegas, after you're feeling better. Fly off right away on a honeymoon, then come back, throw a huge party, and tell everyone after the fact. Keeps the moment about us and no one else."

"You've been thinking about this."

"Eleven and a half hours of surgery is a long time."

"Well, my mother's going to be livid, but it sounds perfect to me. I adore the idea of sneaking off." She started to laugh, then groaned. "That hurts."

"You should be in bed."

"Come with me." She stood and held out her hand. "I know, I know. Just to sleep. For now."

"I've got a big meeting tomorrow. I should go home."

"I thought you were home," she said softly.

"I guess I am." He put his arm around her and they went upstairs, slowly, because she became winded. She sat on the bed and he reached over to turn on the table lamp. A volume of poetry was open on the table. He picked it up. "What's this?"

"Poetry. I haven't looked at that book in years, but I had the strangest thing happen right after the surgery. Must have been the medication, but I dreamed you were reciting John Donne."

He laughed. "Me?"

"Yes, you."

He set the book back on the nightstand and turned, aware he loved this woman more than life. He would live up to all those promises he made to God and heaven and fate and any other deity he'd sought in that waiting room. He took her hand in his. "Such wilt thou be to me, who must like th' other foot, obliquely run; thy firmness makes my circle just—"

She placed her finger to his lips. "And makes me end, where I begun."

His brother reacted to the news of his paternity without a show of pain or anger, just a few questions—most important, *Did you know?*—and long moments of silence. Someone else might have mistaken his silence for calmness, his control for quietude, but Jud knew whatever emotion was going on inside his brother was far from quiet.

Jud drove them to the warehouse and they stood inside the old building where noise from the Santa Ana Freeway hummed in the distance and millions of dollars' worth of art was hidden away. Cale's response was similar to Jud's the day before—complete disbelief. Cale walked from room to room, then stopped, his eyes still taking it all in. "Funny, isn't it? I spent so many years wanting to be like you. Victor saw you differently."

"Now we know why. The immoral old bastard."

"He treated me with failed expectations from the first day we came to Newport."

"That day changed everything, didn't it?"

"It did." Hands in his pockets, Cale turned away, then said, "I want to hate him, and I can't."

"I know. I look at this, think about what he did, and it's strange," Jud admitted. "I spent so much of my life trying to live up to him."

Cale laughed bitterly. "While I tried to live him down. Little did I know."

"I think we can look in this place and see that Victor had more things to live down than either of us." Jud saw an opening and took it. "No one ever has to know about anything. But it's your decision if you want to tell anyone."

"I wish Robyn were here," Cale said honestly, looking for the first time as wounded as he must have been. "She's the only person I would tell, and she's gone. Victor's gone." He shook his head. "There's no one left to know."

"I hated that I had to tell you this. Damn him."

"It's just so strange. To find out your life is a lie."

"It's still your life, Cale. I'm still your brother. Matt and Dane are still your sons." His brother looked so numb and lost, bewildered, like a bird that just flew into a plate glass window. Jud gave him all the time he needed in the room, and he would need more time, maybe the rest of his lifetime, to come to terms with what he'd learned today. If Jud could have borne his brother's pain himself, he would have. "He left the art to us. What do you think we should do with it all?"

"Donate it to museums. Look at this. Her work is still spectacular. That it's been locked away all these years is a crime. Just one of many."

"I was thinking we should do the same with Kathryn's work. He must have bought it out of guilt. If we tell her, she'll think he had a hand in her success."

"It should be auctioned anonymously and donated, too. The money can go to MADD or to help single mothers, something appropriate." Cale took one more long, pensive look around the room and headed for the door. "Let's get out of here."

They locked up and took the old elevator down to the street level, then walked out into the sunshine. Blinded for a second, they both stopped. Parked in front of them was the red car, the first in a long line of things Victor used to divide them. Jud pulled a set of keys from his pocket. "Here. Catch."

"What are these?"

"The keys to the MG. It's yours."

"No. I can't take these. Rudy was your father, not mine."

Jud put his arm around his brother and spoke the

truth. "He was more your father in those few years than Victor ever could have been." He closed Cale's hand around the keys and they stood together in silence and perhaps a final understanding. "It's yours, buddy. You take the car." Jud stepped away and opened the passenger door. "And I'll take the girl."

Three Months Later

The walls in the rooms of the small bungalow on Descanso Street were no longer blue. Kathryn and her granddaughter stood painting, while Laurel did the window trim. She stepped back and eyed her work, then faced Kathryn. "I love this caramel color against the white trim, Mother. It looks so warm. I never liked those blue rooms. They were always too cold for me."

Kathryn just smiled and rolled the last section of wall. "I love the new color."

"See, Mom? Take a lesson from this." Annalisa held up a sponge roller. "People can still change even when they're old."

"What?" Kathryn said as both she and Laurel turned.

"Just kidding."

Kathryn threw an old roller at her and missed. "You there, with all that milky youth. Watch it. Life can still bite you, kiddo." Kathryn knew she had a lifetime of bite wounds. She was still recovering, but she and Laurel no longer tiptoed around each other. There were no more hurt feelings and long silences. Their moments together, like this weekend, were more precious to her than all the lost years. The past was just that—past. Kathryn had learned to live in the now. "Let's clean this mess up."

"That's right," Annalisa said. "Those brownies are waiting in the kitchen. I need chocolate." She left the room.

"God, that child can eat." Kathryn folded up the tarp. "She always amazes me."

"She has her father's metabolism," Laurel said and took the paint can to the back porch.

They sat together at the kitchen table, eating brownies while Annalisa talked about what they could eat for dinner and they made plans to return to the mainland.

"I have to take the early boat," Laurel said. "I need to pack."

"That's right," Annalisa said. "You're going with Jud to Vegas Monday. Your first trip together."

Laurel smiled and Kathryn understood that her daughter was finally happy. She stood. "I almost forgot." Kathryn took a grocery bag from the counter and handed it to Annalisa. "Here. I bought you something."

"Is it chocolate?"

"You haven't had enough?" Laurel asked.

Annalisa groaned. "Mamie . . . *Brides* magazine? Again?"

"Someone in this family has to have a traditional wedding. I'm counting on you, dear."

"Matthew and I are too new. You could do something foreign and date yourself. Then you could have the wedding."

"Me? I'm too old."

"Match.com," Annalisa said and wiped the chocolate off her fingers. "Look at this." She opened her laptop and showed them the dating site. She'd already pulled up prospects for Kathryn, who watched patiently, but thought privately she would rather have her skin flayed inch by inch than try Internet dating at over sixty-five—retirement age. But she listened patiently, promised to think about it, then herded them into the living room to rehang the freshly painted display shelves.

When they finished, one shelf in the center of the wall was still empty. Annalisa stepped back. "What can we put on that one?"

"Something special. Wait here." Kathryn left and came back a few minutes later with a white vase, simple in design, fluid, innocent, perfect.

"That's my vase, Mother," Laurel said. "The one you made years ago that I love. You took it from my bedroom?"

Kathryn set the vase on the shelf and stood away from it. "No. I made it two days ago."

epilogue

Cale found his passion for the fragile, elusive art of healing again. He had originally devoted himself to it with an unyielding drive that came from betrayal so deep and painful he could hardly live with it. So young, with a heart broken by a girl who was destined, even then, for his brother. Funny, how a broken heart would send him to find his calling in medicine that healed the deepest passages of the heart.

And Cale wasn't certain he would be where he was today if she hadn't hurt him so long ago. He'd come to terms with Victor. His father was dead and he could never say to him what he wanted to say, ask him what he wanted to ask.

His early life was filled with tragedy, and later, losing his Robyn was the most tragic of all. He had always thought he never understood his calling. But looking back on it, perhaps he wanted to save lives because he learned of death so young. Some say life prepares you for its tough times, and perhaps he had lost those he loved because he needed to understand what death was. Perhaps medicine and his need to perform it was, and always would be, his way of balancing things.

Less than an hour ago, he'd finished a thirteen-hour surgery, repaired the heart of a seventeen-year-old girl who wanted to go to med school. Cale took off his surgical cap and tossed it on the desk, then signed his name to the patient's surgery chart and finished making his notes.

For just an instant, he glanced back at the operating room, where he had spent those hours under the hot lamps, holding that girl's heart in his hands, a miracle in itself. In his own way, he was saying, *You're not taking this one. We're keeping her.* And in every surgery he fought back with a strength he believed was taught him by his brother. Cale didn't always win, but he fought like hell not to lose.

He heard the call buzzer from CCU, where his patient was recovering. The green light was on, but not flashing an emergency. The internal phone line rang a second later.

"She's awake, Doctor."

"I'll be right there." He sat back, stretching, because his back was sore and his muscles ached. A good ache. He understood he was given a gift. Medicine, lives, people were no longer part of game where he fixed the dice so he could always win.

Cale thought about his father again, the man who wanted to control everything. Poor Victor. Cale understood that he was the living, breathing reminder of Victor's mistakes, of his weaknesses, and for all his power and need to control, Victor was not a man who was strong enough to face that. It must have been terribly hard for a man of his immense pride to look at his son and see what he hated about himself. He was a success in the eyes of the business world, a dismal failure as a father and as a human being, and he knew it. Cale could forgive him for it, because he knew he wasn't Victor, although there were times in his life when he started down the same roads, driven by emotion and pain and self-doubt.

Unlike Victor, he loved his sons and they knew it. He didn't use them as pawns in his life. They were all men in the same family who loved one another openly, in the same way they loved the women in their lives.

Cale stood up, stretched once more, and left the room, heading down the bustling hallways of the cardiac wing. As he walked, he was struck by a memory of Victor, white-haired, his face tanned, walking toward him all those years ago, tall, confident, the power in his steps, the sheer image of him as a man, and the impression he made.

His young patient with her dream waited for him, and like his son, she might be part of a new generation of doctors. He wished for them an easier time of it. So Cale walked a little faster, stood a little taller, a man who had learned to stand on his own, but chose to stand with those who loved him. He paused outside the room for an instant, then pushed open the doors, because he knew he had somewhere important to go.

acknowledgments

Over the years, I've heard authors talk about books that come easily, like gifts from God. Someday I'd like to find one. This was not it.

I must acknowledge my lovely editor, Brenda Copeland, for her brilliant insight, which helped make this book and its prose rise to my vision, for her patience and support, even when that meant leaving me to wade through the story drama, and my own. You are the best.

Thanks to everyone at Atria, especially Judith Curr, for giving me the gift this book needed: time without pressure.

A special thank you to Linda Goodman at the Avalon library and to those islanders who shared their memories of Catalina.

For her medical knowledge and expertise, and especially her time, I thank Dr. Barbara Snyder, the wonderful Katherine Stone.

A special thanks to my support group of writers:

Kristin Hannah, Megan Chance, Jenny Crusie, Christina Dodd, Kim Fisk, Jill Landis, Debbie Macomber, Teresa Medeiros, Linda Nichols, Susan Elizabeth Phillips, and the ladies on RomEx, especially Heather McAllister and Suzanne Forster.

For her friendship and generosity, I owe so much to Meryl Sawyer, who opened her incomparable Newport Beach home to us and showed us the ins and outs of the isles.

For her unflagging belief in this book and my ability to write it, I owe a huge debt of gratitude to Marcy Posner.

For your understanding, patience, and love, bless you, Kassandra Corinne Stadler, Jan Barnett, Kelly Walker, and Linda Crone. A special thanks to Kasey for her keen eye and nod of approval when I was mired in my late-night searches for the right language. You always have been and always will be my greatest gift.

And finally, to every woman who lives with her choice to give up a child. There are no words eloquent enough to thank you. But know that we the women who received your gift understand better than anyone how strong you are.

READING
GROUP GUIDE

THE *Days of Summer*

BY JILL BARNETT

QUESTIONS AND TOPICS
FOR DISCUSSION

1. The Bannings and Peytons are the real victims of the automobile crash that killed Rudy, Rachel, and Jimmy. Victor's grandsons come to live with him and he makes a concerted effort to drive them apart. What is it about Victor that makes him believe in his motives? Do you understand or agree with his reasons? Kathryn moves in with Jimmy's mother for Laurel's sake. Why do you think she really made the move? What is it about Kathryn that does not allow her to separate herself from Jimmy's death? Does this make her pitiable or sympathetic? Why?

2. A recurring theme in the book is about the mistakes we make in the name of love. Describe each character's failure at love and their capacity for understanding what love is.

3. Which characters change? How? Which characters don't change? Name a scene that tells you they can-

not change. What does the characters' ability or inability to change say about the nature of love, family, and loyalty?

4. Victor writes Cale off as irresponsible and too easily distracted by women, and believes there is no potential for greatness within him. Do you think his perception impacts Cale positively or negatively or both? Why?

5. How does Laurel both exacerbate and heal the wounds between Cale and Jud? Do you think she ultimately has a positive or negative effect on their lives? Why or why not? How are Cale and Jud different from Victor? In what ways do they exemplify the lessons he taught them? How does the next generation reflect a growth and change in male relationships?

6. A prominent part of the book describes the experience of young love and burgeoning sexuality. Laurel misunderstands sexual thrill as love and pays a terrible price for it. Is her response believable? Does her failure to love and understand love make her more or less sympathetic? How does a woman know or learn the difference? Do you believe that Laurel's love was true in Part Two? Did you feel differently in Part Three and by the end of the book? Why?

7. Many of the main characters have histories that haunt them. How does the past become an influential part of the present? Discuss the points at which memory and mistakes affect a character's actions or change how a moment is played out. Do any of the charac-

ters ever fully escape their individual and collective pasts?

8. What motivates Jud to pursue Laurel? Were Jud and Laurel meant to be? Should Cale and Laurel have been the destined lovers?

9. Kathryn's grief over the loss of her husband colors everything, including her interactions with her daughter. Do you understand her reaction? Kathryn fears the Bannings will continue to destroy them. When she warns Laurel away from Cale, then Jud—both at the cost of her relationship with her daughter—was she right? Was her intention to save her daughter worth the ultimate damage to their relationship? Do you believe she is a good mother?

10. In Part Three, we come to see who these characters have become after thirty years. How much did the turbulence, the social and sexual influences of the late 1960's and early 1970's affect the earlier decisions of the characters? Discuss how their decisions would have been different if they were facing the same problems today.

11. Laurel's secret about Greg O'Hanlon haunts her for years. How do you feel about her original decision? Even in 1970, was it justified? When she finally seeks him out, should she have told him the truth? Should she have told Jud and Cale?

12. Victor spends years collecting artwork. What drives him to do it? Why does he hide the pieces away? What does that say about Victor? Is he a man capable

of love? How does his relationship with Kathryn in Part Three change or further your opinion of him? How did you feel about Victor by the end of the book?

13. Thematically, what is the purpose of the third generation? How are they like their parents and grandparents? How are they different?

14. Which character learns the most by the end of the book? Which character has changed the most? How did Victor and Kathryn's weaknesses, strengths, and actions influence the biggest changes?

15. At its heart, *The Days of Summer* is about characters who must face difficult choices, terrible pain, and betrayal. This is certainly what makes the characters seem so damaged, yet allows for their dramatic rise to grace. Do you believe the characters are victims of their own self perceptions, choices, and realities? Is there one character you would like to have seen change more? If so, who and why?

A CONVERSATION
WITH THE AUTHOR

Q: Was there a particular place that inspired the idea for you to write *The Days of Summer*?

A: I was born and raised in Southern California, a very idyllic area along the coast, and spent time on Catalina Island, quite a magical place. I remember the first time I went there and saw the flying fish. Amazing. When I was thinking about certain years for the expanse of my idea, I remembered my time on the island in 1970. It is quite wonderful to write about a place you know in your bones. I know California, how the lantana grows each spring and what the air smells and tastes like, the weather patterns and how the state has changed over the forty plus years I was there. But as with any story, once the characters exist inside any place, real or fictional, creative imagination takes over and the setting becomes a place unique to those characters and their lives.

Q: Where do your ideas come from?

A: Every book comes to me from a different place or in a different way. Sometimes something visual will spark an idea—you see something on the news or read an article and suddenly a thought becomes "what if?".

Q: Do you write about your own experiences?

A: Not really. I write fiction. Like most writers I do often write what I know, yet there is a definite line between the imagined and experience. The characters lead you down an imagined path, one that exists inside actual human experience. But the revelation of story comes to me from the craft of writing itself. My stories have themes tied to my vision because I always have something important to say about relationships, the complications associated with love, human nature, and my favorite topic, inhuman nature—the things we do to mess up our lives.

Q: You write about Kathryn and her daughter Laurel, whose lives are changed forever by a single moment of tragedy. Why a widow and her child?

A: I just said I didn't write about my own experiences, didn't I? Well, remember I write fiction and get to lie for a living. Here's my experience: a few years ago, I said goodbye to my husband one morning and that night a policeman stood at my door to tell me he was dead. I know what Kathryn had to face. While her story is fictional, made up completely inside my head, I lived with the same kind of fear, especially when it came to raising our daughter.

Q: The secrets of the characters' pasts and their effect in the present are throughout the book. Why this theme in this book?

A: I write family dramas and all families have secrets. We all make mistakes in the name of love or let feeling color our decisions. Our heads and hearts guide us. While some secrets are born from shame and fear of humiliation, most come from love. Within families and in life, the absolute truth can damage and hurt people. Often the reason to keep a secret is to not hurt someone you care about.

Q: Destiny is an important part of how the Banning and Peyton families are bound together and keep crossing paths throughout the years. Do you believe in coincidence?

A: I believe there is no such thing as coincidence. Certainly not in my experience. Everything in human life is cause and effect. There has to be some grand plan, one that is for some people very complicated. Often in my life I've seen things that disprove coincidence. You move a thousand miles away and meet an old friend on the street. You have a dream about someone you haven't seen in twenty years and the next day they call. I believe all love is destined.

Q: What comes more easily to you, writing the beginning or the end of a book?

A: That's easy. The end. I often know very early in the process what line will be the last in a book. So often about halfway through a book, the last page has come to me quite suddenly and seemingly out of the blue. Emotion is difficult to nail sometimes, particularly in the first draft or when the characters have yet to reveal themselves. So I always write an emotional scene the moment it comes to me because emotion is most honest when in its first pure form.

Q: What's next?

A: I'm working on another California-set book, Northern California this time, about a woman's struggle to keep her family together and about women's relationships with their children and with men. I have something to say about how our society treats women of different ages, something I think all women will relate to. I know the book is like a gift to me. I've never had a story come to me the wonderful way this book is coming. It's great to be a writer.